GENE

Also by Stel Pavlou

DECIPHER

GENE

STEL PAVLOU

**SIMON &
SCHUSTER**

London · New York · Sydney · Toronto

A VIACOM COMPANY

First published in Great Britain by Simon & Schuster UK Ltd, 2005
A Viacom Company

1 3 5 7 9 10 8 6 4 2

Simon & Schuster UK Ltd
Africa House
64–78 Kingsway
London WC2B 6AH

Simon & Schuster Australia
Sydney

www.simonsays.co.uk

A CIP catalogue record for this book is available
from the British Library

Hardback ISBN 0-7432-0859-5
EAN 9780743208598

Trade Paperback ISBN 0-7432-0860-9
EAN 9780743208604

Typeset by M Rules
Printed in Great Britain by
William Clowes Ltd, Beccles, Suffolk

AUTHOR'S NOTE

The Cyclades is a chain of Greek islands sat on the wine dark Aegean Sea and is in effect the eye of a great storm that has been raging for over three thousand years. If you trace the coast of the Mediterranean that runs concentric to the Cyclades you find Greece, Turkey, Syria, Lebanon, Israel, Egypt and Italy. You find Crete and you find Troy. You find that Western history has been shaped by what has happened around the Cycladic circle, almost as though history were the hands on the Cycladic clock; the Trojan War at midnight, the Crusades at 3 a.m. and all the way through until dawn. Even now what happens around the Cyclades dictates the focus of the world. The world's youngest power, America, is drawn to this region it calls the Middle East. Ancient Babylon remains the beast. It is as if we have come full circle – yet the enemies have remained steadfastly the same. Thus is the nature of a clock. The nature of man. The nature of Cyclades, with whom we journey.

Gene is an historical fantasy. Where possible the history and the figures presented within it are real, but on occasion elements have been purposely altered to fit the needs of the story. My characters interact with them, or at times are them, though of course my tale is simply a new weave made from their tapestry.

New York City, too, has been shaped for my purposes. Many aspects are real, but sometimes I have altered them, the size of buildings, for example, or a little geography. I hope the people of NYC can forgive me; I do this with genuine respect and affection. New York Police Department procedures have also been altered intentionally where required, but only a real cop should notice and it is out of respect to the NYPD and the work that they do that I mention this.

Thanks go to William Belmont, Director of Operations at Pinkerton Consulting & Investigations, W. Mark Dale, Director of the NYPD Crime Laboratory, NYPD Detective Peter Dzik (retired), NYPD Detective John Cornicello (retired), Steven Pinker, who did not have to answer my questions on his excellent book *The Blank Slate*, Jim B. Tucker, MD, Assistant Professor of Psychiatric Medicine, University of Virginia, Gary A. Wasdin at the New York City Public Library, Jon Thorpe, MSc, Dr Andrew Holder, James Sprules, Louis and Christina Pavlou, Alex Franke, MA and Carol Anderson. Where artistic concerns necessitated I ignored them all completely and add the caveat that any mistakes that I have made as a result are mine alone.

A very big and special thank you for their enormous help, advice and support goes to Maureen Pavlou and Rowland Wells. Thank you also to my editors John Jarrold and Ben Ball (may his nerves recover) and my agents Sophie Hicks, Jeff Graup, Alex Goldstone and Linda Seifert, all of whom do an enormous amount of backroom work which is difficult to describe and hard to live without.

Last but by no means least, thank you Lise, who kept me sane through all of this, who picked me up when I was down, who encouraged me when I just wanted to walk away. I started this book for me; I finished this book for you.

for Dad

Paul Pavlou
1928-1999

DECLARE THE PAST, DIAGNOSE THE PRESENT, FORETELL THE FUTURE

HIPPOCRATES

GATCAATGAGGTGGACACCAGAGGCGGGGACTTGTAAATAACACTGGGCTGTAGGAA

TGGGGTTCACCTCTAATTCTAAGATGGCTAGATAATGCATCTTTCAGGGTTGTGCTTCA

TCTAGAAGGTAGAGCTGTGGTCGTTCAATAAAAGTCCTCAAGAGGTTGGTTAATACGT

GTTTAATAGTACAGTATGGTGACTATAGTCAACAATAATTTATTGTACATTTTTAAAG

CTAGAAGAAAAGCATTGGGAAGTTTCCAACATGAAGAAAAGATAAATGGTCAAGGG

GATATCCTAATTACCCTGATTTGATCATTATGCATTATATACATGAATCAAAATATCAA

CATACCTTCAAACTATGTACAAATATTATATACCAATAAAAAATCATCATCATCATCTC

ATCATCACCACCCTCCTCCTCATCACCACCAGCATCACCACCATCATCACCACCACCATC

ATCACCACCACCACTGCCATCATCATCACCACCACTGTGCCATCATCATCACCACCACTG

TCATTATCACCACCACCATCATCACCAACACCACTGCCATCGTCATCACCACCACTGTCA

TTATCACCACCACCATCACCAACATCACCACCACCATTATCACCACCATCAACACCACA

CCCCCA**TCATCATC**ATCAC**TACTACCA**TCATT**AC**CAGCA**CC**ACCAC**CACTATCAC**CACA

CCACC**AC**AATCACCATCAC**CA**CTATCATCAAC**ATC**ATCA**CT**ACCAC**CA**TCACCAACACA

CCAT**CA**TTA**TCAC**CACCAC**CACCAT**CACCAAC**AT**CA**CC**A**CC**ATCAT**CATCACC**ACCATA

CCAA**GA**CCATC**AT**CATCAC**CA**TCACCACCAAC**AT**CACC**ACC**ATCAC**CA**ACACCACCAA

CCACCA**CCACCAC**CATCAT**CACCACCAC**CACC**AT**CATCA**TC**ACCAC**CACCGCCAT**CATA

TCGCCACCACCATGACCACCACCATCACAACCATCACCACCATCACAACCACCATCATA

CTATCGCTATCACCACCATCACCATTACCACCACCATTACTACAACCATGACCATCACA

CCATCACCACCACCATCACAACGATCACCATCACAGCCACCATCATCACCACCACCACA

CCACCATCACCATCAAACCATCGGCATTATTATTTTTTTAGAATTTTGTTGGGATTCAGT

ATCTGCCAAGATACCCATTCTTAAAACATGAAAAAGCAGCTGACCCTCCTGTGGCCCCT

TTTTGGGCAGTCATTGCAGGACCTCATCCCCAAGCAGCAGCTCTGGTGGCATACAGGCA

CCCACCACCAAGGTAGAGGGTAATTGAGCAGAAAAGCCACTTCCTCCAGCAGTTCCCTT

CTGAGCTGCTGTCCTTGGACTTGAAGAAGCTTCTGGAACATGCTGGGGAGGAAGGAAC

ATTTCACTTATTGAGTGGCCTGATGCAGAACAGAGACCCAGCTGGTTCACTCTAGTTCG

ACTAAAACTCACCCCTGTCTATAAGCATCAGCCTCGGCAGGATGCATTTCACATTTGTA

TCTCATTTAACCTCCACAAAGACCCAGAAGGGGTTGGTAACATTATCATACCTAGGCCTC

CYCLADES IN THE UNDERWORLD

I remember the day I died.

The details are a fog now. A haze distinct enough only for the nightmare. I remember the scything sounds of metal on metal, the shrill creation of bloody carnage upon a canvas. The bloodlust. The rivulets of sweat running down the channels of my arms. Dirt and animal fat smeared in a marble glaze. The smell of burning flesh. Like strips of rancid swine all crackling and spitting on a split wood fire. Juices oozing. Blood flowing like wine. The human animal makes a fine sacrifice.

They said the horse had worked. I do not know why I remember that. The horse had worked. But that was the way it was. I remember I killed, with my own hands. One I ran through as quickly as one might sneeze and on instinct guard the nose. I remember I took one man's face in my hands as though to caress him and instead gouged out his eyes with my thumbs, until they were sunk deep up to the knuckle. I do not remember if he screamed. I suppose he must have. It's all a blur now. All part of that carnival of terror that ended with my belly sliced clean, and my bowels spilling out like the flowering ribbons of a child's toy.

I remember I was at the top of another blow when the dull thump of a side swipe caught me unguarded, and away flew my hand. End over end. Tumbling in the dust, my bloody fingers still grasping my sword.

What happened next I do not know. The details are a fog now. A haze distinct enough only for the nightmares. Perhaps it is for the best. The horror I witnessed I do not wish to remember, though I know that I met evil that day and was not man enough to stop it.

I returned in time for the darkness, pulled back by much tugging at my clothing. Perhaps they assumed I was carrion. My moaning soon put paid to that. I was dragged through the streets, and loaded on to something, I know not what.

Later there was dripping. An occasional splattering of filthy water caught up in snatches by the feeble flame of cavern fires. I lay, slipping in and out of my stupor for I know not how long. Only she would know. That wild-haired bitch with her hungry eyes and need to see me choke. Wafting the smoke of her strange concoctions, holding me fast so that I could not look away, but was forced to consume her vile magicks.

She perused my innards as though I were a prophecy. As though the meats of my self could tell the future. I do not know what she saw, for there was no future here. I was beyond restoration. But she smeared me in honey nonetheless and patched me with cloth. She fed me berries and brews and the strips of bark and forced every morsel down my withered throat. She recited her incantations and as the flames began to dance, as the cavern began to swim, she hitched up her garments and exposed the thick black hair of her moistened furrow. She squatted down on me, and, much to my surprise, had more control over my parts than I. She writhed and cursed and spat at me to deliver to her my seed. She struck at me with balled fists. And all the while the flames and smoke of the fires rose up around her, a crescendo to her wild hair and her hungry eyes. Until at last I released into her what she sought.

And when she was satisfied she snuffed out the fires and left me to squalor and starvation. And as I lay there, my nostrils filled with the rotting, bilious stench of my dying carcass, she led him in and claimed she had saved me for him. He took up his blade and drove it into my temple.

And as I died I looked deep into those hungry eyes and knew.

I remember the day I died. It was the day I bore witness to my own conception.

My name is Cyclades. And this is my story.

THE SEVEN TRIALS
OF
CYCLADES

BOOK ONE

KNOW THYSELF

PLATO

NEW YORK CITY

He stabbed the first visitor at precisely 10.23. They determined this later when they pulled the time code from the security tape.

It happened like this: he wandered into the Great Hall wearing a plain grey sweatshirt, harmless looking, a regular guy. He passed through the metal detector without tripping the alarm. He loitered under the imposing glass domes of the entrance hall for ten minutes. Didn't take a map from the help desk. Didn't ask for directions.

He watched the staff change the flowers, a continuing donation from Lila Acheson Wallace, for almost three minutes, made a move towards the staircase up to the next floor, changed his mind, turned left away from the stairs, and walking the thirty or so feet towards the Greek sculpture exhibit, never stopping to pay the voluntary entrance fee at either of the two booths, entered the Belfer Court looking – lost. Though not like a tourist. This was something else.

This was when he started to weep.

Not a sudden outburst. If it had been, perhaps one of the blue-blazered attendants might have come to assist him, realizing something was wrong. Instead he made his way over to the *Cubiculum from Boscoreale* – frescoed walls and a mosaic floor assembled as a room from a Roman villa – where

Mrs Margaret Holland (a history teacher from Scarsdale High School who was at the museum as part of a group) remarked, he looked like that boy at her last school who'd smoked all that crack in the student library.

She knew enough to get out of his way.

At the *Grand Sepulchral Vase* over on the right he traced his finger over the pictures of the prone black corpses depicted on its terracotta surface. He touched a number of other objects until he reached the middle of the court.

Surrounded on all sides by marble statues of gods and kings, the young man's attention was drawn to the figure in the centre – *Volneratus Deficiens*, the Wounded Warrior, a depiction of Protesilaos, destined to become the first Greek to die at the battle of Troy, but shown here raising his spear arm, preparing to kill.

Lauren Bergen, a 21-year-old Art History major from NYU, explained that she had been making sketches of the Wounded Warrior when the man suddenly appeared by her side and spoke to the statue. Puzzled, she asked him if he was familiar with the work. He replied that he was not familiar with the work but familiar with the man.

At this point, Lauren Bergen decided to leave the Belfer Court.

It was as she did so, and as the man tried to follow her, that he appeared to notice the special exhibitions gallery through the doorway under the sign: *The Greek Achievement*. Inside, artefacts from the Trojan War to the first Olympic Games had been placed on display in celebration of this summer's games. Hoplons, spears, pots, bowls, coins. But it was the swords that interested him the most.

The swords and the skulls.

Lauren Bergen said that she wished she had never struck up conversation with the man. Perhaps then he wouldn't have done what he did next.

*

At 10.23, the young man picked a three-thousand year old bronze short sword off the museum wall and in the same movement slashed the arm of Richard Scott, the only other visitor in the room. In seconds he had hacked down the room's attendant, and the attendant from the next room who attempted to intervene, both blows of practised ease. The sword seemed still solid and sharp. There was a lot of blood.

Swinging the bronze sword above his head, he brought the ancient weapon crashing down on display case number 43. Inside were a helmet and broken skull.

His hand studded with glass fragments and running rivers of red, he reached inside the case and plucked out the objects.

And then, just as suddenly as his fury had erupted, he began to hyperventilate. The security tape later showed the confusion written across his face as he studied the bleached white human bone and then collapsed in a heap.

For several minutes he remained on the floor, ranting in a language nobody could understand.

He pressed the skull to his chest.

And he wept.

NORTH

The mid-August morning was hot and oppressive, an asphyxiating New York broiler that left the air thick and charged, drenched with the naked fumes of the gasoline and diesel engines crawling down Fifth Avenue like sweat.

Parked behind three oily Scarsdale school buses idling at the sidewalk, North chewed over Bruder's report. He marked up the doer's location on a tattered blue and white museum ground plan before peeling it off the hood of his dark blue motor-pool Impala.

'When does ESU get here?' he asked.

The Emergency Service Unit was the NYPD's tactical branch. Negotiators and SWAT. As a catching detective from the Fourth Precinct, North didn't work hostage – they must be short-handed.

Patrolman Don Bruder's swollen features, about three minutes short of heat stroke, bulged with agitation as the chaos on the steps of the Metropolitan Museum of Art continued to unfold relentlessly. Patrolmen were marshalling the public out the exits. Morbid crowds of tourists pooled around the hot-dog vendors and picture sellers. And though he could hear more sirens trying to squeeze out of the 86th Street Transverse just a block away, so far only two squad cars had made it here ahead of North.

It was now 10.41.

'It's your call,' Bruder replied.

'*You're* the first officer on the scene. Did you put a call in for ESU or not?' North asked sharply, throwing open the trunk.

'Central didn't tell you?'

'Tell me what?' North fished his heavy body armour out and secured the fastenings over his sweat-soaked T-shirt.

'Ah, Jesus,' Bruder trembled. 'ESU's your call.'

'Why?'

' 'Cos the mope's asking for you by name.'

North slammed the trunk shut. Cold sweat beaded down his clammy forehead. He could feel the black city grime thick on the back of his neck as he shook his head.

'Asking for me?'

'Detective James North. That's what he keeps saying. Think maybe you pissed someone off?'

North marvelled at the understatement. 'I'm a cop,' he said. 'Listen, call up Central Park, tell them to get their asses in gear and send more guys to quarantine this area,' he ordered. 'You locked down inside?'

Bruder thumbed at the crowds still fighting each other to exit the building. 'You kidding me? There's over three thousand people in there, and a little kid trapped with this nut. They said it could take up to half an hour just to empty out.'

North watched as a couple of Met staffers were helped out by paramedics to the only FDNY EMS ambulance to breach the midtown gridlock. One held a blood-soaked cloth to his face. Another had a T-shirt wrapped around his hand.

If he's touched that kid . . .

North reached to check his piece but the cloud crossing Don Bruder's face spoke for him. 'I wouldn't want to be you right now.'

'Trust me, we all want to be someone else.'

'Central gave the order: no gunfire inside the museum.'

North was stunned. 'Excuse me?'

'Someone called up the Mayor's office. Said they'd made a three-thousand year old donation to the exhibit. Next thing I know, dispatcher's coming back with the order it's worth more than whoever goes in there.'

North didn't answer. He checked the action then holstered his Glock 21 .45. Eight rounds. Hollow point. All cops knew a full metal jacket pierced the target and went in and out. But a hollow point opened up inside like a lead flower. Its damage was vicious; its stopping power absolute. And there was no risk it would emerge from its target to hit anyone unfortunate enough to be standing right behind. The gun was going in.

'I didn't see you do that.'

North didn't care. 'Anything else you want to tell me?'

'Yeah,' the young uniform said as he surveyed the steps up towards the imposing columns of the vast imperious stone building. 'We found the little kid's mom.'

'Matthew Hennessey,' she kept saying over and over. 'Matthew Hennessey.' But it was just one of a jumble of names that were swimming around inside North's head. Amos Arreilamo, Louis Rosario – he put Louis away for burglary. Was he out already? Michael Francis Duffy was in for double homicide. No way he was out. What about Denni? She looked like Dennichola Martinez's wife. He nailed Denni for grand larceny.

The trouble with being a catching detective was they put you where they needed a pair of hands most. He could know the guy in the museum for any number of reasons, from racketeering to jay-walking.

'Do you hear me?' she was saying in utter desperation. 'Do you hear what I'm telling you?'

North lied and said that he did.

'He has asthma,' she sobbed, her hands shaking, tears staining her cheeks, proving that the five-dollar make-up she was wearing didn't like the wet. She clawed at her Costco clothes, that were old but otherwise immaculate. This woman knew how to make money stretch.

She had another kid with her. A little girl in a pale yellow cotton dress. There was no father around.

'Mrs Hennessey,' North said gently. 'Is he a good kid?' She wasn't listening. She was freaked. 'Mrs Hennessey. Your son, what's his name?'

'I told you, Matthew. His name is Matthew.'

Jesus Christ, North, get a grip. 'How old is he?'

'Eleven.' Her eyes were wandering.

North had to steer her attention away from the situation. He touched her arm. 'Mrs Hennessey, listen to me. All right? Look . . . look at me.' North was all confidence as she made eye contact. 'We're gonna get your son out of there, okay? But I'm gonna need your help.'

She nodded that she understood.

'You said he has asthma. Is he on medication?'

'His inhaler. He has a plastic inhaler.'

'What triggers it? Does he have panic attacks?'

'No. No, it's medical.'

Well, that's something. 'Does he have it with him?'

It was a simple question but one this distressed mother just couldn't answer. She was shaking again, incapable of a coherent response. She tugged at her faded blonde hair tied up in the back, held in place by a ribbon. She couldn't have been more than a few years older than North. Mid-thirties at a push, even though the faint trace of burst blood vessels around her nose suggested otherwise.

'He put it in her purse . . .' the daughter offered. 'He hates carrying it around. It makes him look goofy.'

North turned his attention back on the mother. 'Do you have it?'

She fished around indecisively in her crammed purse until she came up with the small blue plastic device. She handed it over to North. The label on the pre-loaded canister read: Albuterol.

North recognized it immediately. His sister's kid used Albuterol. But this canister was empty and way past its use by date. North smiled, he hoped reassuringly. Little Matty didn't have asthma at all. He was playing his mom, for reasons known only to himself.

'I'll make sure he gets this.'

The sweltering, grease-slicked orange clouds were pregnant with the promise of rain, but North didn't believe them. He would go on sweating.

Heat did strange things to a man's head. Could make him boil to the point of irrational, make him lash out without fear of consequence. Heat interfered with a man's ability to reason.

North had two choices as he entered the museum against the heavy tide of panic-stricken visitors still surging down the main staircase trying to get out: he could either have the air conditioning turned way up and hope the perp came to his senses or shut it down and let the heat go to work on him. Make him sluggish, easier to apprehend but dangerously unpredictable.

How to pacify a hornet?

'What's he doing now?' North joined the next uniform, huddled behind one of the ticket booths.

'Sharpening his sword.'

'Ah, Jesus.' North peered around the corner to take a closer look but there was nothing to see. Instead he could hear what sounded like a stone, slowly, very slowly, being run down the length of an ancient blade.

'Where is he?'

The cop pointed to a side gallery. 'He keeps moving in and out of there. There's an exit the other side.'

North checked the museum plan. He felt the muscles in his jaw flex in frustration. There weren't enough cops, there were still too many visitors. He tucked the map away with dismay. 'This is too fluid.'

At the other end of the Belfer Court a lone uniform directed the confused visitors emerging from the café and the Americas exhibit to head down the stairs, past the coat room and out the 81st Street exit. He had his back to the court. He had no other option. There were no internal doors to lock down, no bars that had magically appeared. The museum prided itself on freedom of access.

The perp had to change his mind just once about where he wanted to be and this whole situation would be turned on its ear.

The sharpening continued. A tangy smell of metal drifted from the side gallery. 'He been doing this long?'

'About ten minutes. The museum people said it's a genuine sword from Troy.'

North had to think. 'Upstate?'

'Ancient Greece.'

Oh. 'Guess it's worth a lot of money.'

Bruder came up beside him. 'Not any more.'

North sized up the exits. 'Has he made a move on the kid?'

'I don't even think he knows he's there.'

But North had no doubt. 'Trust me,' he said. 'He knows.'

Bruder didn't like all this waiting around. His fingertips were white from gripping his radio. 'So what's the deal on ESU? Do I put in the call?'

North chewed it over. ESU would be the primary response if the situation were not contained. But it was, for now. Hostage situations in the city averaged around a hundred a year. The NYPD Hostage Negotiation Team had a ninety per cent success rate talking the desperate, the suicidal and the crazed out of acting on their unfathomable impulses. It wasn't for nothing that they had 'Talk to Me' emblazoned on their equipment.

'Put in a call for HNT,' North ordered. But no sooner had he said it when the situation began to spiral. The crowd at the far end began to surge past the lone uniform and spill out into the court, right where North didn't want them – right through the hostage situation.

North didn't think. 'Get back!' he yelled, running at them. 'Go back!' Before he knew it he was in the middle of the court. The visitors were bewildered. They dithered. North waved them away desperately.

Back by the ticket booths, Bruder and his partner were forced to direct the sea of visitors streaming down the staircase, away from the situation and out the exits.

'Get away!' North pleaded.

And that was when the first girl saw the perp standing just a few feet inside the Special Exhibitions Gallery and screamed.

At around five feet ten inches, maybe a hundred and forty pounds, with close-cropped, light-coloured hair, he stood with his back to his audience, his arms clearly splattered with thick, dark red blood.

The visitors hurried back the way they had come but already the stranger was turning on North.

He was younger by more than a couple of years. He was maybe twenty-five, twenty-six. North worked out but this guy looked like an athlete. He was going to be quick and agile.

North marvelled at his own stupidity. Guess they were right. Guess seven years really was the shelf life of a New York cop.

He clutched the blue inhaler tightly in reflex and tried to work out his next move. He was in the doer's domain now.

And North didn't know him at all.

GENE

The chilling sound of the slow deliberate strokes of the whetstone against the cold, hard metal of the ancient blade continued to echo from wall to wall. Now North could hear that they were accompanied by the rasping of laboured breaths forced through the stranger's dry, constricted throat.

Was he asthmatic too, or was he ill? Was that a trace of pneumonia North could hear; a bronchial infection? Or was the man with the sword just beyond category, save for unbalanced?

Nearby, behind a large marble statue of some long forgotten, long dead, Greek god, stood Matthew Hennessey, sobbing, so terrified he had a puddle at his feet, a deep indigo stain running down his jeans. He'd piss himself some more if he had anything left.

North was too far away to snatch him and run – the perp would hack him apart before he could get there. The boy tried to meet North's gaze for some comfort, but North couldn't afford to give him that reassuring look that he craved. He had to keep this man's attention off the boy, no matter what.

The stranger's feet shuffled as he turned to see Bruder directing the anxious, curious visitors back to the exit, all the while sharpening his blade. North watched his peculiar, faltering gait. What was he on? PCP? Crack? Something new?

He could afford it. His clothes were expensive. Designer pants. Two-hundred dollar tennis shoes. His fingers were neatly kempt and callus free. He wasn't just white collar, he was successful white collar.

What possessed him to rage amid the smashed display glass and crushed human bone littered with earthy modelling clay, artist's materials and glass eyes, strewn all across the hard marble floor? Was that a clay facial reconstruction he'd stomped into the ground, its eyes bulging from the explosive hatred unleashed upon it?

So many eyes. Even North could feel the eyes, the glare of the gods lining the gallery bearing down on him, as though they were watching him. Judging him. Is that what set him off; he didn't like to be looked at? North knew men who'd killed over less.

Do I just say: hi, you were asking for me? No. Then he's got all the cards.

North took the blue inhaler, shook it violently, making sure the small ball bearing inside rattled loudly, and pretended to take a deep hit of Albuterol.

'I get nervous,' North announced without apology.

No response. If the perp had heard anything at all he wasn't letting on. Just continued like a chef grinding a knife on his steel.

North had to take the initiative somehow. Become this man's focus. Do something unexpected but non-threatening that would give him the upper hand.

He noticed a heavy brown leather jacket lying on the floor, abandoned by a fleeing visitor. North waited a moment before slowly reaching for it.

'Hey, is this yours?' he asked, despite the stranger's sweatshirt; anything to start a conversation. Cautiously he picked it up, never taking his eye off the stranger. 'Here, let me get this for you,' he offered with reassurance.

Still nothing but the excruciating scream of stone against cold metal.

The jacket was not cheap and too heavy to be comfortable on a day like today. Habit would have made someone bring it. North ran his fingers quickly over the lining just to make sure, but the pockets were empty.

He tried again. He had only one gambit left. 'My name's James,' he said. 'James North.'

The stranger brought his sharpening abruptly to a halt. His chest heaved as he struggled to take another laboured breath. Was he thinking through a response? It was hard to tell. North could hear he was muttering to himself, though he couldn't understand the language. It sounded perhaps Middle Eastern, North wasn't sure.

How to proceed? 'You want me to set this down over there next to you?'

The stranger brought his curious punch-drunk eyes up to level them on North.

That's right, that's right. Look at me . . .

Yet the man's look revealed a familiarity that North couldn't quite place. A peculiar, circular shaped birthmark sat back from his right eye. North did not stare too hard – he was quick to look away again, quick to show deference to the dominant. He tried to sound pliant. 'Call me Jim,' he said, offering the man his jacket back even though the sword played lightly in the perp's hand. 'You?'

The man thought long and hard. How difficult could it be? Eventually he replied softly: 'I am Satan's Oath.'

North didn't even want to think about what that meant. Was he pushing buttons or did he mean it? *Forget it. Steer it back.* He replied mildly, 'That's not your name though, is it?'

The stranger contemplated this revelation. 'Gene . . . They call me Gene.'

Whoever *they* were, North was sure that wasn't all they called him. He let his expression soften a little. 'Hi, Gene. You don't want your jacket back?'

Gene smirked. He was almost sheepish in his reactions, as if he were simple-minded. 'It's not mine,' he replied modestly. 'You like my sword?'

North went cold, well aware of the blood on the blade and soaked all the way up his T-shirt. *Be careful with the answer. Don't talk about anything substantive to the situation.* Those were the rules. Get the guy's trust. Keep his trust. But nothing substantive.

'These jackets are expensive.' *All the time, steer it back.* 'I had one, left it on the subway. Three hundred bucks for a new one. I don't know about you but three hundred bucks is hard to come by.'

Gene didn't care. He ran his finger along the newly sharpened glinting edge of the broken blade. It had a thick green patina encrusted across much of its surface. It appeared extremely brittle. It should have shattered with its first strike but it was as though the sheer will of its wielder had held it in check.

Gene's fingers danced warmly over the Bull's horn pattern embossed on its surface. 'I haven't seen this in many years.'

North took the opportunity to keep the conversation friendly. 'You come to the museum a lot?' He sucked again on the empty inhaler. It gave him time to think, while it gave the perp something else to focus on.

Gene shook his head. 'No,' he said, disturbingly matter of fact. 'This is my first time.' He raised the sword up and swept it through a crescent, a rehearsed move. Blood spat from the blade and splattered across the marble floor in a pattern of heavy droplets only inches from North's feet.

'You, uh, you from around here, Gene? My folks are from Brooklyn, born and bred. What about you? Where you from?'

Gene hacked at the air in reply, thrusting into unseen targets. Parrying an invisible attack. 'Here and there,' he said eventually, but the curiosity alive in his eyes was reserved only for testing the balance of the weapon.

He repeated the action. Dropping his shoulder to whip around, light on his feet, his reactions sharp, sudden. It was in stark contrast to how he had acted only minutes before.

'I know all about you,' Gene said.

'You do?' North glanced back down the gallery towards Bruder, his mouth dry with dread and resignation. *What's the situation? HNT in five minutes.* May as well be five hours.

'Where, uh, where do you think you know me from?'

'I don't think. And you don't remember.'

'What makes you say that?'

'You have to stop this.'

'Stop what, Gene? You're the one doing this. Don't you think you're the one in a position to stop it?'

Gene stopped his sword patterns. His nostrils flared, his eyes widened, his voice trembled. 'You don't understand.' He hammered at his head. 'Only you can make this go away. Help me.'

'How?'

Gene wouldn't answer.

North watched the glinting edge of Gene's sword swing with menace. Spinning on his heel in a finely practised move, the blade an extension of his arm, his lunge an extension of his reach, Gene's swordplay probed his surroundings with a deftness of touch and a grace of motion that defied his state of mind.

He twisted again, lost in the moment. And he didn't see the jacket coming.

North was swift. He yanked the heavy brown leather down over Gene's head, aware of, yet totally unprepared for, the younger man's poise and explosive strength. Gene's elbow slammed into his gut like a steel piston, but with momentum on his side North followed through on his launch with a heavy boot to Gene's lower back, propelling the man headlong into what was left of one of the display cases.

In an instant North switched his attention to Matthew Hennessey, but the boy was so confused by events he took a step back, just as frightened of the detective. Undeterred, in two easy strides North grabbed him by the collar in one fist and the belt in the other, and desperately hurled the startled kid down the court towards Bruder.

Matthew Hennessey screamed as he landed heavily and skidded across the marble to be gathered up into the arms of the waiting cop.

But that moment was all North got before Gene regathered himself, flinging the jacket to the ground. He struck North hard with the flat of the blade, pounding into his back with such ferocity North collapsed in a heap, gasping for air, still clutching an inhaler that was of no use to anyone.

Only the uniform near the 81st Street exit had the presence of mind to stop it going further. 'Freeze!' he barked, taking aim at a perp who had no idea he was under orders not to fire.

Gene faltered as if momentarily brought to his senses, while North wheezed at his feet.

Wheeling around, struggling to get back up, North fumbled for his gun. He could hear the spiel loop over in his head, but his lungs just wouldn't let him read the man his rights. He gritted his teeth, finally yanked out his piece and took aim, only to find that Gene was gone.

North looked to the dithering uniform, who indicated the direction in which Gene had fled, away through the special exhibitions, heading for the rear of the building towards Central Park and certain obscurity. North stumbled to his feet, waving Bruder away to the other end of the court. 'Get that kid to a medic.'

Bruder did as he was told. The other cop took the route through the Arts of Africa, Oceana and Americas exhibits. North picked his way along the route Gene had taken.

He probed the shadows, searching, flitting, restless, his Glock trained on everything his eye rested upon, his left hand steadying his right wrist. Glass shards crunched underfoot. *What's that smell?* Pungent and all pervading. *Flowers?* Perfume. A sticky puddle of it, pooled around several glass eyeballs like some macabre soup.

He pressed on, his neck prickling at the unrelenting stone gaze from the gods of the gallery, until he emerged into a space dedicated to exquisitely ornate French furniture. Writing tables, commodes and the 'Merovingian' armoire. But no Gene.

Which way did he go? There'd been work going on at the museum. The direct route through the long, vast European sculpture court was blocked. North pictured the ground plan and tried to remember the exits. He kept moving, searching for a short cut through.

At the end of the European sculpture court was a café and a locked revolving door out to the park. To the left of that the Modern Art exhibit, a stairwell – and an emergency exit.

North ran between the tapestries, porcelains and intricate walnut marquetry, bursting out into a dark ochre corridor by a deserted souvenir stand, piled high with guide books and T-shirts.

To his left, back down the hall, the dark foreboding wooden effigies of African Art. In front, the incomprehensible paint flecks and dribbles of Jackson Pollock; and all around him the impenetrable silence of a trail quickly going cold.

North crept further towards the emergency exit, whirling, probing for movement, a fleeting shadow, a distant voice. There were no footfalls. *Is he out already, or hiding?*

The door to the stairwell swung back and forth, somebody was in there. North moved in tighter, closer, and heard the faint scratching sound of metal scraping against metal. It came from inside. *Behind the door? Up the stairs?* He levelled his Glock, moved in and took aim.

A standard issue semiautomatic stared him between the eyes.

North aimed off as the venom of disgorged relief and guilty panic percolated through his every nerve. The cop from the 81st Street exit was clutching his throat, bright frothing red blood gushing between his desperate fingers. He tried to speak but all he managed was a bloody gurgle.

The cop lowered his weapon and collapsed against the heavy door. North launched at him to cradle his fall and yanked the uniform's Motorola radio to life. 'Get me a *bus*! Right now! Officer down!'

He barked their location for the paramedics, his sudden outburst startling someone further off deeper into the museum. Chairs and tables clattered to the ground in the direction of the café. *Gene.*

North had seconds.

Boiling with frustration he ran back to the souvenir stand and grabbed a T-shirt, pressing it to the cop's neck, forcing it under his rigid fingers. But the blood wouldn't stop. Had the artery been severed? North had no idea where else to apply pressure.

'You'll be all right,' he said. But the shameful truth was he had no idea if he was lying or not.

Down the hall he could hear glass smashing as the appalling seconds ticked by like hours. North craned his neck. *Why the café? Why hadn't he used this exit?* North shoved the door: it was chained shut. Awaiting repair. Gene had been doubling back when he encountered resistance.

North was desperate. *I can make that run, I can get him.* But he couldn't leave the scene. Officer down. That officer must be administered to. *But he's right there! Where are the paramedics?* Maybe he could rip the laces out of his shoes and tie the T-shirt to his neck? *Think! You'll just end up strangling the guy!*

North reached a bloody hand into his back pocket and fished out his Nextel, switching it over from cellphone to radio mode. 'Bruder! Where *are* you?'

But no harried or breathless response came; instead the consuming silence of quiet recrimination and anguish began to wrap both men in its worn and tattered blanket.

North clutched desperately at the cop's neck, feeling the man's grasp go slack, watching his hot blood bubble up between his own fingers only to trickle away again. A crimson brook spilling over his craggy knuckles and down into the growing slick at his feet.

He pressed harder, jamming the T-shirt deeper into the wound despite the overwhelming sense of futility.

God, he didn't even know the man's name.

The heavy clatter of booted paramedics charged down the hall. Bruder was with them. 'North! Which way'd he go?'

A swift and surly paramedic peeled North's fingers away from the wound with routine efficiency.

North wiped the blood from his hands on to his dark body armour. Mopping the sweat from his mouth with one greasy palm, he could do nothing to mask that he was shaken.

'North?'

But North had already set off down the hall for the café without saying a word. All Bruder could do was follow.

Thick glass separated the café from the park outside. Steeply angled windows offered a view of Cleopatra's Needle peeking up behind dark trees on the edge of Turtle Pond.

Tables and chairs and heavy wooden counter tops lay uprooted and overturned in a glinting path through the café that led directly to the widely splayed feet of a triumphant bronze archer.

North picked his way through the debris with care, alert to the possibility of ambush. But he knew in his gut that Gene had already moved on. Knew even before he laid eyes on the gaping hole the man had ferociously smashed through one of the toughened panes.

North picked up the pace. 'Radio all units, he's in the park.'

Bruder complied, quick to keep step, but North was already jumping through the hole on to the grass.

Another vic lay sprawled out on the sweating asphalt of East Drive. Slumped face down. Black leather riding boots and a distinctive yellow triangular patch on his upper arm; it was a cop from the Mounted Unit.

Tell me he doesn't have the horse.

North rushed to the cop's aid as Bruder came barrelling out behind him. 'Get going! I got it! I got it!'

But which way should he go? Central Park Precinct was off to his left a few blocks. *Not that way.* Alice in Wonderland was to his right. Gene had no other option; he was going through the park.

North sprinted up the embankment straight ahead to the thwacking sounds of rubber and cork smacking against white ash, echoing from tree to tree – softball on the Great Lawn.

He darted between the trees, holstering his Glock. There were too many people around. Too many chances for things to go wrong.

On the far side of the needle, he could smell horse and followed the fermenting aroma of fresh dung until he could hear chatter; the soothing, intimate discourse between rider and mount.

Gene stood in the cool shadow of the stone needle on the far side of the horse – a chestnut brown bay, sixteen hands high – rubbing the gelding's sensitive white velvet muzzle with easy confidence.

He seemed mildly puzzled that the tack included two bits,

and was clearly nonplussed with the stirrups, which he had tied up under the belly.

North didn't even have time to plan his next move before the gelding heard him, instinctively pricking his ears back at the heavy footfalls of the approaching cop. It gave Gene all the alarm he needed.

Gene swept up a dark messenger bag at his feet, a bag North was sure he didn't have before. He must have left it here – he must have known he'd be coming this way. *He planned this! He has a route!* North broke into a run.

Gene moved quickly, but calmly. He threw himself up into the saddle, tugging on the reins to steer the horse around to face North. He held the sword out at his side.

And he charged.

10-88

The thundering dervish of hooves violently collapsed the distance between them.

As horse and rider bore down, North took refuge between the trees. The ancient sharpened bronze sliced through the air mere inches from his head, its cold breath upon his neck a ghostly reminder of what might have been.

North darted behind another trunk before making a bid to outflank him, but Gene was not coming around for another attack – he began to cut through the trees, heading west across the park. He tucked the sword away into his bag and urged the horse on, jabbing with his heels.

North ran after him, knowing full well that he had no hope of keeping up with a horse and rider at full gallop.

He burst from the shade of the trees, the naked flame of the summer swelter filling his lungs with burning air. Rivulets of saline sweat cascaded down his face, stinging his eyes.

His chest heaved against his tightly bound body armour, but North refused to give up. Barely capable of speech, he reached again for his Nextel.

'Ten eighty-eight! Perp – heading west . . . ! Delacorte Theater . . . !'

'Say again?'

No, I can't say it again!

He stumbled past a couple of tourists and sprinted hard along the asphalt footpath towards the wooden horseshoe-shaped theatre where the grass dipped away. He'd been here before too many times to count. There was a crossroads at the foot of the small depression; a recreation lane.

He could see the tail of the horse swish and bob as Gene's experienced horsemanship brought the gelding down to a canter. Small clusters of concerned park dwellers broke up quickly to allow them passage, a few making gestures of admonition, as they disappeared over the rise.

By the time North arrived the dizzying heat had worked its oppressive effect. He pulled up sharply, clutching his right side as the excruciating spasm of a stitch squeezed the breath from his lungs. He drew his next breath deeply, trying to control the trembling that seized him, and gazed down at the crossroads through a crimson haze.

North forced himself to keep moving, pushing through the throng in spite of the pain, changing his breathing so that he exhaled every time his left foot hit the ground, taking pressure off his right side, where his liver sat banging into his diaphragm.

Which way now?

The recreation lane was inches deep in fine soil. Horse tracks had cut deep and led in both directions. Overlapping. Confused.

There were two dappled grey ponies trotting under the leafy canopy in the direction of Uptown. More people milling around, spilling down from Central Park West, taking an early lunch break.

North heard a whinny from the direction of the road and quickly jogged up the slope to the kerb outside the park.

Gene was across the other side making the horse pick its way through the bumper-to-bumper gridlock. For a moment,

North wondered whether Gene *wanted* him to catch up. With a horse, he should be miles away by now.

A thin young man, a messenger in black spandex shorts and yellow T-shirt, was preparing to push off on his mountain bike when North flashed him his badge and explained who he was. 'Sir, I really need your bike.'

The cyclist hesitated, but the chaos unfolding in Gene's wake spoke for itself. The messenger quickly handed over the bike and North was gone.

It had been years since North had ridden a bike and this thing had more gears than he knew what to do with. He shot between the closely packed vehicles, narrowly avoiding a collision as the traffic shunted forward. A yellow cab honked angrily at him when his passing allowed a car from another lane to steal the space in front.

North kept his head down and just kept moving. *There's a gap!* He surged forward, dodged a truck and collided headlong into the front end of a gleaming silver Chrysler Sebring Sedan.

Slumped across the hood, North looked angrily up at the driver through the windshield. A striking woman with long, deep auburn hair and wearing designer sunglasses glared back at him. She'd been trying to take the turn into West 81st herself.

North shook himself off the hood and bitterly snatched the bike back up. *Where's that horse?*

Jamming his foot down on the pedal, he kicked off before he lost them for good, weaving in and out of the traffic while trying to keep his gaze above head height. *There!*

Why did Gene need to reach this side of town? Where was he going? Was Gene the type of man to live on the Upper West Side? Was he a lawyer, a doctor? Did either of those labels fit?

Where's he going now?

Gene tugged on the reins, pointing the horse south on to Columbus Avenue.

South? What's he looking for south of here?

HELL'S KITCHEN

On the tourist maps they called it Clinton, but everybody else still knew that at its heart it would always be Hell's Kitchen.

North pedalled hard. The sticky, exhaust-saturated air made his skin burn and crawl. But no matter how hard he tried, for block after block, he just couldn't seem to make up any ground. Gene was too fast. The traffic too heavy. Why was it beginning to feel like he'd spent his entire life chasing this one man?

Gene glanced over his shoulder as if he just knew that North would be there and spurred the horse on to a gallop.

The streets had an air of calm from the gentrified veneer of ex-East Village writers and artists, but North, like any cop, knew that scratch the surface and the darker core remained. Inviolate. The writers were nothing but frauds, looking for the next good story to leech. Amid the designer apartment blocks refurbished from nineteenth-century slaughterhouses and glue factories, tiny dishevelled food shops and restaurants still sat on the doorstep of crumbling tenements. It was a powder keg of affluent white mixed with ethnic poor.

And Gene seemed to know the area well. He jumped the gelding up on to the sidewalk, and cleared the barrier to a small parking lot.

North blasted through the tiny gap at the side of the barrier and rode swiftly through the side alley. He shot out on to the next street where the porn industry had taken up residence ever since they'd been moved out of Times Square.

If ever there was a place that defined the city's true nature, it was Hell's Kitchen. They'd tried to Disneyfy it. They'd done a good job, too. But like a grotesque wearing a cheap Mickey Mouse costume, the smile proved false reassurance, because underneath the costume the demon remained. Sharpening his claws. Biding his time. Perhaps the demon had taken to painting his portrait. Perhaps the demon had painted Gene.

Where the sidewalks grew busy with sad individuals shuffling in and out of seedy gilded dollar peep shows, North heard the screams from further down the street as people struggled to get out of the way of the madman on horseback.

The Lincoln Tunnel was a few blocks away – if Gene wanted to make it out of the city and into New Jersey, that was the way to go. In Manhatten a man on a horse would always be conspicuous. But still, it didn't make sense. There were easier routes than this one. Was Gene a stranger to the city?

Without warning two squad cars suddenly screamed out of a side exit, lights and sirens whirring. Gene leaned back so hard the horse reared up on its hind legs.

Ignoring a patrolman's order to stop, Gene turned the horse around and kicked at the gelding to get moving. He looked up and caught North's eye.

The two men were now speeding relentlessly towards each other.

This is it. North's pulse quickened. *I can take him*. He was exhausted, yet his legs pumped furiously. Gene reached into his bag. *Reach for the sword! Go on, just do it!*

The horse bucked his head and pricked back his ears in protest at the relentless pace. His hooves slipped on the asphalt. Gene pressed him on; drawing back his arm.

North leaped from the speeding mountain bike and ploughed into the younger man on horseback. Together they tumbled off the rear of the frightened bay and landed heavily in the road.

The surrounding vehicles screamed to a halt while the horse ran on.

North threw the first punch. His fingers so tightly clenched his hand had gone numb before it had even connected with Gene's face. There was an almighty crunch of bone.

Gene's fingers loosened around the bronze sword. North saw his chance, and hammered on the man's forearm until the sharpened metal tumbled away.

He kicked at it with one foot. It slid across the asphalt as he reached for his gun. Yet Gene was quicker. He pulled his other hand from his dark messenger bag and plunged a flashing metal object deep into North's thigh.

The cop grunted in supreme agony, bursts of white light exploding behind his tightly clenched eyes.

Gene threw him off and staggered to his feet. The patrolmen from the two squad cars were running towards him, pulling out their guns.

North recovered and reached for his Glock. Again Gene was quicker. He instinctively kicked the gun from North's hand and dived between two parked cars. Peering between the windows, out of range of the patrolmen, he looked for an escape route. Spotting a dumpster-filled alleyway no more than a few yards away, he ran.

North was up and hobbling after him, trying to ignore the excruciating pain in his upper thigh. When Gene approached the corner, brick dust exploded above his head as the patrolmen took aim and fired. Hysteria swept down the sidewalks.

North raced through the waves of panic, pushing aside the bodies that got in his way, yet the more he struggled against the tide the more black clouds and rolling thunder filled his senses and obstructed his better judgement. He careened around the corner, his hunger to find this man and capture him once and for all so absolute he gave no thought to what might be waiting for him at the rear of the building. If Gene wanted to be found, North was happy to oblige.

The shadows that were cast across his path seemed to shimmer and move. The deafening roar of bloodlust filled his ears in a cacophony of raging confusion. Like the disconcerting pops of old fashioned flashbulbs, distorted and blurred images accompanied a displaced jumble of sensations in a relentless assault on his mind's eye. The pressure in his skull throbbed with every pulse of his constrained blood vessels.

North ran out into the rear yard to find Gene desperately tearing at bags of putrid, filthy garbage. Access to the alleyway was blocked. Foul smelling dumpsters were crowded against a far wall, but the bags were not allowing him to climb to freedom.

'Freeze!'

Gene tore at another bag. It spilled open as he flung it distractedly in North's direction. Small black ceramic ashtrays, caked in foul ash, rolled across the ground. With the smoking ban throughout the city they had become useless objets d'art.

North grabbed one and palmed it like a discus.

Gene stared contemptuously back at him. 'I am Satan's Oath!'

How could he respond to that? What could North say when all he could see was the vision of a bull standing before him, its hot breath billowing from its nostrils, defiant rage written across its brazen face?

North looked away in confusion. *I'm losing my mind.* He stumbled in sheer disbelief as the Bull dipped its horns. 'You have the right to remain silent.'

The Bull dug its hoof into the ground.

'You have the right to an attorney.'

The Bull took a step towards him.

'Stop right there!'

But the Bull continued to advance.

North retreated, weighing the ashtray in his hand, without being fully aware of what he was doing. He spun on his heel like the athletes of old and launched the weapon at his charging enemy.

The ceramic ashtray exploded above the Bull's right ear in a cloud of fluttering butterflies, its sweat-soaked hide ran dark with blood as it burst upon North, its horn rending a savage blow to North's left shoulder.

North whirled around, his mind and vision clearing momentarily from the fog. Gene stood before him brandishing the broken haft of a mop like a sharpened spear. Then he lunged without warning, plunging the stake into North's aching gut, but the body armour would not give.

Gene ploughed him into a trash can, his gritted teeth clenched with fury. 'Submit!'

North grabbed the lid of the trash can and smashed it down on the weapon, flipped it up and used it like a shield to deflect the blows.

Spots of rain struck his eyes, the first strikes in a heavy summer downpour. Fat droplets lashed against both their faces as they circled each other, the spray becoming a torrent. The torrent became a deluge. Thunder rolled across the sky.

The channels of rainwater cascading down Gene's face

started to writhe and spit, and rise up like snakes. They peeled away from his cheeks and hissed at North with venomous hatred. North cowered. *What's happening?* This couldn't be real. He had to be hallucinating.

A car horn rang out somewhere off beyond the wall. *Did I just hear that?*

Gene cocked his head. *Yes!*

North took the distraction and grabbed the weapon; Gene countered by surrendering it to him.

The surprise of Gene's move caused North to slip as he yanked his arm backwards, allowing Gene free passage to escape. Running at the nearest dumpster, he leaped up on to it, scrambling over trash bags until he vaulted over the wall.

North threw down his shield and tried to emulate Gene's agility. He failed. He was exhausted. He had no sense of distance, no sense of balance. Everything washed in and out of his mind like waves lapping at the shore. Winded, he collapsed in a heap, his only company the sound of the distant car idling away, and the lashing of the black, greasy rain.

After a moment, North heard a car door open and a deadened voice say, 'I can help you. Get in.' He heard footsteps. The door closing. The car driving away. He heard all that. But was it real? He couldn't see the car. He barely knew where he was.

He knew what he had to do, yet he had neither the energy nor the willpower to do it. He just sat in the wet, trying to catch his breath, destroyed and defeated, until the throbbing pain in his leg wrenched him back to reality.

Through his mind's troubled haze, he gazed down at a thin silver spike protruding from his leg.

North reached for it but found that he was disturbingly dissociated from his actions; he had no sense that the hand he saw moving belonged to him at all. Persisting, he felt around the spike for a moment before he tugged it roughly from his aching flesh.

He brought the flashing metal close to his eyes. He hadn't been stabbed at all. The spike was a needle from a large syringe. Gene had injected him. *What did he put in me?* Four inches of cold hollow metal, bathed in his rapidly congealing blood. It was a pernicious parting gift.

SCRATCHING THE SURFACE

Thu-thump.

Not safe. Not safe here. It's coming.

Thu-thump.

Gotta go. Gotta. Now.

North staggered to his feet. His fingers numb. His balance in spasm. A confusing mishmash of tinnitus and gurgling roars punctured the silence only in flashes.

Where are my feet?

The heavy rain lashed his face. He looked up into the chasm of the sky and felt the full force of nature.

Can't breathe. Can't breathe. Air.

He tore at the fastenings on his body armour. Stumbled out into traffic.

Hooooooooooooooooonnnnkkk!

Thu-thump. Thump. Thump.

Not that way. It's waiting.

He melted into the crowd, cowered and stooped. Avoiding the *it*. Staying away from the *it*. But he could feel *its* hot breath on his back. Feel *it* gathering pace, feel *it* pawing the ground. He was the hunted. He was the prey. He clawed at the crowd in desperation. The ignorant and the blind who danced with death.

Watch out! Move! It's coming!

The crowd refused to part. He pushed and shoved. Jostled and clawed.

Thu-thump! THU-THUMP!

A thousand directions. A million choices. Infinite paths.

They found him in a convenience store two blocks away and half an hour later. In an aisle notable mostly for its canned goods, his body armour at his feet, his T-shirt off, he had a disposable nailfile and was using it to apply honey straight from the jar and on to his open wounds.

The honey oozed like a slow ribbon, entangling itself with tendrils of blood.

He was tearing his T-shirt into strips, using it like medical gauze to bind his arm, when the others arrived. The store owner stood with a few bemused customers at the entranceway holding a baseball bat, hoping he wouldn't have to use it.

The cops were hesitant.

Bruder had a clear plastic rain cover over his hat and a poncho over his uniform. As he took the first step, the rainwater beaded down his body in a constant drip, drip, drip.

It made North twitch.

'Detective?'

North didn't respond. He smeared more thick golden orange blossom honey into a deep graze, and bound it tight.

'Hey, man, you left the scene. You're not answering your radio.'

'Cleaning up.'

North said it as though what he was doing was perfectly natural.

With a uniform by his side, the store owner felt more confident. He raised his bat, complaining about the mess. Bruder laid a hand on the butt of his gun and held the other one up to the owner. 'Sir, I got it. Okay?'

He moved cautiously down the aisle.

'Why'd you leave? The Crime Scene Unit don't even know if they put the grid in the right area. Everyone's been looking for you.'

'Things to do.'

North looked up, his eyes swollen and bloodshot.

'Jesus.'

Bruder glanced back at the other patrolman in the doorway. Neither man really knew how to proceed when it was one of their own. Least he wasn't violent.

North looked outside. 'Did you find him?'

'No, he got away.'

North just nodded to himself, or shook his head. He seemed to be having a whole conversation that no one else was privy to.

'You gonna pay the man for his groceries?'

North stumbled over his words. The confusion of his predicament seemed, impenetrable. 'I . . . I bought a bike.'

'You bought a bike.' Bruder scratched his head trying to make sense of the comment. 'Okay, I'll pay the man. You can owe me.'

'Thank you.'

'Wanna take a ride?'

North watched the heavy sheets of uncompromising rain. 'Sure.'

They put him in the back of the squad car. A blanket draped around his shoulders. A haunted and perplexed shell of a man, docile behind the grille.

They drove him slowly past where the Crime Scene Unit was despondently working the area in windbreakers and rubber gloves.

The worst thing that could happen to evidence gathering was to have the rain wash it all away. They worked quickly.

They found the body of the syringe, filthy from where it had rolled under a dark blue, grime-encrusted dumpster.

There was a residue inside the glass, a deep red concoction. They dropped it into a paper bag; like all organic evidence it had to be able to breathe.

One of the Forensic Investigators came up to the car and showed the bag to North through the rear window, like a trophy, but Robert Ash's satisfaction turned to concern when he saw the state North was in.

North didn't even register that he was looking at the face of a man he had worked with many times in the past.

Ash addressed Bruder instead. 'Did he touch this? He needs to get a blood test as soon as possible. God knows what he picked up.'

'So nothing to worry about.' Bruder cracked a friendly smile.

A paramedic came over and checked his signs. North appeared stable, he just needed to sleep it off.

North's mind was elsewhere, his psyche swimming in a sea of confusion, barely registering the moving scenery when they drove him home to his third floor apartment in an old elevatorless brownstone in Woodside.

'I called the Fourth,' Bruder explained. 'They're gonna give you a couple days.'

How long would it really take to return from this darkness?

Alone in the apartment the flashbulbs popped again. Image after. *Pop!* Image. An assault with. *Pop!* No end in sight.

Pop.

Beads of sweat. Liquid ants. Cracks in the walls. Skeletal fingers. The branches of trees. Route maps to darker places fed by despair.

Thu-thump.

Thu-thump.

A searing pain arced across his head, temple to temple. His brain a kernel waiting to . . . *Pop*.

'I got away. He doesn't know I'm here.'

'He doesn't know?'

'He's on duty. We got all night. *All* night.'

He ripped at her clothes. Threw off her bra and devoured a mouthful of her fleshy breasts. Teased her nipples between his teeth and dug his clawed fingers into her hungry, soft white skin. Handfuls of rounded ass, drawing her in to meet his rage. A frenzy of hardened animal lust. Hammering at the gates.

A thousand grunts and screams, the sweet taste of bitter secrecy, the unbridled need.

And before the release, the closeness of the mutual crime, she, stroking the back of his neck, lost in his mysterious eyes, he, consumed with the familiarity of hers.

Yet even that did not stop him.

He released. A shudder so violent that she cried out.

He released into her. His mother.

North awoke sobbing and naked. Cocooned in his bed sheets. Drenched in a three-day-old sweat.

His mother.

PORTER

Samir Farouk swerved to avoid a mangy stray dog on the dusty road to Jbeil at around 8.30. It was Tuesday, 1 April 1997. He was driving an old Isuzu pick-up truck, its white battered paintwork severely scored and dented. Swollen blisters of rust sat feeding on the wings, right above the tyres. Its suspension was so feeble it could barely cope with the heavily laden cargo of spare parts for his small refrigeration business.

It was in no shape to negotiate the potholes sunk deep into the dirt on the edges of the worn-out road. When it hit one, the truck flipped almost immediately. Samir Farouk, at thirty-one years old, was catapulted through the windshield. His unconscious body landed in the path of heavy oncoming traffic. He was dead by 8.32.

When William Porter picked up the phone, the voice on the other end of the crackly line sounded timid and frightened.

They exchanged greetings. She'd heard about him through a friend. She wouldn't give the friend's name. She didn't want it getting back to anyone else. Her English was excellent, luckily, since although Porter had lived and worked in Lebanon on and off for the past twenty-three years, he still couldn't get the hang of Arabic beyond a pidgin familiarity.

Calls like this were rare. Usually he had to go searching for case studies, subsisting on university grants and charitable handouts. But regardless of how, or how often, he met these people, he was always struck that their curiosity and their concern were almost always present in equal measure.

When the caller got to the point – and Porter was careful not to rush her – she was candid.

'They say you are the seeker of the reborn?'

'Yes.'

There was silence on the end of the line. He could hear a match being struck. A cigarette being lit. The underlying distress in her voice was becoming infectious. She said, 'I normally don't smoke.'

They normally never did, these people who found themselves doubting both their beliefs and the evidence.

'How can I help you?'

He could hear the charred match being tossed away, the echo of it tumbling around an otherwise empty glass ashtray.

'My name is Najla Jabara,' she said. 'My boyfriend – my *ex*-boyfriend – has written to me. He says he misses me. He wants to see me again. I have the letter right here.' He could hear her smoothing out the folds in the paper. 'He says he can't understand why I haven't been to see him.

'Dr Porter, Samir has been dead for seven years.'

They met in secret in the stairwell of a small dishevelled apartment block some days later. Porter, six feet tall and thin with age, cut a distinctly European figure among the Arabs and Najla dared not risk being seen with him. She was a married woman now and wanted to give no cause for her husband to start beating her.

Motes of dust swirled in the hot beams of sunlight that pierced the shadows of the dusty stairwell. Standing in the darkness, she handed him an envelope filled with American dollars. He counted out the contents. It was what they'd agreed. He tucked it away. He felt no guilt. Only he knew what other activities Najla's payment subsidized.

Najla was a dressmaker in the narrow crowded back streets of Beirut. Her pay was meagre, but opportunities for overtime came three days a week and she took them. Cutting fabric and pressing garments in the cramped and sweltering sweatshop. She sewed until her fingers were red raw.

She showed him the letter and read out passages she thought most sounded like Samir. The post mark was recent. Though Porter could read only the odd word here and there, even he could tell that the writer did not have a fist for letters. From beginning to end the communiqué was written in a particularly immature hand.

It was exactly as Porter suspected.

The return address pointed to the Chouf, a mountainous region to the southeast where the obscure village of Fawwara sat on the slopes of Mount Lebanon.

For over half his life Porter had dedicated himself to penetrating the veil that surrounded the Chouf. He had known instinctively that what he was searching for lay hidden somewhere in the heart of those mountains. Now he could return and continue the search.

But he was not a dishonest man. He had no intention of bleeding this woman dry. He would investigate the writer claiming to be the deceased Samir Farouk and if he felt there was no merit to the story he would not continue to take her money.

'I must know if it is him,' Najla insisted.

Porter's reply was polite, his English accent softened by years of living abroad. 'And have you given any thought to what you will do with this information if it *is* him?'

His dark eyes, though gentle, were intense. She felt that here was a man who could look right through a person and peer into their very soul.

She seemed almost desperate. There was clearly unfinished business weighing on her mind. 'I will see him.'

In the Chouf Porter was already well known. Those locals who had come to know Porter regarded him as something of a novelty and even appreciated some of his more peculiar foreign habits.

A series of lengthy meetings took place before Porter was convinced there was something to the letter writer's story. The village had been relatively easy to find, and it afforded him ample opportunity to pursue his other work.

He was close. So very close. In that village, he knew, lay more answers.

Najla, in the meantime, saved her money. Porter warned her that when the time came, she should not go with any fixed expectations, but her mind was made up.

On a bright summer's morning, everything was finally set in motion. Najla told her husband about the terrible troubles her distant cousin was having in her reconciliation village to the south. The girl she used to play with as a child in the squalor of the Beirut suburbs during the troubles. It was just credible enough not to arouse suspicion. It was all she needed to get away.

She climbed into the back of a silver Mercedes 500SL sedan, with two men she hardly knew, and trusted they would not betray her.

DRUZE

'There is blood between us, and blood is never easy to forget.'

Ma'mun al-Suri swung the gleaming 500SL dangerously across the thundering road, veering in and out of the volatile traffic. The protesting wails of car horns replaced all need to use the brakes. He sped onwards towards Mount Lebanon and the reconciliation villages.

'We all took part in the war. We all paid the price,' the swarthy translator added. He was a Maronite Christian who had lived alongside the Druze in the Chouf before the war. Then Israel invaded, retreated, and a power vacuum caused the nation to implode. Friends and neighbours turned on each other. It was a bloodbath.

Porter watched the guilt dull Najla's lively eyes. Her cover story had aroused unpleasant memories. The lies did not sit well with her. She looked away, brushing her long dark hair from her face as the hot, dry air blasted through the open windows.

Porter gently clapped al-Suri on the shoulder. He had hired the Lebanese translator many times in the past. They had an understanding. 'Concentrate on the traffic, please.'

Al-Suri laughed. 'Like the motives of women, my friend, these roads obey laws all of their own.' He glanced back at Najla through the rear-view mirror with a friendly twinkle in his eye. He had not been fooled by her cover story, but her affairs were her own concern, just as the traffic was his.

Najla sat wringing her hands in her lap, wrought with uncertainties. 'Druze don't allow marriage into or out of their religion. I don't understand how Samir could be among them.'

'Their beliefs are different from what you're accustomed to.'

'I know very little about their beliefs.'

'Which is just how they want it. The Druze are a people of secrets. Most of their followers are called the *Juhhal*, the Ignorant Ones, who are denied the secret teachings of the *Kitab al Hikmah,* the sacred scriptures known collectively as the Book of Wisdom. Very few are granted full knowledge by the sages. Even then, only after the age of forty can they become the *Uqqat*, the Knowers. It's been that way for a thousand years.'

'How can they be trusted? They deny their own faith.'

The *at-Ta-lim*, or the Instruction, allowed a concession called the *taqiyah*. In the face of oppression the Druze were permitted to deny their faith outwardly in order to survive. Porter considered it an enlightened policy, but then he was of no particular faith. He kept the passions of religious fervour at an intentional distance.

Porter gave neither comfort to Najla nor offence. 'They let Samir send you his letters, did they not?'

Najla had no reply.

Druze belief was founded on a principle few religions of the area found conscionable. Yet it was enough to prompt a simple dressmaker from Beirut to lie to her husband and travel hundreds of miles just to see if they were telling the truth.

The Druze believed in the transmigration of the soul. Reincarnation.

Al-Suri slowed his Mercedes around the sharp mountain

bend. The ground was parched and his vehicle pitched up great clouds of amber-coloured dust. The sweet smell of peaches was strong in the air from the lining groves. Across the dusty green valley small plantations grew apricots, prunes and tomatoes.

Life in the heart of the mountains was hard and poor. A kind of uneasy peace masked an undercurrent of bitter resentment towards all who would come here and flaunt their wealth. Porter wondered, not for the first time, whether al-Suri's Mercedes was the best car to travel in.

The dented old tin sign at the edge of the road read Fawwara. The sound of the gushing spring after which the terraced village had been named was its perpetual voice.

A small army checkpoint stood abandoned and dilapidated by the main road. A throwback to when stability in the area was enforced.

The Mercedes crawled carefully past the piles of rubble, the ghostly shells of houses. The village, though in the early stages of redevelopment, was still grimly scarred and pocked from the ravages of war.

A little way on lay the beating heart of the village, a small roadside café sat next to a souk, a shabby but well stocked convenience store that sold everything from soap to sugar, light bulbs to cigarettes.

A few small children were playing in the street as the car pulled up. Three elderly Druze men sat drinking tiny cups of mint tea at a stained and badly chipped table. They wore Ottoman pantaloons in the traditional style, and sported white fez-like hats. Two had ample beards, their skin dark and leathery.

The third, with his curly moustache, stood when Porter got out of the car. He had been waiting.

'*Ahlen wa sahlen.*'

Porter smiled at the welcome. '*Sabah el khair, kifak?*' he replied. *Good morning, how are you?*

The old Druze shrugged modestly, self-consciously rubbing his left knee and giving it a pat. '*Mnih, mnih,*' he replied, but it was clear from his waddle that he wasn't as well as he was claiming.

His eyes told yet another story. He was apprehensive, and his companions were well aware of this. His gaze settled on Najla, and Porter was quick to make polite introductions.

The old Druze's name was Kamal Touma. He clapped his hands to his sides. It was time to do this thing.

The Touma family all lived together in one house further up the slope of the village where the line of tall pine trees grew dense. They kept chickens in the back yard and a young lemon tree in the front. To the side sat a massive and rare Lebanese cedar which gave ample shade from the withering sun.

Inside, the house was spotlessly clean and the furniture surprisingly modern. The visitors could smell cooking wafting through the house from the kitchen, while the hall reverberated to the relentless ticking of an antique pendulum clock.

Touma ushered them through to the lounge and told them all to take a seat, before disappearing into the kitchen, but only Najla went on through. Porter held back, pulling al-Suri to one side.

'Go to them,' he said. 'Tell them I'm here. That I'd like to see them today.'

Al-Suri was sceptical. 'You know how these people can get. They are suspicious of you.'

'Tell them I've brought the book.' Porter reached into the file he had wedged under his arm and pulled out an old, green leather-bound notebook filled with scribblings and sketches. He forced it into al-Suri's hands. 'They cannot deny the book.'

Al-Suri was surprised. Porter had never let the book leave his side before. He took it, but he remained to be convinced. 'I'll see what I can do.'

He left quickly, leaving the Englishman alone in the hall.

Tick, tick, tick.

Porter joined Najla in the lounge. What was taking so long? Perhaps the family had changed its mind. These things happened.

Najla nervously wrung her hands in her lap once more, curiously in time to the old clock that ticked out their lives one measure at a time. She repeated the action until the door opened, quietly and without fanfare.

Najla instinctively got to her feet, wide-eyed, as two people came into the room. The older was a woman who wore the white *mandeel*, or headscarf, that signified Druze religious devotion.

Porter made introductions but did not offer his hand to the woman. Druze women were not permitted to touch any man outside their immediate family.

Then the woman said simply, 'This is Khulud.'

Khulud stepped out of the woman's shadow, his eyes welling with tears. He could sense something in the air and drunk it in deeply. 'I can smell you. You're wearing that perfume you wore the night we first kissed.' A smile touched his lips. 'I have missed you,' he said. 'So much.'

Najla was uncertain and glanced momentarily to Porter for support. 'What's wrong with him? Why doesn't he look at me?'

'He's been blind since birth.'

Khulud took another step forward, excited. 'Remember, when I tried to feel under your blouse? The blue one with the little birds on the sleeve and my watch caught on the buttons! You said that'll teach me!'

Khulud's mother shook her head with embarrassment.

Najla blushed and backed away. But she was also shocked. 'Stop it. You shouldn't be talking about such things.'

Khulud was confused and innocent. 'That's why you're here, isn't it? Why shouldn't I talk of such things?'

To Najla it was obvious why not. These words were not coming from the mouth of the man she loved, but from the mouth of a boy.

Khulud Touma was a 7-year-old child.

She felt so foolish. Khulud knew it.

'I *am* Samir,' he insisted. 'I'm *also* Khulud.'

Najla's body started to shake. 'Samir is gone,' she sobbed.

Takamous, the changing of the clothes. Reincarnation implied the physical body was clothing for the soul. It had only been seven years. It was always going to be a child. Porter had warned her it would be difficult to be faced with this boy.

Khulud asked to be guided to her. His small frame dwarfed by hers, his blind eyes distraught that he couldn't see her face. He held his pose stoically and took her hand in both of his, stroking the back tenderly. 'You remember when your father bought those ridiculous trousers that stopped six inches above his ankles, and they used to flap when he walked?'

Najla laughed involuntarily, wiping away a tear. 'Yes,' she said.

She didn't want to – couldn't – believe, but how did he know these things? Maybe he had somehow learned the details by rote?

Porter was certain he had not. He had come here several times to determine whether Khulud's memories were genuine or not. To determine whether this was a ruse by his family to extract money from Najla, as was common in these parts. Khulud knew things only Najla had consistently been able to confirm. As far as he could surmise, that made Khulud's memories genuine.

Najla recalled more details of the shared memory. 'It didn't matter what anybody said to him, he insisted on wearing those silly things. They were all he could get. He had no more money.' She gazed down at the boy. 'You remember how you used to tease him? What did you say?'

Khulud went to answer, but he drew a blank. A picture of uncertainty, his face clouded. He reached out to his mother. Najla's tears welled again.

Porter took a measured breath. 'Details can be patchy,' he said. 'It can often make memories seem incoherent.'

'Maybe we're not supposed to remember,' Najla said wistfully. 'Maybe the memories of a past life are a defect.'

'Perhaps.'

Najla wiped more tears away and brushed her damp fingers over the face of Khulud. He had the most curious birthmarks all over his brow and across his eyes.

'What happened to make these marks?'

Khulud seemed not to know. But Porter did. He'd seen many instances over the years. A woman in India who claimed to have been murdered, burned alive in her previous life, left to roast on a woven straw mat. In this life the pattern from that mat had been etched for ever on to her body as birthmarks.

There was Cemil Fahrici, a Turk born with a bleeding birthmark under his chin and a further mark just to the left of his crown, in a line where no hair would grow. Fahrici remembered living the life of a bandit who, when cornered by police, shot himself. Fahrici's birthmarks exactly matched the bandit's wounds recorded in the police files.

Birthmarks represented the physical trauma sustained by a reincarnated soul from its previous life.

In Samir's case, his face was heavily lacerated when the windshield shattered. 'He was blinded before he died,' Porter gently reminded.

Najla tried to retain her dignity. Of course. How could she forget?

'May we have time alone together?' she asked, letting her eyes settle on the little boy she had travelled so far to see.

Porter very much wanted to stay and see for himself the extent to which the connection between these two would be rekindled, but he refused to impose himself.

Khulud's mother quickly explained that he was welcome to sit in the back yard. She had made fresh lemonade and he could help himself.

It was hardly a consolation, but Porter thanked her all the same. He stepped out into the yard and poured himself a drink. He could hear a motor running, puncturing the rural quiet.

Out on the main road al-Suri was returning, but as a passenger in a strange car with three other men Porter didn't know, and who did not have the most welcoming of faces.

Al-Suri shared his troubles as soon as he got out. 'They've been sent by the family,' he said. 'But I don't trust them.'

The most corpulent of the three men, his breathing audible, held up Porter's green leather notebook. 'This is very unusual. No outsider should know these things.'

Porter took it back and tucked it away. 'You have a child who is a *natiq*? He read my notes?'

'The *nataq* was told of them, yes,' the corpulent man replied.

A *natiq* meant literally one who talks about the previous generation. But the man used the word *nataq*, the feminine form.

Porter hadn't guessed she would be a girl.

'My niece will see you.' Porter felt the hairs on the back of his neck prickle. 'She will talk about the *seventh trial*. But after this, you will not see her again. We want no part of this.'

All his life, and finally somebody had confirmed for him the existence of the seventh trial.

The tallest of the three men stepped forward and held out a small cloth sack. It was clear to everyone that he meant to put it over Porter's head.

They could take him to the girl, or they could just as easily take him to his execution. The leap of faith would have to be Porter's. Either way he would not be privy to the route to his destination. They did not want him finding his way back to them, uninvited, in the future.

The ultimatum was made. 'You come now, or you don't come at all.'

Al-Suri cursed in Arabic. 'Don't trust them.'

Porter's mind was made up. 'I have to.' He stepped up to the car. It was black and large. He trusted al-Suri to commit its other details to memory. 'If I haven't returned by sunset, get Najla back to her husband.'

Porter eased into the back seat and waited nervously. A cold sweat crept down his chest when the larger man lowered the rough sack over his head and pulled the draw string tight. He did not check to see if Porter could breathe.

The doors were slammed shut, and before al-Suri could protest further, Porter was unceremoniously driven away.

AISHA

How long had they been driving? An hour? Two? The journey was a bumpy one. After the first few twists and turns he'd lost all sense of direction.

Porter guessed they were driving him across farming tracks. He couldn't be certain, the light that pierced the coarse weave of the hood gave no clue. All he was sure of was they had traversed not a single stretch of road that continued straight for more than a few minutes. They seemed to be still somewhere in the mountains.

The music from the radio was loud, probably also to prevent him from remembering any outside aural cues.

Conversation was thin. He was here at the request of the *nataq* and no other reason. Nobody else wanted him here.

The car rolled to a stop. No one said a word. They waited for what felt like an eternity and then let the engine die.

Porter could hear a door open. Footsteps. Someone walking around to the back. Another door opened.

They dragged him out.

'Stand here.'

Porter did as he was told. He tried to swallow, but his

mouth was parched. He could hear them talking. A decision was being made. What were they going to do with him?

He shook with fear, his only company, his own erratic breathing. He dare not say anything. He simply waited, and hoped.

They pulled the sack roughly from his head and gave him little time to adjust his eyes.

The car roared into life and sped quickly away. He was left in the company of the corpulent man, who handed him his belongings and pointed to the small gate that led into the back yard.

'Aisha is waiting.'

The girl sat in the shade beneath a tall cypress tree, sketching with fixated determination into a large, heavily thumbed incarnadine book. She was no more than nine years old and her hair blew freely across her stern face. It would not be long now before she would have to wear the headscarf of tradition.

Porter approached uneasily. Set back behind the cypress, the doors to a large sitting room inside the house sat wide open, revealing an assembled circle of couches where the girl's large extended family watched them both, quietly suspicious.

'They're afraid of you,' the little girl said.

'I'm a stranger.'

'I am not afraid of strangers.'

A scowling young man of army age appeared in the doorway. Porter had been warned.

'My brother. He says you Westerners are talking yourselves into extinction. He says unbelievers don't get to come back.'

'We're two very different cultures that have long been in conflict. It's our history. Perhaps even our destiny.'

Aisha looked up. Her face brightened. 'Are you sure that we're not the same, you and I?'

She knows.

Porter sat down to watch her draw, a newspaper at her feet. As she swept her pencil across the page, she tucked her thick hair behind her ear revealing the peculiar circular birthmark that sat by her temple, just as his own did.

Birthmarks are the traumas from past lives.

'Why did you choose green for your memories?' She let the pencil flow free, sculpting a face in strokes of dark graphite. She was extremely skilled. More capable than any adult Porter had ever seen.

He was taken aback at the maturity of her conversation. 'I don't understand.'

'Your notebook is green.'

Porter thought about it, but he had no answer. 'I was very young. As young as you are now. It was an instinct. I awoke one morning with an urge to write, my parents thought it was a fantasy.'

It was a portrait of a child, he realized, the face taking shape in the book.

She gave definition to the rounded cherubic cheeks with gentle strokes from the edge of the sharp point.

'Green is an interesting choice. Nothing happens by accident,' she said. 'There are five sacred colours to us Druze. Yellow is *al-kalima*. Yellow is for the word. Blue is *as-sahik*, for the mental power of the will. White stands for what is made reality because of the power of the blue. But you chose green, which is *al-'akl*. Green is *the mind*, and the mind understands the truth. You chose green because you understand the mind.'

'I'm a psychiatrist, if that's what you mean.'

'In *this* life,' she said.

Porter watched her closely. Watched how she held the pencil in an eerily familiar grasp; *his* grasp. A 9-year-old girl doing just as he had done when he was a boy, showing a kind of wisdom and a knowledge that was far beyond her years, struggling to comprehend the nightmares.

Aisha worked in a shadow with heavy strokes of pencil, blackening the page. She set the pencil down and held the book up to appreciate her drawing. 'It is done,' she said. 'The *seventh trial* has come.'

The head of a child, not more than a few weeks old, sat severed and impaled on a stick.

Porter was aghast. He flicked the pages. Leaf after leaf was filled with writing, sometimes in several languages, and always accompanied by a torrent of the foulest, bile-inducing images. He was aghast, not because the images disturbed him, but because these murderous scenes of death springing from the mind of a child matched the ones contained within his own green notebook. They were identical.

Everything that his nightmares had told him growing up as an only child on the leafy dairy farm near Canterbury had revealed that his instincts to leave England's green shores in his search were true. There *were* more like him.

'This is for *him*,' she said. 'The one you will guide.'

Who is she talking about?

'This book is red. Red is *ah-nahts*. Red is for the soul. What I've written, I've written for Cyclades' soul,' she explained.

Cyclades. Just hearing that name on lips other than his own brought indescribable reassurance.

'But there are others,' she said. 'The sixth book is black. Black is for despair, the chaos of mental destruction.'

'And the seventh?'

The little girl's face was pensive. 'The seventh is the book that's within us all. Guide him with the six so that he will know who he is. The thread of Cyclades' fate is like a thick rope that has been frayed. It is up to you to pull the thread back together again.'

She set her incarnadine book down on top of Porter's resolute green one.

Aisha seemed curiously relieved. Like a great weight had been lifted from her slight shoulders. 'I cannot go with you.

But justice must be done and it is up to you to see that justice *will* be done. That is *your* fate.'

He could feel the spring of uncertainty well up deep within himself. It was a sickening feeling and Aisha seemed to be sharing it. 'Who is it I must guide?'

'My goodness, the sun is so strong today.'

Porter was hesitant. 'Yes.'

'Can you see your shadow?'

Porter cast his eye along the ground. He held out his hand and watched the shadow of his fingers dance along the undulations.

'Look closely at it. Do you ever think that you are your shadow?'

'No. It's just a shadow.'

'What if it was a reflection? Or when you see yourself in a dream? Would that be you?'

'Of course not.'

'We Mowahhidoon are defined by the nature of the returning soul.'

Mowahhidoon was one of the many names the Druze called themselves. Monotheists who believed in one God whose qualities could not be understood or defined by men. Who started out as a sect of Islam, though Islam had long since cast them from their ranks.

'Like a shadow or a reflection, we shouldn't identify ourselves with this living body either. Our bodies are the clothes for our souls. But what I feel is not what my family says I should believe.'

She handed Porter the newspaper at her feet. It was a recent edition of the *International Herald Tribune*. An amalgamation of *New York Times* and *Washington Post* articles sometimes circulated free by some airlines.

This edition was printed in Paris. There was nothing remarkable about it. No particular headlines jumped out at him as she flipped through the pages.

Porter did not understand.

'My uncle travels to Europe on business all the time. *Every* week he brings me things to read. Says it's important that I know *the world*. Dear, sweet man. I know it better than he ever will. Tell me, what do you see?'

In the centre of the page was a photograph of two men caught in a moment. Lashed by the rain. Two men fighting in a backstreet of New York City. Fighting like the warriors of old. 'Cop Battles Hostage Taker.'

Porter could feel a chill in his bones.

'The body is but clothes and its face but a mask. Yet I know this face. You know this face. We are both drawn to this face. Once, *we were this man*.'

Porter studied the article. Everything he had felt and known as a child this little Druze girl had now confirmed, that there were people in the world who were both reincarnate and a living paradox.

By the day's end Porter had booked his ticket to New York and had put his affairs in order. He knew he would not be coming back.

In New York City awaited the man of whom Porter was the living reincarnation, a man who appeared younger than he was, a man who was not yet dead.

BOOK TWO

KNOW THYSELF? IF I KNEW MYSELF,
I'D RUN AWAY

GOETHE

AWAKENING

He stirred in the back seat of the sedan, his tongue a fibrous carpet of dried mucus. He had difficulty moving at first, his face had stuck to the black leather interior and he had to peel his skin away with some discomfort. His hair was matted with a congealed paste of sweat, dirt and blood. The car was not moving.

How long had he been here?

'You stink,' the voice announced with irritation. 'He won't see you like this.'

Gene wiped motes of crusty yellow discharge from his eyes and pulled himself out of the car. His voice was hoarse, his face riddled with confusion.

'Who are you?'

She sighed, impatient and uncaring. 'We go through this every time.'

He was unsteady on his feet at first, like a newborn foal. He clutched the doorframe with trembling hands and let his naked feet absorb the comforting cold of the subterranean concrete parking space.

Strip lights buzzed overhead. Air conditioning units rumbled, drawing down deep howling breaths through the gleaming metal duct work.

The woman had long, deep auburn hair and fiercely dark

eyes. She seemed somehow familiar though he could not place her face.

'What you did was foolish. Utterly stupid!'

'What did I do?'

'Don't play games with me. I know you too well.'

Gene was uncomfortable. Uncertain. 'I wasn't thinking.'

'That much is clear.'

She strode towards the security doors, where two large, smartly dressed security guards stood expectantly, and waved her pass at the scanner. The heavy metal doors slid open.

'Come with me.'

'Where am I?'

'Where do you think you are?'

'I'm not sure.'

'It's just a side effect. We've been through this many times before. Once you settle it'll come back to you. Come.'

Gene steadfastly refused to budge. She softened her approach.

She reached out to him, took his scuffed hand in hers and stroked his chipped, blackened fingernails.

'It's as though you've regressed to a feral state.'

He said nothing.

She shook his arm. 'Come,' she said gently, and led him through the security doors as if he were a child.

The surfaces of the walls were the gently rippled grey of unpainted concrete. The windows into the offices were all uniformly large and sterile. There seemed to be security at every intersection. Bright red LEDs shone harshly under the numerous tiny steel security cameras. Too many to count on this level.

She held his hand tightly the rest of the way, passing through checkpoints. Weaving from one warren of corridors to the next. Never saying a word. Never introducing him to anyone of import. Never allowing him to explore further.

It was all so tightly regimented Gene had the gnawing sensation that this was where he was supposed to be. He had glimmers of recollection. He was familiar with this place but it felt as though he was seeing it through someone else's eyes.

In a room lined with unmarked steel lockers, she pointed to a cubicle at the back from where they could both hear running water and said, 'I expect you to be ready by the time I return.'

Gene gazed despairingly at the array of uniform doors.

'Which one is mine?'

'It doesn't matter. They're not locked.'

'I can't just take somebody else's clothes.'

'Nearly everyone here is of similar size. You should find something that fits. I would suggest something smart. A suit.'

The timbre of her voice belied something more. There was a disapproving quality to it. She was angry.

She hadn't even stepped out of the room when Gene turned to her and asked, 'Why do you hate me?'

She didn't reply.

Gene plunged his head under the steaming, cascading torrent of water, the swell of filth at his feet taking time to siphon off down the drain. He picked up the bar of soap and rubbed agitatedly at his hands. He clawed at the softened edges. He put the bar of soap back in its tray, carefully aligning it to be exactly parallel to the geometry of the cubicle.

He repeated the action a further five times, though he knew that what he wanted to expunge was not on his skin, but somewhere altogether deeper.

Where was he? Who were these people? What did they want from him?

How could he escape?

He glanced up at the shower head and took solace in the hot droplets of spray hitting his eyeballs. It made him feel alive.

In the locker room he found a folded towel and threw open the doors to a number of lockers. A mid tone suit was easy to come by, but a pair of shoes was an altogether different prospect.

He tried on three pairs before he found a pair of plain black leather ones that fit to his satisfaction.

He wore a crisp clean white shirt, but decided to forgo the tie. This wasn't a job interview. Whoever had brought him here, clearly wanted him to stay.

The woman with the auburn hair disagreed. She had returned and was standing in the doorway, watching him. She angrily raided another locker and yanked out something stylish, made from sumptuous Italian silk.

She wrapped the tie under his collar and set about tying a perfect Windsor knot with practised ease. 'A tie reflects both the body and spirit of its wearer. You have an image to project.'

'Why?'

'You ask too many questions.'

'And you answer too few.'

Her boiling rage broke the surface once more. In a fit of pique she slapped him hard across the face. 'I am not here to answer your questions!'

On instinct Gene raised the back of his hand and belted her across the face so hard she staggered back and cowered. Rubbing lipstick from her lip. She was sore, but not bleeding.

Gene looked to the corridor. She could call security at any moment. Why did she not have him subdued? Her anger at him had nothing to do with what he had done, he realized. It was far older and deeper than that.

She composed herself. Tears rolled down her soft cheek. But she would not give in to them. She went back to him. 'Please forgive me,' she offered, and kissed him hesitantly on the cheek, just where she had struck.

Gene withdrew with suspicion. 'I wish to leave,' he said forcefully.

'And go where?' she replied. 'You're home.'

LAWLESS

Fifteen security guards patrolled the mezzanine and foyer. At least two more were visible beyond the thick glass doors of the elevator on every floor that they rose through after that.

This was no home. What was this place? Gene could see yellow cabs amid the heavy traffic outside. He was still in the city. But *where*?

A question someone had asked him once echoed through the vault of his clouded mind. *What do you know of your life?* Curious. He could find no answer.

The doors snapped open and the woman with the auburn hair led the way out. She negotiated their way past the next security check without humour or humility.

She had already gauged Gene's reactions as they journeyed. His eyes had betrayed very little. 'Nothing about this place seems familiar to you?'

'Nothing. Should it be?'

She threw open the heavy metal door to a large room beyond. She stepped aside without replying. Instead she locked the door firmly behind him.

How could he be so stupid? Cunning, making him dress for

the occasion. Gene tried the handle but it was stuck fast. Its construction was so solid it didn't even rattle.

He spun on his heel to look for a way out. In the middle of the room a stark white gurney and a counter full of computer equipment sat waiting. Large overhanging glass windows framed an observation room to one side, where the woman with the auburn hair took up a seat amid several busy lab technicians and watched him coldly.

He looked away. She deserved no more attention.

'Please lie down on the gurney.'

The voice was male. Emotionless. When it repeated the command Gene tracked it to a speaker. He didn't comply.

There was a set of double doors at the opposite end. It was his only option. He broke into a run, but they burst open before he could get there. Four burly security guards, a doctor and a sixth, much older man made straight for him.

'Stay where you are!' one of the guards ordered.

Gene ignored the crass stupidity of the request.

He tried to go around them, but they wielded cattle prods and an animal control pole with a steel aircraft cable for a noose. They were intent on cornering him like a beast.

Careful what you wish for.

Gene leaped at the nearest guard, grabbing him by the throat and steering him around in one fluid movement, thrusting the tip of the cattle prod into the thigh of a second guard. A spark of crackling electricity flared white as seven thousand volts shot through his leg.

Gene had been quick. But the other men were quicker. The noose slipped down over his head with barely a whisper. It snapped tight. The sudden crushing force on his windpipe made him bend double. He gagged as his tongue was rammed up into his mouth. He fought for air and fell to his knees.

'Get up!'

A surge of electricity erupted across his back. His muscles shot into spasm. His blood burned.

The animal control pole smashed into the back of his neck forcing him to crawl along the floor like a primate.

'On to the bed.'

Again Gene refused to move. The humming tip of another cattle prod loomed into his field of vision. But an aged hand stayed it. Constellations of pigmented lesions peppered the translucent skin, the speckles and spots of age. The thin flesh sagged over delicate bones and blue veins.

'Gene, please do as these men say or they will be forced to harm you.'

The voice was strong and compassionate. But its cadence betrayed a darkness that did not instil trust of any description.

The withered hand moved in and with a surprisingly strong grip tilted Gene's chin up so that both men might look each other in the eye. Compelling. Wilful. Neither man's gaze was inclined to retreat.

'It is time to continue our work, but we can't have you running amok. We simply do not have the time. Now . . . are you going to comply?'

Gene looked the old man in his harsh cold eyes. 'I'm going to kill you,' he promised.

Surprisingly the old man softened. 'Of that,' he said, 'I have absolutely no doubt.'

The young technologist applied more gel and attached the last of the thirty-two flat, cold metal electrode discs to Gene's scalp. He checked that the contact was good and that he had a strong low voltage signal. 'We're ready, Mr Lawless.'

Lawless held up a small glass vial containing a thick red liquid. 'What did you do with the second one of these?'

Gene tried not to stare but it was clear from the flicker on his face that the ampoule registered somewhere deep within his tortured memory.

He looked away. 'I don't know.' He strained at the

fastenings holding his wrists and ankles secured to the gurney. 'What are you doing to me?'

'Answer the question.' Lawless positioned his aged yet sprightly frame close to Gene, resting both his hands atop a long, ornate ebony walking cane. 'Where is the second vial?'

'I ate it.'

'Considering your recent actions, that would not come as a surprise. We have a strict regime. *One* vial. Once *a month*. You broke our contract.'

'I could care less about your contract.' Gene strained again. It was hopeless.

Lawless raised his cane and set it firmly against Gene's far cheek, forcing him to turn his head. 'Look at me when I talk to you, you ungrateful, repugnant goat. It would be unfortunate if I had to start the process again, with somebody *else*.'

Gene spat at the old man, but achieved nothing more than making a clumsy mess at his feet.

'I told you he was not fit for this.'

Lawless glanced up through the observation window at the fiery haired woman holding the microphone.

'Meg, leave us.'

So that's her name.

'He's not worth it. He's a fool,' she persisted.

'Megaera! Whatever *his* shortcomings *you* will never be fit for this procedure. Leave, immediately. I cannot hear myself think with your twittering!'

He waved a hand. Without further instruction two security guards entered the booth and forcibly removed the woman.

Gene reassessed the wizened old man. He held the reins of power like a king. 'Lawless.' He rolled the name around on his tongue, trying it out as though he were swilling a rich red wine.

'So, you *do* remember.'

'Not really. *He* said it.'

The technologist turned his back on the men and concentrated instead on the bank of flat panel computer screens where the jagged lines of brain-wave activity etched out Gene's turbulent state of mind.

Gene watched the crooked graphs with disquiet.

'We're taking an EEG,' Lawless explained. 'An electroencephalogram. A map of your brain waves. You remember doing all this before, surely?'

'What do you hope to achieve?'

The innocence of the question left Lawless quite astounded. Was there any other answer than the obvious? He rested his withered hand on Gene's young, supple extremities.

'What Odysseus was offered, and like a fool turned down. What Gilgamesh sought and could not find. What Tithonus stole and for his sin was shrivelled into a cicada, which is more than Priam's wretched brother deserved. What Cybele's bitches promised yet refused to give. The gift that the Fates meted out on Cyclades as punishment to *me*. Immortality.'

'You're insane.'

'My dear boy, what a curiosity you are. The difference between insanity and eccentricity is demarcated by wealth, so I am very, very eccentric. Now tell me, *what do you know of your life?*'

Gene shot Lawless a startled look. There was that question again.

The graphs on the screens jumped in sympathy. The startled technologist addressed his benefactor. 'It's working.'

'Progress at last.' Lawless patted Gene on the hand. 'Good. Perhaps your little stunt has borne fruit.'

He raised his cane and poked the tip of it in Gene's face, pushing it hard into his flesh, forcing him to look in the direction of the screens once more.

'Those are alpha waves. The telltale signs that expose the naked truth of your mind.'

Gene was vaguely aware that he could hear the doors opening and footsteps approaching. He looked up to see the auburn-haired woman standing over him. She was wearing a white lab coat and had brought several small glass bottles containing clear liquids, some cotton swabs and a pipette.

'Meg.'

She didn't respond.

She took the pipette and began siphoning off small amounts on to the swabs. Gene was alarmed. He strained at his fastenings, despite the pain from his chafed and reddened wrists.

'I thought you told her to leave!'

Lawless seemed genuinely perplexed. 'I did no such thing.'

'What's she doing?'

'She is providing context.'

'I don't understand!'

'Of course you don't. That's why we're here.'

The auburn-haired woman smiled down at Gene. *Why did she do that?* Was she Megaera or wasn't she? He suspected not when she took one of the swabs and wafted it gently under his nose.

A dazzling scent of pungent spices and exotic flowers filled his nostrils.

'The souls of the underworld perceive *our* world only through its scent.'

Gene fought the urge to breathe it in.

'The underworld is a realm where nothing solid exists, only images, phantoms, mist, shades and dreams. It can be neither seen nor touched. It is experience buried deep within you. It is memory. Drink it down. You *must* breathe deeply if we're to resurrect your soul.'

Lawless whacked the younger man firmly in the gut with his cane. Gene coughed and spluttered, reluctantly inhaling, but the graphs refused to budge. His reactions were not what they were looking for.

'Try another.'

The woman repeated the procedure with a new combination of chemicals dropped on to another white cotton swab.

Lawless stepped closer and brushed the younger man's hair with his bony hand. He ran a tensile finger over Gene's face, guiding his understanding.

Gene tried to fight off the next assault of provocative aromas. *Citrus limes. Lavender.*

'The sense of smell is the most ancient, the most basic, *the most animal* of our many natures. It requires no journey through the gateway of the thalamus to be processed. Smell is routed directly into the centre of our deepest self.'

The auburn-haired woman wafted yet another scented swab above Gene's sweat-beaded filtrum. *Jasmine. Inescapable. Immutable.*

Lawless ran his finger up Gene's face and back amid the electrodes pasted on to his scalp. 'Your sense of smell not only connects directly with the olfactory cortex in the medial temporal lobe, but into all parts of the limbic system, plugging directly into the amygdala, your emotional centre, and the hippocampus, the seat of memory.'

What was this old fool talking about? This was all gibberish. The room seemed brighter. What were they doing to the lights?

'And thus the machinery of your memory is set in motion, like a telescope pointed at time.'

What do you know of your life?

Gene gasped for air, the flickers of unwanted images pricking the darkness of his mind's eye.

'As I speak your brain is recognizing these scent molecules. Firing up myriad chemical reactions, electrifying the network of engrams responsible for remembering the odour. It is becoming so flushed with remembering that it's setting alight every pathway connected to that smell. A wild fire of memory that cannot be stopped. Your alpha waves are decreasing, your episodic memory is activating. Your hippocampus is releasing theta waves in a desperate attempt to interpret this new information, combining it with what already exists. Reinforcing your long-term memory. Strengthening the bonds between neurons. The scent molecules, the missing pieces of the puzzle, finally joining the dots of long forgotten, long dormant experience. A net that has made its catch. It burns. Can you *smell it*? Can you *see it*?'

Gene choked and rasped. Tears streamed down his cheeks. Slave to the visceral assault of memory.

'Do you remember? What do you know of *your life*?'

SHADOW OF THE ORLOJ

The boy stood nonplussed beneath the gleaming golden hands of the Astronomical Clock.

'*Think! Think back! Over all the things you have done. What exactly is it you know?*'

The mechanism thundered overhead, the whirring of gears and cogwheels beating out the rhythm of time's heartbeat measure by heavy measure.

'I . . . I have done nothing, Master Athanatos.'

'Nothing.' Athanatos pulled his cloak over his finely embroidered red silk doublet with disgust. 'You shot out of your mother's womb fast enough. That was quite an adventure. Your first act of gratitude when she fed you was to soil both yourself and her for her trouble. That is hardly nothing.'

'Nothing of consequence.'

Athanatos sprang forward and clutched the boy by the cheeks of his full mouth, searching for something hidden in his eyes. 'I do not believe you.'

His outbursts were always so difficult to contain. He was a man of such unfathomable nature and unpredictability. Sirocco dared not answer for fear it would inflame his passions further.

The clopping of hooves on worn cobblestones punctured

the air. He shoved the boy away harshly yet without menace, but the approaching ride was not for him. It pressed onwards into the city.

He checked the setting of the sun, the disposition of the sky, until finally he settled his intense gaze upon the blazing blue face of the timepiece.

'Where is my carriage, Sirocco? You said *eight*, I cannot be late for the emperor, or it will be *your* head.'

'It is not yet eight, master. See? The clock has yet to strike.'

This amused Athanatos. 'But it struck for Mikulas did it not?'

Mikulas, the clockmaster of Kadan who built the mighty Orloj, had discovered first-hand the insidious nature of a little knowledge.

'Magnificent. A clock that tells three different sets of time. The ring of Roman numerals that bestow upon us the twenty-four hours of the day. The rotating outer ring of gothic numerals which give us Bohemian time. See it approaches twenty-four, and indeed it is time for the sun to set. And finally, Mikulas saw fit to add *my* time. *Babylonian* time. The true time of day.'

The mechanism rumbled deep inside the tower and there followed a great pealing of bells.

'The greatest clock ever constructed by the hand of man, and what did Mikulas get for his troubles?'

'King Wenceslas IV,' Sirocco looked at his dirty shoes with shame, 'had Mikulas's eyes gouged out with a red-hot poker so he would not repeat this remarkable work for others.'

Athanatos marvelled at the bitter irony. 'For a device that merely measures time. Think what retribution awaits the man who would reveal the very nature of the ultimate anti-clock.'

'Master?'

Athanatos cast his eye down the narrow crooked streets ahead. 'Come, it is a pleasant evening. We shall walk.'

'But the carriage?'

'Is no longer my concern.'

Athanatos thrust a finger at the clock as he strode onwards towards the banks of the mighty Vltava. 'Master Hanus must have considered himself quite lucky that a different monarch sat upon the throne when it came time for him to add his astrolabe.'

They walked with good pace and good time, emerging on to the Stone Bridge which led to the vast castle set imposingly on the hill across the river before them. The angry Devil's Stream, which separated the island of Kampa from the river banks, gave a hint of the mighty Vltava's temper, but only a hint. What demon stirred the waters below?

'You trouble me, Sirocco. I'm not sure you can accompany me on this journey.'

'To the castle, master? But we are almost there. I do not understand.'

'*That* is precisely the problem.'

The City of One Hundred Spires looked distinctly unreal wrapped in the cloak of diminishing twilight. This was a city of light and shadow where every street held its ghosts and memories as warning.

'You asked what I know of my life, master. Forgive my impudence, I am but your apprentice—'

'The *emperor's* apprentice, court appointed to watch *over* me. Nothing more.'

'But I serve *you*.'

Athanatos did not answer.

'Master, what know you of *your* life?'

Athanatos stopped there and then on the bridge. The city stood held in the embrace of extravagant sprites, undines and the pensive heroes of legend. They held aloft the turret towers and red-tiled roofs like shelters of stone, yet Athanatos did not feel safe here.

He jabbed a finger to his temple. 'I know everything. From the time I was born and beyond.'

'Beyond?'

'That frightens you?'

'Only that I would ask, how can you be so sure your memories are real? The mind can play tricks.'

'These are no tricks.'

'Then what is the proof? What facts can you point to that would render such a notion unquestionable?'

'You want *facts*? There are no facts to give! Memory is a subjective mishmash of half-truth and faulty recollection. Sense and emotion intertwined like snakes wrapped around truth's neck!

'Look there upon the sphere of the moon and the divided universe in its unchanging perfection, the heavens above and the corrupt degeneration of the earth below. Surrounding the moon, the spheres; the inner planets, the sun, the outer planets and the fixed stars, each cranked by a higher angel. Surrounding them all over the heavens, the house of God, The Great Chain of Being. But I know that this Great Chain of Being is not out there at all. It is *within*.'

Sirocco reflected on this. *It is within.*

'Tell me, Sirocco, what do you think, for revealing the secret of that, Emperor Rudolf will do to me? No poker in the eye for fear of revealing that secret, I can tell you. The secret of the universe exacts a heavier payment than that.'

'So why come here, master?'

'To hide, of course, wretched as that makes me. Though Cyclades is here already. I can feel him within these walls. His eye is upon me. When last we met he almost destroyed me. He brought wrack and ruin down upon my empire and I have been wandering ever since. I have not yet gathered myself sufficiently to face him once more, so I come *here*,to Prague, to hide among the astrologers and the necromancers, the soothsayers and the alchemists. In

Prague, what's one more promise of the Philosopher's Stone amid a hundred?'

Gene looked up at Lawless, his eyes clearing, beating the heart of the faithful. 'I remember, father. I remember.'

Lawless pursed his dry lips and kissed him.

BLOOD

'How you feeling?'

How to answer that? North sat heavily in the black chair and pulled up his crumpled shirt sleeve. He was glad this was a private exam room and not the fish bowl of the ER. He knew the physicians here; his father was in cardiology at least once a month. Levine was young, purposeful, and at the very least sounded sincere.

North felt numb, bowing his head in ashamed frustration. 'I'm not sleeping too well.' He knew that this admission explained comparatively little, but further explication was beyond his grasp.

Levine tied a dark latex tube around North's left upper arm to increase the blood pressure in his vein and cleaned the inside of his elbow with simple rubbing alcohol. 'We were expecting you sooner.'

North had nothing to offer as an addendum to that quiet request for more detail. He wanted this over with. He wanted his life back, living it the only way he knew how. The warped and formless hallucinatory world of the skels was not something he wanted to know in further intimate detail. It certainly wasn't worth dwelling on or discussing.

'Did they tell you what was in that thing yet?'

The syringe. North shook his head. 'Not yet.'

'Pity.' Levine prepared a sterile needle. He had test tubes of different lengths and different coloured tops. Red ones, grey ones. He chose a tube with a lavender top first, loaded it into the vacutainer holder and inserted the needle into North's vein.

The partial vacuum in the tube immediately aspirated his rich, dark red blood in an uninterrupted flow. It oozed up the inside of the tube, thick and glistening.

'I'm going to level with you.' *Well that's a relief.* 'When we run the tests, it'll be too early to say if you've contracted HIV, so there's no reason to put you on the cocktail until we know more. The quickest way you're going to get peace of mind is if they run your evidence faster, okay? Otherwise we have to wait it out, and test you again later on down the line.' He checked his notes. 'Usually we only need about seven millilitres, but unfortunately for you we got a request from the OCME for identical samples.'

That was because North didn't trust anyone down at the Office of the Chief Medical Examiner to perform a venipuncture. They played with cadavers all day. A dead body was unlikely to complain if it all went wrong. Whatever was in his bloodstream was evidence, but only someone he trusted was going to have the privilege of extracting it.

Levine selected another tube and swapped it over. It too began to fill steadily. He made a start on the labelling and paperwork. 'You A or B?'

'I don't understand the question.'

'Blood group. It's okay, a lot of people don't know their blood group.'

North dredged up the memory. 'I'm O. O *positive.*'

Levine's pen nib hovered over the paper. 'You sure?'

North shrugged. 'I'm sure. Why?'

Levine hesitated again, incapable of writing it down. He put his pen back in the top pocket of his white lab coat and switched the test tube over. After he'd filled a fourth he withdrew the needle and took a cotton ball, applying it to the puncture with some pressure.

'Okay, hold that in place. Keep the pressure on it for a minute or so.' North complied while Levine collected up all the blood filled ampoules. 'You taking the samples yourself, or you want us to send them over?'

'I'm taking 'em. It keeps the chain of evidence unbroken.'

'Let me package these up.'

Levine left the room leaving North to his unsettled thoughts. *What did blood groups have to do with anything?*

He checked under the cotton ball, it was still oozing red. He pressed down again and got to his feet. There was a storm brewing out the window, maleficent clouds that just wouldn't go away.

Who was Gene? *Where* was Gene?

The clock on the wall ticked by – *8.43.*

Levine returned, his attention firmly on his file of medical records. 'Your father's blood group is AB, right?'

North tried to rein in his impatience. 'Look, I appreciate you doing this, but I have to get going.'

Levine didn't listen. 'Your mother's blood group is A.'

This didn't mean a thing to North.

'D'you want to take a seat?'

'I'm just fine.'

Levine was hesitant. He met North's stern gaze without the umbrella of impunity, his thoughts weighing heavily on his conscience.

'Have you ever thought about getting a paternity test done?'

North rocked on his heels. 'On who?'

'You.'

North shook his head. 'I'm not following.'

Levine pressed on. 'Look, I'm not going to bore you with the science, but when you have two people, one whose blood group is A and the other whose blood group is AB, the chance of them having a child who is O is nearly zero.'

Levine handed over the OCME samples all packaged up in a pouch. He was having trouble finding the words.

'I'm sorry to have to be the one to tell you, but you need to know this, as a matter of *your own* medical history. *You* are blood type O. That means one of your parents is probably not *biologically* related to you. In all likelihood that means your father.'

North blew him off, tossing the cotton ball on the counter. 'That's insane.'

'You need to talk with them.'

North thought on it; thought on it hard. He was seeing the world through new eyes now, and it was a harsh, sharp-edged place.

This helps me how? What am I supposed to do with this?

He stepped out of the Jamaica Hospital Medical Center and into the savage embrace of another ferocious downpour. He fished for his keys; a 1994 dark blue Lumina. Where did he park the thing?

I'm going to scream.

Oppressive stinging raindrops hammered down upon the hood of every vehicle on the lot, creating a fine mist that was hard to penetrate. He trudged through, his knee aching sharply, his thoughts in turmoil, searching each row systematically.

There it is.

The lock was stiff, the handle worn. The door needed some oil. And it stank, a nauseating mixture of stale body odour and old food. He missed the Impala but the busy motor pool left him little option.

He threw the blood samples angrily down on the passenger seat and listened to the rain. It was a welcome distraction, but it failed to mute the echoes of the nightmare which would not dim or fade. His mother. Insatiable.

Being inside her, alive and vital.

He adjusted the rear-view mirror. *The mirror.* When North remembered the lust he had shared with his mother, he remembered that he had looked in a mirror in the middle of it, that the wretched contorted ecstasy he felt so violently was written upon a face that was not his own. It was almost as though he had been present, but had been wearing a mask.

It was not his face. It was not his father's face. So whose was it?

I am Satan's Oath.

9.56 a.m.

Twenty minutes to find a parking space. What possessed them to move the entire NYPD Crime Scene Unit into a converted old Montgomery Ward department store in Jamaica, Queens, with no parking lots?

With the evidence from all five boroughs coming here for trace evidence testing, it was a busy building, surrounded by many other busy government buildings on Jamaica Avenue. The Social Security Administration building, three court houses, the Department of Motor Vehicles; every side road was filled with government employee cars.

North stashed the blood samples under the dash and grabbed his ID and notebook. He didn't bring a jacket. He didn't own an umbrella. He was soaked through and he didn't notice.

The thick sheaves of glossy photographs and their accompanying pages of neatly typed notes made the preliminary CSU report dispiriting reading.

One hundred and forty-eight separate individuals had left

their fingerprints in varying degrees of clarity on the heavy display glass collected at the primary crime scene in the museum.

All had been run through AFIS, the Automated Fingerprint Identification System. All had returned negative results. Not a single known criminal among them.

'This says you don't have all the glass here. Where's the rest?'

Ash, the Forensic Investigator who had led the evidence gathering of both the primary crime scene at the Met and the secondary behind and in front of the Jiggle Joint peep show, was a much older man with a thoughtful though firm disposition.

He guided North into one of the tiny breakrooms on this level, curious as to the detective's pronounced heavy limp. 'The shards with blood splatter went straight to the OCME. What's up with you?'

'Ah, I dinged my knee.' North was more concerned with the report. 'You found cotton fibres? They could be from anybody.'

'Egyptian cotton.' Ash poured himself a coffee, heaping in sugar and milk. 'Help yourself, by the way.'

North didn't even hear him. 'What's the deal with that?'

'It's imported. It's known as the best quality cotton money can buy. I'm guessing you won't find too many stores stocking imported cotton garments, and those you do find will be expensive outlets.'

'What kind of clothes? Sweatshirts?'

'Possibly. But Egyptian cotton is used more in expensive bed sheets.'

'So, the guy likes to lie down a lot.' North moved on. 'The sword's at OCME in serology and the syringe is in toxicology. Did you lift prints?'

'Sure, did that first, page six. What's up with the postal service you couldn't wait to read this? If you were in such a rush we could have faxed it.'

'I was in the neighbourhood.'

'Look, we got two usable sets off the syringe. One set came up in AFIS. And we got one print off the sword. A thumb print. That came up in AFIS, too, and matched the syringe.'

'Who'd you get?'

'You.'

North felt the cold harshness of the jolt deep in his bones. How was it that he'd woken up in a world today where every finger was pointing at him?

Cop fingerprints were kept on file so they could be eliminated from the investigation as a matter of course. Under the circumstances, it was to be expected that they'd find his prints. Yet this felt different, this felt personal.

Unlike other PDs, the NYPD Forensic Investigators worked out of the Detective Bureau, so they weren't the average scientist. They were cops, they'd worked a beat and Ash knew North well enough to know things just weren't sitting right.

'Jim, what're you bugging about this case for?'

North refused to answer.

'Nobody died. You got the kid out.'

'People are in hospital. Four civilians. *Two* cops, one with his throat cut. You want to abandon two of our own? Next time he could kill.'

'I'm not saying abandon them. Did you hear me say that? But it's been three days already, the trail goes cold in *two*; the doer's in the wind already, and you're taking this on, on your *own*? This guy could be halfway across the country, maybe even halfway across the world, by now.'

North felt the agitation spreading across his chest. He couldn't explain it, he could only *feel* it. 'Let *me* worry about which case I want to work.'

There it was, welling up inside of him, a raging vengeful kind of emotion that had no place on the job.

'Who are they? These two cops.'

'Manny Siverio and Eddie Conroy.' He only knew that

because he'd spent breakfast finding out. The guilt was overwhelming.

'You know 'em?'

North shrugged it off. 'No, they're from Central Park. But that doesn't matter, does it.' It wasn't a question.

Reproach was already written across Ash's features. The older man took his time. 'Y'know, back when your dad was on the force he used to say to me—'

North wasn't going there. He tucked the report under his arm. 'Did you make me copies of the museum surveillance tapes?'

11.03 a.m.

On the second floor of 520 First Avenue, North watched the traffic out of the austere windows of the Office of the Chief Medical Examiner, the spherules of rainwater on the glass panes contorting the grey activities below.

He sat at a desk and filled out the chain of custody for his blood samples. The issue with evidence was always chain of custody. The PD had to be able to account for the evidence from the time it was obtained until presented in court. Detailed logs were essential. Who collected the evidence? Under what circumstances? Every fact specific to how the evidence was found was catalogued. Did they know when they first saw it that it would be evidence or did they have to go back and get it? Every time the evidence was touched or examined it had to be signed out. Every measure was taken to circumvent a defence counsel ploy of claiming that the evidence had been tampered with.

North was meticulous, and something Ash had said kept ringing in his ears: they found his thumb print on the sword.

I never touched it. I kicked it away. One thumb print?

Dan Sheppard, one of the Supervising Criminalists in the Department of Forensic Biology, loomed in the doorway. In his hand he had the photographs North had requested. 'You *know* we take about a week. I'm not sure I can tell you what you want to know in three days.'

North gathered his paperwork up. 'This is important.'

'Every case is important.' He handed the photographs over, but was more consumed in his abnormal fascination with North's head.

North was self-conscious. 'What?'

'If I may?' Sheppard whipped out a pair of cold metal tweezers and plucked a few hairs from North's scalp. He deposited them into a small white paper envelope. 'Whatever's in your bloodstream may have secreted out already. We'll see.'

North rubbed his head. 'Think you'll find much? It's been three days.'

'Depends. You're cutting it fine on some things, you're okay on others. Benzodiazepines, like Librium and Valium, can stay in your system anywhere up to thirty days. Cannabinoids, grass to you, up to *ninety* days. You said you seemed to be experiencing some detachment and psychotropic effects. Psilocybin, the humble magic mushroom, LSD and MDMA can stay in your system anywhere between three and five days. If it's there, we'll find it.'

'You sure you know what to look for? Did you test the contents of that syringe yet?'

'Nope.'

Sheppard always liked to jerk chains. It gave him some kind of sadistic amusement. North wasn't biting. 'I need that done.'

'Then you'll have a long wait. It's not going to happen.'

So he wasn't joking. There was that thunder again. 'Why not?'

To Sheppard it was obvious. 'Too much risk. We're not insured for it. I don't want any of my crew jabbing themselves with it. It's not going to happen. You could go to a private lab but I doubt they'd touch it, and I doubt the FBI has an interest in this case. That's why I asked for blood, urine and hair. We'll figure it out. Where *is* your urine sample by the way?'

North fished out an old Gatorade bottle from a plastic bag and set it down on the table.

'I just need ten centilitres. That's a pint.'

'Knock yourself out.'

Sheppard held his hand out for the plastic bag. He carefully re-wrapped the bottle and picked it up at arm's length.

'It's okay, I wiped it.'

Sheppard headed out the door, expecting North to follow him. 'A PhD in chemistry and I'm reduced to carrying your piss. Aren't you going to take a look at the photographs? Your syringe is in there.'

'Is there any point?'

Sheppard's face lit up. 'It was quite an unusual implement that he used on you.'

North shuffled through the images. The syringe had been photographed actual size, with a rule next to it for reference. It was larger than normal and its glass chamber was capped at each end with ornate silver. 'Looks like something a veterinarian might use on a dog maybe.'

'Better.' Sheppard held the door open for North to follow. 'It's antique. I doubt one of those things has been used professionally in over a century.'

North was surprised. 'How'd you know that?'

'I used to work with a Dr Willoughby down the road at the NYU Medical Center. He used to collect these little medical curios. He had a cabinet in his office that was full of them.'

'Think this was stolen?'

'Either that or he's a collector. The syringe, the museum. Your doer is showing signs of a pattern. He's obsessed with old things.'

Two things didn't make a pattern, but North would take it as his starting point. It was *something. Why an antique syringe?*

'Is it possible I could talk to Willoughby about this?'

'If you own a Ouija board I guess you could. He's been dead about two years.'

North scratched the name from his notebook. 'Well do *you* happen to know where I might be able to get my hands on something similar?'

Sheppard thought on it. 'I doubt many antique shops in the city would stock something like that, but I'm sure there are a couple of speciality stores.'

'What're these letters engraved on the metal end? H-R-S-H.'

'No idea, but a collector *will* know.'

They made a visit to one of the lab technicians at the far end of the hall. Sheppard poked his head around the door and brightly presented the girl with her gift. 'Detective North's illustrious *urina*.'

She took it before North could hide his face. She smiled at him. North had no choice but to return the pleasantry.

Sheppard pressed on. His office was steeped in erudition. One wall was devoted to his numerous academic achievements and accreditations. His desk was surrounded by a vast array of books and journals, notes and photocopies. A cluster of pills sat assembled by his computer: vitamins and aspirins. He worked hard, and the work was not always easy.

He rounded the desk eagerly and lowered himself into a large leather chair. 'We found four different blood samples on the sword. Skin, hair and blood from the glass display case. We haven't run them through CODIS yet, but when we do it'll be in the report.'

CODIS, the Combined DNA Index System, was the FBI national DNA database. It wasn't unusual for someone to have a profile in CODIS but no record of their fingerprints in AFIS, and vice versa.

North didn't enter, he stayed back, loitering in the doorway. He didn't want to be here. He felt anxious. It was as though he didn't want to be *anywhere*. 'Ash told me you lifted my print off the sword?'

'Yes, very curious. We don't know how you did it. There appears to be ancient residue on the haft. Somehow you managed to leave an impression in it, but from our tests it's calcified. One of life's little mysteries.'

2.38 p.m.

The oppressive pressure cooker of the Fourth Precinct was not for the faint of heart. Alive with the seedy business of investigation, it was an altogether brutal world. When North violently slammed a large and heavy Yellow Pages down on his half of the desk in one corner of the busy squad room, the loud thud went barely noticed.

The precinct was the gateway to a parallel world, a sordid, grotesque, distorted world that lived just below the surface of decency's veneer. It took its toll, and prices were paid. In here North was not some loner caught on the outside looking in, because in truth every man on the squad was a loner. North was merely one cloud of anger amid a furious storm.

He opened up the case file and scattered the photographs across the work surface in a conflicted collage that obeyed the rules of his deductions and guesses. Only he fully understood the process – it was all done on instinct, in the gut. His gut was telling him several things were missing.

He pulled out the picture of the syringe and sat it by the phone as he thumbed his way through the directory. His attention flitted between it and the other photographs. He wrote: *Skull?* He remembered Bruder from the Central Park station house saying something about witnesses reporting Gene had picked up a skull. There was no reference to it in the evidence.

He shuffled the pack and laid the pictures out again.

He returned to the directory. There were antiques houses all over the city. He hit the phone and tried Christie's the auction house first; they rattled off a couple of names to try before hanging up. It went like that for half an hour. A few names cropped up repeatedly. He whittled those down some more. Some businesses had moved. Others had changed staff and no longer dealt in certain items. How difficult could it be to get someone to fill in a few details on an antique syringe?

He rearranged the photographs again.

And then someone mentioned a name that kept surfacing repeatedly, an antiques dealer who specialized in more esoteric curios, a gentleman by the name of Samuel Bailey. He would know what H-R-S-H meant.

He'd moved twice. Business can't have been good. Someone said he had a small concern over at the Chelsea Antiques building on West 25th Street as recently as November last year. North called them up. Bailey had a store there, sure, but he could never make the rent and she was thinking about serving an eviction notice.

'Is he there now?'

'No.'

'Can you get him to call me back?'

'I can't even get him to call *me* back.' She sounded exasperated, but wasn't trying to be difficult.

North offered to leave his number but she was already riffling through papers. 'Here,' she said. 'Here's his address. You got a pen?'

When he hung up the phone he was on his feet. He shuffled the pictures some more. *What's missing?* How did Gene get away?

The car.

4.13 *p.m.*

The dark, imposing shadow of the squeaking windshield wipers lurched back and forth across the dash, keeping time like the ghost of a musician's metronome, perfect in its insistence.

He had his phone in his hand, his parents' number displayed on the small screen, all ready to dial. But what would he say? How could he ask if his father was really his father? His thumb hovered over the call button. *No. Not now.*

North watched the street in front of the Jiggle Joint through the haze of memory, seeing the whole incident play out repeatedly in front of him, shadows from his mind's eye imprinted on the rain sodden canvas of Hell's Kitchen.

No one reported anything about seeing a vehicle making a getaway. *I didn't imagine it.* They canvassed the whole block. Even the patrolmen who'd followed him into the backyard didn't recollect hearing or seeing a vehicle.

North threw a stick of gum into his mouth; the simple act of chewing eased his tension. *They're wrong. There was a vehicle.*

He locked the car door and limped his way around the back to where the rear of the Jiggle Joint was still taped off. When he'd first chased Gene here he hadn't even noticed what the place was called. Now, it was impossible to ignore. It was a peepshow for transsexuals.

In the back yard, the tangible memory of what had transpired was still marked out in the greasy black sludge that caked the surface of the concrete. The clawed scuff marks of heavy shoes were the dance steps of the battle.

Along one flaking whitewashed wall at waist height, hundreds of curious yellowed stains mottled the wall, the faint trace of where something had repeatedly squirted. The appalling, nauseating stench of rotting human semen was description enough for what had been taking place back here.

At the far wall, the dumpsters were still lined up, the trash bags still lay arrayed in discarded chaos. North ducked under the yellow and black crime scene tape and poked around.

Why this building had a back yard at all was something of a minor mystery, though not entirely unusual in Manhattan. Maybe this had been a loading area at one stage in its history.

At the back wall, North climbed up on to one of the dumpsters, just as Gene had done, and peered over the top. Where would a car have been parked?

A back alley stretched left to right, not a common sight in midtown. The black iron fire escapes hung ominously low over the road surface below. There was enough room for a car but nothing larger.

'Hey, you're not allowed back here now! Fuckin' cops. We can go inside and do it, or you got a car?'

Do what? North glanced over his shoulder, flashing his badge with acrimonious contempt.

Under the cloak of the rear entrance, a dancer of slight build wearing gold hot pants had ventured out to smoke a cigarette. With extraordinarily pretty eyes, full round breasts and curvaceously inviting hips, North's eye was instinctively drawn. Yet the unnaturally large bulge in her crotch, her sharp jaw and thick masculine neck soon stifled his arousal. *Jesus.*

She simply smiled at him. It was a deceptively powerful response because it was clear that his disgust was her amusement.

North climbed back down. 'What's your name?'

'What would you like it to be?' Her long false eyelashes, caked in thick black mascara and gaudy glitter, seemed to droop in anticipation. Her husky voice resonated.

'You want me to ruin your day?'

Insulted, she dropped the pretence. A deeper, distinctly male inflection answered back. 'Claudia.'

'Your real name.'

Claudia's eyes hardened. The woman was gone. It was just North and a man in gold hot pants now. 'Everyone knows me as Claudia.'

'You working three days ago?'

Claudia was no longer in the mood to play. He stubbed his cigarette out on the doorframe and flicked it away. 'I work every day.'

'You remember the altercation that took place back here?'

'Altercation?'

'The fight.'

'I know what altercation *means*.' He brushed hair from the cheap red wig out of his sullen face. 'I don't know much about it. I was busy.'

'Doing what?'

'Doing *whom*. You want me to draw you a picture?'

'But you know what happened?'

'I heard some of the other girls talking about it.'

Girls. 'Any of them in today?' It was worded like a question, but North wasn't making a request.

Claudia shook his head and rolled his eyes at the inconvenience. He beckoned for North to follow him inside.

4.57 p.m.

At a tiny upstairs bathroom window Mario, also known as Mona, showed how the frosted glass didn't open all the way. All he heard was the engine. You had to lean right out if you really wanted to see, and why did he want to see? He was cleaning up after a show.

North took a look, having to squeeze past a clothesline laden with damp pantyhose and bras. 'No one came and spoke to you after?'

'Ohmagawd, are yakiddin' me? You boys in blue scare easy.'

'It was just a car. Why'd you pay it any attention?'

Mario pulled his white towelling bathrobe in tighter. 'It stood out, yaknow whatam sayin'? Our customers know yacan't get in through the alley, yagotta come round from the front. No one goes down the alley.'

Twenty-one people in the building. Mario was the only witness.

5.22 p.m.

From a small plastic storage box in the trunk of his car he pulled out a roll of silver duct tape and tore off two strips. He stuck one on to the sole of each of his shoes before setting off again.

He had to go down a whole block before he could come back on himself and find the entrance to the alley. It was gated and protected with razor wire at one end. The purpose of this was not altogether apparent at first since the other end was exposed but in all likelihood it was done years ago to stop through traffic.

Manhattan was built on the grid system, but people often forgot that it hadn't always been that way. Manhattan's foundations sat atop much older creations that would occasionally resurface in the form of small oddities that sometimes never even made it on to the road maps. North found himself running into these oddities all the time.

In midtown an alley was a rare thing, a brick road surface even rarer, but not unheard of. Over in Greenwich Village a few small patches of brick and cobblestone surfaces dated back to the 1800s. The debt to history was there if anyone cared to look.

North trod cautiously, his eyes focused on anything that stood out. This wasn't his job, in an ideal world this was the work of a Forensic Investigator, but he had lost time to make up. The area hadn't been swept by forensics at all and the chances were he was going to wind up disturbing something. The duct tape was to differentiate his prints from anyone else's.

Amid the trash, the weeds and the rats' nests North noticed a dark stain spread out across the brickwork of the road, sheltered from the elements under the overhang of a rusted, forgotten fire escape. It was only a few yards down from the wall that blocked off the Jiggle Joint's back yard.

As he drew near he recognized immediately the dark viscous nature of old motor oil, and as he peered closer he saw clean shards of broken plastic, embedded in a visible tyre print.

6.04. p.m

Robert Ash stood directly over the oil leak and placed an L-shaped black-on-white, 30 cm by 15 cm tyre measuring scale beside it, then took another photograph. He was on his way home from the CSU when he got the call, but he arrived in good time and carried out the task without complaint.

North refused to leave his side. 'What do you make of it?'

'Oil is oil. You're not going to trace a car from motor oil, but I will say this; I *doubt* it's from a car. It's at the side of the alley, see? Oil tends to leak from the lowest part of the engine, which puts it in the middle. You can't get a car over to the side down here.'

'So you're thinking a motorcycle?'

'Powerful one too. Over 500cc. Never underestimate the power that dumb luck plays in an investigation, eh? A four-stroke engine uses viscous oil. A two-stroke engine uses thinner oil and it would have washed away by now in all that rain, but this is still here. It's very dark, I'm going to hazard a guess that it's not from a well-maintained bike.'

North let his frustration boil to the surface. 'I heard car doors. I don't care about a bike.' *What's that smell?*

'I talked to your old man earlier today.'

North was suspicious. He turned away. 'Oh yeah?'

'Yeah, he invited a bunch of guys over at the weekend for a barbecue. You going?'

'I, uh.' *Tell him you're busy.* 'I don't know. Hey, d'you smell that?'

Ash sniffed the air. 'Smell what?'

It made North want to gag. His nostrils were now filled with the stomach-churning stench of putrefying meat exposed to a flame. He tried to determine where it was coming from, the Jiggle Joint's back yard perhaps, but it seemed to have no source.

His mouth tasted bitter. 'You sure you can't smell this?'

Ash was down on his knees with a pair of tweezers examining the oil leak. 'Nope.' He plucked out the first of a series of tiny translucent fragments. They were exceptionally clean and had not been ground into the oil in any way. There wasn't just plastic, but glass too and the fragments extended directly from the rear of the Jiggle Joint and down the alley beyond the oil leak for a couple more yards. They were recent.

'You say you heard this guy slam the car door when he got in?'

'Pretty much.' North pulled out a paper tissue from his pocket and held it over his nose and mouth. It didn't help.

Ash nodded. 'Yeah, that's what dislodged it.' He pointed to where the trail began. 'He gets in the car, slamming the door, he dislodges these fragments. As the car reverses, the fragments continue to fall out. It's not coloured, so it's not a tail light. The vehicle you're looking for has a broken lens, and it took its hit in the front.'

8.39 p.m.

The odour just wouldn't go away. The whole precinct seemed to be filled with a ghost of decay that only he could sense. In the break room he found a pot of strong coffee and poured himself a cup. He didn't drink it, he didn't dare, instead he carried it around like some kind of incense and hoped nobody would ask any awkward questions.

What's wrong with me?

He filed his sixty-one. There was already one from Bruder, but North had been there too, there should be a completed incident form from him. It was sloppy – there was no excuse but it was done now. He went upstairs.

In a small room on the second floor of the Fourth Precinct he reviewed the surveillance tapes on a couple of old black VCRs and a television set.

Over and over it went; insert another cassette, press play; same room, different angle, all in fuzzy black and white. Gene's entrance was clear. He entered the museum, alone, at 10.07. He wandered around a little, though whether he was trying to figure out which way to go or whether he was meeting someone was not altogether apparent. He saw something in the Belfer Court, became fascinated with the Greek exhibits. He stabbed the first visitor at precisely 10.23.

North threw his arms over his head and stretched. He'd read stories about people dying of deep vein thrombosis sitting in the same position on long haul flights. Fifty bucks said the same thing happened to cops forced to watch hours of surveillance footage.

In went another tape. Another angle. Again Gene entered the museum.

Something was different.

North rewound the tape and started it over again. *Gene enters the museum. Loiters. He enters the Belfer Court.*

But what's *she* doing . . . ?

North stopped the tape and shuffled it back.

Gene was standing looking at a large vase. A woman with long hair and sunglasses was approaching him from behind. She stops. *Pretty close by. What's she doing?* She has a hand to her face. *There.*

A puff. A cloud. *What is that? Is that smoke?* He hadn't noticed before because the angle of the light hadn't caught it. But here it was perfect.

He peered closer at the screen trying to compensate for the

tiny wobble in the freeze-frame picture. Her face resonated with him, though he was at a loss to explain it.

He heard footsteps out in the hall. Nancy Montgomery, the Police Administrative Assistant for the squad room, had her coat on but was still taking care of business. With an armful of cardboard files she gave North a disapproving look. 'Don't you got a home to go to?'

North rubbed his tired face in his rough hands. 'You seen my place?'

She carried on walking. 'So get a girlfriend.'

That stung. More than she was even aware. North kept it to himself and studied the blurry figures on the screen instead. Was she really doing what she looked like she was doing? He had an idea and poked his head out into the hall. 'Hey, are you busy? Can you come take a look at this? I want a woman's opinion.'

He could hear the photocopier whirring away in the next room. 'What did I just tell you to do?'

He could hear Nancy continue cursing and throw down something heavy. She shuffled out, sweeping her straightened black hair from her flawless chocolate skin. 'Do I get detective's pay?'

'You're *requesting* a pay cut?'

She stood in the doorway and folded her arms. If she thought it was funny she wasn't letting on. 'I don't got all day.'

He showed her the TV screen. 'What's this woman doing?'

He played the tape. The stranger stops by Gene, she raises a hand. A puff. Nancy squinted at the screen.

'Play that again.' North cued it up. She rolled her eyes. 'She's putting on perfume. That's just an atomizer. Did I crack the case?'

North ran his finger over the image. '*You* use an atomizer that way?'

She took another look. Now she saw it, too. 'Why's she spraying it at the guy looking at the vase?'

North threw his pen down, exhausted. 'Exactly.'

He returned to the squad room and riffled through the CSU report in the case file on his desk.

Glass crunched. When he went after Gene. He could *smell* perfume, and the glass crunched.

The report confirmed that the remains of a small perfume bottle *had* been recovered. He pinned a note to it to have Ash rerun it through trace.

Perfume. If only it was perfume he could smell right now, instead of this sickening stench that made him gag.

10.57 p.m.

The hollow street outside his apartment was naked under the spill of the streetlamps. It was a place where the rumble never went away. Faint wisps of steam vented from the manhole covers and grates in the pavement. It was like being in the belly of the beast; a dragon in slumber.

A single red light twinkled in the darkness, a message on his answering machine from his mother. He couldn't help that he winced at the sound of her voice.

He went for the bourbon. The rain rattled the windows and the liquor dulled the echo of an otherwise empty apartment. He necked two fingers without thinking about it, poured a little more into a tumbler and flipped channels on the TV until he found the javelin throwers in full Olympic stretch.

The Games. What was it about the hurl of points that spoke to him? The grip of spears that had reduced war to sport. Why did they inflame him? He'd always stopped to watch the sport, but now he felt hypnotized by it. His cynical mind chided him for perhaps driving through Greek-filled Astoria one too many times, but one of his deeper selves knew that it was more than that. From the darkness it spoke to him, its ebony tones demanding more than just his attention, the fetor of its putrid blackened flesh so vile and intrusive that the reek made him vomit where he sat.

Three days old. Perhaps four. Its skin charred and split exposing the pale meat within, crevasses of cooked flesh opening out down its well-roasted cheeks. Its complexion reddened by the roaring fires of the city, razed to the ground, she handed him the head of a roasted newborn on a spike.

Whose child was this? What pitiable crime had an infant babe committed to be served as a meal to avenging hordes? Was this hell? Or some other place buried deeper than evil?

She moved in close to him, her swollen naked breasts glistening with the fat from cooked human meat. She guided his hand and gently pushed the roasted cadaver towards his mouth.

'Eat.'

His stomach turned at the thought, twisted in excruciating knots, yet he could not resist her power. He opened his mouth and took a bite of crispy, salted cheek.

North awoke screaming. Before him, daubed on one wall of his apartment, in a paint that owed as much to human excretions as it did to any ink, the face of the Bull that haunted him.

It was the Bull that filled him with fear and dread and rage.

It was the Bull that told him to kill.

THE GILDED CAGE

Dawn's disrespectful glare burned into Gene's brow, waking him from an otherwise unyielding, unknowable blackness.

Not for the first time he found himself conscious, yet starkly lacking in any recollections that might persuade him of his surroundings and his predicament.

He lay in a bed that was simply vast. Its sheets the softest cotton he had ever encountered, with fine feathered embroidery fit for a prince.

He had absolutely no earthly idea how he had come to be in it, or whose it was for that matter. Perhaps it was his. He would pretend it was until someone informed him otherwise.

He could hear the faint music of angels, a choir singing in baroque revelry, at a volume level so low it was almost inaudible. The music was being fed into the room, but from where he couldn't tell and there appeared to be no way of stopping it.

He sat upright. The room was opulent beyond the point of excess. The carpet deeper than any he could remember having walked on. His toes sank their height in the light-coloured pile.

There were mirrors on the walls, and recessed light fixtures in the ceiling. There were artworks, and silks. Naked, he stepped up to the broad windows that looked out across the Hudson beyond. He was many floors up and apparently still in the heart of downtown Manhattan.

A few loose thoughts tumbled down the rocky escarpment of his mind. He checked his wrists. Still sore and bruised. He ran his fingers through his hair. It was matted from dried conductive gel.

He could feel the remnants of powerful sedatives striking hammer blows to his senses as they wrestled with his blood. What had they done to him?

He could not remember the details, but he had the sense that every day was another experiment and another unnerving journey into bewilderment. He would sever these suffocating bonds one day. He was sworn to it. He made it difficult for them, and with a brutish frequency, yet still they refused to let him go and as their black activities continued he found it increasingly difficult to deny them.

He threw on a robe and fastened it in a single knot. He was hungry. He opened the first door. It was a bathroom, lavish and ornate. A second led to a spacious dressing room filled with suits, shirts and shoes. A further door led from here but it was locked. There was no key.

He returned to the bedroom. There was a third door. It had no lock of any classic kind, instead a small numerical keypad sat mounted next to the handle.

What was the code? His mind drew a blank. He approached with little trepidation; he refused to be cowed by a simple numerical value, and keyed the first set of numbers that entered his head.

Without fuss the heavy door swung open.

'He's left-handed this morning.'

'Interesting,' Lawless replied with ruminative approbation. 'The idiosyncrasies of *the process* never fail to delight.'

'He seems to be affected more by the variation in personality than we had anticipated.'

Lawless's gaze was unwavering. Savage was not a man who could be intimidated easily but Lawless was a force of nature. Savage shifted uncomfortably in his chair at the long mahogany breakfast table.

'Are you suggesting that we chose the wrong successor?' Lawless asked.

The other men sat in silence. Savage was on his own. 'Not at all. I'm simply pointing out that what we're attempting is completely new. It was bound to have consequences.'

Lawless admired the man's deft defence. 'It's not *completely* new.' He studied the faces of his tabulatory men, the doctors and scientists that perfected and invented, experimented and refined, the men who kept *the process* alive.

He dipped a toasted soldier into the rich yellow yolk of a soft-boiled egg. 'What are the latest results?'

Megaera sat at the other end of the table. She snatched up the remote control and switched the channel on the wall-mounted screen to the security cameras monitoring Gene in the lower apartment.

He had ventured into the circular lounge and was studying a large collection of portraits hanging over the fireplace. They were all of old men; Lawless was among them.

Savage said, 'The EEG results show he's experiencing two distinct personalities. Each one is vying for control and trying to establish dominance over his memory function.'

'Is there any sign of convergence?'

'No.'

The hesitation in Savage's voice was not what Lawless wanted to hear. 'Why am I suddenly forced to drag information out of my kindred? Continue.'

'We are lucky that convergence is not taking place, but no one personality has yet to establish its dominance either. He's proving to be particularly stubborn.'

Lawless smiled, though his face lacked any warmth. 'That's what I like about him.'

Savage got to his feet and presented Lawless with a graph. 'We spent all of last night stimulating the CA3 region of his hippocampus.'

Lawless munched on his egg-sodden toast. 'Ah, his access to long-term memory. How are you stimulating it?'

'Sound. Specifically music.'

'How very charming. What did he respond to?'

'Given his current state of mind, the music of the late fifteen hundreds and early sixteen hundreds; the madrigals of Josquin Desprez and the opera of Claudio Monteverdi proved the most positive.'

Lawless sat back in his chair with a sweeping air of contentment. 'My favourite music while I was in Prague.'

Megaera was less than enthusiastic. 'That's what worries me. Prague is the last time we encountered Cyclades. And *Cyclades* is left-handed.'

Lawless threw down his napkin. 'That music was *my* favourite. Not his.' He snapped his fingers for the table to be cleared.

Servants appeared from the darkened corners to sweep away the china dishes, the marmalades and the cutlery. Enquiries were made into any further service.

Megaera didn't even look up from her paperwork when she issued the order to set out the passels of Lawless's daily regimen. A vast array of pills and potions were laid before him.

His tonics prescribed to stave off age included iron for the blood, aspirins for the heart, anti-inflammatories for the brain, and for the kidneys and the liver, Tribulus Terrestris. He took vitamins B12, B6 and red ginseng. Ginkgo biloba and zinc. It was such a pharmacopoeia of pilular rejuvenation he had reached a minor crisis. In truth, he no longer had the faintest idea what purpose some of it served any more. If his tabulatory men had taken the trouble to source an ingredient and include it on his list, he took it without question. He was far beyond second-guessing them at this stately age.

Megaera watched stonily and deliberately. 'He plays at something you know. I have proof Gene has been searching the genealogical records. No permission was issued.'

'And what *does* that prove, my girl? That he's a keen librarian, perhaps?'

'Don't be so flippant.'

'Or you'll do what, precisely . . . ?'

The faces of the men around the table showed clear embarrassment. Lawless rather enjoyed that.

'How did you come by this information?'

She seemed jolted by the question. 'By means.'

Lawless considered what she had to say for a moment. She was planning something. 'The same means by which you just *happened* to be at the museum when Gene had his little outburst? Your jealousy is pathetic. He *must* familiarize himself with the records at some stage, wouldn't you agree? Curiosity is the very essence of who we are.'

'Not like this!' Megaera slammed her palms down on the polished solid mahogany table. 'Has it occurred to you that he may be searching for the others?'

'The others?' Lawless genuinely struggled with such an amusing concept. 'What others?'

'What an arrogant man you are. You know to expect others.'

Lawless wagged a finger. 'Yet again you tap dance on the edge of my restraint. You forget *I* have been through *the process. I have been that animal.* I understand him. Give him time and he'll understand too.' He turned on Savage. 'Would you say he's ready for a little more freedom or must we keep him caged?'

'I couldn't possibly say. Megaera is right in that he is unstable.'

'Good, that's settled. Give him freedom of the building once again.' He took a sip from a glass of water and waved the men away. 'You may go.'

The scientists and doctors got rapidly to their feet and left with clear relief.

Megaera, however, refused steadfastly to budge. 'Compared to our previous experiences this is nothing but a grand experiment that may be failing before our eyes.'

'You know nothing.'

'Really? Well, remember these words, because I will never be able to pass them on.'

'No,' Lawless chided with glee. 'No you won't.' He chuckled to himself as he took his glass of water and resumed his morning ritual, working his way through his medications one at a time, pressing each pill into his overwet mouth with one wretched, bony finger, chewing on them one by one with weakened, brittle teeth.

His choices were naturally skewed towards clarity of thought and the strengthening of memory, for that was what *the process* required. He was quite simply nothing without memory.

He used alpha lipoic acid with acetyl l-carnitine to help stave off the onset of Alzheimer's disease, though there was, of course, not a shred of evidence that he was at risk. Those masses of protein tangles and inflamed lesions in the brain had yet to make an appearance, but one couldn't be too careful.

He chose concentrated sage and the amber capsules of omega-three fish oils to enhance his memory and increase his mind's plasticity this morning. A side dish held the remedies of male want, pure extracts of Yohimbe tree bark and the roots of the African violet.

Megaera checked these all off on her list as he gorged his way through them, making sure that the old man completed the regimen.

She stood at the screen with quiet exasperation. 'What are we going to do about him?'

Lawless seemed to find the question absurd. He wiped his mouth on a white napkin and rose to his feet. 'Megaera, you are bitter and resentful. You find nobody suitable. Each one you determine to scupper before proceedings can even begin. Yet this wily snake of a man has outdone you, and he fuels your vengeful ire. Why do you fuss so?'

'It's not too late,' she pleaded, stroking Lawless's white hair above one ear. 'We've made so many advances. We can find a way that restores my rightful place.'

Lawless drew her attention to Gene, projected on the screen. 'Perhaps *he* can, but my time is limited.'

'I should be the one!'

'Megaera, there is nothing that either of us can do. You are confined by the fate of your birth. It's not me you're battling, but biology. Women cannot achieve my kind of immortality; you are but a vessel for the next generation of males.'

What were all these things? Trophies or trinkets? Did he know them? Was he supposed to know them? Were they objects of interest? Or tangible symbols of a life lived?

Gene appraised the paintings above the fireplace, a murder of old men gazing down upon him with harsh, expectant want. Lineage in an unbroken chain; they were the proof, while he was the formless clay. The cheeks of one man might be higher than those of another, the ears slightly bent or the nose marginally clipped. But there was a definite progression from one man to the next, an evolution of facial morphology.

He looked in the mirror and studied his own face. If he was a link in their evolutionary chain he could not find it. Perhaps he did not want to find it.

He examined the books along the shelf. Something still didn't feel right, but for the time being he would keep it to himself. This was for his mind and his cataloguing alone. He knew they were watching him. He could feel their probing judgements. *Let them watch. I do not hide.*

He possessed distinct memories, imprints of more than one self. Yet none seemed more real than any other. All he wanted was to understand *this* life and his place in it, but he could feel a jumble of former beings, pressing behind his eyes, scrambling for his attention, destroying each other to control him.

He had trodden this path before. What remained to be seen was whether he could reach its end; whether he could understand it.

Where was the past? Was it in this old dagger that had lived a thousand years and perhaps stabbed as many men? Was it the past? Did it feel its pull like he did?

Did the act of remembering alter the past in any way? Or was the past merely a figment of his fancy; a sprig of figments, like dried leaves on a brittle twig, crumbling in the dust?

Gene worked his way through the objects beneath the pictures. With each shelf, and each new artefact and ornament, came the unlocking of a further deeply rooted vault that spilled forth images and sounds from a distant past.

He could hear the rumbling of something opening, disturbing the creaking, dusty cobwebs of the repository of his mind. And through each heavy door, the musty smells of memory. Something tangible, half buried beneath the dust, like a fine old book, all but forgotten, its leather used and worn with age, waiting to be revealed by a quick sharp breath.

The floorboards creaked in this place, they creaked and they whispered. They shrank from the sunlight and sighed in the shadows, straining with the burden of so many memories. He could hear them, smell them, taste them, the crumbling pieces of himself, longing to complete the jigsaw.

Who was it who said that the body may move forward, but the soul moves in circles towards itself as if always coming back to the beginning?

Gene took barely a moment to reply. 'Plotinus. It was Plotinus.'

Where that information suddenly sprang from was a mystery. Clearly the machinery of his mind was in perfect working order – he simply was not party to its actions. He was merely a spectator. He had cracked the spine of memory, but someone else was reading its pages.

Yes, Plotinus. We wish we had met him. It's a pity—

The act of living does not reveal the crucial figures of the age. Only hindsight can do that.

Gene knew exactly what they meant. He stood in front of the mirror and opened his robe. His bare chest seemed peculiar somehow: empty.

Something is missing.

'Oh, yes,' he commented. 'I agree. Where are my breasts?'

IN THE THEATRE
OF MEMORY

'All bow for His Majesty, Emperor Rudolf, the Holy Roman Emperor, at all times Expander of the Realm; King in Germany, King of Hungary, of Bohemia, Dalmatia, Croatia and Slavonia; Archduke of Austria; Margrave of Moravia; Margrave of Lusatia; Duke of Silesia; Duke of Luxembourg; Ruler of the Hapsburg lands of—'

'Yes, yes, yes, yes, yes!' Emperor Rudolf waved his hand at his guards to stand by the door, not waiting for his entourage to assemble behind him properly before descending upon Athanatos.

'What do you have for me today?'

Athanatos bowed, long and low. 'Visual mnemonics, Your Majesty.'

'To what end?'

'So that in here, Your Majesty, you may stand a little closer to infinity.'

Athanatos dutifully guided the emperor to a polished stage at the heart of a large wooden construction that occupied an entire room on the top floor of Emperor Rudolf's Powder Tower.

Rudolf had built the imposing addition to the mighty

Prague Castle especially to house the most noted alchemists of the age as they performed their calcinations, mortifactions, putrefactions and sublimations; all labouring on the Great Work which would yield the thousand names of the Prime Matter, the Philosopher's Stone, the secret of immortality.

The emperor was perplexed. 'If this is infinity it is a strange one.'

'All shall be revealed, Your Majesty.'

'You have been in my employ for how long now?'

'Just over a year, Your Majesty.'

The Holy Roman Emperor reached into his back pocket and plucked out the set of blackened fingers he kept about his person as an amulet of reckoning. Athanatos watched the Emperor stroke them in gentle contemplation as though they still lived.

'It is certainly the most *novel* approach I have yet seen.' There was that troublesome sibilant arriving into the conversation again; Emperor Rudolf's pronounced lisp was present with alarming force today. *Thertainly. Theen.* 'This bears no resemblance to any work I have seen before. Most curious.' *Bearth. Rethemblanthe. Curiouth.* It was no effort on the emperor's part. The work was all done for him by his overlarge chin, miserably hidden beneath an unkempt beard, a gift from his Habsburg ancestors along with a preposterously overfull lower lip that seemed to flap with a life all of its own.

Emperor Rudolf was not an attractive man. With his short stubby legs and his deep black troughs of melancholy, some said it was a wonder he wanted to live at all, let alone for ever.

'With respect, Your Majesty, some of those you have entertained in the past have been charlatans, at best.'

An uneasy cough echoed from beyond the walls of the wooden structure; Athanatos' barbs did not have to travel far to wound.

'Really, Tycho,' the emperor called out. 'I am satisfied the assault was not directed at you.'

Athanatos bowed graciously, as though he had meant no offence, but others knew differently. Tycho Brahe, the emperor's Danish astrologer, stood on the outskirts of the structure, listening with intent while his scrawny German assistant Johannes Kepler took notes. Athanatos had protested, but the emperor had insisted they accompany him to witness Athanatos' invention.

Sirocco, ever the watchful apprentice, kept a keen eye on them both.

Athanatos pressed on. 'I was thinking more of that English rogue, Queen Elizabeth's cumbersome scrying vizier. What was his name? Dee, was it?'

'John Dee ...' Emperor Rudolf appeared lost in the memory. 'Yes. Turned up in my court proclaiming that a vision had told him that I must reform or God would put his foot against my breast and throw me down.'

'What impudence!'

'It was just a ploy; a message from his queen to resist Catholic domination. In return he promised me the Philosopher's Stone. But I know a charlatan when I see one. I had him imprisoned for his failure to produce it.'

'Indeed, Your Majesty. Then it may interest you to know that his doubtfully psychic lackey, that ear-clipped forger, has returned to this great city.'

'Edward Kelley is in Prague? Without Dee?'

'It is my understanding they no longer communicate.'

'Why ever not?'

'One evening while scrying, it seems that Kelley conveniently struck up a psychic encounter with an angel, though truth be told it sounds more like a demon from the telling of it. This angel then *instructed* Kelley to tell Dee that they were required to exchange wives.'

'There's a sin that should damn both their souls to hell.'

'Quite. The curiosity is that Dee agreed. It is well known that Jane, his wife, despised Kelley, but the exchange proceeded and she fell pregnant. They have not spoken since.'

'Athanatos, you sound as though you do not believe this angelic interdiction.'

'Simple manipulation, Your Majesty. I have seen it all before. Kelley could tell Dee anything, and all that was required of Dee was to believe him. Now Kelley walks your streets again, having brought with him, by accident or by intent, Inquisition spies.'

'My city is full of Inquisition spies. They seek out that arrogantly rude monk, Bruno, and they may have him. They already stoke his pyre. But come, we are not here to chat in idle gossip about your rivals in the art.'

Athanatos bowed his head and through the gaps in the woodwork met Sirocco's gaze. He winked at his apprentice with a trace of a smile. His work was done, his rivals would not be haunting the Powder Tower in the foreseeable future.

Emperor Rudolf strutted across the stage and threw open his arms to embrace the vision before him. Constructed from mighty oak with all the convoluted undulations of a Vitruvian amphitheatre, Athanatos' Theatre of Memory was a semicircular auditorium dissected into seven sections by seven arches supporting seven rising tiers. Yet instead of a living audience each of the seven sections housed paintings – coded motifs, some from classical mythology, some from the emperor's life. Further sections contained scrolls and ornaments, emblems and curios.

'These items, these mnemonics, allow a person to stand here and recount in exquisite detail every facet of your life, Your Majesty, details that perhaps even you yourself have forgotten. These items can be replaced to allow a person to know, for example, every detail of every work of literature.'

Athanatos guided the emperor's eye. 'Memories are but a succession of changing stage settings. Like the actor playing a part. In here, Your Majesty, we have access to the knowledge of the whole universe, should we desire it.'

The emperor was transfixed. 'Is this, perchance, inspired by the work of Simonides of Ceos?' *Thimonideth of Ceoth.* 'I have been reading some newly acquired works. The world should be forever thankful that the Florentine Cosimo de Medici rescued so many of Greece's ancient manuscripts from the clutches of those vile Turks who dared to breach Byzantium's walls. Even now those unworthy animals sit on my borders, taunting me. The world of the west seems to be forever at war with these eastern barbarians.'

Athanatos' nostrils flared with rage. To be insulted on so many levels was almost more than he could bear. And by a man who was barely capable of speech!

'Simonides spoke of memory being aided by spatial allotment, Your Majesty. Nothing more.'

'And that is what we have here, is it not? I see on one shelf you have paintings of my forefathers, on another shelf manuscripts and proclamations. Aids to memory. Such a fascinating people, the Greeks.'

'They are an insufferable people!'

Athanatos' rage echoed around the curved walls of the Theatre of Memory and became trapped between the spaces confined by the Powder Tower's outer walls.

Sirocco remained silent, tending the small fire where, amidst the alembics and retorts, a dark liquid frothed in a small glass beaker, and watched Brahe and Kepler wince at Athanatos' outburst. He would be lucky if the emperor did not have him killed. To raise his voice to the sovereign was surely madness.

Yet the emperor's response, in spite of his insipid melancholy, was to laugh. 'Such arrogance! I am awed by you, Athanatos. Pray tell, who would you rate better?'

'Why I would rate myself, Your Majesty, greater than any Greek.'

Rudolf clapped his hands in enraptured amusement.

'Athanatos, you could live for a thousand years and never better a Greek. The Greek gives to the world. The Turk takes from it. The rest of us are caught in between.'

Sirocco had to end this. The apprentice cried out: 'Master Athanatos, the brew is ready!'

Inside the Theatre of Memory Athanatos composed himself. 'With your permission, Your Majesty, we shall begin.'

Sirocco entered from one of the five available doorways and presented the emperor with his bubbling brew.

The Emperor kept his eyes on the pale, rosy-cheeked apprentice. 'Such a fresh face. Such full lips.' Sirocco refused to meet the monarch's gaze, trembling nervously. Rudolf lifted the apprentice's chin. 'Taste it.'

Sirocco dutifully put glass to lip and drank down a mouthful of the strange concoction. There was no poison. 'It is your hot chocolate, Your Majesty. I crushed the beans myself all morning. See, my knuckles are raw.'

The emperor took the glass. 'You do not like it?'

'Perhaps the addition of cane sugar would make it more palatable, Your Majesty, but I do not think this new beverage will catch on.'

'I should hope not. This is my family secret.'

Athanatos shot Sirocco a look and the apprentice scuttled back out to the wings.

The emperor raised his glass with some cynicism. '*This* is your elixir, Athanatos?'

'The butter from the cocoa bean does not spoil, Your Majesty. That in itself is a magical property we would all like to harness. But hot chocolate is but a small cog in the machinery of my scheme.'

He waited for the emperor to start drinking before carefully directing his gaze towards a painting of a woman. 'This is your Aunt Maria, Your Majesty—'

'I know who she is for goodness' sake! Why do you hang that miserable old crone's face before me? I yearn for my lost teeth whenever I look at her. I had a full set before I went to Spain. She hoped to knock out any Protestant notions my younger brother Ernst and I may have acquired in Vienna, by subjecting us both to the strict Catholic court of Madrid.'

Athanatos appeared genuinely pained for the monarch. 'It must have been very . . . difficult.'

'I withdrew into the gloom of depression and the light of fantasy. This little brew they had retrieved from the new world always gave me comfort. When I left Spain I brought the recipe with me.'

Athanatos suspected it was the brew that had lost him his teeth.

A silver object glinted in the sunlight that shone through one of the slitted windows. Rudolf's eyes lit up in sheer delight. 'My foil!'

He surged forward and grabbed it, waving it in the air. 'After the misery of Montserrat, that decrepit old monastery, my Uncle Philip took Ernst and me to Aranjuez, where we practised our fencing all summer! I haven't seen this blade in many a year.' He beamed with the memory, but the joy was soon to wane. 'Uncle Philip was gravely ill that summer. Bedridden with the fever. Ernst and I would go hunting. All was well until we met him . . .'

Athanatos urged the emperor on through sly probing. 'It was not your fault, he was unbalanced was he not?'

The emperor turned on the magus. 'You have no right to speak ill of my cousin Don Carlos! That is *my* privilege.'

'As you wish, Your Majesty.'

Rudolf laid the weapon carefully back down in its allotted compartment. 'After my sister Anna married Uncle Philip, I returned to Vienna. I was seized with such joy that I could not bring sleep into my eyes.'

'The years in Spain marked you deeply.'

'My father said I had become cold and distant. That I exhibited *Spanish humours*. He ordered that Ernst and I change our bearing, but it was too late. We were set.'

A long black cloud hung over the Theatre of Memory and embraced the two men. The emperor was disturbed. 'I thought I had bathed in Lethe's waters long enough to banish such memories. I had not thought of them in so long. Yet here they well up with no warning.'

'All that memory, Your Majesty, dredged up from Lethe's slimy bed with just a picture, a foil and a cup of hot chocolate.' He took a step forward and led the emperor's gaze around the amphitheatre. 'And we have so much more of your life left to explore. Yet these are only some of the memories I wanted to reveal to you, Your Majesty.'

'Perhaps the Greeks were right. Perhaps life is easier if on the journey one wades through the river of forgetting. Do you really think there is a Lethe in Hades?'

'Without memory, Your Majesty, then who are we?'

Emperor Rudolf found himself moved by the theatre, so powerful were the memories it elicited. 'Now I understand what you have built here. Please go on.'

'What we have discussed thus far are the memories you carry with you from *this* life. Yet you carry with you memories from further into history than that. You carry memories of *previous* lives also, and it is this aspect which truly offers immortality.'

'This is a theory?'

'It is a fact. And I shall prove it to you.'

'I have travelled far and wide, Your Majesty, and I have seen many things. I have been to the source of the Nile.'

The emperor was astounded. 'The source?'

'There, a certain crocodile resides which must hide itself in deep earthen burrows without food or water if it is to survive the long dry summer. Yet before its descent it breeds and leaves its eggs on the surface. Every year, without fail, the eggs of the crocodile hatch. Yet without the aid of a parent to teach it, its first action is to seek out the darkness of the burrow and crawl to safety. At birth, Your Majesty!'

'Without tutelage? That is nothing more than instinct.'

Athanatos wagged a finger. 'Precisely. But what *is* instinct? In the world of beasts, instinct *is* memory. Take the goose. Newly hatched goslings are born with innate perceptions. If a shape moves across the sky and the gosling can see that its wings are at the rear of its body, the gosling knows that it is seeing a goose and it is safe. A hawk's body is of similar shape to a goose, only its wings are forward, close to the head. A gosling, at birth, can recognize this difference in a bird in flight, and if it sees a hawk, will hide.'

'Hippocrates said that the nature of animals is untutored. You find the Greek unsavoury, for reasons unfathomable, yet you know the work of the physician Galen in the second century, do you not?'

'Why that was my next example, Your Majesty. He delivered a goat kid by cutting it from its mother's womb so that it would never see the one who bore it. He put it in a room with bowls of wine, oil, honey, milk, grains and fruits, and the very first thing it did was instinctively stand, shake off the moisture from its mother, scratch itself and sniff the bowls. It then drank the milk.

'Does a cow eat meat when it is first born? No. Without learning it suckles from its mother before moving on to grass.

'We humans have an innate fear of spiders and snakes that when drawn out is difficult to control. It is an old instinct that has served as well for survival. It is a memory from ancient times. But it is not the only type of memory that we carry.'

Athanatos guided the emperor over to another portrait. Guntram the Rich was, in AD 950, the first of the Habsburgs.

Emperor Rudolf studied the image, his keen eye taking in every nuance, every deformity.

'See his chin? See his lip, Your Majesty? Do you not carry the scar of his memory upon your own face? We are all, each of us, a jigsaw of our ancestors, a familiar nose, a mother's smile, held together by a firm thread. But are these not memories written in flesh?'

'It is unavoidable. It is in the blood.'

'Yes, Your Majesty, in the blood. And what if all that you are could be conveyed just as easily? All your memories of youth and beyond. A form of immortality worthy of the ancient gods. Perhaps even better.'

The emperor whirled on the alchemist. 'Better?'

'Consider this. What if you broke your leg, Your Majesty, so violently was it shattered that it was impossible to repair. You were forced to use crutches because a great plague had destroyed your courtiers and there was no one left alive to carry you. Would you still seek immortality if you were trapped in that one useless body?'

'There is no alternative but death!'

'No, Your Majesty, there is another way. Tell me, what would life be like to be in a newer, younger, virile body? To be born anew, to start over, when the old fat husk has outlived its usefulness? We live through our children, do we not?'

'What are you suggesting?'

'Let not Lethe cause us to forget. Let us surge forth with new rivers from our loins, rivers of self that carry us into every generation, alive and with vigour.'

The emperor was truly shaken by this notion, his face ashen, his cheeks waxy and pale. 'But what of the soul?'

'The soul enters the body at the moment of a child's first breath, as you know. But the blood arrives many months before. What are we, but a collection of memories and experiences? If they are transferred to a child, upon its birth it cannot take on a new soul, for it is a vessel that is already filled.'

'But what of *my* soul? If I live, yet so does the child which is also me, would it be but a mirror of myself, or me in actuality?'

'The soul will have been merely shattered, and the child has but a shard of it. Upon your death the pieces unite and you shall be whole once again.'

'What do you propose?'

'I propose a test, Your Majesty, a test to confirm that what I say is true. I propose that I shall take a concubine, hand-picked by yourself. You and I will then have a conversation. You shall reveal to me certain information that only you could possibly know. It shall not be written down, and no one else must be present at the time of the telling. A feat of memory will be required on your part as well as mine. I will then breed with this concubine and she shall produce a son. When my son and heir reaches the age of five, you will administer my elixir, and when his fever has broken you will test him, you will probe him with questions about the subject you and I will have discussed, and the man within will reveal himself.'

'If you are his father, you could have trained him.'

'Not at all, for he shall not be raised in my presence.'

'You will banish him?'

'No, Your Majesty, I propose you banish me; with means at my disposal to live a comfortable life and continue the course of my work. But the child stays with you. And when the time is ripe for the plucking, you shall summon me and perform your tests.'

'And what if you are wrong?'

'Then kill me. For I will have betrayed you and there can be no other punishment.'

'And if you are right?'

'The decision is yours, of course, Your Majesty. But if I am right and you still kill me, then I live on in the growing body of my progeny. But *if* I am right and you let me *live*, I will be able to provide you with an heir, who is nothing short of yourself *reborn*.'

THE BLACK ART OF DECEIT

This was the worst of all possible occurrences.

Athanatos marched to the alehouse to gloat among his rivals, but Sirocco still had work to perform. The apprentice desperately ran down Golden Lane, but was so fearful, a quick stop in the shadows was called for. The contents of an evening meal spewed forth and ran into the icy gullies between the cobblestones.

Athanatos had vowed never to reveal his secret to the emperor for fear of alerting Cyclades, yet he had done so after much planning and preparation and had kept his entire intention secret from his apprentice whose work with the theatre had kept him distracted. It was a masterful deception.

As the goldsmiths hammered out their creations before their furnace doors, their fingers curled, blackened and clawed, like crocodiles'; as the smell of wood smoke wafted from house to house down the lane, the glow of their tinctures lit up their glass and wax-paper windows with the blossoms of rubedo and citrinitas; as the swirling of their opus brought forth creations blacker than the crow, whiter than the swan and redder than any blood, Sirocco staggered to the home of Athanatos, and barricaded the door shut.

The emperor demanded answers, and Sirocco had thoroughly failed to furnish them.

The apprentice tore through the house sending wheels, gimbals, cylinders, cogs crashing to the ground. Scrolls of vellum appeared defiantly blank and though the cauldrons sat distilling their deadly powers, nothing could be found to satisfy the emperor's demands.

Week after week, month after month the secrets that Athanatos held remained firmly elusive, despairingly untouchable.

The game was at an end. The marching boots approached outside. A mighty hammering on the heavy oak door and a calling out of Sirocco's name soon followed. 'Come out! Emperor Rudolf awaits!'

Apprentice and spy peered through the ice sheet that blanketed the glass window, to see the distorted faces of the men who had come to fetch him.

'The conceit of man is to believe that he shall find a way to outdo death. Cheat the finite clock, beat back the ticking and stave off that final chiming of the bell. Tell me, *Sirocco*, what is the conceit of woman?'

In the emperor's bedchamber, Sirocco stood nervously, shaking like a sapling while the emperor fiddled with one of the bejewelled clocks that stood on every surface.

'You came to me a year before Athanatos' arrival, did you not? Told me to expect the *sol niger*, the black soul of alchemy, a Lucifer, a prince of the east; a man of despicable tricks who has risen from the worms time and again. You told me not to trust him, and told me the tale of an eternal struggle between a man of eastern evil and a brave Greek named Cyclades.'

The emperor shuffled over, a glinting knife in hand. He grabbed Sirocco and ripped away the fine doublet with savage wrath, slicing through the bindings beneath until two rounded breasts spilled out to his satisfaction, revealing a woman beneath the sheath of male clothes.

'A hero who is reborn time and again? Tell me, witch, why would Cyclades return as a feeble woman?'

Bitter tears flowed down the young girl's face, exposed for all to see. 'Perhaps I am a plaything of the gods; a cruel joke that has lasted longer than they have. All I know is that time circles round me and offers unrelenting madness as its gift. I tell you I am Cyclades, and Athanatos is like a many-headed hydra – when one life has outlived its usefulness he moves on to the next, resurrecting his bloodline at a stroke. But I cannot uncover Athanatos' secrets for he keeps no record of them. They are locked away deep inside his mind where I cannot reach.'

'Oh, but you can. You are the perfect vessel.'

Cyclades clutched her breasts in desperation. 'You cannot mean that!'

The emperor waved his knife at her. 'You promised me his secrets of eternal life and failed to deliver! He now offers them to me freely requiring nothing more than a concubine!'

'The mixing of our two bloodlines, his and mine, is exactly what he wants! If a child of our union would reveal his secrets to you, it would also surely reveal mine to him!'

'Then you should have thought of that when you decided to return to this sublunary world using womanly wiles as your weapon. You are either unskilled or a liar.'

'I will not be reduced to a limb of the arch mage.'

'You have no choice, my dear. This is a deal signed in blood and it will reveal itself in the veins of youth – or shall I instead throw you to my lions? Guards!'

They lunged forward and grabbed Cyclades by each arm, while the emperor toasted her departure. 'Here's to immortality. Time held fast by the filament never ending. Take her to Athanatos. He has his wench.'

What possible cure was there for the maddening realization that in living forwards, understanding could be reached only by looking backwards? How would anyone ever know where they were going? It was only natural to keep bumping into things.

Gene held the dagger and knew where he'd seen it before. Its delicate hilt protruded from its elaborate sheath, while its sharp blade remained hidden and protected within.

These accursed memories were a problem. They spoke to him from multiple perspectives, in many voices, all his own.

We were a girl.

He could see the girl through the eyes of Athanatos. Yet he could see Athanatos through the eyes of the girl.

He held within himself the memory of a woman. That was something Athanatos had vowed was not possible in his scheme of immortality.

It is a contradiction—

It is a life of contradictions—

We're not sure you're ready for this—

'Be quiet!' He attempted to set the dagger back down on the shelf, but as he did so a small crumpled piece of paper dropped to the floor.

Don't—

They're watching us—

Be aware—

They observe us with dark purposes—

He fumbled the dagger, letting it tumble to the carpet. He took a step back, eyeing the slip of paper and palming it when he stooped to retrieve the blade.

Clever—

Nicely done—

He kept it hidden between his fingers, and returned to his study of the other artefacts dotted around the lounge. He did this for half an hour before returning to the bedroom and preparing to take a shower.

Only when he hung the bathrobe up on a hook did he take the opportunity to read what was written on the slip.

It was a set of numbers. Were they the code to a lock? But he had already opened the door.

Another door? Perhaps he could flee this prison. He'd done it once, perhaps again.

A bank account? Or was it a telephone number? He could be certain only of one thing; the digits were written in his own hand.

'One of you knows more than you're saying.'

Yes, but I cannot say—

'Why not?'

You swore me to secrecy—

Why had he chosen to leave himself such a cryptic message? To let himself know he was in trouble? That seemed absurdly redundant – that much was obvious. His concerns had to run deeper than that.

He remembered the childbirth, the agony, the screaming; and the knife to his throat upon delivery. *Cyclades? Athanatos?*

Which am we?

BOOK THREE

THE UNEXAMINED LIFE IS NOT
WORTH LIVING

SOCRATES

MANHUNT

Porter arrived at JFK at 2.30 a.m. on Air France flight AF8994. Despite the throng of people, the terminal building was a lonely hollow experience. He was glad he'd taken a flight with a connection in Paris. Anyone arriving on a distinctly Middle Eastern carrier, with or without a swarthy complexion, seemed to be taking appreciably longer to get through passport control.

He had one bag, on wheels. Dazed from such a long journey, his ears still ringing and sore, Porter dragged his luggage behind him, and joined the line outside. Three or four people, each of them a different race, said something to him in thick accents that he didn't understand. He was so used to the Lebanese inflection, English in any other accent was incomprehensible.

Forty-five dollars plus tolls, the flat fee for a yellow cab into Manhattan, put him on a journey through the back end of Queens. The twinkling bulbs of the city were like thousands of children's night-lights, defining the depths of the darkness.

For a city that didn't sleep, Manhattan seemed to be at the very least dozing, and from that Porter took some comfort.

On Seventh Avenue, across the road from Penn Station, the cab deposited him in front of the Pennsylvania Hotel. He pulled his bag off the empty street and through the hotel's worn glass doors. At the far end of the deserted grand lobby, he was greeted by a strange shimmering sound reminiscent of a hundred tinkling orchestral triangles. Emerging from amid the stained and dented brass fixtures, he found two men up ladders by the utilitarian reception desk, washing a colossal chandelier, one long dangling crystal at a time.

Porter paid for a room, the cheapest they had, collected his key and made the lonely journey up to the ninth floor. The green-tinged hallways were the widest he had ever seen; the room was cramped and tatty, but perfectly clean and serviceable. He had the choice of two double beds, both squeezed flat against one wall. The bathroom was box-like, the tiles peculiar little hexagons that served only to accentuate his feeling of exhaustion.

In its glory days this would have been quite some hotel, a place of splendour. But in its autumn years it was creaking and faded, a shell of its former self, barely alive, its rooms the desiccated leaves of fall, dropping one by one.

He kicked off his shoes and unpacked his notebooks on to the narrow wooden desk. Armed with a small grey New York guidebook he'd purchased in Paris Charles de Gaulle – a curious little thing with a foldout map and a plastic compass on its spine – he set about drawing up a plan of action.

More than seven million people lived and worked within the five boroughs of New York City, speaking eighty different languages. The guidebook cheerfully informed him that there were more Italians than in Rome, more Irish than in Dublin and more Jews than in Jerusalem, but that didn't deter him.

It was only during the long flight that Porter's intense scrutiny of the photograph in Aisha's newspaper revealed the full implications of what she had been trying to tell him. That one simple picture held many surprises, and he had marked up the accompanying article with zeal. It contained a lot of information – names and places – but nowhere did it mention the name of either man in the photograph or who was in charge of the investigation.

If he started at the beginning, the Metropolitan Museum of
Art might have some of the clues he was searching for. But he
required more than mere clues, he needed answers. He knew
very little about the city outside of what he'd seen in feature
films and on the news. He didn't have the faintest notion of
how it operated. He needed a detailed list of all the police
precincts in Manhattan and perhaps one of them might be
able to point him in the right direction. And then there were
the other news publications. Perhaps they would help.

He opened out the map and circled 42nd Street and Fifth –
New York Public Library.

Breakfast was not at Tiffany's but rather at the Dunkin'
Donuts next door to the Pennsylvania lobby, served to him by
a pretty Russian girl named Irina. It wasn't his first choice,
indeed it wasn't any kind of choice, but without his bearings
there appeared to be remarkably few options on this stretch
of road. He decided to eat and walk at the same time, the
drizzling rain making a welcome change from the arid hills he
was used to.

In the harsh reality of daylight, New York was another city
entirely. The bleak urban chaos overwhelmed him, swamping
his virgin senses with vertigo. The heavy tides of pedestrians
and vehicles ebbed and flowed to the moods of fickle traffic
signals. Where the tides converged it was like the dance of the
bees, bodies and vehicles communicating in voiceless
movement, pattern and rhythm.

The guardianship of the impassive twin lions at the foot of
the New York Public Library came as welcome relief.

Porter walked up to the Astor Hall on the first floor, where
he left his raincoat at the library checkroom and asked for
directions. *Room 108.* Passing under the cathedral of

marble-clad arches, he headed down the hall that led to the Current Periodicals Reading Room. Newspapers, he was informed, were generally held there for between two and four weeks.

Porter suspected that most of what he needed was right here in front of him. He began assembling his finds on a table in week-long piles. The last seven days of the *New York Post* and the *Daily News*. A week's worth of the *New York Times*. The *Wall Street Journal* was unlikely to have run the story, and he also discounted the *Observer* and the *Village Voice*. But there were other journals that might prove useful, community-based publications that he had never heard of but that could possibly contain some of the missing details.

His approach was systematic. One pile at a time, scouring even the front pages, though he doubted the story was important enough to appear there. When he made his first discovery it was tucked away on page eleven, an artist's impression of the perpetrator. Slowly but steadily he assembled a more detailed picture of the places and events, until eventually he had the name of the man he was searching for. Now to locate him.

Under the painted ceilings of the cavernous Rose Main Reading Room on the top floor, Porter used every minute of the maximum half an hour allotted him to use one of the online computer terminals. He found what he was looking for surprisingly swiftly, though it took longer to sift through the exhaustive list of addresses and telephone numbers. He printed off maps and further details.

Downstairs, Porter took out his stash of quarters and picked up the receiver of the public payphone.

'Fourth Precinct.'

'Yes. May I speak with Detective James North?'

'Who's calling?'

'My name's Porter. Dr William Porter.' The agitation in his voice was hard to stifle. If the lady on the other end noticed at all, she certainly wasn't giving him any indication.

'What's this regarding?'

'Can you ask him whether the nightmares have started yet?'

H-R-S-H

7.21 a.m. Wednesday.

His apartment was a suffocating furnace, redolent with despair. For every turbulent minute that he remained confined by its walls he felt the slow march of inevitable decay inch deeper into his bones, his fate a sword waiting with Damoclean malice to cut him down; he teetered on the edge and he was afraid.

Where was his mind? And why with bare fingers and with his own shit had he painted the portrait of a bull? He could feel its furious hot breath upon his skin and dared not meet its incriminating gaze.

North shrouded himself in a winter coat and slogged through the mist, envying those who still enjoyed their uneventful slumber.

He had parked nearly four blocks away; good street smarts said it was reckless to do otherwise. He never liked to use the unmarked cars as a take-home when he didn't have to; they were so easily recognizable. It was like sending up a flare to the public at large declaring that a cop walked among them. It made life complicated and dangerous.

The driver's seat was cold and damp. He whacked the heat on and wrung his hands over the blower.

The streets were deserted when he pulled out on to

McGinnis Boulevard, he'd make good time to the Williamsburg Bridge if he was doing that, but today he wasn't heading into the city. He had business elsewhere. He turned on to the I-278, heading north.

8.13 a.m.

It was on East 187th Street, west of Belmont Avenue, where someone from the Forty-eighth Precinct had recommended a small bodega with a parking space that had eyes. If he parked there the chances were he would have a car to come back to when he was done. Oh, and welcome to the South Bronx. As Tim Dog once said: 'Fuck Compton.'

Through the nostalgic haze of the notorious seventies when the South Bronx looked like Berlin after the war, it was perverse comfort to know some landlords still weren't averse to fire bombing their own buildings for the insurance money. A burned-out shell here, sheets of corrugated tin there, all waiting to collapse, houses of cards sat in among fresh hands dealt from new decks, new single row family housing, doused liberally with plenty of abandoned cars, angry tags and bitter eyes. It set alarm bells ringing. *Fuck Compton.*

North knocked again on the grimy front door of apartment 2C. He heard a chain being set, a lock slide back. The darkened wooden door cracked open.

'Whadda ya want?'

'Samuel Bailey?'

A hesitation. 'I don't know.'

North fumbled left-handedly for his gold shield. 'Sir, I suspect you know whether you are or are not Mr Bailey.' All he could see was a shock of grey hair and a pitted and scarred nose. 'I apologize this is so early.'

'Are you crazy?'

North didn't answer. In all honesty that was something *he* didn't know.

'You with the IRS? I'm not talkin' wid ya if ya wid the IRS.'

'Sir, I'm not with the IRS. I'm NYPD. I tried calling—'

'I don't answer the phone.'

'I just need five minutes of your time.'

'Why zat?'

North fought his frustration. 'Sir, could we conduct this in your apartment?'

'I in some kinda trouble?'

That remained to be seen. 'You were recommended to me as an expert. I understand antique medical equipment is a specialty of yours?'

'Might be. Recommended, huh?'

'I want to ask your advice.' North fished for the photograph of the antique syringe and held it up at the door for Bailey to see.

'Consultations I charge for, y'know?'

Here it comes. 'What do you want?'

He could see Bailey licking his lips. 'I, uh, I ain't eaten in two days. A sandwich? And maybe sumpin to wash it down wid. A good strong bourbon.'

There's an old saying: it's impossible to starve in America. It's a lie. It's perfectly possible, it just needs work.

Samuel Bailey clutched the sandwich box to his chest as though someone was going to snatch it from him, and eyed the can of soda with disdain. He picked his way through the masses of grey scrap metal and seedy tattered junk that made up his inventory.

The apartment made North's skin crawl. The stench of body odour and stale urine was overwhelming, all pervasive. The tiny living room wasn't big enough for a separate kitchen so a counter with a stove sat at one end. He could see Bailey hadn't cooked in weeks, a hardened thick brown greasy crust caked the ceramic around the hotplates.

Bailey found what he was looking for and snatched up a heavy directory. He sat on a pile of magazines and thumbed through, keeping the photograph close to hand.

'This is in excellent condition. Zit belong to anybody?' He was in his boxers and a threadbare bathrobe that flapped open at the crotch presenting a distinctly unwelcome view.

'Unless we can get it back to its rightful owner it'll stay in property until there's an auction.'

'Wonderful workmanship. Sterling silver fittings. Hand-engraved volume numbers on the glass barrel. Manufactured around 1870. 'S a Ferguson from London.'

'You ever see too many of these? I mean where can you get these things?'

'These days ya just go on eBay.' Bailey's lower unshaven lip trembled in sympathy with the value he clearly placed on this otherwise unremarkable object.

'eBay can be traced. What if you didn't want to be traced?'

'Brimfield.'

'Who's he?' North reached for his notebook. It wasn't in his coat pocket.

'Brimfield, Massachusetts; biggest outdoor antique show in the area. Five tousands dealers from all over the country. Eight hundred square acres a tables. Ya wanna unload or pick up widdout anyone rememberin' who ya are? Brimfield.'

Not in his other pocket either. 'You got directions?'

'Sure, but nobody'll be there. It's a five-day event every May, July an' September. September's meet ain't for anodder tree weeks.'

Dead end, forget that. North fumbled around, he had a pen; *where's my notebook?* A pen and a copy of Gene's photograph that had been lifted from the surveillance video tape; he showed it to Bailey. 'You ever seen this guy before? Had any dealings with him?'

Bailey looked up from what he was doing for a moment. He squinted as he took a good look but in the end he shook his head. 'Sorry.'

North turned it over and wrote his notes on the back. 'What about the lettering? H-R-S-H?'

'Gettin' to that.' Bailey thumbed through more pages of his directory with cantankerous irritation. 'Interestin'.'

He pulled another heavy directory from the shelf. There were pages and pages of names and phone numbers. Some places underlined in thick ink. The pages were yellowed with age. North could only trust that the information would be current.

'H-R-S-H. Hudson River State Hospital. It's a nuthouse.'

North took notes. 'Does it say where it is?'

'Dutchess County.'

'Is it still there?'

'Better. It's a museum.'

A museum? Is Sheppard right? North tried to picture the scenario. So Gene visits the museum, steals the syringe, maybe a few other items. What does he do next? Come to the city to look for a fence?

'You hear of anything else from this place coming up for sale in the city?'

'Nope. But y'know, I know this place? They got this priest who still does these exorcisms on the insane.'

'I thought you said it's a museum?'

'Old part is. I dealt widdem years ago. But they still got a wing open. Calls itself the Hudson River Psychiatric Center.'

Revise scenario: so Gene's a patient? North was on his feet, much to the surprise of Bailey.

'That it?'

'Thank you for your time.'

Bailey showed him to the door. 'Detective, if you don't mind me sayin', you look ill. I mean *really* sick. You thought about takin' somethin'?'

North didn't appreciate the advice but he kept his reply to himself. His thoughts lay elsewhere; a priest that still performed exorcisms? *I am Satan's Oath.*

9.55 a.m.

He pulled out his road atlas from the dash and thumbed through the index. Dutchess County was upstate. If he left now he could be there by lunchtime.

Was that where Gene was from? Had he made the trip deliberately to do what he did? If so, who else was in the car? Had they travelled together?

He'd call up the house en route and get Nancy to trace the number for the nearest sheriff's office to the hospital. Maybe they had record of a theft.

He threw the atlas on the passenger seat. There, next to it, was his black notebook lying out in the open. He cursed his addled memory and jammed the notebook into his coat pocket before starting up the engine and swinging the front end of the Lumina out into the road. A flash of motion swept across his mirrors.

Hoooonnnk!

He jammed on the brakes as a bright red Toyota swerved to avoid contact, running wide so as not to crush the cyclist that was caught in between.

The cyclist for his part simply sailed on through, oblivious to how close he'd come to death.

North was shaken. *You idiot.* He watched the receding bicycle and instinctively rubbed his battered knee until sharp pains jabbed through his skull.

He cradled his head in his tired hands as flashbulbs of searing pain exploded behind his eyes. He could feel his nerves set on fire, an agonizing, blazing chain that stretched deep inside to the back of his head.

A yellow cab honked angrily. There was a gap.

The front end of a gleaming silver car reared up at him.
The driver through the windshield.
A striking woman with long, deep auburn hair and wearing designer sunglasses.

North shook off these memories and gripped the steering-wheel; his breathing ragged and tortured.

The woman spraying perfume at Gene in the museum.

He'd seen them before. The car. The woman. Outside Central Park.

Were they one and the same? Was it an accident? Or had she *intended* to run him down?

His Nextel was ringing. North was slow to respond, the revelation already crumbling in his hands.

'North.'

The quiet voice hesitated on the line. Lieutenant Hyland sighed as if the words just wouldn't come out. When they did arrive, his tone was grave. 'Central Park just called. Manny Siverio's dead.'

So I did lie to him.

Manny Siverio, the uniformed officer he'd tried to save, whose hot blood gushed in the stairwell of the museum. The force of the blow was crippling. 'When?'

'Couple hours ago.'

North was quiet. All the rules had changed the moment his hunt had turned to homicide.

DD-5

The walls of Hyland's confined, circumscribed office were made from thin wood and sheet glass. As in an aquarium, everything outside appeared magnified – the sea of dented steel desks on three sides, the tattered flotsam of the bureaucratic, peeling blue squad room that roared with the wash of investigation. And there was nowhere to hide.

It was an assault that North could not fend off. He felt under seige.

'Funeral's this Saturday. You going?'

'I don't know. I really didn't know the guy.'

'You tried to save his life.'

'But I failed.'

Hyland, sat behind his desk, his patience as rickety as the creaking machine he was using, jabbed at the keys with powerful stabbing motions. He did not look up. 'I think you should go.'

North remained silent. The lieutenant was not issuing an order, North wouldn't have listened if he had. Supervising a squad room was a political process and he was offering the political solution. It was up to North if he wanted to take it.

The lieutenant looked slowly through the manila folder like

an arthritic secretary. His slight build and less than average height had worked to his advantage in the dim and distant past when he'd worked vice. But his non-threatening demeanour was an illusion. He was sharp and meticulous.

'Department of Transportation give word yet on how many traffic cameras lined that route from the museum?'

'DOT says the Traffic Management Center only has eighty-six cameras citywide; they're putting the tapes together, but I'd be surprised if it's more than a couple.'

'Think you'll get a hit?'

'If I don't I'll go back and check for store cameras with a view of the street, and ATM machines.'

Hyland didn't relish the prospect. 'That's a lot of work.'

North answered with some reticence. 'I figure I need just the cameras covering the collision at the corner of West 81st Street and Central Park, and the cameras from in and around Hell's Kitchen.'

'You got anything on make and model?'

What is this? 'It was silver. CSU's looking at trace and tyre marks now.'

Hyland riffled through the case file again. He thumbed sheet after sheet of handwritten notes and neatly typed paper, setting each one aside with precision. 'That's not in here.'

'I just got it yesterday.'

'I need the DD-5.'

A DD-5? It was the investigator's notes detailing his progress on the case, a follow-up to the sixty-one. *It hasn't even been a week.* 'Are you serious?'

'A DD-5 once every six months is not appropriate on homicide; especially when it's a cop.' Hyland expected signs of steady progress.

A thunderous cloud shadowed North's thoughts. *Let's settle this.* 'Why are you telling me how to work?'

'There's a whole squad out there. Use them. You working alone on a homicide investigation is a liability.'

'Is that a threat?'

'It's just the way it is. If I can't demonstrate you're good for the job it gets reassigned, your old man could tell you *that*. DD-5, tomorrow morning.'

My old man? There was no retreating from that darkness.

'I spoke with Martinez.'

'What's he got to do with this?'

'He wants to help.'

'He already has a partner.'

'He knew Manny. He's prepared to put in the extra hours, pick up the slack. It's not a partnership, but he'll watch your back. It's a good deal.'

North got to his feet. 'For who?'

11.37 a.m.

At the PAA's desk, Nancy Montgomery presented North with his faxes, phone messages, letters and bulletins. 'Ash called back from the CSU. Said the perfume bottle's being dealt with. The mountain bike you borrowed is already transferred to property.'

'Did he mention how long ago?'

'Nah-uh.'

North took a breath. 'I need that bike back in trace.'

'I can take care of that.' Vincent Martinez didn't have his gold shield yet. He was twenty-six years old and had been a detective for three years. He knew the deal. Was it sincerity North could see in him? If so, it was an odd feeling.

'Are you sure?'

Martinez was a few desks away. He stood in his cheap though well maintained suit at a white board he'd set up with a map of the city and Gene's photograph taped to it. He was retracing every step, going over every move, marking it in detail. 'I can do it. I wanna do it. It's just gofer stuff.'

North acquiesced mildly. 'Thank you.'

Nancy wasn't finished. 'You got a visitor, by the way.'

That's new. 'Who?'

'A psychiatrist. Left you a buncha phone messages. Finally got tired and came down.'

A psychiatrist? The prickles on his skin tingled. Had Bailey contacted the museum? 'What's the message?'

Nancy pointed out the stack of Post-its already in his hand. North shuffled through them.

Have the nightmares started yet?

It hit him in the pit of his stomach. *What kind of message is that?* He stumbled over his words, shaken. 'Does he have any ID?'

'You can ask him, he's right down the hall.'

'Why don't *I* ask him?' Martinez was already hurriedly making his way over. 'You're the assigned, you shouldn't be so easy to get to. Let him jump through hoops.'

North was not enthusiastic. 'We have to talk.'

'So we'll talk.'

Martinez headed out into the hall.

North watched as the old man sat quietly, producing from a worn leather briefcase a single sheet of paper; his life in two hundred words. He slipped it to the homicide detective with nervous hands.

His wasn't a face North recognized, even when the comparisons were plucked from the torment of his mind, but he knew about the nightmares and that was familiarity enough.

Martinez stood at North's desk and read directly from the résumé. 'William Porter. Age sixty-two.'

North took the sheet of paper and read through it himself. Porter was British. He claimed to have been a student of medicine at University College London before receiving his PhD in Psychiatry at Oxford. Until very recently he was receiving extended funding to conduct research from an organization called DOPS, the Division of Personality Studies, which in turn was a unit of the Department of Psychiatric Medicine at the University of Virginia.

'Think he's legit?'

'Anyone can type up a résumé.'

'Have the nightmares started? What's he mean by that? That ringing any bells with you?'

The nightmares. North gave nothing away.

'Maybe this guy's just a whack job. Read something in the paper. You want I scare the shit out of him and put him back on the street?'

North sat down heavily at his desk. 'I'll take care of it.'

'Look, I uh, I got a few hours, I can assist.'

North logged on to his computer. 'Where's your partner?'

'Maternity leave.'

That explains a lot.

'You got direction on this?'

Yes I have direction. 'Gene wasn't alone.'

'He wasn't?' Martinez pulled up a chair.

'That's why I need the bike back in trace.'

'What you looking for?'

North set Porter's résumé down on the table, his reservations plain for Martinez to see. He took a long moment and reflected. *How do I handle this?* He tried to sound patient. 'Talk.'

Martinez didn't appear to know where to start at first. His eyes clouded over, this was troubling him deeply. 'Manny and me, we're cousins.'

There was nothing North could say to that. Nothing worth saying; nothing worth hearing.

'His Mom, y'know? I see her in church. I promised I'd look in, keep on top of this. I know it's a conflict, investigating your own family. I just want to help out. Me, Manny, my uncle; we're a family of cops, y'know? Like you and your pop. It's in the blood. It's what we do.'

A family of cops. And what do you do if you discover you've been living a lie?

'What's the story between you and the doer?'

He moves fast. 'Nothing.'

'Not some old case?'

'I didn't know him. You could go through old case files for a month, you will never find him because we never met.'

'But he asked for you by name.'

'Yes he did.'

'And that set him off?'

Is he looking for someone to blame? 'What's your point?'

'It makes no sense. Guy just walks up, says he got a beef with a man he's never met?'

North had an easier answer. 'Maybe he hates cops. Maybe you're right. Maybe *he's* the one who pulled the first name he saw from a newspaper. I've seen things make less sense out there.'

'What about this shrink, Porter? Think he could be treating this guy?'

'We'll find out.'

'You canvassed anyone else? There must be ten thousand shrinks in this city.'

'I have a lead. I'm going there this afternoon.' *I might even check in.*

Martinez took the details down, adding it to the list. 'Hey, want me to badger the OCME while you're gone, see if they got your blood results?'

He's already been through my case file. North was quietly furious. Martinez had overstepped his bounds. It was improper for him to even touch the case file without permission. Yet North found he could not blame him for his zeal; besides, it smacked of Hyland's doing.

'And that woman on the security tape with the mace pepper spray or whatever. I was thinking we should get TARU to see if they can pull a clear mug shot off the tape so you can go through the books.'

The NYPD Technical Assistance Response Unit had already produced clear shots of Gene from the tape, so they were already set up for the case. North agreed it was the right thing to do.

'Got anything else?' asked Martinez.

This one kept getting pushed to one side. Maybe he did need the assist. 'The skull.'

'What skull?'

'Exactly. Witnesses reported Gene snatched a skull from a display case. They say that's what set him off, started him weeping. The skull's missing. It's not listed in the evidence.'

'Did he take it?'

'Not that I saw. I guess one of the museum people tampered with the scene, but I'm not certain. We need to talk to them.'

The younger detective noted that down too. He'd reached the end of the list. 'That everything?'

North thought about it. 'You are working other cases, right?'

Martinez hauled himself out of the chair. 'Oh yeah. Don't worry, I won't crowd ya.'

UNDER SCRUTINY

12.01 p.m.

North had neither the time nor the budget to pay a visit to Porter's alma mata, but verification of his credentials was essential. He directed his web browser to a site called UMI, University Microfilms, which was based out of Ann Arbor and provided varying services from access to newspapers, books and periodicals, to university dissertations.

The database was not mandatory so it wasn't foolproof, but it was substantial and dated back to the 1860s. The chances were high that if Porter was genuine, his PhD dissertation would be listed here, and for thirty dollars, North could purchase an actual copy.

North had no intention of purchasing anything. The dissertation abstract would be enough.

William Porter was listed. Oxford. Nineteen seventy-two. *Abreaction, Memory and Delusion.*

Abreaction? What does that mean? North Googled an online dictionary and searched for an entry. The result was a disconcerting puzzle.

He consulted Porter's résumé again for his last employer. There was no contact information for the Division of Personality Studies, but the University of Virginia would be in the phone book. He doodled on a Post-it while he waited for the journey through the maze of the university switchboard to complete. He got right to the point.

Yes, came the reply, William Porter had been a faculty member. No he was no longer eligible for funding.

Why was that?

He'd stopped publishing. He had years' worth of research but was doing nothing with it. Researchers in the field who withheld their research could not be funded by the University.

North took note. So Porter was a man with secrets. Did he set up practice somewhere else, like say, New York City?

No, came the swift response, as far as the department knew he was still conducting research in the Middle East.

Middle East? 'Out of curiosity, what kind of research is it the Division of Personality Studies specializes in?'

The voice on the other end of the line seemed taken aback by the question. 'We're the foremost national scientific centre conducting research into the validity of past lives.'

'Like people who think they were Marie Antoinette? And there's scientific evidence for this?'

'Not necessarily Marie Antoinette, but you'd be surprised.'

Have the nightmares started yet?

12.36 p.m.

North wanted privacy. Uncertain of whether this man's information would be personal or case related, he opted for seclusion rather than the glare of the squad room. Under the dim light of the small interview room, the smallest that the station house possessed, North began his questioning. 'You're a psychiatrist?'

Porter rested his hands on the wooden desk. 'Yes.'

Do you know what's happening to me? 'You were a medical doctor previously?'

'I was a doctor for six years before things changed.'

'What things changed?'

A thin film of anxiety misted over the old man's face, emphasizing the hallmarks of his age. In the grip of his demons, he hadn't expected the question and clung to the moment of hesitation. 'My wife died.'

The old man offered the detective a wistful smile as though he appreciated the silence and North recognized in him a guilt that fed self-loathing. The stark shadow of something quietly hidden from public view. It was primal. It was like looking in a mirror.

'I know this must seem unusual.'

North attempted to be noncommittal. 'People read the papers. They get an idea. I can't stop them.'

'You don't have to humour an old man, detective.'

'I don't have the time to humour anyone. I don't have the inclination.'

'It's not my intention to waste your time. I came here to help.'

Now this was the crux of it. 'Help who?'

'You, of course.'

North was matter of fact. 'Because of the nightmares?'

'Yes.'

'I'm not having any nightmares.'

'I don't believe you.'

Porter's conviction was solid though he gave little else away, except a flicker of curiosity when North laid his black notebook on the desk. *He wants my case notes? He's pulling something.*

North let his pen dangle provocatively over the closed book and reached for a prepared sheet of psychological notes. 'I understand you think Gene *abreacted*, is that correct?'

'Yes.' There was an excited edge to Porter's voice. 'You're fully aware of what an abreaction *is*, I assume?'

North bluffed it, hoping it didn't sound too much like he'd simply memorized the dictionary definition. 'Sure; the spontaneous release of repressed emotions, often apparent with dissociative disorders, multiple personality, that kind of thing.'

'There are fewer than thirty genuine cases of multiple personality disorder in the United States. Have you given much thought to what we're dealing with here?'

'There is no *we*, Doctor Porter.'

'You suspect my motives.'

'I suspect everybody's motives.'

'That's quite a pessimistic world to inhabit.'

He's hiding something. 'It's a realistic world. Let me let *you* in on a little secret. There are two types of people in my line of work. Those who get caught, and those waiting to *be* caught. Which are you?'

Porter was clearly uncomfortable with the question. Whatever he had expected to happen when he came to the station house, this wasn't it. He offered a faintly nervous smile. 'The royal *we* then.'

North said nothing. It was up to Porter to swim against the tide.

'An abreaction progresses. At first it occurs solely in the imagination; a daydream, or a nightmare.'

North's face remained flat; Porter didn't solicit a response.

'In time an abreaction begins to manifest itself; a sufferer will take to copious writing or painting, until at its *most* heightened it causes the sufferer to act out.'

'Act out? Like psychotic behaviour?'

'It mimics a psychosis – the sufferer is not aware that what they are experiencing is not real. The illusions are extremely vivid. But the state is not psychosis. The sufferer will talk to people who aren't there, his voice will assume the tone and vocabulary of the time of the memory being experienced, yet these people exist solely within memory. From his perspective he will believe that *that moment is actually being relived.*'

'What does memory have to do with it?'

'An abreaction is the net result of reawakening long

forgotten memories, and the intense emotions associated with them. It has a profound effect causing disorientation and confusion.'

North shifted uncomfortably in his chair.

'This is familiar to you.' It wasn't a question. Porter's comment was sharp and precise.

'It's interesting.'

'It's what Gene was doing.'

North had spoken to mental health officials before – this was New York City. 'He could be delusional; a symptom of his schizophrenia.'

Porter was dismissive. 'To the untrained eye it might appear that way.'

'Why would it appear any other way?'

'Why would a man suffering from delusions be administered medication that actively seeks to augment the effects of his condition?'

He knows what was in the syringe? A bluff? 'Go on.'

'Delusions are random. They're a fantasy. Abreactions are much more practical. People suddenly acquire skills they didn't know they had, speak in languages they didn't know they knew. These are the marks of memory, not fancy.

'Did you ever stop to ask yourself why Gene was so obsessed with the skull in the museum? Is it possible he knew the man?'

North hesitated at the mention of the skull.

That's absurd. 'That thing was thousands of years old.'

'Or why did he ride that horse through the city without using the stirrups? He was perfectly comfortable in the saddle. His actions were consistent with a genuine knowledge of horsemanship.'

'So he's a trick rider. Maybe he grew up in a circus.'

'Is that really likely?'

'More likely than him remembering a past life.'

North's words clung to the air, dividing them. Yet Porter,

caught off guard, his truth laid bare, did not stop. 'Then why are you experiencing exactly the same thing?'

It was North's turn to feel the silent, creeping agitation of guilt; the rush of blood ringing in his ears, powerful enough to blot out rational thought.

Porter had to be guessing. Maybe he was sent here by Gene to determine the state of the case. There was no point in honesty. He didn't know this man. *I have to be careful.* 'I don't know what you're talking about.'

Porter was unruffled. He clearly sensed North's unease and it bolstered his confidence. He reached into his briefcase and pulled out a newspaper and a green notebook. The newspaper was folded to show a picture of North and Gene that had been taken on the street outside the Jiggle Joint. He laid it out flat on the desk. 'You were exposed to the same medication that he was. There's a hypodermic needle hanging from your leg.'

North looked at the newspaper. That information hadn't been made public. North refused to comment.

Porter leaned forward. 'I know what's happening to you. I know because I've been through it. *Gene* is *going* through it. You don't have to be ashamed. A witness in the *New York Post* said he heard the detective cry out that he thought a bull was chasing him. *You* thought a bull was chasing you.'

North felt the tightening grip of fear. 'He was mistaken.'

Porter cracked open his notebook. A few pages in and he laid it out, presenting the images he had scrawled many decades ago.

The Bull. North reeled from it.

'Is this the image familiar to you?'

It was eating him from within. The Bull. The pen strokes could almost have been his own.

'I was seven years old when the Bull came to me.'

Porter planted the book in North's hands and slowly guided him through its yellowed leaves filled with images and crammed writings, layer upon layer in different inks. *Different languages.*

Porter could sense the recognition on his face. He looked across the desk to North's own notebook. 'Have you always written in a black notebook?'

North would not respond. The Bull consumed him and would not let him go.

The Bull.

Close the door on this man. Close it now.

North slammed the green notebook shut and tossed it back at the old man. 'I don't want this.' His fingers danced with his pen; flipping it over and over in an endless nervous rattle both irritating and soothing.

'No. No I don't suppose you do.' Porter reached into his pocket and fumbled for a pen. He wrote the number of the Pennsylvania down on the back of his business card, laid it flat on the desk and slid it closer to North.

'Imagine what you're going through, through the eyes of a 7-year-old boy; the strange contortion of reality, the peculiar mishmash that both sickens and reveals; the nightmare of remembering having sex *with your own mother*. That nauseating, guilt-infested sense of pure elation you feel because the emotion of that memory tells you that *you enjoyed it.*'

'Shut up—'

'You don't have to feel guilty. Those aren't *your* memories. They belong to *your father.*'

North lurched forward with such explosive rage Porter sat back in his chair. 'Fuck you!'

The silence was a chasm between them. Porter did not move, he was waiting for North.

'I don't have my father's memories. I *can't* have them.'

'Why not?'

Where do I start? 'Because he's *not dead.*'

'You don't understand.'

'I understand enough.' It was obvious to both men that this wasn't going to go any further.

Porter was clinical in his appraisal. 'We've talked enough for today.'

'Just get out.'

Porter stood and tapped the card. 'If you want to talk some more, here's where you can reach me.'

North said nothing.

'Good day to you.'

North watched him walk out, if only to settle his own mind about his definite departure. He sat alone in the interview room and was haunted.

This is crazy. I'm crazy. Have you always written in a black notebook? *What does that have to do with anything?*

It sat in front of him, a taunting reminder. It was just his notebook. *What's there to be afraid of?* But North knew deep down what he'd find, what he was trying to deny. *Make a decision.* He flipped the notebook open with defiance, more bluster than genuine desire. At first he found the comfort of simple case notes, page after page of conversations. Details. Place. Time. But he knew there was more.

His own madness awaited him; a bitter rage imbued with spite that had leaked from himself and soaked into the paper.

THE PYRES FROM ACRE

We rode with the blood of the Saracens up to our horses' knees, thus was the wake of our victory at Acre; the tenth day of August, the year of our Lord, 1191.

From there we ravaged the land. The stench from the raging pyres sought out its prey in an oily smoke that filled the nostrils of every man; the encampments were littered with Saracen carcasses, dripping fat on their spits. I listened to the crackle of the fires, and drank down the smell of cooking human flesh. It stank of swine.

Christians had lived among them, but we glorious crusading knights had not stopped in our slaughter. This was the seventh such village since the time of our arrival. When first we had arrived we had wondered how to sort worthy from savage.

'Kill them all,' I said in the end. 'The Lord will know his own.'

We feasted that first night, like beasts manifest from the depths of hell; under the cloak of darkness that blanketed this rocky land, we huddled together, scorched by the pyres, and when I was sated they brought him to me.

The spy said: 'This is what I have heard. Barbarossa sent an envoy to Damascus prior to our arrival.'

King Frederick of Germany, Emperor of the Holy Roman

Empire, lay dead; drowned to the north leading some one
hundred and fifty thousand of his men across traitorous
waters. They fought magnificently, yet leaderless were
ultimately humbled. All but the smallest of bands turned and
went home, never to set foot in the land of ancient Phoenicia;
destined never to fight the third great Crusade.

Even so, in death Barbarossa had been no fool and his
preparation had already proved useful to the impetuous
Lionheart, King Richard. He knew Syria had many faces.

'What did this envoy find?'

'He said that between Damascus, Antioch and Aleppo there
lives a certain race of Saracens high in the mountains. This
breed of men lives without law. They eat swine's flesh against
the law of the Saracens. They make use of all women without
distinction.'

'*All* women?'

The young man nodded. 'Mothers and sisters alike.'

'They are abhorrent.'

'Yes, to Christian and Saracen alike. It is said they have
deviated from the book.'

'They have a name, this breed of Saracen?'

The young man was cautious, as if to speak that dreadful
name would bring ill fortune. He looked around the tent,
making sure he was not being overheard, and drew closer.
'They have many names.'

The young man held his breath. He knew by the gleam in
my eye that I would not ask again without bestowing upon
him my gift of retribution.

'I have heard tell that in their own language they call
themselves the Heyssessini, still others say the Ashishin, until
I chanced upon a scholar. I let him live so we may question
him. He is over there, he can tell you yet more than I.

'He said that in their tongue they are known as the
Hashishi, for their leader's love of a form of dried herbage I
know not what. But the Christians hereabouts find their

tongue a hard one to master and have taken to calling them the Assassins.'

The Assassins.

'They thirst for blood, kill the innocent for a price. They care nothing either for life or for salvation. They are like the devil, imitating the ordinary folk hereabouts, in gesture, in deed, in garment, in language. They hide away; a wolf among sheep, until it is time to strike. This very village was filled with them just as you supposed.

'Their profession is perverse. They are an abomination. What kind of man would willingly conceal his identity in so cowardly a manner? These are who you seek?'

'Undoubtedly. By what name is their leader known?'

'He is a mystery, that one. Some know him as the Old Man of the Mountain. He is as old as time. Others yet say that he is called Sinan—'

'*Sinan*? He ridicules me.'

'That name has meaning to you?'

'In the distant past. Today it matters not. Sinan is not his real name. He has many names, though he keeps his true identity hidden from age to age, but I know it. He is Athanatos, the great deceiver from the east.

'I have hunted him since time's thread first spun me out and it will be my pleasure to murder him in his bed. The killing of this devil will be the beginning of bliss. Under the heel of perdition, I will crush him. With the fuel of his carcass, Hell shall roast his followers.'

There was fear in the spy's eyes, and I enjoyed it. He stumbled over his words. 'Their fortress is impregnable. I do not know how we shall infiltrate them, let alone bring them to their knees.'

'We will march, and raze to the ground every Assassin encampment that we encounter until we tempt this snake from his lair.'

For five hundred miles we rode with the blood of the

Saracens up to our horses' knees. And with every roasting pyre of Assassin flesh we let just enough voices flee terrified into the night telling tales of the depth of my fury. Once more I had an army, but as I ravaged his lands, still Athanatos would not come to meet me.

We slaughtered and we planned as we marched further towards the mountains, until on the night of the seventh pyre I chanced upon a trader making his way to Byblos.

As I waited, contemplating that fetid mountain of burning flesh, they brought the Saracen before me; a small man who shook with fear. I asked for solitude with him and I was given it.

'What is your name, trader?'

The small man hesitated. 'I am called Samir.'

I looked to his cart. It was piled high, much of it blackened with soot. He had been looting.

'You trade with these Assassins. You are one of them?'

'I trade, but I am not one of them, oh great knight! They believe they have a common interest with me, is all.'

I probed further, dissatisfied with his explanation.

Samir the trader was reluctant to reply, shame was wrought upon his face and he was pallid. 'I am Druze.'

I was aghast. These vermin were as bad as the Assassins. Every Frank knew the Druze, they worshipped one man as though he were a god: al-Hakim, sixth caliph of Cairo.

Just as Nero had murdered Seneca, so al-Hakim butchered his teacher, the eunuch Barjawan. This instrument of evil would frequent the streets of Cairo accompanied by his bear-like African slave, Masoud, who would publicly sodomize any shopkeeper caught cheating his customers.

Though I had no proof and could not be certain, even this tale reminded me of my first encounter with Athanatos. It was all too familiar.

Though al-Hakim's mother was Christian, he was not and persecuted Christians with relish. How these fools had come to worship such a man was truly a mystery. Perhaps they did it to taunt us.

It was al-Hakim who marched on Jerusalem in the year of our Lord 1009, and razed the Church of the Holy Sepulchre to the ground. It was al-Hakim who invited the first great Crusade.

If al-Hakim had been yet another one of Athanatos' former lives, what great justice that he had provided me with the perfect excuse to raise my army.

Samir the trader cowered from the seething hatred in my eyes. He was ignorant of my true intent and the target for my heated venoms. I asked him, 'Why would Sinan feel any kind of kinship with the likes of you?'

He could not look me in the eye. He gazed instead upon the earth. Perhaps he knew that it would soon become his bed. 'It may be because of our belief, oh great knight, that with every generation we are reborn; it is my understanding that these Assassins follow the same path.'

I felt those words like poison eating its way through the lining of my stomach. 'You will take me to this Sinan.'

'That would be suicide, oh great knight. They have killed princes and generals alike. The price on *one* Assassin's head is equal to the slaughter of *seventy* Greeks, and you would have me take you to their heart? I cannot. Besides, I do not know the way.'

I took him in my fist and promised him marks upon his hide. 'You lie as easily as you breathe.'

'No! I swear I do not know the way. They have ten strongholds. I can only guess at which one he commands. But – they are men, and men have urges that must be met. I know where these *fida'i* can be found when they stray from their fortresses.'

It was clear from my expression that that word was unfamiliar to me. The trader obliged.

'The *fida'i* are the foot soldiers of the Assassin order. The

name means "devotee of the actual murderer".' Only now
was his true emotion vivid enough to see. 'Perhaps there, you
may find a way to join them. They may lead you to the source
that you seek.'

'Take me and you will be rewarded.'

'A reward? I do not think you have enough dinars to cover
such a risk. Though I thank you and I mean no disrespect, oh
great knight, but how will you join these Assassins? What can
you offer them which they cannot already offer themselves? If
you are going to kill them, then I am dead already and your
reward is but hollow words.'

'If allowing you to live is a hollow reward then come, run
on to my sword here and now. I offer these Assassins a way
to purge this land of their mortal enemy.'

Samir trembled like the twitching of a thicket alive with
grouse. The offer was too tempting, even to be beaten by fear.

I was amused. This trader was a fool. The ruse was
swallowed as surely as honey. Still within his earshot I gave
instruction for my fellow Hospitallers to meet with King
Richard, for the task ahead was for me alone.

I had sown fear and doubt into Athanatos' mind – ten
thousand of his men lay dead at my hand – but if I was to
draw close enough to slit his throat my visit could not be
heralded by the march of heavy feet across the plain. It would
have to remain a delicious surprise.

DANCE OF THE HOURI

We journeyed for six days and six nights, under the glare of a withering sun, and under the canopy of twilight's stars, forever wary of bandits along our path. Syria was a broken landscape of mountains and valleys where the deserts sheltered the forts and citadels of Seljuk armies, yet they themselves were surrounded on all sides by Turcoman bands roaming free, preying on the fractured people of this barren land.

Samir's treasure was considerable and tempting. He had done well from my work. Eight satin cloaks, a few hoods, some furs and two capes, one lined with satin and the other with Chinese crepe, sat in a great cedar box under twenty-six robes of honour. He had acquired two belts of a hundred dinars' weight, ninety-three pieces of cloth and three caparisoned horses with saddle and harness. He had seven thousand dinars in gold and had taken possession of a string of Bactrian camels which formed the backbone of our caravan.

At first he said nothing. We would make camp, he would catch desert hare, I would skin it quickly and cleanly for I did not trust him long with a blade, and he would cook it, his face pale and afraid. Which night, he wondered, would I choose to skin *him*?

By the second evening his tongue had loosened a little and I was able to learn a little more about the nature of these Assassins.

'They are taught Latin, Greek and Saracen. From childhood they are educated as though they were princes, but trained to obey the Old Man's commands as though he were a god with power over gods. Some of them are even the children of his enemies. When they have reached the age of manhood they are given a golden dagger, and with it they must perform their first murder and kill whomever the Old Man has marked down. It is not unknown for an Assassin to find that he must kill one who brought him into this world without ever considering either the consequences of his deed or the possibility of his escape. Only his zeal, his toil and his labours will bring him to paradise, and he will wait a lifetime, if that is what it takes, to perform his actions.

'The daggers of the Assassins have struck down many a Saracen prince, for Sinan entices with promises of such pleasures and such eternal enjoyment that the *fida'i* prefer to die rather than live.'

I found nothing surprising in these tales, which seemed to disturb the trader further. Indeed it struck me that perhaps Athanatos had learned a little something over the ages. It mattered not. I reaffirmed my vow to kill him and destroy all that was his.

On the third night the trader sobbed like a child, and with his cheeks awash with terrified tears that ran streaks through the dust upon his face, at last he braved his question. 'Why are you so filled with hate?'

It had been so long, I had grown weary and I almost did not know. But then the flashes would return, moments of time caught in the raindrops of a storm, illuminated by that heavenly spark that fuelled my demon spirit within.

I knew.

On the sixth day, at noon, as he drew the bumping cart over

rough, stony ground, he said, 'We are in their *jazeera* now, their island, their domain. You must make yourself ready if you are to disguise that you are a Frank.'

With the last of the precious water he bid me strip naked and handed me a brush so that I might scrub my parts. I was not so foolish as to forgo keeping a blade in my other hand, but as he drenched me in cold water, I complained bitterly. 'What is this?! What are you doing to me?'

'Were that you a dog, oh great knight, I would be ashamed to let you wander in the presence of my neighbours. In this land, we bathe.'

'It is a despicable act! Treachery!'

'Be still!' He raised my arm and rubbed the surface of a strange pale fatty block across my hide. It possessed the faint smell of rose petals and left its trace upon my skin.

'Trickery and witchcraft!'

'Soap.'

I tasted it. It was foul and I spat it out with haste.

'It is the very latest invention of our great thinkers and aids in the removal of dirt from the body.'

Such ridiculous notions. 'I do not think such a thing will catch on,' I chided.

'With animals,' he replied, 'perhaps not.'

I rounded on him so swiftly that his eyes became quite frozen. I pressed my blade to his throat and he whimpered. Did he think to ingratiate himself with me because he had offered his help? He knew me not at all. He said no more after that.

With the long hours of the afternoon behind us we arrived wrapped in twilight at a town on the banks of a stream, awash with the cacophony of shrill street traders. While Samir set about selling off his camels, three to another trader and the one with the lame foot for meat, I took it upon myself to distinguish Assassin from Saracen.

It was no easy task. As my efforts remained fruitless I

became aware of faint music through the din, the beating of a drum, the faint buzzing whispers of reed instruments like insects in rapture; I heard laughter, young, vivacious, joyful laughter.

I carved my way through the bustle and stole a seat on the edge of a square where an audience had gathered. If these Assassins had needs I had found one myself that I had not expected to discover in such a wretched place as this.

Her dress shimmered as it twirled above her ankles, a diaphanous blue that revealed her hidden passions as she danced before the trembling of the oil lamps. Her face was downcast as she moved rhythmically to the music, her familiar long, thick, raven-black hair flowed out from under a gossamer headscarf, alive and free. Her full hips swayed to a rocking motion that enchanted and intoxicated, and when she opened her eyes, such clear bright penetrating eyes, I was captured.

Did she see me? Was I the one that made that smile dance upon her lips?

I had not considered this. I had not expected *this*. I had banished such beauty from my thoughts and from my heart. There was nothing left within but bitter enmity. Yet I felt the stirrings of something I had forgotten. I thought it had been ripped from me. How could she touch what was not there?

'The delights of a simple harlot are enough to inflame any man, are they not?' Samir took up his perch next to me. I was startled. I had not heard him approach, though I could smell the pall of sweet drink all around him. He had been spending his new-found wealth with foolish relish. His loose lips might prove valuable now that my journey faced a crossroads.

'What is her name?'

'Who can say? I am sure for a few dinars she would take whatever name you asked her to.'

I rounded on him. 'I will hear no more of your foulness.'

'Please, be reasonable. She is hardly a houri.' My scowl

once again belied my ignorance. 'One of the virgins of perfect beauty who lives in blessed paradise.'

A few of the other men overheard our exchange. Their laughter was explosive. 'He thinks she is a houri!'

I could not do what my instinct would bid me and lash out, not here and not now. Instead I sat quietly, but my words had not gone unnoticed. She had heard them, and they seemed to affect her deeply. She danced this time with an inspired dignity which I knew was meant only for me, the man who had mistaken her for an angel.

'You knew this *physician-astrologer*, this man named Sinan?' Samir shuffled forward bearing dates and more drink.

'Knew him when?'

'Before today; before any day that you have lived in *this* life.'

Was it so apparent that I had lived more than one? 'I am not Druze,' I said.

He watched me carefully. 'But you knew him?'

'Yes, I knew him.'

'And would you know him again, if you saw him now?'

I did not reply. I feasted on the sweet fleshy fruit and I listened.

'He has lived many lives, has he not? He has, therefore, been born many times and had many faces. How would you know him, this man that you seek? How can you be certain that he is who you think, and not here among the crowd? How can you be certain that *I* am not *him*?'

I felt the cold eyes of the crowd and I pulled my cloak around me. In my own arrogance, had I marched too quickly to my death before the deed was truly done?

The music seemed discordant now. There was nothing heavenly here. After many a dance and when the moon shone brightly she drew near, but having watched her work her charms from man to man, the spark in my heart had quietly died as quickly as it had been born. By the time she had come to sit and talk a while and discover the man of such compliments, the wonder upon my face had faded, replaced with harsh realities. Disappointment at my inactions weighed heavily upon her. I had offered her hope and had cruelly withdrawn it. And I did not care.

She was only a mirage, a distant echo. I could see that now. She was as ephemeral as the clothes that she wore. She was an idea, an embodiment of a distant memory that served to remind me only why I was here and why I must continue, but she was not *she*.

She took my hand in hers, and hoped to find some warmth, but I had long since turned my attention towards the jagged mountains a few miles hence. 'What must I look for amid those rocks?'

'A paradise,' Samir answered, 'where there should be none. It is said the Old Man created a hanging garden to remind him of his youth. It is held within the palace of his fortress, so impregnable, with high walls and small points of entry that only cunning or invitation can gain access to it. Look around, do these men strike you as fools?'

'Not at all.'

'Then do not expect an invitation.'

My faded houri, filled with concern, took my hand and pressed it to her breast. She knew what we were discussing. 'There is paradise here, if you so desire.'

I felt the softness of her skin under my rough hand and was confounded to discover that I was again filled with longing, and for the first time in this life, I was uncertain.

Had the flame really died, or had I been suppressing it?

Samir staggered dismissively to his feet. 'Paradise! *Paradise with his houri*! Do you not have needs like any other man?'

In the hushed velvet of the cool night air I was led by the hand through the quiet backstreets of the town by the stream, to where the scent of jasmine was strong. I welcomed our retreat into shadow and slipped quietly behind her into the confines of her small house.

She led me to her bed and sat me down among the silk cushions. She took my hands and ran them inside her dress until I embraced her full round hips. She expected me to pull her close, but I was frozen, racked with guilt for what should not be.

She leaned closer, her thick sweetly scented hair cocooning me from a troublesome world, and as she pressed my face to her warm flesh such tenderness moved me to tears.

Why now? I was not worthy of this, not even from a harlot. That I should know something of love again, even a whisper of it, after the things I had done in the name of retribution.

Her fingers ran gently across my shoulders, her soft kisses eased my torture, and when it was too much, when the fire that scorched my heart could stand it no longer, I grabbed her thighs with surging lust, saw that she was wet and thrust into her.

We collapsed into the pillows, her cries sweet music for my rage. She was not *she*, but for this moment, she was my pain come to life.

I crept back inside Samir's dishevelled tent, listening to the heavy guttural snoring of his drunken slumber as I prepared for bed. I lay on my side, my eyelids heavy, and tried to shut out his squall, with thoughts of strangulation still running vividly through the veins of my shaking hands. When the drum of my blood faded, I heard the distant barking of a hunting dog chained up inside the town.

Its disturbance could be for no other reason than for the prowling of men. I moved quickly.

Outside I saw in the distance the retreat of a lone rider

heading deep into the foothills, galloping a path that could lead only to the mountains.

A Saracen? An Assassin? But no slow packhorse for him, instead a stout Arabian, no less than fifteen hands high and with a depth of chest that boasted of its power.

Here was my chance to follow him. I made haste, gathering my blades, two wineskins and a gourd of water. I kicked Samir, but he did not cease snoring.

'We must leave at once!' I kicked him again and when he would not move stooped down to make him. 'Trader, awaken!'

His reply was a curiosity. His head rolled off the pillow and into the dust at my feet, while his snoring continued unfettered.

'Even if you start now, you will never catch him.'

The snoring had stopped while the voice from the darkness lay somewhere behind me.

'My brother will be most pleased with his gift,' he said, tossing a basket next to me. 'Your head.'

'Brother? Athanatos has no brothers, only dogs.'

From the shadows the Assassin stepped into the pale moonlight so that I might see his eyes. 'We are an army, and you are but a fool.'

No amusing allusions was he peddling here. I could see clearly his close connection to family. I bowed. 'My apologies. You are worse than a dog.'

The Assassin lunged, his dagger a chink of gold in a black pot of treachery. I sidestepped quickly and pulled him forward, sending him off balance and tumbling to the ground, but he was no novice. He flipped back on to his feet and swiped with such precision that blood spilled from my cheek.

As fat droplets of scarlet splattered into the dust, I sunk my fists into his gut and brought my elbow against his jaw. One shattered tooth tumbled from his mouth, yet still he persisted.

His kicks were swift, his skill impressive. My knees buckled, I sank to the floor and again his dagger flashed before me.

'Do you have any message for my brother before I return you to the ground?'

'Yes,' I said in quiet reflection. 'I trust he appreciates the effort I went to, to bring him his gift.'

The Assassin grabbed my hair and lifted up my head to expose my throat, and in so doing, exposed his own.

I did not miss. I ploughed my blade deep into his neck and did not stop even when it met hard bone. I roared with rage and rose to my feet and still I ploughed it further. Through gritted teeth I spat my insults and drove him to the ground, and with tears of unfurled anger I ripped his head from his body and spat in his still warm face.

RAMPARTS OF THE ASSASSINS

I rode through the night following the fresh tracks until at last the heavy climb into true mountain terrain became passable only by following a steep, narrow, winding ledge which took me at first through a narrow gorge. A river lay somewhere below. I could hear it though I could not see it.

Before me, overhanging cliffs of rock obstructed my path; on more than one occasion I was forced to duck else I would have smashed into them and tumbled into oblivion.

Upwards we travelled, perhaps more than a mile above the great plain of the barren land behind me, until at last, by dawn's first caress, I came upon the dominating castle high upon seemingly inviolate rock. I could smell citrus and other fruits and knew that the tales of the garden were true.

With the wind billowing through my stolen robes I galloped for the main gates holding aloft my would-be killer's golden dagger. I heard a great whistle go up in recognition of the sign and saw many faces rush to see me advance.

In answer I tucked the dagger into my bloody sash and held up the basket for all to see. In their language I cried, 'He is dead! He is dead!' And for my show I was met with an eruption among them, a tumultuous cheer which echoed out across the valley as the heavy gates were thrown open to greet my ride to victory.

Within those mighty walls I discovered the largest and most beautiful garden that I had ever seen, lined with trees and filled with every variety of fruit. And in the distance the most elegant gilded palace. It was not hard to imagine that wine and milk, honey and water flowed freely here. If Athanatos desired to make people believe this really was a paradise, then he had almost made a believer of me.

Yet despite the marvel of this Elysian field, I could not shake the certain knowledge that evil and corruption stood at its heart.

Along the lawn in front of the ramparts I rode up and down, holding the basket aloft and yelling in triumph. Assassin after Assassin came to greet me, unaware that hidden beneath the headscarf of their brother was the face of their sworn enemy.

In time, Athanatos himself was tempted from his palace and, in so doing, the cold truth of Samir's words struck me. I knew Athanatos only because others had called him Sinan. I did not know his face. In truth, I recognized him not. Any one of them could be he.

The Old Man who marched towards me was flanked by viziers in elaborate robes. His face was a mask. Did he know me? If not then he would know me now. I reared my steed up on its hind legs upon his arrival and slung the basket at his feet.

It bounced across the ground, its lid flying off, whereupon the head of Athanatos' brother was flung out.

There were gasps, but from Athanatos and his closest advisers there was only a sigh and sense of genuine sadness. 'Oh, Cyclades, my friend, why do you do this?'

'Assassins? Would that you invented murder.' I drew my sword. I was met by many blades, but Athanatos stayed their hands.

'Murder? Our killings are done with purpose, and for that some lend it our name.'

'I shall put an end to the fetid juices of your inbreeding. You shall become but a tale on men's lips, a rumour sewn with the thread of doubt.'

'Why do you persist? Did my gift not touch your heart? Did her beauty not bring a simple moment of happiness back into your life? Did I not do as a father would do and share with you my all? I would have paid you a visit myself, but only women can get so close to distant men.'

I thought of my houri and I was suddenly disgusted. He lied. As easily as he breathed, he lied. She was not his gift.

'I have walked this earth now for over two thousand years. Gods have been born, gods have died and gods have been forgotten while I endure. Do you think that if you slay me now my life will be at an end? There are so many more like me; those who carry my face, and my will.'

His advisers stepped forward and one by one they each exposed their faces, the many faces of Athanatos.

'I am not a magus. I am a *magi*. I am the very *plural of a magician*. Cut off *one* head and I will grow *seven* more. All this death is meaningless to me.'

I surged forward and took his closest adviser by the neck. He dangled, his legs kicking as he choked. 'I will kill him.'

'So kill him. I have many more.'

'Do not taunt me!'

'I do not taunt you, Cyclades, I want only that you understand. Would you prefer that *I* kill him? Perhaps kill *more*? You three, my kindred, sons and heirs, leap to your deaths. Demonstrate for him here and now. Shatter your skulls and die miserable deaths if that will bring happiness to my friend.'

I watched in horror as three of his finest *fida'i* did as he asked without question and without hesitation. They strode to the ramparts; they stared down at the abyss below and, stopping only to ensure that they had my attention, without a sound, they jumped.

'You are the devil!'

'The most blessed, so he affirms, are those who shed the blood of men and in revenge for such deeds themselves suffer death.'

'So be it.' I twisted the neck of the man in my arms and he fell to the ground, his thread cut.

The certainty in my action caused some alarm as Athanatos slowly pieced together what his spies had told him of my movements. 'You are not here alone.'

'I am not.'

Across the mountains, my army of Hospitallers was advancing; having followed at a distance. I had served as perfect bait and decoy. They would be upon this stronghold within hours.

I aimed my sword at Athanatos, I charged and I ran him through, but as he promised, there was another to take his place.

I fell from the horse and his Assassins were upon me. I cut a swathe but I was a mere mortal. It would be a glorious battle. My only wish is that I could have seen it.

5.40 p.m.

Such rage. Such *hatred*. From what depths *did* it spring? The incandescent prose scrawled in the notebook felt as raw as the emotions inside him. But how was it that *he* could have written this, yet barely have a memory of doing so? What else did he do in his disconnected moments since Gene had pricked him with this gift? North tried to rationalize it, classify what he'd read as some kind of macabre witness statement, yet each line, even when written in Old French, elicited within him some murmur of a hidden passion he was only just beginning to recognize in himself.

He recoiled from his pale and shaken features in the bathroom mirror, afraid of what he saw within. The skin around his eyes was bruised and sunken as though the darkness was trying to seep out. Here he saw himself as a young man, yet his shell was filled with the spirit of something ancient.

He retched. What little he'd had for breakfast was an acidic purée in the sink. He washed it away and splashed his face with cold water. He dried himself off with a rough paper towel.

His father's memories? Perhaps, if his father was hundreds of years old. These must be delusions, fantasies, not memories. He clung to that notion because the alternative was despair.

Did I do those things? Memories from a former life?

It felt so real; as though *he had*, and in so doing, he was everything that he despised.

Was it the killing that repulsed him the most? Seven years in law enforcement hadn't sheltered him from that. Or was it the fact that in this life, too, he'd slept with a whore just to make himself feel better?

Was this the irony of his life? If what he'd written was true then despite the inevitable march of time some things never changed. He didn't need a past life to know that relationships didn't work. Not for him. He wouldn't allow it. Thirty bucks for a little tenderness without the complications. It was the smart thing to do, wasn't it?

Then why did it still make him feel sick? Why was he racked with so much guilt? Were there such things as fate and destiny? He'd drawn the grim conclusion long ago that whomever he was meant to be with, she didn't exist. Yet still he felt he'd betrayed her, that nameless faceless someone.

Had he really been making the same choices over, and over, *and over*, like a machine incapable of learning?

He saw a deep fundamental truth about himself in his terrified eyes and he didn't like it.

Had the nightmares started? They wouldn't stop. They were the ichor of a beating heart that was unreachable and unrepentant.

ATHENAEUM

It took only four security guards to escort him through the building. He took that as a sign they were beginning to trust him.

Gene watched the two in front; the shape of their necks seemed somehow familiar. Their ears cocked at every rustle from his clothing. They expected him to do something, anything but watch them.

Who am we today? It was so difficult to tell. Who are *they* today?

He watched their blemishes, floating on a sea of warping skin, parted only by the forests of their hairlines. Demeanour, build, gait; it was difficult to tell them apart.

'You all look alike.'

Gene could hear the faint scoffing sound of amusement behind him.

'Are you brothers?'

The reply of their collective footsteps gave nothing away. He should know the answer to that question. He'd asked it before, hadn't he? One of him had.

They ushered him into the elevator, surrounded him on all sides and keyed the third floor. Access to that floor required a numerical code to be entered on the keypad.

Is that what the numbers are telling us? He could feel his discovery, that slip of paper, scratching at him from its hiding place deep inside his sock. He memorized the security guard's hand movements and worked out the number while the elevator descended the shaft. His fingers twitched at his side as he reconstructed the sequence in his mind. It didn't match.

When the doors opened again a large expanse of plush carpet stretched out before him. This place seemed serene somehow, wrapped in a deadened calm. He didn't trust it.

They escorted him to a set of heavy doors. He had asked to be taken to the library, they explained. They would wait for him at the threshold. *When* had he asked for this? Every Wednesday afternoon, they explained, for the past seven months. It was part of his routine. What else did he know that he wasn't telling himself?

A building that held apartments, research laboratories and now a library; what kind of labyrinth was this place?

Inside he found the vast repository; all hand-carved oak and gleaming brass, filled to excess with row upon row of hefty tomes; this was the way that mortals were supposed to remember their past. This was *their* immortality.

As he stepped deeper into its confines he noticed the cameras immediately. They were leaving nothing to chance. He did not stare; instead he went right for the heart without hesitation and found the long reading table at the centre of the room.

Stretched out upon its surface were rolls of vellum, parchment and paper. They looked like slices of the marbled flesh of carcasses, each sheet covered in thousands upon thousands of deep red, intricately thin and delicately drawn lines, like veins that traced the routes of blood. Thousands of names and dates blossomed across their surfaces, fields of baleful poppies that betrayed the slow march towards death; they were the roots of a sanguine tree.

He sat at the table and slid one of the family charts across to study it. If this was his routine he had been studying his lineage for a reason, though that reason, elusive as it may be, was not entirely out of his reach. He could feel it lurking in the darkness somewhere, like an itch.

He traced his finger across one of the branches and found his name at the top. Fathered by Lawless, whom, it appeared, was father to many. Yet the curiosity went deeper. There weren't just many branches to this tree, but many offshoots which led to further brothers, sisters and cousins, who had not been mentioned by name. Were the missing a secret being kept from him? Or a secret to all of them?

'Every one of the Chinese Hani people can recite their ancestry back through *fifty-eight* generations; that's a thousand years.'

The man entering from the far end wore delicately framed glasses and carried a ledger. Had he met this man before? *Think. Yes.* Savage.

'The royal families of Europe can trace their lineages back even further; but when we're done *you* will beat them all.'

How?

Savage stood at the end of the table and surveyed the ancestral trees with what appeared to be simple pride. He smiled. 'What do you think of your ancestors?'

'There are too many.'

Savage took a seat. 'How many should there be?'

He's about six feet away. We could break his neck—

He's strong—

He'd call for the guards—

Not if we're fast enough. He might have a key—

Gene looked away and buried the impulse. *He's not the one.* He concentrated instead on the feathered red lines. *How many ancestors should there be?* 'I don't know.'

'There are many more than in an ordinary family.'

That made little impact; he had no idea how many ancestors there should be in an ordinary family either.

'With so many ancestors did it occur to you that you have even more *living* relatives?'

Gene said nothing. Savage had been watching. If he wanted to truly probe his thoughts he would have to try harder than simply watching him via surveillance cameras.

Savage could sense his tension. 'Let me give you an example. A hundred and thirty-one years ago a Brazilian millionaire named Domingo Faustino Correa died leaving his estate to be divided equally among his relatives, with instruction that this only be done one hundred years after his death. How many people do you think filed a claim in 1973?'

Gene remained impassive.

'Nearly five *thousand*. I believe the case is still being contested. Your lineage is an unbroken chain that stretches back over three thousand years. The number of your living relatives reaches into the *millions*.'

Millions? 'Everyone has a million living relatives,' Gene said. 'But not everyone else's relatives carry the memories of that chain all the way back to their source. If we were to resurrect our memories in every one of our relatives, we would be a legion of one mind.'

Gene got to his feet, fighting a wave of buckling claustrophobia. It felt as though every book in the library were suddenly a man, every page a woman, every word a child.

Is that what he could hear?

Yes—

A million voices for a million people?

Yes—

He teetered, gripping the nearest bookshelf and clinging to it; his breathing uneven.

Savage sat forward with alarm. 'Gene, breathe deeply. Slowly. This is just the side effect. Your memories will return in a day or two. I know this is disorienting. Are you okay?'

'You tell me.'

The grip of his nausea eased. His eyes settled on the volumes ahead; the numbers along their spines.

613.48.

613.49.

The Dewey decimal classification system. The numbers hidden in his sock suddenly made sense. Somewhere in the library, he'd earmarked a book. But which shelf had the book with his number on it?

This wasn't serendipity; he *knew* they would bring him here. He'd been trying to send himself a message.

He couldn't look for the book now, not with Savage in the room. He would have to come back. *Every Wednesday. We can't wait a week.* He turned away and returned to the table. 'What do you want? Why have you come to see me?'

'When I saw you were in the library I assumed you were ready to return to work. I can see now that I was mistaken. In any event *the process* has a schedule to meet. It's time to take more samples from you.'

'What kind of samples?'

'The usual. Blood, urine.' Savage was concerned, though he didn't voice it. 'It's been two weeks so we also need your latest sperm sample.'

Sperm? 'Why?'

'It's what the project requires.'

'What *is* the project?'

'*You* are the project.'

We are the project?

Savage was on his feet. Did he see that Gene was unsteady on his? 'Don't be alarmed. We've been here before. This is what happens when *the process* begins selecting some of your memories over others.'

We don't understand. If he takes us away how do we get

back here without arousing suspicion? We must see that book.
'I'm in no fit state to work.' Gene had no idea what his work
was. 'It'll interfere with my studies.'

Savage took a measured breath. The library seemed to
amuse him. 'Soon this will all be redundant to you.'

'My future doesn't concern me. My present does.'

'I understand that you're not feeling well but this'll cause an
inconvenient delay.'

'My apologies for being inconvenient.'

'You issued direct orders many months ago not to allow
that to happen.'

We issued orders? He's a liar—

He's trying to confound us—

It was clear Savage hadn't come here to make a request; he
simply had methods different from Megaera's. It was another
instance where in reality Gene had no choice. He hated Savage
for it.

Savage edged closer. 'The schedule cannot be changed.'

Gene fought the urge to turn and run. He drummed his
fingers on the heavy oak table. How to get the upper hand?
Threaten him. 'I *will* remember, when *the process* is
completed, whether you have complicated my life needlessly
or not, *Uncle.*'

Savage seemed to take that to heart. *Interesting.* He smiled
ruefully. 'You've been causing us some concern. Your response
to the treatment has been – patchy.'

Gene edged away. 'Is that normal?'

'We don't know. Your condition is unusual.'

Gene didn't know what Savage meant but he wasn't about
to reveal yet another facet to his ignorance. It didn't matter,
Savage could read him and seemed to be taking perverse
pleasure from his plight.

'Would you like me to tell you what the project is?'

'It'll come back to me.'

'Your DNA contains a very special piece of genetic code.

You are the greatest book that we possess and we will continue to read from your pages until we understand what we need to know.'

I am the greatest book? Little wonder this scientist seemed to find it so amusing that Gene spent his time *here*, in the library.

'You initiated the project that was designed to look for markers that will indicate to us whether or not you possess a certain gene, and whether or not it's being expressed.'

Gene was alert; from the darkness came a glimmer. 'Expressed? You mean if it's active.'

Savage was wrong-footed by the surprise. 'You remember your science.'

'And if it *has* become active?'

'Then *you* will be a stunning success.'

Gene considered the implications. 'If it hasn't?'

'Then you will compete like everyone else.'

'Compete for what?'

'Your survival.' Something of great import was weighing on Savage's mind. 'You are aware that a police officer is dead? It's all over the news.'

'No.'

'Did you kill him?'

He thought back to the museum. It was all such a blur, a hazy, drug-addled mishmash of unreality. 'I doubt it.'

'The NYPD disagrees. You study these archives like you're hunting somebody.'

North. We were looking for a man named North—

Is North dead? Why were we looking for him?—

I asked for his help.

'This will all have serious repercussions.'

'This is America. When has a little murder ever been an inconvenience to those of us with money? If I'm so important you'll make the problem go away.'

Savage was apprehensive again. 'So you *did* kill him.'

'I killed nobody. But I *do* want to kill somebody.'

Savage involuntarily took a step backwards as he reflected on that. His collar felt a little tighter. 'Who?'

Gene tapped his finger on the table with some unease. This multiplicity of mind clouded everything, but the urge was undeniable.

Gene's focus settled on Savage. 'I don't know yet.'

BOOK FOUR

The blood that lives in memory, glistens age to age

AESCHYLUS

ON THE ROAD TO THE ASYLUM

3.30 a.m. Thursday.

At first it was because he was afraid to go to sleep; then it was because he couldn't. Afraid of what he might see, afraid of what he might do, North wanted no part of the insanity that controlled him when he wasn't looking.

No more bull.

He stared bleakly at the uneven surface of the wall, watching the contorted shadows that crept in through his window dance for him like a Rorschach puppet show.

No more bull? Did I say that out loud? He could hear it grunting in the darkness. Did it hear him too?

He lay on his side, his arms wrapped around a pillow, clinging to it as though it were his only anchor in this world.

His eyes ached and his lids burned. Exhaustion had long since given way to reason, but reason was irrelevant now.

Each thudding movement of the hands of his wall clock measured out his despair second by miserable second. He felt it in every nerve. Each tick with its invisible thread tugged at his lashes, refusing to let go.

His body wanted to rest. His mind knew better.

*

3.52 a.m.
Still no sleep.

4.17 a.m.
I wonder what it's like to be sane?

7.38 a.m.
The skin on the back of his trembling hands was pale. His nose felt cold, his forehead clammy. In the rear-view mirror his eyes were shot with blood. *Watch the road. Don't wrap yourself around a tree.*

He found the sign for Poughkeepsie an hour and a half up the hypnotic monotony of the Taconic Parkway. Where the forest grew thick, he nudged the Lumina off the fifty-five and on to the nine and fished for directions on the passenger seat.

The museum sat just to the north of the town and was maintained by the Hudson River Psychiatric Center. He had a number for the director of research, a clinical psychologist he'd called twice before but with no luck. The third time and he was greeted with an officious tone. 'The museum is seen by appointment only.'

North's voice shook. 'What kind of museum needs an appointment?'

'This one.'

He negotiated the traffic lights and followed the signs for the centre. 'So when's good for you?' He heard paper being rustled; a diary of some description.

'Next Tuesday between nine and ten would be okay I suppose.'

'I'll be there in an hour.' North hung up the phone and used all his concentration to put it back in his pocket.

*

9.57 a.m.

Downtown Poughkeepsie was in the grip of a great depression. Main Street climbed up long and steep from the Hudson River, to where North was greeted with boarded-up store fronts and the deserted sidewalks of the main mall. He drove slowly through; looking for the best way to get from Fulton Street and up to Cheney Drive, but the desolation was suffocating. He wanted out of Poughkeepsie as fast as he'd arrived, and even though his wish was soon granted, the place remained with him and hung there like a portrait of his soul.

A chill wind howled amid the tussling branches on top of the hill where he found what used to be the Hudson River State Hospital. It was an unnerving imposition of stained and crumbling Victorian red bricks, its eerie towers stark, and its gothic windows boarded up with sheets of weathered plywood. A few windows here and there had required more permanent alterations; they had been bricked in, some more recently than others. It gave North the undeniable impression that although the wings now sat quietly empty, the work that had been undertaken here reflected less the need to keep people out, and more the need to keep something else in. Compared to the more modern building of the working hospital just over the far side, obscured by a few trees, this was a ghost that steadfastly refused exorcism.

An unpainted picket fence marked an empty parking space and as he got out and took his bearings he noticed that all the caution signs were posted upside down.

He welcomed the warning.

10.20 a.m.

The administration building was small and littered with bleak confined spaces. The passageways meandered in a twisting maze of dead ends and crossing paths. Despite his confusion North found an office door marked with the ghost of a name on the grimy glass: Dr C. H. Sullivan. Was this still the right room?

North took a moment to compose himself. *Play the part. You know the part.* He took a breath, his heart pounding furiously in his chest, his pulse racing. He knocked quietly on the door and stepped inside.

He was greeted by a tall, wiry man, perhaps only a couple of years older than himself, who started at the sight of North.

'This is very irregular,' the psychologist complained, fussing over the papers on the desk.

North waited for the man to finish but he seemed disinclined to do so. 'It's a very tidy desk, Dr Sullivan. I'm sure everything's in order—'

The man seemed suddenly a little less awkward. 'I'm sure it is, but I'm not Dr Sullivan.'

North waited.

'I'm Dr Oak. Dr Sullivan retired last year. And you?'

North introduced himself by flashing his badge. 'My information must be out of date. Sorry to interrupt your morning,' North replied, forgoing even a hint of sincerity.

Oak eyed his visitor with more gravity. 'I see. What's this about?'

North took the photograph of the hypodermic syringe and set it down on the desk. His voice was tired and warbled with the strain of exhaustion. 'Is this yours?'

'You mean the museum's?' Oak picked it up warily. The image of its polished glass and silver surface was clear and crisp. Sure enough he noted the H-R-S-H engraved clearly on its surface. Hudson River State Hospital. Oak was surprised and didn't mind showing it. 'How did you come by this?'

'I ran into it in the city.' He was reluctant to go further. Oak didn't need the details, but he got the picture. He winced.

'Could have killed you.'

'So they tell me. Are you missing an antique syringe?'

'I doubt it. We *do* have an antique syringe in a set on display from around the time the hospital first opened.'

'Which was when?'

'Eighteen seventy-one. The syringe, two needles, extra plunger washers, some wire cleanouts all in a little box with a purple silk lid. It's quite attractive.'

'You seem to know it pretty well.'

Oak took the compliment. 'Not many psychiatric centres have a psychiatric museum on site. We all take something of an interest.'

He handed back the photograph.

'Surely you haven't come all this way just to investigate a petty theft?'

'A cop is dead.'

The set of Oak's face hardened.

North produced Gene's mugshot and slid it towards him across the desk. 'I'm trying to trace this man. Do you recognize him?'

Oak considered the likeness carefully; his response measured. 'No. I've never seen him before. Why would a young man like that break into a museum just to steal a syringe? If he's a drug addict there are more accessible clinics and pharmacies.'

'Opportunity maybe. I'm thinking he either worked here, or he was a patient.'

'I see.'

'You're *sure* you don't recognize him?'

'I'm sorry.'

I'm going to kill this man. I'm going to reach over and gouge out an eye. 'The museum's by appointment only. Do you keep visitor records at least?'

Oak riffled through his desk momentarily. 'Unfortunately it's not here. Do you have a name to go with your face?'

'Gene. That's all I know.'

'That's not much to go on.' Oak grabbed his coat and a set of keys that dangled provocatively next to it and ushered North out of the office. He checked his watch. 'I can give you half an hour, but then I really need to be getting on. Let's see what we can find, shall we?'

Hidden behind the heavy door, the museum was a lone cavernous room where large snowflakes of ceiling paint lay scattered along its thickly varnished wooden floor. The light was poor, the air was damp and the smell was of rampant decay.

A high-backed wooden chair with straps at its base and on its arms stood just inside the doorway alongside other terrifying devices of restraint. The chair looked like a commode with its hole in the seat, but at head height a screen-covered box protruded ominously. It was designed to prevent whoever was strapped into it from biting or spitting at anyone close by.

The sign read: 'The Benjamin Rush tranquillity chair; circa early 1800s'. North regarded it queasily. *Tranquil for who?* It was a strange invention for a man who had signed the Declaration of Independence.

The other devices appeared, on the surface at least, to be no better. 'What's this one?' North asked warily, eyeing a coffinesque box with bars instead of a lid that hung suspended from dull heavy chains.

'That's a Utica crib,' Oak explained proudly, 'named after the New York State Lunatic Asylum at Utica. The patient slept inside and was swung back and forth, mostly for calming purposes; it reminded them of the safety of being inside their crib as a child.'

I wonder where I can get one.

On the wall behind it hung a straitjacket, further down from there was what looked like a horse's bit. A female mannequin wore the blue student uniform from a nursing school that once was attached to the asylum. There were old writing desks and medical books. And there were the dusty glass display cases containing bolts of cloth, bottles, fans, combs, even straight-edged razors.

North was starting to sweat. He could feel the chill running down the back of his neck. *Is this what I'm in for?* What did they do to people these days who were losing their mind?

'Back then the hospital was a self-sufficient community of course.' Oak ran his finger along the display cases trying to find the one he was looking for. 'They ran a farm with livestock, made clothes, shoes and—'

Inside the display case a lone rectangular clear patch sat exposed amid the dust where a box once sat.

'It would appear your Mr Gene has been here.'

The small brown ledger sat on a shelf near the front. Oak cracked it open and began leafing through the visitor entries, starting with the most recent. It didn't take long.

'G . . . G . . . No, I'm sorry. No visitors with the first initial G. Are you certain you have the correct name?'

'Yes.' *Why would he tell the truth?* 'What about a surname?'

Oak looked again, but he was soon shaking his head. 'Gerard. Goldstone. No Gene.'

He's not looking hard enough. 'How far back are you checking?'

'We don't get many visitors. The list goes back maybe five years and not everyone signs in.'

Gene. What am I missing? He peered over Oak's shoulder and traced his finger over the names. *D. B. Cole, Ed Dybbuk, Janet Courtlandt M.D., A. H. Romer, Ed Dybbuk again. Jane Shore. Jay—*

Is that it? Had he been spelling it wrong all this time? 'Jean, with a J. Look under J.'

Oak did as instructed but the harsh reality soon became apparent. Only four people had visited the museum in the last few years whose first initial was a *J*. All had signed in using their full first name. All had been women. None was Jean.

Oak closed the book. 'I'll make inquiries with security, see if a break-in has been reported that I wasn't aware of, but I can't see your man here. I sympathize, but you've had a wasted journey, detective.'

11.00 a.m.

North sat in the car by the administration building, wondering whether he should go home or check in there and then, and watching the bruised sky over Dutchess County close in over the Hudson River and the Shawangunk Mountains. The lush woodland that cocooned most of the hospital and which made the complex so secluded began to startle with the first fat droplets of rain.

It was a thing of beauty a wide open space, a type of freedom he wasn't used to in the city. This was an Elysian field he could call his own. From up here on the hill, it wasn't quite enough to give him vertigo, but it was enough to offer him a glimmer of a fresh perspective. In his apartment all he had to do was look out the window and he'd be treated to the sight of three total strangers scratching their genitals.

He rubbed his burning, blistered eyes. Here he might at least get some rest. Be out of sight for a while. *Out of sight and out of my mind. I'm seeing beasts of burden for God's sake.*

The ringing from his Nextel wasn't entirely unexpected. He was just surprised the call hadn't come sooner.

'I told Hyland you're out working the case.'

That *was* a surprise. It was Martinez. 'I *am* out working the case.' North started the engine and slowly began to roll the Lumina around the loop towards the exit.

'Good, so you didn't make me out to be a liar. Dig up anything new?'

'No, the nuthouse is a bust.'

'Damn. Listen, two things: first, Hyland wants to know what happened to his DD-5.'

'Tell him it's on his desk.'

'He knows it's not on his desk.'

'So tell him I'm a liar.'

'He's gonna go fucking nuts.'

'Good for him. Is that it?'

'No, I've been saving this one. Ash came back with your trace evidence on the car. The tyre tread matches a Michelin MX4.'

North slowed the Lumina down and pulled up on the side of the road. He whipped his notebook out and thumbed to an empty page. 'Go on.'

'It's pretty common. The glass fragments from the scene match the left front lens of a 2004 Chrysler Sebring sedan. And – Sebring sedans come fitted with either Goodyear Eagle LS tyres or MX4s.'

North wrote feverishly, his mind racing. 'Got it. What about the bike?'

'Ash says on the front column he found flecks of paint consistent with a collision with a vehicle. The paint is silver, the exact colour's called graphite metallic clear coat. It's one of the colour options for a Sebring sedan.'

Now we're getting somewhere. 'What else?'

'Glass fragments were found studded in the front tyre of the bike. Some of them were also consistent with glass from the left front lens of a Chrysler Sebring sedan.'

North was alive with possibilities. 'That a match or is it just the same make of car?'

Martinez was quick to respond. 'The damage on the two sets of fragments corresponds. It's the *same* car. Someone was following you.'

Gene got *in* that car.

North had a flash of earnest panic. 'Has the Department of

Transportation sent the tapes over from those traffic cameras yet?'

'I'm all over it.'

'We *have* to pull a set of plates off one of those cameras.'

'Hey, I said I'm all over it. In the meantime I got the DMV sending over a list of registered owners of Sebrings that match the description. What's the worst that can happen? We go door to door.'

North felt alive, like a load had been lifted and he was suddenly free. He had to get back and go through those tapes. He checked his mirrors.

A large dark figure was standing right beside him in the mist of drizzling rain.

The man hammered on his side window.

'Detective North? Detective North!'

Startled, North ended his call. He peered out at the man bending over to get a better look at it him. It was Oak. North wound the window down.

'I'm so glad I caught you.'

'What can I do for you?'

'It's this register of visitors.' The psychologist brought the brown leather book out from under his coat to show him. 'I was looking back through it and I suddenly realized I recognized one of the names.'

Oak handed it over. North opened it up at a random page while Oak leaned in and guided him further. 'For several weeks *last year* we were treating a patient with an unusual condition by the name of Cassandra Dybbuk.'

'And she visited the museum?'

'No, but around the same time there are these records of a visitor to the museum with the same last name. Here, see? Ed Dybbuk.'

North was polite. Dybbuk had visited a number of times,

far more than anyone else, but he didn't see the significance.

'I phoned across to the psychiatric centre. The visitor was her son.'

'But you already said you didn't recognize the photograph, doctor.'

'*I* never met her son. However, a couple of clinicians over at the main building did. Her son checked her in. He's her guardian but his name isn't *Ed* Dybbuk at all.' Oak directed North's attention to the ledger and the faded entry. 'It's the way he's written it, see? He omitted the periods. It actually reads E. D. Dybbuk.'

North closed the book and handed it back. 'I'm not sure I'm following you.'

Oak smiled warmly. 'The name of Cassandra Dybbuk's son, detective, is *Eugene*.'

North hurriedly followed Oak into the main building. *Someone give me a positive ID, please.* The gloom from the rainstorm outside cast a pall over the spartan reception bay. Oak left him alone while he went off in search of the clinician who had dealt with Cassandra Dybbuk.

North bided his time by showing the photograph to the receptionists. They drew a blank. However, when Oak eventually returned he had with him a small gaggle of irate psychiatrists.

One clinician, a small woman with dark red hair, confirmed from the photograph that Gene certainly bore a striking resemblance to Eugene Dybbuk but would say no more. A senior administrator arrived shortly thereafter. They huddled in a heated debate.

Oak appeared embarrassed. Voices were quickly raised. The administrator broke ranks.

'I'm sorry, we just can't give you any further information.'

This is unbelievable. 'I don't want access to any medical

records. I just want Cassandra or Eugene Dybbuk's contact details.'

'We have to abide by HIPAA. Privacy of the patient is paramount. It's our policy not even to *confirm* that a patient is here.' The jab was aimed squarely at Oak. He shouldn't have opened his mouth.

North could feel his frustration taking hold. This wasn't the first time he'd run foul of the privacy law.

The Health Insurance Portability and Accountability Act was well intentioned. In practice it had run riot. He remembered a gunshot victim that he'd tried to interview. He needed a description of the shooter. Not only would the hospital not even confirm she was there, it took two days to get a warrant to see her. By that time, she'd already left.

North gripped the counter. *I have to try.* 'Perhaps I'm not making myself clear. This is a homicide investigation. A police officer was killed.'

'And perhaps I'm not making *myself* clear: no.'

11.38 a.m.

North stormed back to the car and pulled out on to the main road. *That can't be my only option.* He headed back into the centre of town. *I don't have time to get a warrant.*

Dybbuk, Dybbuk. What kind of a name is that? Polish? Dutch?

He tried to picture the ledger. He hadn't copied it down. *How did he spell it?* He could see the entries where Gene had scrawled his name. *Dybbuk. D–u . . . ? D–y . . . ?*

D–y–bb—

He was close. He could smell it. Without looking, without caring, he swerved around the bend in the road as he fished out his Nextel and dialled four one one.

He gave the operator the details.

'Which city?'

'The whole state.'

'Sir, you are aware with that kind of search there could be hundreds of entries?'

I doubt it. 'With a name like Dybbuk?'

Reluctantly the operator did as he asked. He heard the plastic keys tap away on the system. 'Sir? I have three entries under Dybbuk. Do you have a first name or an initial?'

It can't be that easy, can it? Go for it. 'Try Eugene.'

The wait was painful. It also proved fruitless.

'Okay, try C. Full name: Cassandra.'

'I have that name listed. Cassandra Dybbuk. Area code five one eight—'

Five one eight? That's further out from the city. He cradled the phone in his shoulder and wrote the rest of the number down on the back his hand. 'What's the address?'

'Address: two-fifty-two, Sixth Avenue. Troy.'

SHADES OF THE SANGUINE TREE

Was he in truth just a rat caught in a maze; set another test for another piece of cheese? Savage led Gene through a series of laboratories past great vats of volatile chemicals such as acetone and butanol. In one cubicle they took blood, at another the rough end of a plastic sample brush was roughly scraped against the inside of his cheek.

As the nurses tended to him, one, her hair neatly tied up in a bun at the back, let slip that she had seen him talking to himself in the shower.

Gene froze, though he said nothing. Somehow he wasn't surprised. *So we are being watched.* Had they seen him make his little discovery of the number sequence? Gene stepped from the room and regarded the scientist quietly. '*How many* watch me?'

Savage was clearly uncomfortable even though it appeared to strike him as such an obvious question. 'Everyone. We're all interested in you.'

Everyone.

Each laboratory was successively higher up the ziggurat until they reached the upper floors where there was no possibility of escape. *What does it matter? Let them take their samples.* He had been trapped before, confined to the tower, a prisoner of whim. He would just have to be patient. He would bide his time.

On the thirty-third floor they put him on a treadmill and hooked him up to myriad machines that measured his breathing, his heart rate, and when he was sufficiently sweat soaked, collected his perspiration. While the medical staff swarmed around him, Savage took to writing in a ledger and asking a series of questions.

'You feel lost?'

How can we not? The truth was a nightmare that had no end. 'You mean like I don't know who I am any more?'

Was Savage apprehensive? He responded by cranking up the speed and the incline. 'You don't know who you are?'

Gene struggled to increase his pace. The thud, thud, thud, and the whir of electric motors became deafening. 'Of course I *know* who I am!'

Savage was circumspect. 'I understand you forget things. You do something and forget why you're doing it.'

'Yes.'

'Like the art museum.'

'Yes.'

Savage nodded, pleased that he was getting somewhere. 'So you didn't intend on going to the museum?'

'Why would I want go there?'

'You tell me.'

On the thirty-fourth floor their meticulous dissection of him required a urine sample. Affording him little privacy except for an opaque screen, they discussed their hunt for the concentration of neurotransmitters they anticipated finding in his system. He listened while he peed into a cup.

Neurotransmitters guided the emotions and memories of the mind. They were trying to induce in him memories that stretched back into the dust of antiquity, but something else troubled them. Here they were more guarded, and gave nothing away.

He strained to gather any detail but he was given no time. One of them was tired of waiting and demanded he get on with producing his sample. He took a moment to deliver.

On the thirty-fifth floor he was escorted through a series of toughened-glass walled corridors exposing the machinery beyond. It came as a shock when at last he saw something he recognized.

This he knew. It was at his core.

Hooded cubes of machinery sat in clusters around computers, manipulating the very fabric of his DNA, a twisted double helix of molecules like two intertwined snakes that trapped his soul between their fangs, two snakes each with three billion scales in four different colours: adenine, cytosine, guanine, andthymine; A, C, G, T, the four bases; the alphabet from which was written his fate.

This was his work. It called to him, tugging at his psyche as the host of technicians loaded their DNA scanners with gene chips – small squares of glass carrying genetic material instead of electronic circuits.

Like two halves of a zip, the twisted double strands of DNA bonded perfectly to each other: A only with T; C only with G. A sample of DNA had been unlocked and the individual strands placed upon these chips and fused to fluorescent markers, so that as the unlocked threads of Gene's DNA washed over the gene chip in a solution, they bound to the gene chip sample making it glow and exposing which of his genes were active in any one of his cells at that instant.

Yet in order for the hunt to succeed Gene's DNA had to be compared not only to a control sample but to a DNA sample known to contain the gene they were seeking. A gene only Cyclades possessed. The one that unlocked true immortality.

The question was, whose DNA had been used to create the gene chips? Had they hunted down a living donor who was just like him, or had they used an older source? A relic perhaps, from a former life, such as pulp extracted from the tooth of the skull.

He could feel the press of complication filling his thoughts. He remembered the museum and the commotion he had caused. Had he truly held his own head in his hands?

'The gene you're anxious to find renders all of this obsolete, doesn't it?'

Savage seemed pleased that he understood. 'Athanatos has kept his essence alive, from body to body, for thousands of years, kept it alive by continuous alchemy. But you contain that which will render his rebirth automatic. We will either find it by sheer persistence, or the process you are undergoing will be successful and his offspring will reap the rewards by virtue of simply being born.'

What does he mean by that? 'If this process has been working for millennia, why change it now?'

Savage rued the question. 'Is this any kind of life?' he asked upon reflection. 'That immortality is achieved only through relentless endeavour? What stops it from being our right from birth?'

Gene understood. 'His system is flawed.'

Savage found it painful to admit. 'Yes, it is flawed. Ultimately there are gaps. The selective resurrection of memory from generation to generation means Athanatos cannot be certain his entire self has been passed on at all. There has been the lingering doubt that . . . he is dissolving.' Savage put his hand on Gene's shoulder. 'You will change that.'

Alarmed, Gene followed Savage into a busy office complex, where at the end of the hall stood an imposing black door. At its threshold stood – was that Megaera? He had been fooled before. In this place he could be certain of nothing.

She held a small child in her arms. It was perhaps barely two years old, what hair it had was fair and thin and inadequately covered its misshapen head. Drool cascaded down its small chin, and though its eyes sparkled brightly it did not respond to the stimuli around it.

Megaera bore it no love and seemed to find its very presence insulting. She thrust it back into the arms of the waiting nanny who complained bitterly. 'He just wants a little time with his mother.'

Megaera was not moved. 'Who knows what *it* wants? Get it out of my sight.'

Did she see him? Would she have cared if she did? Gene remained firmly rooted where he stood as she stormed past him. He watched the doting nanny offer the babe a little of the affection that the flame-haired woman who was marching away refused to give. The nanny struggled to reach for her ID card and swipe it through the door lock. No one came to help.

As the looming black door opened Gene craned his neck to see what lay behind but he was not allowed to probe any further. Savage ushered him away from it all as quickly as he could. 'Not that way.'

'What's down there?'

'Nothing.'

'A nothing that requires a security pass.'

'Nothing *important*.'

That isn't true either.

He regarded the hall and its offshoot annexes. 'Which way?'

Savage led him further on until at the furthest end of the hall they stood before a large executive office, its door firmly shut. The panes of glass either side of it were frosted opaque. The name upon the door read: 'Eugene Dybbuk'. He had *an office*?

'I thought we could conduct our business in here, with your permission.'

Perhaps in here he might find some answers. He tried the handle. *Foolish.* It required yet another code.

He could feel a host of eyes burning into him. Another test to show he really had returned to them?

He tried to relax and cleared his mind. On instinct he entered the first set of numbers he thought of.

The precision lock mechanism buried within the fine wood smoothly released the bolt.

'In my condition you're lucky I remembered that.'

Savage's eyes lit up in satisfaction. 'Not at all. You were never taught the combination. Like everything else, it's encoded within every fibre of who you are. Even if you're not aware of it, your memory function is intact and accessible.'

How do we use this to our advantage?

Savage handed him another cup. 'I think you'll find you still have a magazine in the top drawer if you need some assistance getting *in the mood*, so to speak. Take your time. I'll wait right here.'

Gene tried the handle and swung the door open. Inside, he found Megaera waiting for him.

She was sat on the desk, her legs crossed, apparently delighted that Gene had made it this far. He didn't believe her.

A magazine was laid out on the desk. Lazily Megaera flipped from page to page. Naked rounded women stared back from its leaves, their young agile bodies set in provocatively contorted positions. 'You're keeping yourself busy today, I see?'

She had been watching too. Gene closed the door behind him. 'At least you don't hide behind a camera.'

Megaera looked at the cup in Gene's hand. 'Oh, don't stop your crude fumblings on my account.'

'I doubt I'll start on your account either.' He set the cup firmly down on the desk next to her.

As he did so, he noticed the framed page of spidery handwriting that sat next to the computer screen. It sparked something. He picked it up to study, if only because it afforded him the opportunity to turn his back on her.

'You're always so obsessed with that picture.'

We are? It was an example of Darwin's handwriting. While

outlining his theory of evolution, Darwin had made a note to himself that his own handwriting looked remarkably like that of his grandfather, Erasmus. Was it chance that it appeared so similar? Or was it a trait? Even Darwin couldn't decide.

'Remember when I gave that to you?'

'No.'

'Your memories are still in flux. A pity. They will settle and come back to you. You said to me: genetically speaking Erasmus' handwriting was an expression of his motor coordination skills. It was *that* aspect which he passed on to his grandson. You said: and who was to say that Erasmus' handwriting didn't look like *his* grandfather's? You refused to believe it was genetic memory.' She laughed. 'You were so funny.'

Then why did her laughter sound so hollow? It was as though she wore a shroud of bitter jealousy.

He set the picture back down. 'Your mothering skills are astounding.'

'What do you care?'

'Why do you hate your son?'

'I don't hate him.'

'But you don't love him.'

'I don't think about him. He's a lump of useless flesh. Do you get so attached to *your* experiments? What would be the point? He eats, he excretes, and he serves no useful purpose.'

Gene resisted the temptation to revel in judgement. Yes she was callous. But why was that? He probed further. 'Much like his father?'

She rose to her feet coyly. 'My, aren't we clumsy with the bait? In any event,' she said, 'that would be too much of a compliment to his father.'

She ran her finger along the desk. 'How are the voices treating you?'

Touché. 'I don't hear voices,' he lied firmly. 'I have memories.'

'That's the whole point of *the process*. In time your shadow personalities will coalesce until you feel whole again. You will be more than just the sum of your parts.'

'But you won't?'

That got to her. The simmering envy that she kept barely contained beneath the surface came rushing to the fore. She grabbed the picture from his desk and slung it at the wall. The glass shattered into a thousand jagged fragments.

'I am *not allowed* to be! Despite everything, despite all the complications that you've caused, our glorious father has decided that *you* will be the next Athanatos. Despite all my work on our elusive CREB Linked Hypothesis—'

CREB? Gene thought quickly. The CREB1 gene was on chromosome two. *What does it do?* Memory, one of its functions had something to do with memory. He'd have to refresh his own when she was gone. 'Despite my progress in locating your clock, *you* get the glory. *You get to go on.*'

There were tears in her eyes, large and filled with genuine frustration. This had eaten away at her for so long it was as though there was nothing left.

'My hard work, for nothing; all for want of a Y.'

What was it about the essence of the male that reduced her to this? Gene made no move to comfort her. He wasn't even sure he wanted to. She reached for a tissue and dabbed at her eyes.

'And there you are the eternal liability. You may very well languish in jail for what you've done. You've jeopardized everything. And *still* he chooses you.'

'Savage isn't certain of that.'

She treated his comment with derision. 'Savage is not in charge here. He's a dreamer, and not a particularly good one. He's quite the runt of the litter.'

She tossed her copper hair back over her shoulders and regarded the broken glass on the floor bleakly. She grabbed the wastepaper basket and began cleaning up her own mess.

'You will be the next Athanatos. It's been decided, so I'm here to pay tribute and pledge my allegiance to the king.'

Gene was suspicious. Like a creeping hand that sought to guide him merrily to his downfall he watched her collect the glass and knew that her motives, as ever, were not pure.

He had been outmanoeuvred before. Outmanoeuvred and rendered impotent. The memories of it were a scar that even *the process* couldn't remove. The duplicity at the heart of Athanatos's scheme made him ill. *Enough of these games.* 'What are you planning?'

She threw the pieces of glass forcefully into the trash, not content with their fractured nature, she wanted carnage. She sliced her finger open. Spots of glistening crimson dripped on to the discarded white paper below.

She edged towards him and held out her finger gently. 'Will you kiss it better?'

Gene remained impassive. She smiled. She liked that. She edged even closer and wiped the blood across his lip. He felt compelled to lick it off.

She whispered in his ear. 'What do you think I have in mind?'

Gene refused to answer.

She wiped her bloody finger down his virgin white shirt.

'Oh come along my dear brother, we both share the same memories. We're both splinters of the same soul. Surely you can see what I have in mind?'

She was flushed; a rose-tinted mist had crept up her neck. Her pupils dilated. She took her other hand and ran it gently up his leg until it rested on his crotch. She squeezed and was delighted when she felt a response.

'Come, let me give you a helping hand. They want their sample. There are two of us here. We're the same, you and I. Just look on this as glorified masturbation.'

He could feel the throbbing in his penis grow stronger. *Why don't we push her away?* Her grip tightened. Taking the zipper firmly between her thumb and forefinger she teased his fly open, and as he fell out into her hand she firmly pulled back his skin and began the long stroking motion that set his nerves on fire.

His breath, like hers, caught in his constricted throat. This was all so familiar, all so frighteningly reminiscent. He had been trapped before. He couldn't let it happen again. Not again.

'You repulse me.' Yet he could not pull away.

'I have *ample* evidence that you're lying.' She smiled and whispered breathlessly in his hot ear, 'Enjoy it, my *dearest* brother, because I'm going to destroy you.'

THE COLOUR OF GREEK FIRE

When he was nine years old, his father fell ill. The great Byzantine Emperor Leo IV, Leo the Khazar, was fevered and took to his bed. Great boils and monstrous weeping carbuncles had erupted across his forehead, yet still he clutched at the crown that they said was the cause of it. Oh his love for his crown.

They said to him: 'Do not go in there. Your father is sick. He will not wish to be seen when he is so frail.' So he stood in the shadows of his father's bedchamber and watched him die from there.

His mother never came.

Cyclades stood in the gloom of the Porphyra and awaited his fate. It was a cold night. A chill wind was blowing in off the Bosphorus and digging its claws into all of Constantinople, but he was not afraid. There was little to be afraid of when he knew what the inevitable was to bring.

Nearly eight hundred years since the birth of Christ and this was where Cyclades had been *reborn*. This was where his son was born. This was where they thought he had died. A pavilion made from the porphyry stone, in hues of the deepest red and the purest purple. A chamber adorned with exotic and luxurious purple silks and dyed purple wall hangings. This was the colour of empire.

In here his mother the Empress Irene had given him life. He never thought that he would be born into the arms of his enemy.

His memories were long.

'Where is she now?'

The voices from the gloom of the Porphyra answered: 'She will come.'

When he was nine and a half years old, and the forty days of mourning had ended, they told him he was not old enough to rule alone, so they crowned him co-emperor and his mother too.

They paraded him around the streets and held festivals throughout the city. The Greens and the Blues brought on the dancing bears, and when they grew tired, brought on the dancing acrobats. From the mighty dome of the church of Hagia Sophia, to the Acropolis hill that jutted out into the wine dark Bosphorus and the sparkling Sea of Marmara, from the four gilded horses of Chios that guarded the Hippodrome, to the mighty Theodosian Walls, from the Forum of Constantine the Great, and to every colonnaded street, the chant went up:

'This is the day of the salvation of the Romans! Glory to God who has crowned your head. May He who has crowned you Constantine VI, by His own hand keep you in purple for many years, for the glory and the exultation of the Romans!'

Constantine. He answered to that name only because it was expected. He knew he was someone else. Someone trapped, a man's thoughts in a child's body, yet since his body was still developing, only a child's intellect to help him make sense of it all.

It was so very confusing.

After the ceremony they ushered him through the Great Palace, but the whisperings had already begun before the proclamations had even stopped ringing in his ears.

Many years. Many years. Such duplicity. Even at the age of nine and a half, he knew that it was a lie. This was the era of schemes. On every street corner from the bath house of Zeuxippos to Chalke, the glorious bronze gates of the Great Palace itself, there was always some disaffected exile from some far away land plotting with Roman help to win back their lot.

Like some great malady, the need to plot and counter-plot infected everyone and everything and no one was immune.

His father had five half-brothers that also lived with him in the Great Palace of the Queen City. The eldest of this gaggle of schemers was called Nikephoros. One evening, when the shadows were long and the sun was an echo in the sky, he cornered the young emperor. 'Come here, boy.'

The little emperor was intimidated by his uncle's pendants and jewels and layers of fine silk. He made a great show of puffing up his chest in return, aghast at such rude manners from his uncle. 'I am Emperor. I can have your hide.'

'And I am a man, *boy*. I can have yours.'

He drew the boy near and forced him to listen to his musings. 'Why does your mother consort with eunuchs?' he asked. 'What do they give her that your feeble father could not? *You* are the rightful ruler of this land. Not they. Yet they are the power behind this throne. You call yourself an emperor? Then tell me, *nephew*, where is *your* power?'

'I have power,' the boy replied. But there was an uncertainty behind his voice.

'If you want power, my little emperor, I can *give* you power. All you need do is ask.'

The boy-emperor was shaken. What did his uncle Nikephoros have in mind?

He ran through the Great Palace, frightened and alone. Sprinting from shadow to shadow, hoping that he could somehow disappear. It was a child's wish, a dream that had consequences that came with its granting.

I am not ready for such schemes. I am not yet a man.

He heard laughter coming from his mother's quarters. She would know what to do. She was the empress. She was strong. He listened to her merry sound and was drawn to it, like an ant to honey.

Lost amid the fluttering festoons, the slow steady heartbeat of silk hangings undulating in the sigh of twilight, he crept towards his mother's voice, and from the womb of ivory and pink pearls, he chose a gap through which to spy. He listened and he watched.

'We have done it!' So was the jubilant cry. He heard them twitter about the plan they had hatched many years before he was born, when Constantinople (so he had been taught) had been decimated by a great plague and besieged by Saracen armies for a whole year.

'We have an empire we can call our own.'

They had an empire? The boy wondered. Why did his mother not correct them?

But then came the footsteps and the terrible shame of being discovered.

'What are you doing in the shadows, little one?' the voice asked.

Aetios was the closest of all his mother's eunuchs. His face was set as he crept out from the darkness. His eyes were as hard as marble.

Little Cyclades was afraid.

Aetios said, 'This is my domain, not yours. Didn't you know that the darkness is where the dangers lurk; troubles piled heap upon heap?'

'I came for my mother.'

'She cannot see you.'

'But she must. I am the emperor. She must see me! Uncle Nikephoros—' The words caught in his throat. Who to trust? Who to turn to?

Aetios smiled and kneeled down beside him. He held him firm by the shoulders. 'Your Majesty, you can trust me.'

The little emperor lifted his chin. He could?

'You are the emperor here. What is your want, your will be done.' He bowed his head in deference. 'What did your uncle tell you?'

Little Cyclades said, 'Uncle Nikephoros said that if I wanted true power then all I had to do was ask and he would give it to me.'

Aetios took the news with a thoughtful nod. 'I see. And what did you say?'

'I said I already had power because I was the emperor and nobody could touch me.'

Aetios laughed. 'Nobody can touch you . . . Yes. I suppose youth does have a certain naïve charm.' He got to his feet. 'That's good. That's good.' Dismissively he patted the boy on the head and disappeared back into the darkness.

The little emperor was confused. He retreated to the shadows, but still watched his mother from afar. Her beauty was unmatched, and the men around her were clearly in awe.

Aetios came in to sit with her. Why did she stroke the hair at the back of his neck?

'What of the boy?'

'What of him?' Aetios replied.

'He survives,' Staurakios, one of the taller of the stern-faced eunuchs advised.

'He must,' Aetios said firmly, much to the young emperor's relief. 'If we are to hold our positions, he must.'

His mother sat forward. 'For now.' She spoke coldly, like a wine that had spoiled. 'For now . . .'

The little emperor could do nothing except give a horrified gasp and retreat from that terrifying surprise.

Cyclades stood in the gloom of the Porphyra and awaited his fate. The eunuchs had surrounded him. There was no escape from here.

Whatever had become of his uncles? They lived to the north, somewhere on the coast, the last he heard. His mother had called them into one of the great meeting chambers and had had them sink to their knees. She had them tonsured, their heads shaven roughly and without their consent like worthless criminals, and sent them off to become priests. *Poor Uncle Nikephoros*. He got off lightly.

Cyclades wished he could shave off what was stuck inside his mind. He spent his childhood experiencing waking nightmares and vivid dreams. As he grew so too did the visions. As each new experience in his life unfolded, so each old memory was unlocked.

A child should not go through that alone.

Cyclades watched the eunuchs gather close. It was obvious they were not eunuchs like any he had seen before. They had body hair and deep voices. And though it was not unusual for men of a mature age to be made a eunuch, it was unusual for there to be so many in one place.

They had many faces, these eunuchs. But only one will. It was unfortunate that he had trusted the worst of them.

'Where is Aetios?'

The eunuch stepped from the gloom of the Porphyra and answered: 'I am here.'

When he was ten years old Aetios had become his tutor. They would walk the streets of the city and conduct lessons.

One day they came to the Pillar of Constantine and the

little emperor was drawn to it. He said, 'Aetios, I am confused.'

'How so, Your Majesty?'

'We are Romaioi, are we not? We are Romans.'

'Yes, Your Majesty.'

'Then why is it that we speak Greek and not Latin?'

'Time moves on, Your Majesty. Nothing stays as it was. We are Romans, but this is not Rome. We stand upon the land that was once the ancient Greek city of Byzantium, but we are not they. We are the Romans of the east. We are what is left when the empire once split.'

The boy considered this while he stood under the looming shadow of the towering pillar, imagining the mighty Constantine the Great erecting it when he founded the city nearly five hundred years before and declared it his Novo Roma; his New Rome. 'Before Latin, we spoke Greek again. And other languages.'

'What know you of other languages?'

'Last night I dreamed of an ancient form of Greek and a tongue from ancient Phrygia.'

'How intriguing.'

'And under here, Aetios, under this pillar is the Palladium from Troy itself!'

Aetios chuckled. 'You've been reading your history.'

'It's true!'

Aetios cast about for somewhere to sit and spurred the excitable child on with backhanded humour. 'I doubt you even know what the Palladium is.'

'I *do* know! I have *seen it*!'

'With your own eyes, no doubt.'

'With my former eyes.'

'And what did your *former* eyes tell you?'

The precocious little emperor paced in front of his tutor as though he were giving a lecture at the Forum. 'Across the Bosphorus and down along the coast sits Troy. Or it did. It is lost now. The Trojans worshipped Minerva, whom the Greeks called Athena, and whom the Trojans called Pallas. In honour of Pallas and so that she would protect mighty Troy from all invaders the Trojans built a statue of a horse and named her the Palladium, which they kept at the heart of their citadel.'

Aetios smiled at the passion with which the little emperor told his tale. 'But that is in Troy, Your Majesty. How did the Palladium get here?'

A cloud passed over the boy's brow. 'I don't remember. Not properly. I only read about it.'

'Why is that?'

The boy looked his tutor in the eye. 'I think I died.'

The eyes that looked back at the boy were dark – hooded and suspicious.

The boy did not notice. The tale was not ended for him. 'After the battle and the city were lost, there was a great storm. It was ferocious and unforgiving.'

'Yes, it was terrible.' Aetios looked again to the boy. 'I mean, I had read it was terrible.'

'Many triumphant Greeks and fleeing Trojans alike were drowned in the tumult. The storm lashed the ocean for week upon week, month upon month. Odysseus was doomed to wander, Menelaus and Helen took refuge in Egypt and a Trojan prince named Aeneas led the Trojan survivors on a journey towards a new home, but the storm was so violent he was washed ashore in Carthage and forced to seek help.'

'But he made it, Your Majesty. In the end.'

'Yes. To the hills near the River Tiber where he started a new city which he called Lavinium, and from there sprang Rome. He took the Palladium with him, and when Constantine came here, he brought the Palladium from Rome. So you see, Aetios, we descend from Troy; the whole Roman Empire descends from Troy. But when we Romans brought the Palladium, we also brought the storm. And do you know why there was a storm? Because of one man.'

Aetios got to his feet. He appeared circumspect. 'One man, eh?'

'One man who battled a mighty magician called Athanatos, a magician who had done him a great injustice. I was that man, Aetios, and his crimes against me were grievous.'

'Grievous? What were they?' He gathered the boy out of the crowd and ushered him forth. 'Come, let us return to the palace.'

'I . . . I don't remember. Not yet.'

'Grievous crimes, but you don't remember. And still you have told me nothing that confirms to me that you saw the Palladium with these eyes or any other.'

The boy was confused, struggling to keep up with his tutor's march. The uncertainties weighed heavily upon him. 'I did see it. You must believe me. If we could dig it up you would see the scars upon its flank from where I fought a great battle.'

'Scars, eh? And did you have a name in this former life?'

The boy emperor took his tutor by the hand. 'Yes. I was called Cyclades.'

Aetios tightened his grip. They cut through the crowds, Aetios' impatient step getting quicker and quicker.

'And when I was dying and my justice had not been meted out, I roared on my deathbed, Aetios. I roared. And from my mouth came the storm.'

Aetios yanked at the boy's arm as he charged through the heaving crowds. 'Ouch! Aetios, you're hurting me!'

Aetios said nothing.

'I even think he might be here, Aetios. Here in the city. Will you help me Aetios? Will you?'

The tutor patted the boy on the back. 'I will help you, Your Majesty. I will help you on your way.'

The rains came that night, like tears from the gods who wept for his fate. He had dreamed once more of the storm and stole up on to the Theodosian Walls to watch the mighty lightning strikes.

But what he could hear was not the rolling thunder of night, but the beating of drums.

As he stood on the ramparts, the rains lashing him from head to toe, the sound of an almighty horn went up. He saw the flaming amber torches of soldiers in boats, stealing their way across the Bosphorus. Who were they this time? The Bulgars? The Saracens? He supposed it made little difference.

All along the walls the soldiers took to their stations. The archers were made ready while on the prows of every ship in the Byzantine fleet their siphons were engorged.

At the Golden Horn the great iron chain that stretched from the city to Pera, protecting the mouth of the harbour, was raised, trapping all the merchant vessels held within. The spices and the ivory from Egypt, the silks and the jewels from China, the furs and the amber from the north, all sat piled on the docks, tempting the enemy to advance.

The black boats drew near. The order was passed along the walls. The archers took aim with flaming arrows, while the fleet converged from the flanks.

Attack!

In unison the flaming tongues of incandescent naphtha were unleashed from siphon to siphon, smothering the advancing black boats in a torrent of sticky flame. The greatest of all Byzantine powers. Greek fire. The fire that not even water could extinguish. The rage that not even history could snuff out.

Like a host of burning angels the flaming bodies of the soldiers and sailors were flung into the cold dark of the water and lit up the spitting Bosphorus, shrinking from its surface and descending into the murk below, appearing as though stars in the sky before blinking out, one by one.

From the shroud of the rain a soldier emerged and put a hand on the boy's shoulder to bid him go back inside. 'Come, Your Majesty,' he said. 'It is not safe here. You are surrounded by enemies on all sides.'

*

Cyclades stood in the gloom of the Porphyra and awaited his fate.

Aetios stood before him. He pulled his robes up to expose his parts to the gloom.

'I think you'll agree I am not much of a eunuch.'

Cyclades had other concerns. 'Athanatos—'

Athanatos bowed, truly aglow with the compliment. 'I am humbled that you remember my true name.'

Cyclades ran at him, but the eunuchs soon held him fast.

'This is my brew, my dear Cyclades. My elixir. This is how I go on. I drink this and my essence is transferred to my progeny and so I continue, but you? *You plague me.* You have no elixir. Yet you return to haunt me like a ghost that will not die. Every few hundred years, as regular as the setting of the sun and the seasons in the fields, you return. Time after time, after time. What is it you have, that I do not?'

'Soon you will not even have an empire. I have seen to that.'

Athanatos slapped him across the face. 'What have you done?'

Cyclades smiled and licked the blood from his split lip. 'I have written to Charlemagne. He guards my son. Even now he prepares to declare a new empire, a Holy *Roman* Empire that will displace yours. Get used to these Saracens, Athanatos. You will be forced to live among them.'

The voice that replied from the dark was feminine and sharp. 'No matter!'

'Mother.'

The Empress Irene strode in to join with her consort bearing a glowing dagger that had been fanned in the flames by a blacksmith. She handed it to Athanatos, who held it with some glee.

His mother kissed him on the cheek. 'No matter, my beloved son. You have grown to be quite a man, but in this life you are no threat and by the time you return, the world will have cycled round again, and you will be just as confused as before.'

Without warning and with savage brutality Athanatos drove the red-hot dagger into Cyclades' face, sliced around the sockets, and cut out both his eyes.

Gene stared bleakly at the puddle of fate that was his sperm sample; a cup of memories waiting to be sown. He snapped the lid in place and cleaned himself up with a tissue.

Megaera's scent still clung pungently to the air in his office; her will just as palpable as ever. He was to be the next Athanatos? She was a liar.

We are Cyclades.

LIFTING ILIUM'S VEIL

4.12 p.m.

He had no idea where Sixth Avenue was. North buried his aching head in his hands. The coloured lines of his Rand McNally map were mocking him. Quivering like the vibrating strings of a musical instrument. Threatening to abandon the sheet of paper entirely, forsake their purpose, and steal off without giving him any directions at all.

Just past Chatham the Taconic Parkway joined the I-90; a toll interstate that veered off towards Albany. It wasn't where he wanted to go. Troy was perhaps twenty minutes further north of the state capital, but from this side of the Hudson it was a more circuitous route to reach. Wasn't it?

At least, that was what the map was telling him. Perhaps. But then the map was telling him Troy itself was just a dot. How could he find his way around a dot? *I can't think. I have to sleep.*

His hands shook as he lifted the mug of strong dark coffee to his lips. It made him feel like a skel in cold turkey. The sweet rush of sugar brought a haze to his mind that helped his nerve, but the caffeine wasn't giving him the boost he wanted. He had no edge. The excitement of getting a lead was a faded memory. Finding the energy to see it through now seemed somehow impossible.

A taunting roar went up from the greasy black television set bolted to the wall up in one corner. *Do these games ever end?* The crowd didn't like that. He could feel them turning on him. The jeers of a hundred thousand Olympic spectators packed in and around the ancient monuments of Athens. They chanted a message meant only for him. They were disappointed. They expected more.

The wind and the rain outside rattled the window around his booth. Sheets of thunderous downpour drove across the busy road like sharpened blades cutting into the traffic. North staggered to his feet. He dug his hand into his pocket. He tried to pay but a cascade of coins bounced across the floor instead.

The waitress came over, a chewed-up yellow pencil stuck behind her middle-aged ear. She stooped to help him. She asked if he was okay but North declined to comment. Instead he mumbled, 'I just need directions.'

She took him over to the counter and pencilled the route in on his map. 'You needed to stay on this road,' she said. 'You join the I-90, then get on to the I-87 *north*, and take exit twenty-three. Okay? That takes you on to the I-787, and you take exit twenty-three into Troy.'

Wait a minute. Was she rattling this off fast or was he no longer capable of following? 'Exit twenty-three? You already told me to take exit twenty-three.'

The waitress patiently explained it all again. 'You take exit twenty-three *twice*.'

What?

She told him he should be careful. The weather channel was saying a storm was coming. Doesn't she ever look out the window?

As far as North was concerned it was already here.

4.41 p.m.

The brake lights of the cars in front bounced across his eyes.

It was a struggle just to stay on the road. He followed her directions as best he could. They turned out to be perfectly accurate. His exit off the I-787 put him directly on to Route 2, on the western banks of the storm lashed Hudson, and only a bridge and a few short blocks from Sixth Avenue.

The whole neighbourhood was a collection of well-maintained Victorian row and town houses. If they were in the city the rent would be through the roof. Somehow he doubted that was the case here. Like Poughkeepsie before it, the streets were disturbingly quiet. Despite the cars parked at the kerbs and in garages nobody was going anywhere.

He rolled slowly down Sixth Avenue and pulled up behind an old bronze 1981 Camaro. Whoever owned it wasn't much of an enthusiast. The decaying bodywork was infested with bubbling blisters of weeping rust and the tyres were bald. It was probably the only car they had ever owned.

As the rain bounced violently off the hood of his Lumina, obscuring his view of the street, he found the number for the Troy Police Department back across the river at fifty-five State Street and gave them a courtesy call that he was in the area.

Just talking to them helped focus his mind and clear that unwanted clutter that pressed in from the sides. They sounded eager. North figured they didn't have much to do. Did he want help with the witness?

It suddenly occurred to him, Cassandra Dybbuk had been a patient in psychiatric care. He had absolutely no idea what she'd been treated for.

He said he'd call back if he did.

God, I hope she's not violent.

He pulled the lapels of his coat up tight around his neck and with heavy feet trudged up the grey cement steps. He folded his map into a square and held it over his head while he searched for the doorbell. The button was an off-white ceramic set deep into an ornate though tarnished brass flower.

He couldn't hear it ring.

Under the arched front entrance was a set of aged mahogany double doors with insets of long clear glass and brass kick-plates. This certainly wasn't New York City. The metal bars were missing.

Autopilot. You can do this. When she comes to the door, just click it into autopilot.

He couldn't see anyone inside. He took a step back. There weren't any lights on. *Maybe she's still at work.* There was a bay window to his right. He leaned over the black wrought-iron hand rail and tried to peer in.

'May I help you?'

North took a moment to work out where the voice was coming from. Down at the side of the steps was another entrance that led to the yard at the back of the house.

The woman shielding herself with the door exposed just a little of her face. He could see her fingers where she gripped the painted wood. She wore heavy duty gloves that were caked in dark soil.

North came down the steps to her. 'Mrs Dybbuk?'

She seemed curious that she had a visitor, though it was tinged with some suspicion. He looked for some kind of familiarity in her features. A connection to the man he had confronted in the museum.

Her eyes were soft. Not like Gene's. Her skin was worn and pale. Her hair, which she obviously kept dyed darker than it naturally was, was exposed only in wisps from under a dark green headscarf that she kept tied under her chin. She was in her early fifties. She was certainly old enough to be Gene's mother.

North repeated the question, trying to not let his exhaustion make him sound sharp. 'You are *Cassandra* Dybbuk?'

'Yes. Sorry I took so long to answer the door. I was just doing some gardening.'

In this weather? North peered up through the pelting rain at the vault of the thundering sky.

She regarded him mildly. 'I have a greenhouse.'

Right.

'How can I help you?'

He kept the map above his head while he reached for his shield. 'Detective North, NYPD.' That was always enough to darken anyone's face.

'You're a long way from the city, detective.'

'I wanted to ask you a few questions – about your *son*.'

Her reaction was immediate. She pulled the door open a little wider. 'You've heard from Eugene?'

He was cautious. *Right name at least.* 'That depends.' He showed her the photograph. 'Do you recognize this man? Is *this* Eugene?'

There was fear in her eyes. She was frightened even to touch it. North couldn't fathom why. Did she recognize his face? Was it her son or wasn't it? Had he done something to her? He couldn't tell.

She made no attempt to remove her gloves. Instead she watched the water cascading down from his soggy map for a hat and said: 'Let's get out of the rain.'

Under the echo of the rain-hammered glass Cassandra Dybbuk's greenhouse was alive with scented blossoms, delicate flowers and a profusion of rich greenery.

North could barely keep a cactus alive.

The dizzying array along the workbenches left him feeling unsteady on his feet. He took a moment. The damp air was so clean. Despite his hemmed-in surroundings he breathed it in and felt a little freer than he had before.

A few plants North thought he recognized, an orchid and maybe a geranium amid the bustle of black plastic container boxes burgeoning with bulbs and shoots. For the rest he had to rely on reading the labels when there were any: delicate petals of gardenias, the white crowns of cyclamen and the eerily familiar spicy aroma of jasmine.

What's with all the jasmine? Jasmine at the museum. Jasmine here.

He complimented her on her work, but Cassandra Dybbuk was lost. She eventually removed one soiled glove and held the photograph of Gene in her slender, crinkled fingers. She ran the flat of her hand over the lines of his face.

'When was the last time you saw your son?'

She shook her head. *Is that a hint of regret?* 'Months. Years.'

Strange. What kind of mother wouldn't know exactly when and where she'd last seen her child?

'He *looks* the same. His hair's the same.' Her expression was becoming increasingly impenetrable. 'Those *look* like his clothes. And that birthmark by his eye?' She was caught in a moment in time. 'Eugene has one just like it.'

'So this *is* Eugene?'

Cassandra Dybbuk refused to consent. What was it that disturbed her so deeply? She set the photograph down and turned her back on it. 'So you say you like my plants? My son grew those ones right over there.' She pointed towards the small green plants at the far end next to some dying peas.

'They're very nice. What are they?'

'They're called heliotropes.'

'So you and he share the same passion?'

'Oh, no. I do it for the enjoyment. Gene is always experimenting. He reads everything he can lay his hands on. I don't know where he gets it from. One day he came in here and he said, "Mom, if de Mairan can do it so can I."'

'Who?'

'That's what *I* said. He explained he was a French scientist, I don't know. He told me all about it, but frankly I switched off, if you know what I mean?'

North understood. 'I'm not big on science. Whatever makes him happy, eh?'

'Did you know we have an internal clock? What did he call it? A circadian rhythm. It means if you or I were to spend any time in a dark room our body clock would run a little slower. We'd end up working on a twenty-*five* hour day if we couldn't see the sunlight.'

North didn't know that.

'It's funny the things you remember. The heliotropes were because he wanted to prove that plants have a sense of time, too. Every morning their stems and leaves unfold and point towards the sun. And every night they fold up again. I remember he put them in a box with a hood so only he could see inside.'

'And what happened?'

'They couldn't see the sun, but they still opened and closed, as regular as clockwork. He said to me, "Mom, that's what happens to our souls. We die and our leaves close up. We're reborn, and they open again."'

This is the right man.

Cassandra Dybbuk went back to the photograph. She picked it up carefully and handed it back to him. She said, 'That's not him.'

North felt the blow in his heels. 'What?'

'That's not my son. I *know* my own son and *that's* not him.'

Can't be. She's wrong. 'Are you sure?'

'Are you calling me a liar?'

There was anger in her eyes and a pair of garden shears only two feet away. He listened to the thudding of the rain and measured out his response to its beat. 'You know your son.'

'Yes I do.'

'I don't.' He looked at the photograph, its corners now so worn and ragged. He tucked it away inside his coat. 'Do you have any recent photographs of him I might take a look at, so I can see for myself?'

Her face instantly brightened. 'Of course. I think I'd like to show them to you.'

They came in through the kitchen. The wide hardwood floorboards out in the hall were as polished and dark as the wainscoting on the walls. They all appeared to be the original features to a well-ordered house that was not short of money. Perhaps too well ordered. This place felt nothing like the greenhouse. It was oppressive and claustrophobic.

The wallpaper was an endless chain-link grid of diamond shapes on a teal sea. A facet for every hidden fear. An army of eyes that bore into his soul. As she led him slowly up the hand-carved staircase North realized that there were very few pictures on the walls, and those were abstract bursts of colour and texture. No portraits. Everywhere was devoid of warmth and comfort.

North trod carefully. 'I was surprised to find you home today, Mrs Dybbuk.'

'Oh?'

'You have the day off work, or you got off early?'

As they reached the top of the stairs she hesitated. It wasn't a question she was comfortable answering. Without warning she paused, almost causing North to run into her. 'I don't work,' she explained.

'Really? What's your secret?

As Cassandra Dybbuk stepped up on to the landing North was met with a stony glare that sent a chill down the length of his spine. Her eyes betrayed her. Her sense of reason seemed misplaced. There was a watery quality to the paleness of her gaze. A minute inability to focus. In that one moment North saw beneath the veneer, to what had kept her in the institution. Underneath, something had cracked.

North stood at the top of the stairs, acutely aware of the

sudden drop behind him. He ran his fingers along the polished handrail and gripped it tightly. His knuckles were white. 'What I meant was, this is a great house. How do you keep it going?'

'They send me money once a month.'

They? 'Your ex-husband?'

'I was never married to him.'

'I see.'

She shuffled on down the hall as though nothing had happened. He had to be careful that his aching need for sleep wasn't forcing him into making convenient assumptions. Even so, North followed her only at a distance and was in no hurry to see what she revealed to him when she threw open a door to one of the bedrooms.

She beckoned him closer. He stood at the threshold and peered inside.

A small neatly made bed sat just by the door. The open closet at the far end revealed that most of the clothes were gone. The bookshelves were still filled with heavy tomes. And in front of the window a long worn wooden desk sat covered in grimy glass tubes and what appeared to be some dusty old fish tanks.

'This is your son's room?'

She stepped inside without turning on the light. 'It was. It's just a copy now.'

'This isn't how he left it?'

She pulled the long gardening smock that she wore tighter around her body. 'It's *exactly* how he left it,' she replied, upset.

North stumbled over his words. 'I don't understand.'

'I wouldn't expect you to.' She folded her arms defiantly. 'When he went away to college *they* came.'

North still wasn't following. Carefully he asked, 'Who?'

She was disgusted. Was it at him, or at what had happened? He couldn't tell and that was what frightened him the most. 'They were looking for something.'

'What were they looking for?'

'I don't think even they knew.'

The way she said it. *They.* Were *they* the ones that had picked Gene up in the car?

'They came when I was away. They tore the whole house apart from top to bottom.' Her words caught in her throat, tears welled in her eyes. She was sobbing, quietly at first, but then without control.

'That's terrible.'

'Those bastards. They went through everything. They even went through my underwear drawer. What did they want with my underwear?'

North could tell her a few stories. The pervert he'd caught breaking and entering with the vic's panties on his head and masturbating on her bed. Or the number of times he'd turned up at the crime scene to a burglary to find that the doer had taken a dump in the lounge.

'Did you file a complaint?'

'With who? Nobody cares.'

'Well, if they took something—'

'You want to know the sick part? When they were done? They put everything back *just the way it was.*'

'Exactly the same?'

'Exactly. Not a thing out of place. *Inch perfect.*' She sniffed back her tears and dried her eyes on her sleeve. 'But I'm not an idiot, detective. I knew they'd been in here.'

Is she paranoid or frightened?

'Was your son mixed up in something?'

'I got him into this, it's my fault.'

'How is it your fault?'

'Because I agreed to have him.'

This was a minefield but North had no choice. As gently as he was able he probed deeper than perhaps she was willing to go. But no gentle voice could soften what he had to ask. 'You wanted an abortion?'

Shame and guilt took her. She looked at her feet, shaking her head. 'I wanted the money.'

She had a kid for the money? For who? The father? This wasn't an interrogation, she didn't have to answer his questions, but he had so many. He pressed her further. 'Did Gene find out?'

She nodded, ashamed to look him in the eye.

'Is that why he left?'

'No,' she said. 'But it's why he never came back.'

'Do you ever hear from him?'

Her face suddenly brightened with the warmth of the memory. 'Oh yes, every now and then he telephones. It's so *good* to hear his voice. I want to talk for longer but he's always so busy. And he *always* sounds so sad.'

'Do you ever call him?'

She shook her head. 'I don't know the number.'

The phone company will. 'You didn't think to star sixty-nine him?' Again she was vague. 'What about his address?'

'I don't know where he is.'

She could be lying. 'Would you have any objection to me taking a look at your phone records?'

She seemed startled. 'I do if he's in any kind of trouble.'

As it stood, he didn't have a positive ID. That had implications. If he lied right now it would fall apart in court later on. 'I just want to make sure that he isn't.'

'Well, then, I suppose you can. If you think you really need to.'

North tried to sound friendly. 'That depends on what he looks like in his photograph.'

Her tension eased. She hinted at a smile and apologized for keeping him waiting. She ventured back out, intending to go and find the photographs she'd promised to show him. She said he was welcome to stay in Gene's room while he waited.

North thanked her. But as she got as far as the doorway she gripped the frame, her fingers nervously drumming on the wood. She turned to him and she said in a hushed voice, 'He said he would come and visit me once.'

'And he didn't show?'

'I'm afraid it was worse than that.' She cast a look over her shoulder. Her voice was haunted. She lowered it even further as if to stop herself from being overheard. 'They sent an imposter, you know?'

Did she couch it as a question because she thought it would make it sound more plausible? *An imposter?* 'How did you know?'

'He was a pleasant enough young man. Identical to my son in nearly every detail; he even mimicked his mannerisms. But he wasn't my son.' She looked around, making absolutely certain it was just the two of them. 'They think I don't know.' Her voice became a whisper. 'But I do.'

Cassandra Dybbuk left a vacuum in her wake. North couldn't identify her condition, and her instability haunted him. Only when he was certain she was gone, did he make the most of the opportunity.

He always kept a few things in his coat pocket for handling evidence but he didn't have time to put on the disposable latex glove. He pulled out his handkerchief instead and made straight for the glassware on the desk. What had Gene been working on?

He picked up one of the grimy convoluted tubes and held it up to the light. It revealed the faint familiar pattern of layered whorls and ridges.

Even if the physical evidence couldn't place the murder weapon directly in Gene's hand, there were a pile of unidentified prints on the glass fragments at the museum, and a positive ID would at the very least definitively place Gene at the crime scene. How many times had North sat in court and watched defence attorneys demolish surveillance evidence? He'd lost count. It was harder to argue against a fingerprint.

He didn't have any standard kit with him. No black latent powder and certainly no clear lifting tabs. He'd have to improvise. He pulled open one of the drawers. There was an old roll of Scotch tape. It was a start. He cursed the fact that he didn't smoke – if he could burn something, like the end of a pencil, the soot would stick to the print and he could lift it with the Scotch tape. He rifled through a few more drawers and went through the cupboards.

He found a candle and a book of matches. He had to hurry.

The first one wouldn't light. He panicked and tried again. The next failed strike seemed brighter than the first and destined to alert his host. He tried a third time. The sparks blossomed into a small yellow flame. He held it to the candle which produced a thin wisp of black smoke.

Quickly North held the flame beneath the glass tube and wafted it at the prints. Waiting for enough soot build up seemed to take forever.

He could hear Cassandra Dybbuk rooting around down the hall. Cursing as she dropped boxes and fought with stacks of clothing.

The seconds ticked by like thunderous heartbeats. He blew at the smoke, hoping to speed it up. The invisible was becoming visible. It was faint. It would have to do.

He blew the candle out and threw it in the desk drawer, tore off a piece of tape and pressed it to the exposed print. *One, two.* He peeled it away again, and used the excess end, doubling it over to preserve what he'd found.

He hurried to check it. The print was usable. He slipped it inside his coat pocket and suddenly felt a breath across his neck. He glanced quickly over his shoulder.

She wasn't there. *Now I'm paranoid.*

He stepped quietly up to the door and peered out. The unmistakable sounds of Cassandra Dybbuk still rummaging away echoed down the hall.

That suited him just fine.

North had never seen so many books on genetics and neurobiology. There were books on Mendel and his genetic discoveries using peas. North wondered if that explained the greenhouse. There were books on Watson and Crick's discovery of DNA; there were research papers by even more scientists he'd never heard of, Seymour Benzer and Eric Kandel. And long-drawn-out descriptions of how genes controlled both memory and time.

Gene had an interest in the workings of memory and time that went beyond fascination. It was obsession. One whole shelf was full of notebooks.

North plucked one at random. The pages were full of notes and neatly drawn pictures of glass boxes and tubes. Inside each contraption were hundreds of tiny black dots labelled *Drosophila*. They were fruit flies which, through a process of elimination using the glass tubes, Gene had sorted into strains that exhibited different mutations, while the dusty fish tanks were the farms he had once used in which they'd bred.

The entry in the journal read:

The sense of time is innate. It is the oldest of all our instincts. Every creature experiences it, every creature succumbs. Even bacteria with a lifespan that can be measured only in hours, pass on to their next iteration a perfectly calibrated sense of time. The signs within us are there for all to see. At 4 a.m. asthma strikes with its greatest fury. At 2 a.m, ulcers flare without mercy. At 1 a.m. death from surgery is almost a certainty. The body has a clock and our lives are slave to it.

North flipped through more pages, skipping whole swathes of

detailed notes until he came to another passage that was clear enough for him to understand. It described in intimate detail the physical workings of the biological clock.

> Within the nucleus of a nerve cell that sits within the brain, the Clock gene and the Timeless gene weave their proteins. When their armies have been raised these legions of proteins enter the nucleus and urge their kings to stop. They stand guard, resolute, until one by one these proteins reduce and decay. And the kings, left alone, receive word from a messenger, a third gene called the Cycle who bids them raise an army once more. This cycle takes twenty-four hours until it is repeated. This is what creates the sense of time. No gods involved here.

The notes continued, parts of them rambling, other parts clear and concise. If he understood them correctly, the Clock gene was 3,600 letters, or nucleotides, long. If a single letter was changed, it could have remarkable effects. Gene had discovered that if the 1766th letter that was normally a G was changed to an A the body clock ran *five hours faster.* But if the 734th letter, which was a T, was changed to an A, the body clock ran *five hours slower.*

Gene seemed to be looking for a way that the body clock could trigger other internal events. Most of it went straight over North's head. Gene by name. Gene by obsession.

Gene Dybbuk was far smarter and sharper than North had ever anticipated. He'd known what he wanted to look for, he'd gone out and he'd found it. Now, if his notes were to be believed, he was intent on repeating his success with *Drosophila* by peering into the essence of the human animal.

North put the journal back where he found it and hesitated about selecting another. How long had he been standing here? Cassandra Dybbuk had been gone a long while. Eventually the compulsion was too much. He went for the blue book on the shelf this time, the one on the end, the one in shadow.

He opened it up at the first page. It read: 'I am Satan's Oath.'

I am Satan's Oath? What did that mean? He'd said it at the museum and it didn't make sense then. What was Gene trying to tell him?

He opened up the second page, keen to see if there were any more clues to his thoughts.

The Bull stared back.

North was winded.

Thu-thump.

He wheezed. His throat constricted.

Thu-thump.

He staggered back, his knees buckled. He collapsed on the bed.

The pages of the blue book fluttered beside him. They taunted him.

The Bull.

Its breathing grew louder its heartbeat grew stronger.

His hand shook violently. His knee bounced up and down. *Thu-thump. Thu-thump. Thu-thump.* He looked around.

Cassandra Dybbuk was nowhere to be seen.

He wiped the sweat from his face; he looked at the book and he slammed it shut.

North got to his feet and paced up and down. The book in turn did nothing. It sat there.

What answers lay within its pages? What did it know that he did not?

What the fuck's going on?

What do I do with this?

What do I do?

He knew what he was going to do would change things for

ever. The shame already had him in its grasp. North snatched the book off the bed, stuffed it inside his coat pocket and in that moment was no longer a cop.

'No! No! No! No!'

The screaming rage from the room down the hall pierced the silence of the suffocating house.

North rushed out into the hall and made his way towards Cassandra Dybbuk's bedroom. He loomed in the doorway and watched her from there. She was sitting on the floor, beating her fists into a lockbox turned upright at her feet; hundreds of pictures had been tossed all around.

'They changed them! They changed them! They came back and they changed my pictures. Where's my baby boy? *Where's my baby?*'

She flung handfuls at the wall. One fluttered at his feet. He stooped to pick it up. It was without question Gene. It was his graduation photograph from Columbia University.

North didn't know what to do. He was barely in control of his own mind. He said, 'Mrs Dybbuk? Mrs Dybbuk, please calm down.'

But Cassandra Dybbuk was far from calm.

With tears rolling down her weathered face, she looked up at North and was horrified. She recoiled across the floor and curled up in the corner. 'What did you do with the detective? What did you do with him, you imposter.'

BOOK FIVE

ECHOES OF THE DEMON

8.27 p.m.

With the hot breath of the Bull an inferno on the back of his neck, he left her screaming in the bedroom.

Nothing he said would calm her down. Nothing he did made a difference. Her mind was made up, and he wasn't who he claimed to be.

The irony was, she was right. She saw him for who he really was. She saw beneath his mask. She saw his horns and he felt naked and exposed.

Should I call for a paramedic? No. He got the impression that they'd been out here a thousand times before. If they could do anything for her, they would have done so long before now.

He left the misery of Pandora's box behind him. Although he made certain that the front door was securely locked, he knew that he brought a pack of hounding ills with him, buried deep inside his coat pocket. He could hear the echo of four strong hooves at his back. The rain was heavier than he'd left it and the sky was much darker than before. Yet it did not dampen the reek of animal. The stench of rain-soaked hide and the sweet smell of coarse grass. The Bull was on top of him and he would not let him go.

North listened to the electrical buzzing of the streetlamp

overhead as it struggled to flicker into life. Under its spill he returned to his car and collapsed in the driver's seat feeling a little safer. But only a little. The shadows were circling.

North needed a drink.

He pulled away slowly, recoiling from unexpected movements, and drove carefully through the centre of the dead town looking for a bar and somewhere close by where he could park.

For twenty minutes he was successful only in uncovering one ancient Greek building after another, one Doric column after the next, and upon each one, the shadow of the Bull keeping pace with his journey, ever watchful, waiting for that moment when he might flee.

When he was greeted by the sight of an edifice that looked remarkably like the Temple of Athena, the Parthenon in Athens, that haunted every channel on television, the effect was as eerie as it was unsettlingly familiar, and for a moment, the Bull retreated.

As well as the brick buildings, all the signposts kept telling him he was in the home of Uncle Sam – Uncle Sam lived here. Uncle Sam died here. Uncle Sam was real? It was news to him. It seemed Uncle Sam was a meat packer named Samuel Wilson who had supplied troops during the war of 1812. Was Uncle Sam a Greek? That didn't make sense.

Troy was a town with an acute identity crisis. He knew how it felt.

He needed a bar. He found a spot on the corner of 4th Street and Fulton, right next to the Ilium building, and decided to walk from there. But no sooner was he out of the car than the Bull began following him in the windows along the way.

It wasn't long before North found a dark hole in which to take refuge. Its few gaudy lights were welcoming. Yet he knew even as he stole off out of the rain that the Bull, ever watchful, would be waiting.

*

North sat heavily at the small bar and slid a twenty across its surface. His fingers bounced on the dents and grooves in the aged wood and were soon damp from the spillage of old beer.

He asked for a whisky. Neat. He didn't care what kind just as long as it was the right colour and it set his throat on fire. Anything, just as long as it blocked out that animal.

The lone bartender was young. His hair was light and short. He wore a grey Rensselaer Polytechnic Institute T-shirt and kept himself hunched over a newspaper as he agonized through the crossword.

He didn't look up when he took North's money, and he wasn't in a hurry to serve him either. With the exception of three or four others, the bar was empty, the lights and the sound of the television were down low. Everyone liked it that way.

North rested on his elbows and watched the rain hammer down outside.

The bartender set his drink down on a white paper napkin and scuttled off to the far end of the bar where two other men were sitting.

He said, 'Nine down. Seven letters. The madness that is in a cult.'

'What?'

The one with the thick moustache asked, 'The madness that is in a cult? What kind of clue is that?'

'Got any letters?'

The one with the moustache took the paper from him and spun it around for a closer look. 'Something, Union, something, Adam, something, something, something.'

Union. Adam. Those were phonetics used only by cops.

North listened to them struggle over the answer until quite unexpectedly it came to him. He quietly lifted the paper napkin out from under his drink, took his pen and wrote it down.

He slid the paper napkin along the bar towards them. The

nearest of the three picked it up and read it out loud. 'Lunatic?'

North slugged back his drink and set the glass down heavily on the bar. 'Sorry for interfering.'

The young bartender didn't seem to mind. He ran his pen over the crossword with relish. 'It fits.'

'I don't get it.'

The man nearest North understood. 'It's an anagram; the madness that is *in a cult*. Lunatic.' He raised his glass to North in salute. 'Thanks, buddy.'

North nodded politely but he couldn't make eye contact. The man's smile seemed to lift to his ears and his skin seemed a devilish red under the glow of the Budweiser neons. North slid his glass forward. He demanded another drink.

While the college kid fixed it for him, the man at the end of the bar lit a cigarette. He tossed the match into his empty glass and swirled it around in the bottom. His eyes were slits as he peered through his own smoke. 'You just been out to the Dybbuk house?'

North felt the touch of creeping anxiety. How did *he* know? Cassandra Dybbuk's insane ramblings were still fresh in his mind. *Is he one of them?*

North stole a quick look. The satanic man with the cigarette flipped his fingers around his chest by way of explanation and nodded at him.

North looked down. His gold shield was still on display. He sighed and tucked it out of sight.

The demon with the cigarette came over and sat down next to him. 'Roy. Roy Conner.' He pointed out his partner at the end of the bar still helping out on the crossword and stroking his moustache as he pondered the clues. 'Central said you called the station house. Up from the city?'

North nursed his drink. 'Yes.'

Roy Conner shook his head. He knew all the signs. 'That crazy old bird. Man she's nuttier than a fruit cake. Hey, did she do that thing where you're standing in the room and she suddenly says you're some kind of clone? Ask ya what ya did with the real cop who came to see her?'

North admitted that she did.

Roy Conner wasn't surprised. 'I don't think no one drove her crazy, it's a condition.' He flicked the smouldering ash from his cigarette. 'Hey, A.J., what did that, uh, that head doctor say Cassandra Dybbuk had?'

His partner didn't even look up from the paper. 'Capgras syndrome.'

'Yeah, that's the one. Everything and everyone's been replaced. Y'know she even filed a missing person's report on her son that last time he came back from college to see her? She refused to believe he was the real deal.'

North tried to find some enthusiasm. 'When was that?'

'Oh, must have been six, seven years ago. Poor bastard. Had to go to a motel. Lemme tell ya, he started out a good kid. She tell ya what she did to him?'

'No.'

'Yeah, I bet she didn't. She forget to tell ya about the time she thought he was more than just an imposter?'

North was loath to ask what happened but he couldn't help himself.

'She comes into his room at three in the morning, convinced he's a robot. Her 17-year-old kid. Tries to open up his head with a tyre iron looking for all the microchips. I think that's how he got that job down in the city: susceptible stock. One too many self-experiments.'

'What job?'

'I dunno. Brain stuff. Whatever. That kid's had it rough.'

North slugged the last of his second whisky. 'I don't care how rough he's had it. I'll nail him.'

Roy Conner was intrigued. 'What he do?'

'Killed a cop.'

'Holy fuck.' Satan snuffed out his cigarette, hardly surprised by the turn of events. 'Yeah, well, the apple never falls far from the tree.'

10.54 p.m.

A motel. That sounded like a good idea. The bartender told him about the Super 8 a block away on the corner of 4th Street and Grand. The room was forty-five bucks for the night.

He paid cash at the front desk, asked for a receipt and slowly made his way up to the second floor.

He heard nothing. That alone gave him pause. Had he lost him? Had he broken free? By the time North collapsed on to the cheap bed he'd been awake for more than forty-one hours. Still he was afraid to go to sleep.

He could feel the sharp corners of the blue book inside his coat pocket, digging into his ribs, refusing to give. With trepidation he reached inside to pull it out and flung it across the room. He heard its impact. He heard it land. He couldn't bring himself to look at it. Not at first. But when the minutes decided that they would not tick by he felt the glare of the blue book staring at him from across the void. It knew things. About him. Secret things.

Things that even he didn't know.

The blue book drew North to the edge of the bed and goaded him. He kicked at the table that held it but it never blinked. The blue book was the one in control.

North would see about that. He pulled himself to his feet and watched his fraught features in the mirror as he got undressed. He ripped his tie from his throat and threw it down in disgust. A button pinged across the room as he struggled to remove his shirt.

What were those red marks on his forehead? Two red protrusions. He touched them. They were sore. He tried to ignore them.

He flipped the light off and he dragged the covers up around his neck. His eyes flickered with his prayer for sleep. His tongue sank deep into his throat, constricting his breathing. He turned on to his side.

That was when he heard the rattling of the door.

They tried the handle first. Had they followed him from the bar? North was certain of nothing except the cold metal of his gun on the bedside table.

He put out his hand into the darkness but could find nothing there. He sat up. The light seeped in under the door where the shadows of hesitant feet were dancing.

North slipped out of bed. They tried the handle again. It twisted and turned but it would not give. The scraping of metal implements soon joined the play upon the lock. It wouldn't be long now.

North probed again at the bedside table. Where was his gun? The door rattled impatiently. They were getting nowhere and it was unacceptable. He could hear voices as they reviewed their options. A dull thud followed next, a shoulder, then a heavy boot.

They had come for Cassandra Dybbuk and now they were coming for him. Well, they were in for a surprise. He wasn't a helpless old woman. He grabbed the chair that stood in the corner. He raised it up to his chest, the legs sticking out like pikes. North cried out into the darkness. 'I'm warning you! I'm armed!'

The rattling did not stop. There was no hesitation. No fear. His threats were meaningless. The door was going to open whether North agreed to it or not.

Thu-thump. Thu-thump.

The bellowing and the snorting were going to get him whether he was ready or not. Whether he fought it or not.

The door shattered before him, its splinters showering his

feet. Head bowed, eyes ablaze the Bull had come and was here to claim his soul.

Swollen tangles of rippling muscle undulated across his terrifying, powerful shoulders as he poked his head inside the door. His horns, sharp as razors, sawed through the wooden doorframe as he forced his brutish way inside.

North's legs buckled and his arms shook. The Bull saw him and was enraged. He charged, sweat dripping from the lustre of his thick black coat. North screamed, smashing the chair across the angry beast's heavy brow. He leaped on to the bed but the Bull was not content to circle.

He bucked his head atop his mighty neck and reared up after him. His dusty hooves crashed through the stuffing of the mattress.

North struggled to get away, caught in the springs and the mayhem. He screamed and kicked and rolled across the floor. He bolted from the room but the horns were close behind.

The horns were dipped and deadly. The horns were coming for him bearing their promise of savage blood lust in a swirl of blackened spite.

North ran down the hall, his chest alive with the fire of frenzy. But inch for inch half a ton of angry animal closed in and gave him no room to spare.

The terrible thunder of stampeding hooves deafened him. The spray of hot spittle bursting from his gnashing mouth soaked his back. The cloud of dust which filled the hall choked him. The agony of the rage that claimed his prize.

The Bull sunk his horns deep into North's flesh and tossed him into the wall. He clattered to the ground, his body a mess of aching bones. The Bull kicked and bellowed, stamping his hoof, demanding that he get back up. North cowered on the ground and tried desperately to crawl away. The Bull angrily ploughed his horns once more into North's hide and drove deep furrows down the centre of the floor. The carpet ripped. Its bloody fibres veins and mangled sinew.

And when he was done he flung him again. North crashed into the mirror at the end of the hall and sprawled across the intersection. In the shattered pieces of glass he caught a glimpse of his broken face, of the red mounds that were sprouting from his forehead.

North looked up. The Bull's black tail swished back and forth while his gimlet eyes bored into him. He dug his hoof in hard and rough and dipped once more to charge.

North leaped up and, grabbing both horns with agile hands, somersaulted over the charging beast. It shook him off with unbridled fury but North landed on both feet and ran.

The Bull slammed into the wall. His body rippled with the severity of the impact. Reduced to his knees he scrambled to regain ground. He was winded but would quickly recover.

He wheeled around but North was faster. The labyrinth stretched before him but his wounded prey was already in hiding.

Into the depths he fled, into the maze of tunnels and doors. North listened to the breathing that echoed from wall to wall. The magnificent power of the brute that hunted him, fleet of foot and sure of purpose. He was close and he would not submit.

North scrambled to find his way, to find some method of saving himself from the wrath of this horned vengeance. What had he done to raise its ire? What could he do to stop it?

His feet were leaden. His arms without power. His chest heaved to meet the unreasonable, impossible demands of breathing.

He rounded the corner. The Bull stood before him. Waiting. He changed direction. The Bull was there, too. Inexorable and eager to charge. Whatever avenue North chose, there it stood. Impassable. Unavoidable.

North threw open the nearest door. He was met with a wall of dusty stone blocking his path, denying him freedom. He pounded his fists on the unyielding surface. He clawed at the mortar until his nails were torn and bloody. And when he was exhausted and left only with his despair for company, the horns of the Bull drove through from the other side of the stone and cracked the bones of his chest.

Punctured, North collapsed to the ground, clutching at his ragged wounds. Immobile, he could do nothing but stare in terrified torment as the stone shuddered and collapsed and the Bull climbed through, shaking off the dust of defeat.

He bucked and he bellowed and he snorted. He took one immense hoof and drove it down, burying it into North's chest, cracking and pulverizing the feeble human bone. He dipped his immense head and shook it with furious might, hooking his horns and lifting up each one of North's ribs, peeling them back one by one, exposing the bloody mess within.

Still the Bull was not satisfied.

Unable to breathe, unable to move, North was forced to watch the beast jam his uncompromising snout deep into his organs and ram his head into his spine. He kicked and mutilated and bathed in his blood.

He dug a hole and he climbed inside.

The Bull was within him. The Bull was rampant. The Bull could not be quelled. He felt the pressure inside his head and felt the horns smash through the bone of his skull.

North wept. Wept so much that he drowned. Drowned so much that he could not hear himself screaming.

1.06 a.m.

North awoke spluttering on the grey cement steps in the emergency stairwell of the Super 8. The dousing from the fire hose was freezing and relentless.

He struggled to breathe. He held his hand up and begged them to stop. It took a long while for the fire hose to be switched off.

He focused on the sound of its dripping and through painful eyes peered up to see the night manager from the front desk looming over him.

Between his legs and through the door North saw the motel hallway beyond. The room doors were open wide, unnerved guests using them as shields as they watched him.

North didn't know what to say. He shivered and tried to stand upright. He slipped and fell against the wall. The night manager was not sympathetic.

'Get yourself cleaned up,' he said. 'And get out.'

North nodded. It was the least he could do.

4.47 a.m.

The hammering on the door was loud and impatient.

Lost in the darkness, Porter stirred from his fitful sleep in his room at the Pennsylvania. He struggled to find the switch for the bedside lamp and sat for a moment to collect his bearings.

The hammering would not stop. He squinted at his watch. Perhaps it was a fire alarm.

Porter pulled his thin white T-shirt down to meet his underwear and made his way over to the door. He peered through the small cracked lens of the spy hole.

A man was standing outside in a long soaked raincoat. He appeared agitated but in no hurry to leave. He would wake Porter's neighbours with his unwelcome racket if he stood there any longer.

Dubiously, Porter slid back the bolt and cracked opened the door to the visitor. 'Yes?'

The man in the coat shuffled on his feet. Porter could hear his laboured breathing. His gait was unsteady. *Is he on drugs?*

It was difficult to tell, but at this hour the likelihood was high. Perhaps it had not been wise to open the door.

It was only when the man shuffled into profile that Porter felt the first glimmer of recognition. He pulled the door open and peered at his dishevelled guest. 'Detective North?'

The detective's face was awash with confusion and ripe with desperation. He carried a blue book with him. His eyes announced that he was fighting for sanity as he raised the book up to show Porter and opened it at the first page.

Porter recoiled as the book was thrust in his face. Cautiously, he edged back to read it.

Coldly, the writing proclaimed: 'I am Satan's Oath'. Underneath, in different ink, had been posed the question: 'Am I Athanatos's?'

North's limbs shook, his fingers trembled as he took back the book and tried unsuccessfully to close its fettering pages and deposit it back into his coat pocket. He was lost and he did not know what to do.

Porter believed him when he pleaded, 'Please help me.'

IN SEARCH OF A SOUL

They never did let him go.

When Gene arrived, cup in hand, they offered him an opportunity to learn more. It was a powerful seduction. They knew his Achilles' heel well. Though his urge was to flee, his fascination could not be conquered. Long into the night he followed the activities of Lawless's scientists amid their Petri dishes and test tubes. A drop of his well-mixed specimen was placed into the centre of a Makler Counting Chamber, a small round metal device which kept Gene's spermatozoa sandwiched between two sheets of glass where they were still free to wiggle and writhe, but not escape.

Under microscopic magnification they appeared large on the monitors, like pallid tadpoles. The flagellum of each one, the tails that moved in frenzied whipping motions propelling each chariot of DNA forward, did so in healthy zigzag patterns. A few swam in weak straight lines. But many were malformed.

Despite that, the sample was declared good and half was placed in storage. An indigo coloured metal vat cooled by liquid nitrogen was rolled out. A wheel of test tubes was extracted, the oldest sample removed and unceremoniously discarded and the newest sample added. Gene had been busy for well over two years and he remembered it.

All this so they could peer deep inside a single reproductive cell and pull apart the twenty-three individual chromosomes it possessed. And yet Gene still didn't see how those chromosomes contained his memory.

'What are you thinking now, my boy?'

Gene had not expected to find Lawless here. He said, 'I was wondering where my soul came from.'

Lawless handed him his ebony walking cane while he slipped into a starched white lab coat.

Gene held the cane with fascination. *We could hit him.* The ornate metal end was weighty. *One blow to the head.*

Lawless was amused by the quandary facing his heir apparent. 'Such a simple question.'

'I still don't know the answer.'

'To date *no one* has succeeded in answering it, despite all this science and all this religion. Doesn't that strike you as a little remiss?'

Cane in hand, Gene asked, 'Does it strike *you?*' There were several guards within easy reach of him. *We'd never make it.*

Lawless held out his palm in silence. After a moment of hesitation, Gene handed the cane back dutifully.

'Not today, it would appear.'

Lawless leaned heavily on the cane and led Gene around the bench to behold the large laboratory at work. An army of his scientists worked in the harsh light of clinical sterility, glancing furtively at Gene in between their procedures and experimentations. It was unnerving.

'By any definition wouldn't you say that your little soldiers are alive? They move do they not? They possess an instinct to hunt and to breach walls.'

'They can't survive on their own. Only one endures through the moment of conception.'

Lawless cracked his cane on the hard marble floor. 'Ah the *moment* of conception. And how long is that moment? A second? A minute? *Two?*'

Gene dug his hands into the familiar deep pockets of his own white lab coat. His response was clipped. 'Twenty-four to forty-eight hours.'

'This *moment* of conception takes *two days*? And where is the soul in all that time, just hanging about? Floating in the ether twiddling its ethereal thumbs?'

'The creation of life is not a light switch. Even once a sperm has entered an egg, it can remain separate from the egg's genes for over a day. I don't know about the soul.'

'Perhaps you don't know about a soul because you don't have one?'

'Then I have you to thank. I thought transference of the soul is what we were trying to achieve.'

The barb caused several scientists within earshot to wince. It garnered an altogether different response from Lawless. He smiled. 'I see you *are* a worthy choice. But don't be too brash, my boy, this can all change.'

'What are you afraid of? Anarchy?'

'Oh, nothing so vulgar. Merely a little death.' He jabbed his cane at Gene. 'We have rules. We have an ordered system that has served us well for many centuries. In time it will serve you.'

Gene said nothing. Lawless clearly did not know what Savage had told him, that his ordered system was not working. Megaera joined them at the far end of the workbench. While Lawless calibrated the machinery to his personal settings, she distributed sheets of paper with strings of numbers and intricate diagrams.

Her long thick fiery hair was tucked inside a net. She gave Gene a curious smile that he recognized as she went about her business. It made him uneasy. It was as though she didn't know him. She said, 'We've encountered over three million sites in Gene's DNA that vary from his last sample. His encoding process is still fully functional despite his recent hiccups.'

The mutation rate in the human genome was five times higher in men due to constant sperm production. Were these mutations part of how memories were encoded?

'Excellent.' Lawless did not look up from the results. 'Tell me, Gene, what on earth would happen if, disaster of disasters, *more* than one of your sperm were to enter an egg? How many souls would be created then do you think?'

'The egg naturally rids itself of all the extra genetic material until one set of male chromosomes remains to merge with its own.'

'Ah, but what if one embryo decides to *split into several embryos* creating, for example, identical twins? What of the soul then? Do twins get half a soul each? Or merely one which they are forced to pass back and forth like a football?'

'I don't know.'

'You don't know.' Lawless did not sound convinced. 'Let's try something a little easier. What happens in those instances where two embryos become *one* person. Twins merging into the singular. A grotesque chimera. Does that creation receive *two* souls? Does he become a roaring chorus? Is the singular identity of his cell tapestry but an illusion? Is he no more than a man with a multiple personality?'

Us? Does he mean us? Gene felt the chill in the depths of his bones. 'I think he might.'

'You *think* he might? Yes. There's the rub. The truth is, all this talk of a soul is utter nonsense. *You* were defined in all your glory long before you encountered *any egg*.'

Lawless redirected Gene's attention to his specimen still displayed on one bank of screens. He regarded it triumphantly. 'This microscopic mess, this string of amino acids,' he remarked with eagerness, '*this* is your soul. This is the life you forged in chains.'

Lawless tapped his cane impatiently between his legs, perched as he was on a stool overlooking the slick controls of his devices. 'Letha, are we ready yet?'

The woman didn't answer. Clearly from her activities she was not ready. Gene watched her closely. She was double- and triple-checking everything. As she did so her twin came to stand beside her and help her with her tasks.

Megaera and Letha were identical in almost every way. The same fiery hair, the same resolute face. Did it just stop at two? Had he been caught by a procession of flame-haired women, believing them to be just one? In this mirrored place it was more than likely. He spoke to the one Lawless called Letha and he saw that there was a cloud in her eyes; a dull disconnection. That, he realized, is what set her apart from her sister.

'*Before*. You were the woman with the scent swabs when I came back,' he said.

Letha smiled wistfully. 'I was?'

'You're not Megaera.' He watched Megaera carefully as she assisted Letha in her work. She knew his eyes were on her and she enjoyed the attention.

Letha's warmth seemed fickle, but permanent. 'No, I'm not,' she said. 'Though something tells me you're a little obsessed with our sister. I can't put my finger on it, but it's there.'

Gene ignored the comment. He was fixated. 'You're very quiet, Megaera.'

Megaera did not look up. 'I'm very amused. I'm so glad we've grown closer together these past few days.' Only now did she make her move. 'Did you hear, Father, what Gene and I did this afternoon?'

She's going to belittle us. Stop her. 'It was nothing.'

'Nothing? We worked out our differences. I thought you would have appreciated the helping hand. Father? Why must I always clean up after Gene's messes?'

Lawless was focused on his task with ruthless single-mindedness. Their petty exchanges did not interest him. His response was flat and cold. 'Because that's your job.'

Neither Gene nor Megaera was satisfied with his reply.

Gene took his seat. 'How close are you to proving my CREB linked hypothesis?'

Megaera's face was thunder. '*Your* hypothesis?'

'I am to be the next Athanatos, we are all splinters of his tree. It's as much mine as anyone else's. Perhaps more so.'

Lawless found great mirth in the exchange, much to his daughter's dismay. It was exactly as Gene had anticipated.

The more he emulated the old man's relentless arrogance, the more he mirrored his condescending attitude, the more he won his trust. Lawless bade Gene to participate in the procedure.

Just as a surgeon guides micromechanical forceps and scalpels through endoscopes to perform intricate keyhole surgery, so Lawless used laser tweezers and laser scissors – highly focused beams of light which trapped molecules and cut their fate-filled bonds – to begin his manipulation of Gene's DNA as though it were an anagram strung out on lengths of twine.

Gene found that he knew instinctively which genes inhabited which chromosomes, and Lawless was concerned with the five hundred or so dedicated to personality and their intertwined function with memory.

It was a world he could see in his mind's eye as clearly as though he were there.

The interactions between the myriad of memory-forming molecules in the mind was a process worthy of the greatest Olympic relay race ever staged. Instead of the Hippodrome, the hippocampus was its arena and the race to memory began when a stressful moment of tension clung to the air. A moment to which the body responded by releasing a hormone.

That was the starting gun. The race was on.

In the first lane was vasopressin, with epinephrine coming up on the inside. The neuron receptor was in sight.

Baton change!

The hormone bound itself to the receptor and now cyclic-AMP was in the race, running for glory, running for memory. From the surface of the cell cAMP carried the baton, racing around the inside of the wall. Ahead of him his relay partner was waiting and ready. Jumping up and down, keeping limber. He had a mouthful of a name, cAMP Response Element Binding protein – CREB.

But there were *two* of him, CREB activator to create memories and CREB repressor to forget! Together he and his brother sealed the fate of memory, but which race was cAMP running? The cell nucleus was in sight.

Baton change!

CREB *activator* was away! Down the winding ropes of DNA CREB hunted for a partner, but in this race he had many, for CREB had a secret. CREB was an admiral. CREB had a navy.

One by one he selected his shipbuilders, genes that came to life at his command, and one by one they gave their messenger RNAs the blueprints for the proteins they were to go and build.

Baton change!

The sailors went to work! Running the lengths of the neurons, heaving to the ropes that tightened the bonds between them, they defined the pathway according to CREB's plan until the sails of memory were unfurled

It was with memory set in flesh that CREB hoisted his baton aloft. It was with memory made permanent that the race was won.

And yet for Lawless it was not yet won. For Lawless there was another mechanism that defined him and those around him as the facets of Athanatos. Not only did CREB command from the glorified telephone exchange, the great memory switching station that was the hippocampus; CREB also issued orders from deep within the hypothalamus, the capital of the sexual empire.

In the hypothalamus, where sexuality was defined, the mysterious workings of the circadian cycle, the thundering body clock to which all are slave, also ticked out its rhythm, day by inexorable day. It was here, only when the body was under the influence of daylight, that CREB received his orders.

Megaera's theory stated that somewhere in the hypothalamus CREB or one of his lieutenants sent out a second navy to order and structure memories, but this time it was sent on a different journey, to the staging post where sperm was created.

This was the process Gene was witnessing, the transference of Athanatos' memories from a dormant state encoded in his DNA, to a living state made vital by CREB in his mind, overriding any other personality that resided there.

But the more he watched the more Gene became aware of another process. A systematic hunt. And as Gene sat there, he realized what it was Lawless was looking for; the trigger that would make all this imprinting, the centuries of elixir and the years of laboratories unnecessary. He was searching for the man who had the trigger to eternity buried in his genome already. He was searching for Cyclades.

Gene realized, if he possessed Athanatos' memories, but also Cyclades' trigger, then that explained the voices in his head; the ultimate battle waging war in his scarred mind. Gene was a hybrid in turmoil, a conjoined soul being ripped apart.

Yet should they find what Cyclades possessed in the many samples Gene had given, he, and *the process* he was undergoing, would be entirely expendable.

REAWAKENING

Friday.

'Where are you?'

Good question. North kept his Nextel pressed close to his ear. Delicately he dragged himself up. He was in bed, fully clothed except for his shoes.

What's the time?

Sharp pains surged through his head. He wasn't at home. An old man dressed only in a T-shirt and his underwear sat fast asleep on a chair in the corner, his towel for a blanket had slipped quietly to the floor in the night. *Porter.* What made him turn to Porter? Instinct or desperation? *Maybe a little of both.*

A cocktail of Nyquil and sleeping tablets sat on the bedside table. They were a powerful tranquillizing combination that made him suspect that the sleeping old man was a little wiser than he was.

The spill of ugly daylight glowed brightly behind the curtains. It hurt his eyes. 'What time is it?'

'Noon,' Martinez replied. North listened to the fury of the squad room behind him as the young detective went about his business. He added, 'The Chief Medical Examiner's Office's been trying to reach you all morning. I'm just passin' on the message. Sheppard said it's pretty urgent.'

Blood and urine results. 'Does he want me down there?'

'No just give him a call.'

'What else have you got?'

'Video tapes.'

North felt the flood of relief. 'The DOT came through?'

Martinez didn't sound so excited. 'Yeah, now I just got to go through them all.'

'How many did they send?'

He heard the rattling plastic cassettes being stacked roughly and counted. 'Fifteen. Twenty.'

North didn't envy him the task.

'What *you* got?'

'I have a name.'

That was the trigger for Martinez. 'Really?'

North's joints ached; his muscles were stiff and uncooperative. Gingerly he swung out of bed clutching the phone and without thinking gave up the details. 'Eugene Dybbuk. Formerly of Sixth Avenue, Troy, New York. University of Columbia alum.'

North recognized the sound of tension in the younger man's throat – the quick grasp of cold resentment. 'You been busy. You got a positive on that?'

This was what North had been afraid of. He had his own demons to contest with. He didn't need another man's too. Tentatively, North fished for the Scotch-taped fingerprint he'd lifted and kept in one of his coat pockets. It was still there. 'I have to run something over to Jamaica, but I'm ninety, ninety-five per cent certain.'

Martinez was firm. 'I'll go with that percentage.' *I bet you will.* 'If I get time I'll take a trip down to the campus, see what I can dig up.'

'Go easy, yeah?' Martinez didn't respond to the warning. 'Hey, and sign me in?'

'Already taken care of. See? Working with a partner ain't so bad.'

'Sure.'

'You coming in today?'

North turned his attention to Porter who was still fast asleep in the chair.

'Yes,' North replied uneasily. 'I just have to take care of something.'

He hung up feeling more disoriented than he had before. He listened to the restless sound of Porter's breathing and paged through the menu system on the phone for the OCME number. The switchboard put him on hold. It was not for long.

Sheppard came swiftly on to the line. 'How are you feeling?'

North didn't like the question or the seriousness with which it was being asked. 'Fine.'

'Any lingering nausea? Dizziness?'

'A little.'

'Vomiting?'

'Yes.'

He could hear Sheppard scribbling something on a piece of paper. 'Look, I recommend you go back and see your doctor. The results were a little, how can I put this, concerning.'

'How concerning?'

'Rolipram.'

North was none the wiser. 'Never heard of it.'

Sheppard said he would be surprised if he had. 'It's a failed antidepressant that was being worked on in the nineteen eighties.'

'A 20-year-old drug?' North scratched around for something to take notes on. 'How would anyone get their hands on that?'

'There are a few drug and biotech firms working on it again. It transpires it's a powerful memory enhancer. A high level of Rolipram will induce vomiting. The other side effects are not quite as benign.'

North wrote it down, repeating it out loud to check the spelling as he went. 'What else did he put in me?'

'A very nasty cocktail. Some herbal remedies; the list is extensive. Some of these are *nowhere near* ever meeting FDA approval.'

'Do you think Gene's an amateur or a working professional?'

Sheppard couldn't decide.

'These herbal remedies. Can you get them from an ordinary health food store?'

'Depends on the store but anything's obtainable. You were injected with a *vast* dosage of ma huang, for example. That's freely available even though the Food and Drug Administration has classified it as an herb of, quote: undefined safety.'

North jotted that down too. 'Ma huang?'

Porter stirred from his chair in the corner. 'Ephedrine.'

North glanced over to see the tall gaunt Englishman looking faintly embarrassed that he wasn't covered up better. Porter said nothing further; he looked like he didn't even know where to begin. Instead he set about getting dressed.

Sheppard's curiosity got the better of him. 'Who's that?'

'William Porter,' North explained. 'He's a psychiatrist helping me on the case.'

There was a shift in Sheppard's attitude. Was it the sound of relief? 'Then he'll be able to tell you,' he said. 'You should have been taken straight to the hospital the day this happened. It's a minor miracle you didn't slip into a coma.'

North thought it through. He was barely functioning. *Maybe I did.* 'Where could someone get a hold of ma huang in the city?'

'Chinatown. I can't think of anywhere else you can lay your hands on some of these things. And the suppliers there are eager and silent. Listen, I'm having the results faxed over to you now—'

'Can you put it in an e-mail? I'm out of the squad room.'

'Sure.'

Before North hung up, Sheppard urged him for the second time to see his doctor again.

Sure, like I have time for that.

North gave Porter his full attention. The two men sat uncomfortably in each other's silence. It wasn't what North wanted. When he kept himself active, when he kept the questions alive and frequent, he felt marginally in control. The silence was when the memories came flooding back, the bitterness and the guilt.

On the desk beside the Englishman sat the collection of coloured journals; Gene's dusty blue book was on top, Porter's reading glasses were folded neatly on top of that. What did he think of it?

North clutched his phone between both hands, conscious of the bed and the medication that had helped him to rest properly for the first time in days. He gave Porter a humble gesture of thanks. He couldn't find the words to accompany it, his shame and embarrassment wouldn't allow it.

Porter finished tucking in his shirt and politely let him know that he was welcome.

North felt overwhelmed. He couldn't look the older man in the eye.

Porter waited patiently but North would not move. He sat back down and scrutinized the detective in every detail. He knew the signs. 'You're angry.'

'Yes.'

'How long have you been angry?'

North was resigned to the answer. 'All my life.'

'All of *this* life.'

North wasn't ready. He drew back across the bed. 'Please, don't.'

'If you burn your hand it's no use blaming the fire; it's just being true to its nature. The source is what feeds the flame. Would you agree?'

North didn't know how to.

'Can you place *why* you're so angry?'

'No.'

'You must have thought about it.'

'It's just one of those things.'

'And what if it isn't?'

'I don't want to think about it.'

Porter sat forward. 'You asked for my help. My help *requires* you to think about it.'

North would not answer.

'Do these feelings frighten you?'

Yes. Is that so wrong? North drew breath, deep and slow.

'The problem,' Porter observed keenly, 'is that you spent your time running from this. And now that it's caught up with you, you don't know how to deal with it.'

Running from the Bull. Running from the animal. Is that what I truly am? North needed an answer. 'Is the Bull a symbol?'

'No. It's very real.'

It's real? Then what does it mean?

'Think,' Porter urged. 'Is *that* really where you're most afraid to go?'

No, there was one other place that frightened him more deeply than that. North struggled to find his voice. 'Am I Athanatos?'

The wait for an answer was a long and painful one. 'No.'

That was not what he had expected to hear. *No.* He met the psychiatrist's gaze head on. 'How can you be so certain?'

'I can't. Why do you think that you *are?*'

Eating a child's cooked flesh? Watching bodies burn on a pyre? *Swimming up to my neck in the blood of the innocent?* What possible need did he have to remember all of that if it was not because of some inner darkness over which he had no control?

North felt the haunting chill of memory wash over him. It did not cleanse but corroded.

'I smell evil. I *taste* evil.'

'To know evil is not to *be* evil.'

'How do you know?'

'Because it's all in here.' Porter pinched the flesh of his sagging arm. 'And here.' He drew his finger to his temple. 'And *here*. Written in the thread of our flesh, like a ball of unravelling yarn that stretches back through time, *we* are its frayed end. Loose strands that when woven together create the whole. You and I are shades of the same person. Fragments of one soul.'

'I'm not related to you.'

'I can assure you you are. Your blood and mine are branches of the same mighty river – our streams simply diverged a very long time ago, but the memories are within each of us. Sporadically they can be thrown back up, such as in my case. Or they can be enforced, such as in yours. But you and I, though strangers now, have the same genetic origin.

'We share a grandfather from over four hundred years ago. From that moment back our history is the same. How we remember it is the same.

'We are the same man.'

CHINESE WHISPERS

1.28 p.m.

North couldn't take it. *Doesn't this place have air conditioning?* His collar was soaked. He tasted the acidic bite of bile in his throat. *Six feet to the door.* He struggled to keep it down. *Two steps.* He was out.

Porter pursued him out on to the sidewalk.

It was trying to rain but the furnace had returned, reducing everything to steam. A charge clung to the yellow air. The greasy haze infected the streets like a sickness. It burned the concrete in every direction.

North searched for his car keys. 'First I have memories of lives I didn't know I'd lived and now you're telling me I'm not even a complete person. I'm a fragment?'

'I understand this is difficult.'

North tried to laugh it off. He yanked open the door. 'Sure.'

Porter climbed into the passenger side and fastened his seat belt. North didn't object; he drove out into traffic and joined the flow towards downtown.

North's knuckles were white when he gripped the steering wheel.

'Do you know how old my mother is?'

Porter shook his head.

'Fifty-six. She gave birth to me when she was twenty-two. It was my Dad's second year on the job. I've seen pictures of her with her long dark hair and wearing this short, tight candy cane dress. 'She was—' *Hot?*

He could hear her moaning. He could see her contorted and alive with pleasure. He felt the familiar surge of hate from which there was no deliverance.

'She was a pretty girl,' he finished lamely. His control was gone. He could feel the ebb of chaos bucking under him; a dense, shifting mire with a will of its own.

North pulled up at the red set of traffic lights and turned on his passenger. 'But I never thought about *fucking* her before now.'

Porter refused the confrontation. He kept his eye on the road ahead and listened to the ticking of the engine.

You don't get off that easy. 'Do you have an explanation for that? Because I run from that. I *want* to run from that.'

Porter was clearly uncomfortable. He glanced out at the mass of traffic and at the traffic signals hoisted overhead. The lights were changing.

'It's green.'

'Fuck the lights.'

The herd of traffic honked in anger and jostled to move past the obstruction. The furious admonitions of the passing motorists gave Porter nowhere to turn his face. He asked, 'What disturbs you the most? That you have these memories at all? Or is it that you remember you enjoyed it and did these things eagerly?'

North embraced the disgust that he held for himself. *He knows what I'm thinking.* 'My mother, Doctor Porter. I had *sex* with my own mother.' He set the car in gear again and joined the trail of migrating traffic. 'Reincarnation, that's one thing. But why would I do *that?*'

'Isn't it obvious?'

'Not to me.'

'Because we're talking about genetic memory, Detective North, memories that are passed along the patriline, handed down from father to son.'

Father to son. Not his father. Not the man he thought was his father. *That wasn't who I saw in the mirror.*

North struggled with the unwelcome paradox that if he was to accept these memories as real, he had to accept their content.

'It's our biology,' explained Porter. 'The biology of our memories that are created in our minds, held in our minds and, every day, *renewed* in our minds needs a process that *also* undergoes constant renewal so that our memories may be inherited by our children.'

North was impatient. 'A science lesson now?'

'You wanted an explanation.'

'I want to know *why*.'

'Sperm.'

North was confused. He made no apologies about showing it.

'Women are born with their eggs *already* locked firmly away inside them. They go through life insecure in the knowledge that they get only what they've been given. *We* on the other hand produce semen in a constant cycle. Week after week. Each new batch so different from the last that the implications are critical to our memory.'

So critical I don't even know what they are.

'The creation of new semen occurs because either the old sperm is no longer viable, or the owner managed to offload some.'

'Sex.'

'Memories are made to last by the processes of stress and excitement. The signal to create new sperm occurs because the conditions of a sexual encounter create the same excitement that forms those memories to begin with. I believe you and I share the same genetic anomaly; we create our sperm – in the moment.'

North took the next turn ahead under the glare of frustration. 'You *believe*? That's not telling me anything.'

'It's telling you everything. A child's first genetic memory in *this* life will frequently be the actions of his father in the last – having sex with his mother.' Porter was struck by the cruel nature of the twist. 'It's all terribly Freudian.'

He's told me nothing. 'Do you want to know what's terrible?'

'What?'

'That you didn't answer my question.'

A perplexity settled over Porter. He tried to respond but North wouldn't let him.

'You're telling me *how* this happened. I don't care how. I asked you *why*.'

A silence descended between them like some unscalable wall. Porter watched the city blocks streak by, the jumble of cultures blending in to one.

'Where are we going?'

North wasn't listening. He made another turn, swinging the Lumina wide into the next street. Porter watched the circle of black pass through his strong naked hands. There was tension in his fingers; fingers that wore no rings.

'Do you have a girlfriend, detective?'

'What?'

'Do you have anyone to go home to?'

North tried to shrug it off. It was a personal blow that he had no shelter from. He tried to hold firm. 'No.'

Porter didn't seem moved by the answer. He watched the growing throng of people scuttle along the sidewalks as they glided past.

'You never wonder why?'

Of course I wonder why.

'No,' he lied. But in truth it just never felt right. There had always been this deeply rooted impulse that he didn't fully understand which stopped him from committing.

'Perhaps it just wasn't meant to be.'

North chose to shift the uncomfortable focus. Porter had said his wife had died. Had he moved on? Delicately North asked, 'You?'

Porter made hardly a sound. It was hard to tell where his thoughts lay or what secrets they held. When he answered, it was with another question. 'Why is that, do you think?'

Everybody deflects. North gripped the wheel. 'Why is what? That I'm not with someone?'

'Yes.'

That's easy. Bitter, but easy. 'I work stupid hours. I see things that stay with me for months. I don't work the kind of job that lets a relationship breathe.' All he saw was liars and violence; the hidden darkness of society that cast long shadows from its matted underbelly. 'I don't find it easy to trust.'

'Your parents do. They're still together.'

North was stung. *What does he know?* North didn't like where this was going. He stumbled over his words. 'That's different.'

'You weren't always a police officer. What about before?'

What about before?

North found a place to park under a burned-out lamppost. They were on Canal Street. Not far away from where the gaudy banners with their exotic script hung over the jostling chaos of Chinatown.

North killed the engine. He felt the tug of resignation pulling him under in his struggle to grope for an answer.

'Things just never seem to work out.'

He retrieved his phone and keyed the menu to access his Nextel Mobile Office. He waited for the familiar sound that let him know he'd retrieved his e-mails. Sheppard had sent the list as he had promised.

North quietly opened up his notebook, searched for a blank page and started copying it all down.

'Sometimes,' he said, 'I think the right girl's just not out there.' He ripped the page from its firm binding and tucked his phone out of sight. 'Sometimes I don't think she's anywhere.' He stood on the edge of an abyss and wondered what things lay hidden in the unfulfilled depths below.

'Curious, isn't it?' commented Porter. 'That you seem to have someone so very specific in mind.'

North wasn't certain he knew what Porter meant by that. 'What about your wife? What was she like?'

Porter retreated into himself. 'I don't remember.'

What kind of man doesn't remember his wife? 'But she changed the course of your life.'

'I don't remember the love that went with her, only the loss that came without her.' The spark within him seemed to flicker and fade. 'I don't know anything else. I don't think I've ever known.'

North threw open the door and stepped out into the street. He felt the slap of fat rain hitting his face. He peered up into the sky. *What a miserable summer.*

Looking back at the psychiatrist sitting inside his car, North saw him in that instant through changed eyes. He was an old man, tired and beaten. Was it relief that North could see etched deep into the lines of his face; relief that he finally had someone with whom to share the burden of a life in pieces?

It terrified him. *Is that what waits for me?*

North couldn't leave him sitting there so he offered him no choice. 'Are you coming?'

2.16 p.m.

The two men fought their way through the narrow, overcrowded streets and alleyways of Chinatown where the rain shone in the glare of incandescent shopfronts. The torrent bounced heavily around their feet, but its tirade was lost, muted by street merchants engaged in their furious Cantonese trade in every doorway along their path.

Both North and Porter felt the familiar glimmer of memory raise its hackles, though neither man voiced it openly. The smell and the noise provided enough reminders for now.

When the shops weren't neon-enshrined video stores heaving with imported movies, they were small cramped bakeries overflowing with tawny mango pudding and the bird's nest delights of fried taro. Or they were chaotic, eclectic marketplaces packed with ice boxes oozing silvery fish and menaced by canopies of smoked ruddy ducks, hanging dark like autumn leaves impaled upon sharp metal hooks. Restaurants steamed with dim sum and slick noodles wrapped in thick wafting envelopes of garlic, ginger and deep pungent wine. Amid the acupuncturists and herbalists, where incense was being burned and engorged ginseng roots sat like cadavers left to bloat in some festering lake, discoloured with age, victims of a forgotten crime, North and Porter arrived at the door marked Fong Wan Peng, MD. North knew him simply as Jimmy Peng.

Porter asked quietly, 'Can you trust this man?'

North thought the question redundant. Of course he couldn't.

They were entering the complex rotting carcass of Chinese organized crime, the noxious pit of slave-trading Snakeheads, Tongs, Triads, secret societies, and putrescent gangs like the powerful Fuk Ching, the Ghost Shadows, and the Tung On. This was where corrupt shepherds, grandfather figures called *ah kungs*, or uncles called *shuk foos*, protected their flocks with a pyramid of other cancerous organizations like The Fukien American Association.

That North and Jimmy Peng had a history and a bad one didn't matter – any history meant that the door was not closed. Coming here, however, was going to have lasting effects, whichever way this was concluded.

Porter loitered near the front of the long narrow store. It was North who crossed over its threshold, just a short step up out of the rain. The room consisted entirely of an access way and a never-ending glass counter top that was crammed with boxes of herbs, roots and powders.

Jimmy Peng emerged from the back room with small paper parcels for two of his customers. Peng was slight, his short black hair touched with grey, his fingers deeply stained with nicotine. Jimmy Peng, MD, gave advice. He rarely followed it.

He saw North but said nothing. North waited while Peng rang up the sale. Only when he thanked his two customers with a broad grin did he turn his attention to his visitor. His smile dropped almost immediately.

'You arrive under a black cloud.' His Shanghai inflections were a strange, barely noticeable idiosyncrasy buried beneath decades of his received American accent. It made him sound refined. It was a carefully cultivated lie. 'It must be your winning personality.'

North ignored the comment. He ran his eye over the assorted scrapings that filled box after box. *It's another world.* 'What's that?'

'Willow bark.'

'What's it used for?'

Peng was in no hurry to answer his questions. Instead, Porter edged up behind him, his hands planted deep inside his pockets. 'Aspirin comes from willow bark.'

North eyed the ingredient with some suspicion.

'You seem surprised, detective. Your friend knows his medicine.'

'A little,' Porter mused. 'You're the real expert.'

A twinkle appeared in Peng's dubious eye. 'How very gracious.'

Porter knows his thing. Good. North felt a little better that the Englishman was with him.

'A third of all *Western* medicine still comes from plants. If one includes moulds, the proportion is even greater,' Peng explained.

'In ancient Chinese medicine mould was often rubbed into wounds as an antibiotic,' Porter added with some relish. 'Penicillin is a mould.'

North was disgusted. *Mould?* He'd seen the black speckles creeping up people's walls. He produced his sheet of paper. 'Let's talk drugs.'

All civility hurriedly left Peng's pointed features. 'I don't do that any more. I'm clean.'

Sure. 'I just need your help.'

'*My* help?' Peng laughed. 'There's a turnaround.'

North had trouble opening out the sheet of paper. His fingers were tense. The paper quickly ripped.

'You're angry.'

He tried to shrug it off. 'No more than usual.'

Peng appeared to enjoy the weakness. 'Is someone getting to you?'

North laid the sheet out flat on the glass. 'I'm wondering who I pissed off in a former life.'

Peng's instinct was to ignore this as a jibe, but after a moment of reflection he saw something in North that he'd never seen before. 'You're serious.'

North did not look up. Peng's attention settled on Porter. The older man exuded quiet concern but he, too, was denying nothing.

'Ah, but you are still struggling against it.'

North refused to answer.

Peng said, 'I have eyes. I can see. We have all lived many lives. If you were in the East you would not even be questioning such accepted facts.'

'Did you read that in a fortune cookie?'

Peng smiled as he glanced back out the store to the carnival that was Chinatown. 'My sister just opened a restaurant. She found a wonderful supplier for her fortune cookies. They're so popular with the tourists.'

Peng returned to his work and began neatly packaging up a herbal remedy, dropping small ingredients on to a set of weighing scales.

'You're bitter. I get that. I did miss them when I paid my unexpected visit to Sing-Sing.' North held back for fear of making the situation worse. He took the sheet of paper and turned it around, sliding it into Peng's clear view. 'But does this look familiar to you?'

Peng looked at it thoroughly. The list of ingredients found injected into North's blood from Gene's syringe appeared to hold his interest. 'Why should I help *you*?'

How about I see what you're hiding? North glanced towards the back room. *Will that make him sweat?*

No. The look on Peng's face told him he was expecting that. North had to find another way. 'You get to feel superior.'

'Feelings are transitory.'

Something else then. Make him bite. Make a trade. He only had one other thing that he could offer. He said, 'I'll be in your debt.'

'Ah, debts. Yes, they can be very useful.'

North held out a finger to illustrate his point. 'Just the *one*,' he said. 'So play the card well.'

'Yes, but which card?' Peng accepted the deal. 'What do you want me to do with this list? Do you want it prepared for you?'

'I want to know if you've ever put anything like this together before.'

Peng took a pencil and ran it down the list. 'No.'

'Do you know who might have?' He watched as the herbalist began to circle the ingredients he was most familiar with.

'I'm not sure. I will need to make some discreet phone calls. My suspicion is that this wasn't manufactured here in Chinatown, though somebody may recognize part of the shopping list. There's one large dose of ma huang here, is this for someone with asthma?

Asthma? That kid at the museum. 'No.'

Peng took North at his word and said he wouldn't be long. He made his way into the back room.

North waited. There followed the familiar sound of the telephone being picked up and numbers being tapped into the keypad. Before long Peng's native tongue surfaced.

Satisfied, North turned to Porter. 'I had an Albuterol inhaler—'

Porter shook his head. 'Albuterol works in a different way. The ephedrine in your system was from the ma huang elixir.'

North was uncomfortable with his choice of words.

'I don't know what else to call it. It does what an elixir is supposed to do; it prolongs life.'

'What else does ephedrine do?'

Porter explained flatly. 'It's similar to adrenaline; in large doses it causes agitation, even psychosis. As the veterans who returned from the Vietnam War will be able to tell you, it triggers violent and uncontrollable flashbacks. But you don't need them to tell you.'

No, he didn't. *What did he call it before?* 'Like an abreaction?'

Porter agreed. 'They're two sides of the same coin, induced resurrections of memory. All that separates them is the degree.'

The degree. Whatever they were, they were unwelcome. They were horrific, dark and perverse.

'There must be something I can do to stop it.'

Porter considered the options. 'Propranolol would counter the ephedrine at least. I don't know if you could get a doctor to prescribe it to you though. I think in this country it trades under the name Inderal. It's—'

'It's a beta-blocker.' North knew it well. Inderal was the medication his father used for his heart.

Dad.

North watched the thundering rain and reflected on the implications. As the water gushed down in torrents he could reach no other conclusion. 'Gene *wanted* me to remember.'

Porter had some sympathy. 'Yes, he did.'

'*What* did he want me to remember?'

'Who you are.'

Peng returned from the back room with his observation firmly in hand. 'Equally, he may have wanted you to forget.'

How long has he been listening?

Porter was curious. 'I don't understand.'

'There is someone who is familiar with this list. He has an occasional purchaser who visits on an ad hoc basis. He often has him source items that he doesn't want appearing on his records. He said he thinks that the purpose of this concoction is to draw out memories, as one might draw out a bruise.'

Like a bruise? 'Why would they do that?'

'So that after prolonged exposure they can be expunged, leaving behind a tabula rasa – a blank slate.'

North noticed the slip of paper between Peng's fingers. He went to take it but the herbalist first wanted to make sure that the deal was still in place. North agreed reluctantly.

'Some men from a biotech company are stopping by. I'm told you should hurry.'

North didn't question the advice. He checked the slip of paper as he stormed out the door. The name and address pointed in the direction of another herbalist who resided just a few blocks away.

3.40 p.m.

North hurried briskly through the pelting grey wet, and Porter strained to keep up. The asphalt was hard underfoot, its surface slick and treacherous.

'This would certainly explain why Gene lost control in the library, wouldn't you say?' Porter reasoned. 'If he's been subjected to the same elixir; the turmoil of remembering one moment. To draw a blank at the next.'

North put out a hand to feel his way roughly through the mass of dark bodies that blocked his path throughout.

'I don't have to wonder. I have to find him.'

Porter wrestled with the jostle of feet and elbows. North was ahead of him by some distance. When the gaps presented themselves he was forced to run, the drizzle streaming down his cold face.

'When I was a clinician, a few years younger than you are now, I was forced to watch a patient of mine suffer the indignity of Alzheimer's disease. He had his memory eaten away from the inside.'

North checked his note. Without warning he changed direction.

'Every day I trudged to work, consumed with his misery. I read him the morning newspaper, monitored his progress, fed him pills that were of no use to anyone, and watched in sheer terror as the lesions and tangles relentlessly unravelled his mind as though it were a cheap sweater.'

'I'm sorry to hear that.'

Porter matched his stride. 'This man forgot his own children, slowly, one at a time. Gradually the memory of his life dimmed year by wretched year until his achievements and his tragedies were gone. In time he forgot his wife and she wept for a month. Until one day he woke up and he didn't even know who it was that stared back at him in the mirror.

'He breathed, he slept, he ate. But without his memory he was no one. He was a machine with no purpose. Memory is the very core of who we are.'

North understood the pain and he understood its value. 'Sometimes,' he said, 'it's good to forget.'

'I thought so once. Now I'm not so sure.'

North indicated that they should cross the street. The traffic refused to slow to their request. The filthy spray left in the wake of each relentless vehicle was bitter and spiteful.

'We should run.'

'Why is it good to forget?'

Isn't it obvious? 'Because it sets us free.'

'Freedom is a different question. Free to do what exactly? Free to do what we want?'

'Yes. Without being haunted or held a prisoner.'

'So *you're* not bound by fate?'

The traffic hissed past. North's features were set. This was beyond question. 'I can do *whatever* I want.' He saw his chance and shot out into the road. The traffic responded with indignant protest.

Porter struggled to keep up. 'Then why are we hurrying?'

North leaped up on to the kerb on the other side of the road. Porter had not been so swift. He was now just a ghost hidden behind the veil of the rain.

Porter called out to him. 'You're hurrying only because you were told to hurry, you didn't question why. Is that doing *whatever* you want?'

North didn't know how to answer that. Not in the way Porter wanted. *I'm doing my job. What's there to understand?*

The crowds were just as dense on this block, the sounds and smells just as confusing and all pervasive. He searched the store fronts looking for the right sign. *There.* He forced his way on through the jumble of bodies.

Porter was right behind him. 'If you have free will, why can't you control your actions? Why can't you stop your nightmares? Why do they make you run?'

North pulled up short. He did so with reluctance. He reached inside his coat pocket and impatiently retrieved the ingredient list and his photograph of Gene. His intentions were clear. What Porter had to say was secondary.

Porter knew it, but he pressed on anyway. 'We are all confined by our physical nature. Depending on *which* genes you were given at conception, you have no control over the colour of your skin, or the blood in your veins.'

Don't talk to me about blood.

'Memories are who we are. Not what we are. They give fate her voice. You are an orchestra whose strings are being plucked by forces that you cannot see and do not know. When my patient lost his memory he wasn't free. It altered nothing about his world. It rendered him impotent. It *robbed* him of his will because he didn't know who he was, or what he was capable of.'

North studied the worn photograph of the man he was in pursuit of. 'Am I supposed to feel sorry for *Gene?*'

Porter took a moment to consider his words carefully. 'He asked for your help. Like you asked for mine. He's being stripped of who he is. You *know* who he is. He's a part of you.'

Part of me? The very idea was noxious. It hadn't occurred to him, not even a glimmer buried deep in the gloom beneath a heap of unwanted possibilities. Porter's suggestion was offensive.

North's instinct was to deny. 'He's no blood of mine.'

'He knew to look for you; he knew to find you, as I did.'

How did he? 'You had a newspaper to work from. What did Gene have?'

Porter had no immediate answer. Instead he reached into his pocket and pulled out his green notebook. 'Abreactions begin with the compulsion to write. You, Gene and myself; there are probably many more of us than just three, but each will be compelled to write, and each will write the same things.'

North refused the book.

The rain beat down upon both men in a lashing tumult. Every face in the sodden crowd seemed to know him; every eye teased at some connection. He felt so overwhelmed he clutched his moistened pieces of paper close to him and said, 'I have to go.'

He felt Porter's hot probing search of his features. Had they reached an understanding? Porter was not certain and North could give him no assurances.

Porter touched his arm as one might a son. 'I'm stopping you from your work. We'll talk later?'

North agreed, but only because he doubted there was anyone else he could talk to.

He turned his back on Porter, eager to forget the complications he had been presented with, eager to plough on with his duty and follow this new lead. He set himself in motion leaving Porter to his own devices, but in leaving one old man, he walked straight into another.

North apologized but the man with the black umbrella would not move. He stood, his face tilted at an angle, transfixed by the picture of Gene that he saw in North's hand.

North intended to move but the trembling of the black umbrella that showered him with its cascading runoff held him firm. The tremble was in the hand of the man who held it. The tremble was slight. But it grew.

The man with the black umbrella seemed to recognize the man in the photograph.

Was this who Peng had warned him to expect? North sensed he should move quickly or waste the opportunity. He flashed his badge and pressed him. 'Sir, do you know this man?'

The man with the black umbrella said nothing.

'Sir, I understand if you're anxious. It's okay to talk to me.'

There were others approaching, eager men in dark coats who did not agree. They thrust their arms through the scrum of the crowd and tugged at the man with the black umbrella to return with them. *Not that way*, they admonished. *Not with him.*

North grabbed one of them by his gloved fist and held his badge furiously aloft. 'This is a police investigation! Get your hands off him!'

The man with the black umbrella looked up.

In his other hand he held his purchase from the herbalist. In his eyes he held the secrets of his intent. Though his face was tired and his dishevelled hair three shades of grey, behind his glasses no faded shadow peered back. His gaze was penetrating and erudite. He knew the man in the photograph like he knew the man that was holding it.

Yet still he remained resolutely tight lipped as his protectors bundled him away.

In that instant North was left floundering.

I know him.

He felt the blood drain from his limbs. He succumbed to the feeble state of panic. His mind reeled even as Porter saw his predicament and fought his way back through the scurrying horde.

'Wait!' North scrambled to catch up. 'Who are you?'

That face. Aged over the smoke of three long decades; the grimace in the mirror, the mask that he wore when he lusted with his mother.

The face of his real father.

It was all true.

North struggled through the haze of grim reality, trying to see which way they had fled. The bowed heads of so many rain-soaked people anxious to fulfil their needs rendered it impossible. Even when he jumped for a better view no telltale partings of the crowd gave him a trail to pursue. They were lost to a sea of faces.

He heard Porter's voice. His desperate cries. 'No!' he yelled. 'No!'

North spun around, a blur of confusion. Emerging from the distorted din he heard: 'You breed like vermin.'

The familiar scraping sound of metal being drawn against its sheath cut through the rain like the gnashing of teeth. From his blind spot one of the men in dark coats had returned and lunged at him, his short blade a glint in the heavy soak of day.

North reacted quickly. Porter was quicker. He threw himself on to the knife and took the blow not meant for him.

The hard metal sliced through his belly and tore a ragged gash through his gut. A swirl of cascading scarlet wept through his rigid fingers. He kept the blade for himself and tumbled with it into the slosh of rain at his feet.

North lashed out, the papers tumbling from his grasp. The vicious trade of blows stung in the wet. When the man lunged again North gripped the lapels of his coat, but his fingers slipped on the soaked fabric. His clawing grasp failed to wrestle him into submission. The man wriggled like a fish leaving North with just a souvenir.

The man fled without his dark coat.

North flung it to the ground and reached for his gun. He screamed at the crowd in his pursuit and threatened a warning shot, brandishing his Glock with menace.

The mass of dishevelled pedestrians retreated before him like an outgoing tide.

North ran through the street unimpeded but the men in the dark coats were gone. Vanished, like the long fleeting shadows of cockroaches scattering from a burst of lamplight leaving only the whiff of decay.

Where did they go? Where?

He turned full circle but nothing would reveal them. Instead just the faces of the crowd stared back at him, huddled in fear in the doorways. North was alone, left with just the heap of a dying man collapsed on the ground.

My blood. My soul. An aspect of me.

North ran to the end of the street, tucking his gun away and reaching for his phone. Porter held his disgorged intestines in place, his waxen skin stretched taut in remorseless agony.

North raged for an ambulance and stooped to cradle him in his arms, bathing in his river of blood, a flood that fanned out into the drains, carrying the tattered photograph of Gene along with it.

THE PHYSICIAN AND THE GLADIATOR

My wounds were deep, my torment deeper.

That was not enough payment to sate the greed of this braying crowd.

The Samnite lunged again, a feint to make me jump. Instead I bulled right in, smashing his gladius back and meeting his scutum instead. With it, he ploughed into me, using the vast foursquare shield to hide his flank from my reach. He shunted me until my balance was broken and tipped its leading edge for a crack at my jaw.

I flew to meet the cold sand and gazed despairingly up at the awning of azure blue that flapped over Nero's arena in the biting winds of winter.

A beam of one hundred and twenty cubits so they said. And two cubits wide. It was the greatest beam in Rome, they said, that held that roof aloft. I wished they would just nail me to it and hang me there to die, anything but more of this tortuous misery.

Left leg leading, strapped meatily into a boiled leather greave, the Samnite rushed me. I rolled to fend off his frenzied blow. The whisper that his edge blew into my ears thudded into the ground.

His sword was stuck fast. I saw him struggle and took my chance.

I ploughed my gladius into his trailing knee and sliced the cap clean off.

His scream was a terrible gurgling thing to bear; a rage of agony erupting from his burnished helmet so shrill and desperate that it almost made me weep.

My deed was not well met.

The jeers of the crowd were accompanied with the gnawed bones of animals that smacked my face with derision. *You Fool!* they cried. *Why won't you die, you dog? I had wagered upon on him!*

His pain was such that he could not nurse his gore, nor even embrace the presence of mind to plead for tender mercy. So I did it for him.

I looked for the editor in his box, but the man who held these Saturnalian Games was not there.

I paraded my sliced carcass around my plot, peering at the captivated crowd who sat beyond the sharpened tusks, as big as any man, which lunged out into the arena to defend the wall all around. No order came.

I saw above the carved ivory rollers and through the golden hanging nets – there to foil the claws of any wild animal fighting the bestiarii that had the commendable idea of launching itself at the spectators – but still I could find no one who would give me their command.

The arena was enthralled by its orgy of blood. They had forgotten me as quickly as they had chastened me. The fate of just one man meant nothing.

A hundred other pairs of gleaming gladiators sought savage consequence to their exploits in the ring. They sawed and hacked, stabbed and choked and sliced without regard. I saw one man, a dark-skinned andabatus, fighting blind behind his sealed visor, swinging so wildly that by sheer luck he carved the arm from his adversary. The roar of laughter from the incongruous hordes grew with each spew of the wounded man's cruor. The sweeping scarlet patterns that he left in his wake were his fleeting legacy, tribute to his talents as an artist. They laughed still, long after his death, long after his stump had ceased to gush.

I saw another, a nimble-footed retiarius, hurl his black lead-weighted net with such savage force that the secutor who chased him dropped his spatha. So confused was this man, so consumed with his fear, that as he tore at his face to remove all impediment he did not see the three sharpened prongs of the trident lunge towards him. At first it was like watching Poseidon – the Greek in me could not stand to call him Neptune – toying with a crab. The naked retiarius kicked his quarry on to his back, planted a strong heel on his chest and probed for the soft spot between his hard plates. It did not take him long to work apart the gap between the secutor's dull round helmet and his feeble cuirass. He ploughed straight into his throat. A great sucking sound went up in place of a scream. In the end it was like watching the skewering of swine, whole and salted and ready for the roast.

The manic zeal for bloody cruelty gathered all to the great harlot's mangled breast. I saw men have their gazes fixed and their souls made drunk with the endless brutal bludgeoning.

War for pleasure. What a perverse world that I had been born to this time. The Greeks had games, but not like this. What was in the Roman nature that made them lust for blood? If it was not Athanatos's reek that had scoured the fields and infected the hearts of so many with his bilious plague, then what hope was there for any man?

Behind me, the greasy sound of chains and wheels and pulleys was set in motion. The stench of the burning flesh and the singed fur of the tiger-horses and the bears being rounded into their cages at the end of glowing pokers wafted from the confines beneath the stands with the first glimmer of darkness that came with the opening of the gate.

The slaves within bent their backs to it, turning the heavy circle of mighty timber, winding the ropes and sturdy shafts to bring the gate to open. But the warrior behind it was impatient to launch himself into this madness. He rolled beneath the opening, neatly as an acrobat, and came to crouch before me. I was met with the face of the Etruscan demon Charun, torturer of souls in the underworld.

Was he here to fight or not? I could not tell. We orbited around the fallen Samnite and clashed a little metal. The laughter this brought to the crowds seemed to win me some favour at last – it seemed Charun was here merely to singe the body and see if there was fakery.

The Samnite, who had long since passed out with grief, stirred in the sodden sand as red-hot metal sizzled into his flesh and crisped the fat around it. He screamed and in so doing sealed his own downfall; for his cowardice Charun lunged at him. His throat was slit in one.

I wheeled, my gladius at the ready, but Charun had not come for me. He leaped off into the carnage to stir the dead that littered the arena wall to wall.

Amid the catcalls and the ill-humoured rumblings, a voice called out to me from the darkness. 'Get out of there, you fool, your bout is done!'

Oh, that my wretched life were as simple as that.

I had nailed my soul to flesh. There was no rest for me. I had peered through the eyes of my ancestors and shared the moments of a score of lifetimes, until like the flaming comet that shone this very night over the Seven Hills of Rome, I had returned.

This was not the first night that I had stared bleakly out at the tempestuous sky through the bars of my cell at the ludus, and I had no hope it would be the last.

From beyond the graffiti scratched into my wall by a host

of dead combatants, a voice asked quietly, 'You looked for him again in the arena today, Aquilo?'

The Judean Samuel was alive. It came as something of a surprise, with all that I had seen. Aquilo, my name in this life; in truth I still answered better to my other.

I held fast to my bars, overcome that somebody I knew was still with me. 'You live.'

'Barely,' was the faint, pain-strapped reply. 'Ah, my melancholy Greek with his malady of the mind. You should not worry so. You will find this Babylonian magician with whom you have such issue.'

'Issue?' I laughed as I sat upon the frigid hard stone floor. Under the snap and hiss of the flickering red torchlight that lined the walls outside of our confines, I drew my fur close to me on this stark December night. 'It is more than an issue, our feud.'

'You say that your gods did this to you?'

'Do not talk to me of the gods,' I replied with contempt. 'They are anathema to me. Their gift is no longer welcome.'

The Judean Samuel struggled with his injuries. I listened to his gasps of sharp pain from the darkness. Only when he had settled did he resume. 'Yes, but consider: if, as you say, your gods did this to you, then would they not place you here upon this earth close to this man?'

I thought on what he had to say.

'You are like brothers by gods' standards; two snakes pitted one on one. It makes little sense to place you in separate arenas. Where would be the fun for the spectators in that? Whether they sit in the stands of Olympus or the amphitheatres of Campus Martius, which is quite a distance by the way. Marching us through the streets to get there; it is undignified. If we are to be cattle herded for their amusement the very least they could do is put us in camp there.'

'Complain loudly enough, my friend, and they may do just that. Or they may tear down the walls of the temple to *your* god in Jerusalem and build an arena right here at the ludus just to satisfy your command.'

'Do not be so perverse!'

'It is not I. It is the Roman nature to humiliate.'

I could hear the Judean Samuel moving about, grunting with his agony as he lowered himself on to the stone shelf that passed for a bed. 'Oh this straw is filthy. I shall be diseased by the morning.'

I settled my glance again on the comet in the sky. It shone with such pure brilliance, never deviating from its course. Its life was all mapped out.

Athanatos always had the advantage. How could I turn his tide and lay this to an end? I said, 'I am Futility's bastard and she bears me such malicious love.'

'You will find him, as I hope we shall both find some food very soon.' I heard him lunge for the bars and strike them. 'What keeps these goats?'

By the main gates to the courtyard two soldiers stoked the fire to their brazier. We shared its wafting promise, it brought our ravenous tongues to our parched lips, but theirs was not meant for us.

The Judean Samuel staggered restlessly back to the bars. I could see his bloodied and blackened hands but no more. 'You should see the feasts I would present to you and all my honoured guests were we at my palace.'

'Your palace *again*?'

'You have an invitation to another?'

What were they cooking, these soldiers? It was torture. 'What would we have?'

'The very finest!' He spoke with his hands in gestures as though he were tearing hot greasy meat. 'We would begin with the most succulent tender green leaves of lettuce, drizzled with olives and oil. I would take a tuna, young, no bigger than a lizard fish, and pickle him until his flesh hung from his white bones. He would be joined with the small soft eggs of a pigeon wrapped in dark rue leaves.' The Judean Samuel reflected on that for a moment. Something was missing. 'And perhaps a few nuts.'

'Ah.'

'And these we would cook slow, over a low flame. We would crack imported pepper down his back and eat him with the most delicious cheese from Velabrum Street while mulsum would whet our appetites for the finer wine yet to come.'

I smiled. I could almost taste the mulsum now, that heady rich mix of sweet wine and thick honey. 'It is a good dream.'

We listened to the crackling and the spitting of the flaming torches and I wondered about our feast. I grew more hungry and I asked, 'And for lena? What would you serve us for our *main course*? We are in your tricilinium and I am your honoured guest.'

'Of course!' The sound of his voice told me that he grinned as broad as an oar.

'Dionysus cavorts with maidens in the wondrous mosaics upon your dining floor. You have nine tables—'

'*Nine*? Ten! Eleven!'

'And guests from every corner of the world!'

'I see it!'

'I recline upon your couch. I lean upon my elbow. What do your servants bring me?'

'I see now you are the clever one – here is where our feast truly begins. At first your nose is filled with the fortifying aroma of the salt of the sea. From under a waxing moon they bring you the coral flesh of Misenum's blackened sea urchins, salty slithering oysters from Circeii and fleshy Tartanum scallops sizzling in olive butter and rich in Egyptian spices.'

'And garum, don't forget the garum to dip them in.'

When I was I boy I had helped make garum by the Bithynian recipe with the foul-smelling entrails of salted fish left to rot in a sturdy vat under the blistering sun. The juices we then sieved and to this dark potent liquamen we added wine to create garum. Its taste was intoxicating.

'But then what is this? You smell garlic and citrus and are presented with the roasted carcass of an Umbrian, acorn-fed boar! His skin is brown and snaps to the touch, his flesh tumbles into your hands.'

I felt the objections of my belly most severely. I nursed a little grief.

'They bring you sow's udder and stuffed wild fowl, a heathcock meant for two but served only for my honoured guest. Trays littered with baked peacock's brains, flamingo tongues and pike livers garnished with chick peas, their tendrils curled like rams' horns, and fat African figs. They would serve you roast pigeon dripping with white sauce and a bit of hot crusty bread to mop it up with.'

'Oh, my stomach begs you to stop.' We roared with laughter, but it was soon quashed.

We watched one soldier spoon two bowls of steaming grain porridge from his hefty cooking pot and followed with our eyes the keen exchange as he handed one to the other.

But there would be no food for us tonight.

We stared at them glumly through the bars of our dank, flea-ridden cells. 'Come,' I said. 'Let us dream of this wine with no end.'

It was unusual though not impossible for it to be so cold in Rome that it snowed, and so it did this night. It would be settling on the hill tops though here it would remain a rumour. Through the bars of my cell the muted snowflakes danced their festive celebrations and fell softly down upon my face, like tender fingers brushing against my eyes, a whispered lullaby leading me towards quiet sleep. My lids drooped, my head sagged. Slumber had me in her embrace.

I would not sleep so well again. In the coming months and through the hard slog of winter I fought and killed many a man, both in combat and once in training. I sliced the noses of convicts and the ears of downtrodden slaves. I carved great gashes into the limbs of paid men, citizens who sought their fortune and who wished to bask in glory.

The last time I spoke with the Judean Samuel he was lamenting that if he ever got to return to this earth for *his* second life he would live in a tower and surround himself with trinkets. That would make him happiest of all. We were in a cage awaiting our mutual combat. He asked me, 'Please, when the time comes, strike quickly.'

He was my friend. How could I not? As he slid off my sword and rolled in the dust I wept for him and prayed to the gods in whom I did not believe that they would see fit to grant him his wish.

The young murmillo skirted my reach though he edged a little closer with each step. His face was deathly white in the grey light of harsh day. He was inexperienced. He was so very terrified.

He lunged, his head so close that I saw the grimace on the face of the ugly metal fish that sat upon his tarnished helmet.

I battered him with my parma, a strike so vicious that it broke his nose with one clean blow.

His bowels loosed in reply, a torrid release of the blackest slop with a stench so foul that I gagged and staggered my retreat.

His own filth made a humiliating dressing for the deep gouges that ran down both his legs. He hung his head in petrified shame and was met with a howl from the arena. *Verbera!* The people urged. *Strike!*

How could I kill a boy who was merely in fear for his life?

I raised my short curved sica above my head and paraded around him. This place disgusted me. This child was not who I sought. I roared at my audience. 'Athanatos! Do you see me here? Where are you, you coward? I am your Cretan comet returned! Why do you not come to face your Trojan memory?'

Disquiet rippled throughout the crowd. I did not know why. I certainly did not have time to consider it.

The smash of the young murmillo's broad oval shield against my back brought me swiftly to my senses. I turned on the young man, a chink of light caressing my sword, and cried in terrible rage at his treachery. 'You come at me when I give you time to breathe? Is that what they teach you at Capua?'

We exchanged swift spiteful blows. Fast, furious and brutal. Hot blood spluttered from his nose like the blossoms of early spring.

Another cheer erupted all around, this time for the match well fought not ten feet away. The carved meat of a man lay at the feet of a dimachaerus, his twin blades whirling, waiting for the order to give a final slice.

Was the mood in the arena a forgiving one today? The distraction of the thought was my undoing.

The young fearful murmillo, his eyes wide like eggs, saw his chance, ploughed his blade deep into my side and gave it one almighty twist.

My breath caught in my throat as I touched the icy waters of the underworld. I buckled with the pain, victim of both this whelp's blade and my own arrogance. Doubling to the waist I dropped to my knees and prayed it would not end like this.

I had not even seen Athanatos in this life. Was he even alive? Had he been humbled in the long years of my absence? Did I rage for naught?

A lone cry went up. 'Do not let this man die to one who would soil himself to victory!'

The vulgar laughter that followed brought my finger up for mercy.

The young murmillo convulsed as he awaited his instruction. He spewed his porridge down his chest. I listened to his whispered incantation in a language I could barely fathom. I did not think he had killed before. Certainly he did not have the taste for it.

When someone cried '*Mitte*!' he welcomed the voice of reason. When the crowd cried '*Mitte*!' I grew fearful of a lie. Was I saved?

I looked up. The thumb did not go to the chest. I was spared.

My loss of blood leaked me towards my crisis as they dragged me not through the Porta Triumphalis, but through the murky gate reserved for losers.

The moaning of the young brides who lined the blackened course hoping to have their long wet hair parted by the firm spears of the defeated and ensure a fertile marriage was a deafening wail of melodious misery. The scum who clawed for a drop of my blood, licking from my wounds in the blind hope it would restore to them some vigour to their withered arms and drooping members, caused me to roar in fury and kick them in my struggle.

They did not take me to the sanatorium, or to the spoliarium where the dead were being rudely stripped of their armour. Instead six proud Praetorian Guard chained me and piled me into a cage like an animal and drove me screaming through the heaving streets of Rome.

I pinched the carnage of my flesh in a bid to staunch my innards from slopping at my feet. I yelled through broken teeth: 'Where are you taking me?'

The reply was returned with glee. 'Caesar wishes to know why you declared war on his physician.'

Athanatos was physician to Nero?

They sped me past the Palatine Hill where the Galli, the effeminate priests of the temple of the mother goddess Cybele, brought from far-flung Phrygia and transplanted in Rome, watched me with eyes of satisfied knowing.

For thirty leagues we sped on apace until we reached Sublaqueum, where upon the shore of the Simbruine Lake Nero had his villa.

With the hem of twilight descending upon our arrival, the once fearsome comet had been reduced to but a stain in the evening sky. Nevertheless, the omens did not sit well with the soldiers. A comet meant revolution and the people had already begun to ask if Nero was dethroned.

They muttered about it to themselves while they dragged my rotting shell by my scuffed heels into a darkened hole, where by the flicker of torchlight they threw me on to a sturdy table.

A surgeon came rushing in. I did not know his face, but I sensed his nature. Like a snake that tasted the air I knew he was Athanatos.

'Quickly,' he said, directing his slaves to lay out his vast array of glinting metal implements. He checked my eyes and felt for my heart. 'He is not sedate. Have you given him no henbane? No opium?'

The Praetorian Guard did not care. It was Athanatos' job to heal, not theirs. They retreated to the fresh air without comment.

He moved with rapid speed, cutting the filthy cloth from my body and examining my wounds with practised haste.

It made me sick to see such false concern. 'Athanatos, still alive I see. Has not the world tired of you yet?'

'No Cyclades, it has not.' That was not compassion in his voice, merely restrained irritation.

I choked on my own blood. 'How do you do it?'

'I move freely because people choose not to see.'

He drove his hands deep into my stinking cavity and probed the very nature of my self. He teased the route of my bloody entrails and determined the course of ragged puncture. For my part I accompanied him with a scream of such curdling ferocity that it forced him to wring out his curled ears.

With his arms drenched up to his elbows in my hot blood he reached for his bronze scalpels and sliced at my flesh without warning. Ragged, blackened chunks of rot he flung to the rats as though he were preparing a meal from spoiled meat and saving what parts that he could.

'Look at your wounds, islands of torment. Cyclades, you are a map of misery.'

He probed with his spindly hooks and dragged up my guts for a better look. And when the course of my fluids was determined he clamped them with a filthy finger.

'Oh the things I could learn from you. Your blood is such a very special fluid. Wouldn't it be wonderful, Cyclades, if you and I could be one some day, if I could find a way to mix our blood, erase your thoughts and steal your power?'

Delirious in my uncontrolled agony, succumbing to the shiver of Hades' grasp, I whispered, 'You want what I have? Then take it. I want it no more. I am a man trapped in a moment. For my own sanity it is not a burden I can carry any longer. *You win*! Now, help me to die.'

'Ha! I wish it were that simple. I am required to piece you back together, you reeking halfwit.' He clicked his fingers though he did not deign to look at his slaves. 'Bring me my sutures.'

With every ounce of strength I possessed I lifted my hand and held his wrist. 'Put a blade to me. Finish it!'

'By order of Caesar I cannot! One mention of Trojans, one whiff of a Greek and the man is mad with passion for another tale of ancients, you effeminate malcontent. If I have to sit through the dirge of his lyre one more time I swear I will garrotte him with its strings. You have an option; you can disappear for a few hundred years and return at whim, while I must endure these absurdities. No, my dear Cyclades, stay a while. Share in my grief.'

He plucked a leaf or two from his small supply and ground them into a globule of honey. He held it to my mouth.

'Take this.'

I refused. He held my nose and waited until I gasped before shoving it in and massaging my jaw until I swallowed.

'It's for your own good.'

I doubted that very much.

His slave returned, a tall gaunt-looking man with clouded sunken eyes and sallow skin. He set down a large russet clay pot and plucked the lid from it while Athanatos fished inside with a pair of long steel forceps.

'Look upon my works, Cyclades. Look at what I can do; look at what I have achieved in your absence. This slave had cataracts. I removed them and now his vision is restored. You bleed, and I will staunch it.'

He clamped around an object and plucked it out. It was an ant the size of my thumb. Its thin, translucent legs kicked in protest. Its glinting segmented shell twitched and scratched against the metal that bore it its torment. He brought it closer to show me. Its mandibles snapped at my eyes. The pot teemed to the brim with these scuttling creatures, each clambering over the next to escape.

I was panicked. 'What are you doing?'

'Giving you your sutures.'

He grasped one sanguinary slice of my flesh and thrust the ant down on it. It bit without mercy and clamped my wound shut tight. The pain that shot through my every fibre was a fire that could not be extinguished. But he did not let it bite again. One swift motion left the head in place and twisted off its body, which he duly tossed aside.

'I call them staples.'

I did not care what he called them and I doubted very much that they would catch on. 'Get that foulness out of me!'

'Your juices will ensure that they dissolve out of you! Now lie still! I have many more to apply.' He rewarded me with another ant in his sadistic generosity.

Bitter tears of unbearable agony wet the dust that caked my

sunken cheeks. I raised my head up off the table, the sweat of years my venom. 'You will answer for the crimes of your past.'

He waved his bloodied forceps at me. 'Which crime would you choose? Every man has a past. Mine is a thousand years long. And it will go on for another thousand years. And another. Can your heart truly sustain and nourish such hatred for so long?'

It had brought me this far. 'Why did you do it? Why did you take her from me?'

Athanatos had no answer. His face became slack with the dredging of his memory. His puzzlement was genuine. 'Take who?'

He did not even remember? I grieved every hour of every day, yet the horrors that he meted out were nothing to him. I was lost. My life was empty; a gaping hole existed from where he had ripped out my worth. Yet he did not even have the good grace to remember. He was contemptible.

I spat at his feet. 'Moira,' I sobbed. 'My life's course. My love. My wife.'

Did *that* make an impact? Had I reached at least *some* part of his obscene mind that would allow him to comprehend my anguish?

He was not touched. 'Oh, spare me. That? Over a thousand years have passed since then. She is dust, you fatalistic fool, and would long have been so even without me. She was dust before and she will remain dust. She will not rise.'

'She is risen.' I clutched at my heart. 'She is in here.'

'Cyclades, you have been given a gift. A gift that is rightfully mine, but no matter, I will see to it I shall get it in the end. You wait seven hundred years for five minutes with me? I hope you consider it time well spent. Your vengeful hunt cannot settle this. It is done. Move on.'

His voice was flat. His tone utterly controlled. But the shimmer on his instruments as he packed them away told me that his fingers were trembling. He feared me more than he ever wanted me to know.

When I was sedated and stitched, my meat oiled and scraped, my rags were discarded and I was met by Athanatos' surly slave. That anyone had an interest in me seemed to cause him much bewilderment. He tossed me a crumb of bread and told me to follow.

I could barely stand, Athanatos' magicks had robbed me of so much fight. I remember the grass felt cold and damp under my naked feet. The scent of flowers had not yet made their returning presence felt, instead the rot of decay hung in the air, the mulch of fetid leaves, a pall of wood smoke, and the moist black heart of sod which grew as the rain began to pour.

Nero's villa made little sense to me; its brightly coloured walls seemed to undulate as if they were engaged in the process of breathing. The rooms were filled with music and the faint sound of raucous laughter.

The slave made me stand in the darkness, a shadow wrapped in the echoes of raindrops until a Praetorian Guard appeared and ordered me on.

I walked through the marble halls until the cracked and uneven feel of mosaic dug into my hard skin. What creature was it that peered up at me from that multifaceted floor? A bull?

'Answer when Caesar addresses you!'

The swift kick to the back of my legs felled me to my knees. The laughter that it brought shook me from my daze. I was being addressed?

I looked around. I was in Nero's dining room, and feasting had begun.

My senses were assaulted not with fine meat and rich wine, but with the puddle of bile that I found myself kneeling in with its putrefying pieces of undigested flotsam. This was not like any banquet I had imagined in an emperor's palace. The gluttonous frenzy to eat here was not hindered because of something as trivial as a loss of appetite. When the guests were sated they had taken to heaving up their fill on the floors behind them, before resuming their work at the table.

I staggered to my feet but found I had nothing on which to wipe my hands, for I stood before them utterly naked.

Which one was Caesar? Who was my great leader who had murdered his mother, murdered his wife, and was bound to murder more. I looked for purple and saw a plump young dark-haired man with a strong nose and soft chin. He was reclined and looking upon me through drunken eyes.

'I asked you your name.'

'My name is Cyclades.'

He washed his mouth with wine. 'That's not what your lanista told me. He was quite adamant your name began with A.'

It was well known that he paid audiences to applaud his artistic endeavours. This appeared to be just such an occasion.

One fattened hag spied my parts with glee and reached with greasy fingers to probe my constitution. She took a full firm handful of my buttocks and giggled when she put in her request that when Nero was done, she would gladly have me. I preferred death. I had swum in her bile. That was quite enough of her for me.

Rolling thunder from outside infected every corner of the room. The slaves who were preparing something on the lakeshore came rushing in from the drenching, trying to save the food.

'What race are you?' Caesar inquired lazily over the din.

'I am from Crete.'

Nero sat up boisterously. 'This puzzles me. Your lanista insisted that you were a prisoner of war captured in Lycia. So are you Greek, or Lycian?'

I had not considered this. I began as a Greek, but my line

had led me to be reborn in Lycia. Did that make me Lycian? I suppose it did. Did that mean that I was somehow diluted? How could I call myself Greek if I had not set foot there in hundreds of years?

I said with some concern, 'I am both. My body is Lycian. But my soul is Greek.'

'How extraordinary.' He beckoned to me. 'Come, stand with me.'

The Praetorian shoved movement into my feet. The fattened hag slapped my rump as I went. Oh that I was that frightened young murmillo at that moment.

Nero picked up his lyre. 'I'm writing a song,' he said with a loud belch. 'It is about the burning of Troy. You told my physician that you were his Trojan memory. His slaves tell me that you fought there and are reborn.' He plucked a few strings. His skills were truly awful. He fixed me with a leer and smiled. 'Tell me, is that true?'

'It is true.'

Nero giggled like a child. He reached for a piece of fruit and looked to his guests. 'I told you he would be good fun!'

They made great show of agreeing.

Nero said, 'Troy is the tale of kings. But I have never heard of a King Cyclades. If you are not Achilles, if you are not Agamemnon, if you are not Odysseus or even King Priam, then who are you? You are but a man and you should know your place.'

I said, 'I served under a king.'

'Everyone serves under their king.'

'I served under King Idomeneus in his palace at Knossos on the island of Crete.'

I could see it now, as clear as though I had just stepped under the shade of the mighty red columns of the inner courtyard. The blue dolphins danced on the walls and the gates were open to let in the sun. Such memories.

Nero cut them short. 'So you are used to slavery.'

'I am used to being bound to fate.'

There was mischief in his eye. 'Tell me, did you go into the Labyrinth?'

'Where else was I to fight?'

He turned on me like an impetuous child. 'Did you battle the Minotaur?'

I was reluctant to answer. 'King Theseus of Athens and his exploits were before my time.'

'You must have other tales to tell.'

'Some.'

'Tell me them. I love tales. Why, I wonder, when his exploits have left barely a mark on history, would a warrior slain in the Trojan War return?'

'To deliver justice.'

Nero scratched his head and threw down his lyre in disgust. 'What a wretched little tale.'

'I am sorry I cannot provide more amusement.'

'Athanatos can, can't you, my humble physician?' I had not seen him standing in the shadows. He bowed to his Caesar. 'What was she like, your wife?'

I was cut to the quick. I said nothing. The rains grew heavier with each moment of my discomfort. The drumming of the roof tiles quickened with my pulse.

'My physician here tells me she died screaming. Though he did not shed any light on whether it was in agony or in ecstasy.'

I flinched glistening muscle. The rush of blood was so swift that I felt it in my groin. A Praetorian blade was under my chin before I could act. But the odious sycophants at the table had a clear view at what pleasure I took at the thought of slaying him.

'What book did you read that in, Athanatos, that has my guest all excited?'

I did not give him a chance to speak. 'He read it in no book for he was there.'

Nero laughed. 'Oh yes! My physician is a thousand-year-old magus! Oh you are too much!' He took to more drink. 'Everyone knows that the Trojan War began when Paris stole Helen from Argos.'

'Many wives were stolen, from every Greek land. Year upon year our towns were raided. We made it stop. Helen was the face for many.'

'But if you were on Crete, you cannot know what happened in Argos, only that war was declared when Helen was taken.'

'Paris took Helen and the wealth of Argos. He was offered this chance by *his* evil deceptions enacted on Cretan soil when her beloved husband, King Menelaus, was called away to a funeral in my land. Is that not in the history books?'

'Oh, yes, somewhere. Who was it who had died again?'

'King Menelaus' grandfather, Catreus, son of Minos, who had journeyed to visit his son on Rhodes, was killed on the beach when he got there. Mistaken, they said, for a raider.'

'And what does this have to do with Athanatos?'

'It was Athanatos who laid in wait to murder him at Rhodes. It was Athanatos who brought his body back to Crete for burial. It was Athanatos who caused his diversionary funeral and gave us *ten years of war.*'

Nero smiled. He drank his wine and nodded to his guests. They burst into applause. He looked to Athanatos with glee. 'He really does believe it. This is wonderful. Did someone write that all down?'

He got to his feet and swaggered about the room, slopping his wine as he went.

'Allot half a million sesterces, there will be more if needed. I want all of Troy reconstructed. Campus Martius will be too small. Stage it at the Circus Maximus. I want *ten thousand* on each side.' He turned to me and clasped my shoulders. 'And you, Aquilo, or Cyclades, or whatever your name is. You know the story so well; *you* shall lead the Greeks into battle.

But please, pick a name people will know. Can you do that for me? Show me Troy, how it really was?'

I seethed. Athanatos was out of reach, and leered at me sardonically when I spoke. 'You deceit-filled bastard.'

A final bedraggled slave spluttered in from outside. 'Caesar,' he said with fright. 'There has been a lightning strike. Your table. It is cut in two.'

I watched the Praetorian Guards. A comet and now this. These were dark and fearsome portents.

Nero's corpulent face clouded with misery. His guests took to chattering with alarm. Caesar threw his cup at the wall, and stormed off without another word.

We who are about to die, salute you!

About to die? What perverse humour. How many times would I have to die before my return was halted?

After the blast of trumpets had come the parade of the mighty; the charioteers and the gladiators marched in rank and file. Teams of archers stood in gilded howdahs upon the backs of sturdy elephants. Nubians rode on horseback beside Nero's cavalry troops. Chained lions, bears and tigers were led out by their handlers, while snake charmers with pythons kept the giraffes and antelope at bay.

For lunch amazons fought herds of dwarves and pygmies and Praetorians hunted hyenas. Men were gored and women beaten and raped for sport and play.

In the afternoon Troy was rolled out and assembled around the spina, while the chariots raced on and on and smashed stout men to pieces.

When the time came, I led my Hoplites into battle. We cut and we hacked and we savaged. And when, after hour upon hour of mass slaughter, Nero had had his fun, he had me impaled and dipped in pitch and torched as a candle for the night games.

I had taken my oath. I was a gladiator by Rome's design. I

had sworn that I would endure to be burned, to be bound, to be beaten, and to be killed by the sword. And I had done so.

I had learned my lesson, though I doubted it was the one they intended to teach me.

As I gazed down upon the Circus Maximus through the blistering inferno of my own blazing carcass, I took with me from Rome the hatred that I needed to endure. Athanatos had ensured that though I tired now, I would renew. I would rage on after him, relentless through the ages, while the rest had reaped a special storm that they had not asked to see.

As I burned over Rome I knew that once they put me in the ground, Rome would burn over me.

10.41 p.m.

North was woken by a nurse. Porter's green notebook was laid open across his chest. As he stirred it fell to the floor with a loud slap that echoed down the hall of the waiting area of the ER at the NYU Downtown Hospital.

It had been in the Englishman's coat pocket. With him at all times. When they'd stripped him of his belongings and given them to North to look after he'd needed no prompting to read it this time.

Less a string of pearls, than a chain of iron, each link from another life, he felt its pages dragging him down with the full weight of his history. The agony was still very much alive, locked away inside his bones.

The nurse stooped to pick it up for him and asked if he'd like to talk in private. North knew what that meant.

'What time did you pronounce?'

'Ten minutes ago,' she said.

North got to his feet. He wasn't prepared for this. He felt cheated. He could feel himself filling up. He shook it off. 'Can I see him?'

The nurse said he was already being transferred but she'd see what she could arrange.

11.13 p.m.

She led him through the sterile hallways and silently negotiated the many interior doors before descending to the basement and into a refrigerated room. Through the double doors beyond was the darkened morgue.

The nurse switched on the lights and waited for their eyes to adjust to the unforgiving neon strips above them.

The body of William Porter was laid out on a gurney in a dull black body bag waiting to be picked by the OCME for an autopsy.

'We need to contact his next of kin,' the nurse explained as she reached for the zipper.

I guess that's me. North said he'd take care of it.

She opened up the bag to expose Porter's face. This wasn't a funeral home, he hadn't been made presentable. There was still blood caked across his skin, filth from the streets matted in his hair. Even the dents and grooves from the tubes and other medical equipment remained quietly visible. But a little of the man still remained; the birthmark down the side of his eye.

It was only now that North felt truly alone.

I have so many questions. What do I do?

North became only vaguely aware that the nurse was speaking. He tried to listen. It was difficult.

'He just wouldn't heal,' she said. 'His body was riddled with scar tissue. He had a very rough life. In the end it was like he just gave up. He lost all his fight.'

Lost all his fight.

'Did you know him well?'

North thought about that. 'Yes,' he said. 'All my life.'

BOOK SIX

IN A DARK TIME, THE EYE BEGINS TO SEE

ROETHKE

THE MEIOSIS OF MEMORY

He had never witnessed so much panic in them before.

They had moved on to another laboratory to continue with their work when the message came through from the front desk. Megaera had taken the call. Her slim elegant fingers gripped the white plastic receiver and would not let go. There was a problem.

Lawless got up; faintly irritated it seemed at first, though not unduly alarmed. But when he wrested the phone from his daughter and interceded in the proceedings he was soon peeling his latex gloves from his withered fingers and tossing them violently on the hard floor.

His cane cracked with each beat of his step on his march to deal with the complication.

When Gene asked what was wrong, he did so because he knew that that one single act of concern, that one glimmer of kindness, set him apart.

He was not greatly surprised when Megaera simply dismissed him and said that it was nothing. Her beauty was great. Her intellect was considerable. It was everything else that was missing.

This entire sterile environment felt like it had been rubbed clean just through the sheer force of their hyperborean personalities.

Suddenly it all became very clear. Gene was no more than a tolerated pet, made to feel king because it suited them. At this moment, it no longer suited them.

Lawless and Megaera stormed into a large empty boardroom and closed the doors abruptly behind them. Security guards barred Gene's way.

What had happened? *How can we use it?*

So many deep holes in his memory, so many long dark gaps as the voices in his mind raged. If he could just plug a few more he might be able to understand them better. It was that or do what he had done before, and flee.

We will not be expendable.

Gene heard the faint hum of heavy oiled machinery, the whine of pulleys and motors. The elevators at the end of the hall were moving. Was this his chance?

He loitered, away from the boardroom but in plain view of the elevator doors. When their clean mirrored surfaces rolled slowly back he did not expect to find Savage standing behind them.

Savage's face betrayed his thoughts. He stepped from the car a swirl of his own despair. The men around him appeared no better. One in particular had been severely beaten. Dark plum-coloured bruises and crusty bloodied marks cut up his cheeks and around one swollen eye.

Savage was startled when Gene spoke. 'Where have you been? I didn't see you leave.'

Savage's mind was a haze. What had shaken him so? The crinkle of paper grew as his grasp on the crumpled bag he was carrying tightened.

'I had an errand to run.'

'Don't we have people for that?'

Savage saw him clearly for the first time. '*We* are the people for that.'

Keep him off balance. Make him run.

He drew Savage's attention back to the end of the hall.

'They're waiting for you,' he said, his face was a dark shadow.

Savage didn't know what to do. His couldn't think. He watched the closed heavy wooden boardroom doors and his feet turned to so much clay. Whatever it was that awaited resolution, it filled him with dread.

He remained cautious, wary of Gene, incapable of determining what level of trust to afford him. He tried to sound confident when he spoke again, but the crack in his voice was evident. 'Are you coming?'

How was he to play this? He couldn't admit he'd been neglected. 'No,' Gene said. 'I have work to do. Megaera wants our new results set up in one of the other offices. I've misplaced her key.'

Savage's indecision grew destructive. Gene saw his opportunity. 'Perhaps you can help me.'

Savage gazed down at his hand and at the single plastic security pass he had produced. It dangled from a metal chain, retaining its tight control over its secrets.

Without further deliberation he promptly tucked it away again. 'No,' he said. 'I can't give it to you.'

He resumed his long walk to the boardroom.

Gene did not give up. 'I don't need the key,' he assured him. 'I just need someone to open the door. Besides, it's on *your* head if I can't continue with our work.'

Savage winced. There was the nub of the entire issue. What had Savage done?

The older man rubbed at his aching forehead, massaging his thin pale skin with embittered fingers. The weight of making a decision was too great. Perhaps it was easier just to accept the request. 'One of you: go with him and open the door.'

The man with the bruises and the sharp features stepped out of line first but Savage had other ideas. 'Not you.'

When the selection was made Gene thanked him, but the security guard came with an unexpected sting. 'Don't leave his side.'

When Savage reached the destined threshold the large wooden doors were briefly cracked open. The argument erupted between all three of them almost immediately.

'Gene *did* find another one,' Savage announced.

'Whose?' Lawless raged.

'*One of mine.*'

Neither Lawless nor Megaera stood to greet him as the boardroom swallowed Savage to his fate.

We found another one?

Gene looked to his chaperon but he knew he would get nothing forthcoming from him. He did not linger. There would be little chance of them letting him eavesdrop and the attempt would be foolish. He would have to find his answers elsewhere.

The security guard watched him circumspectly but said nothing. He awaited his orders.

They rode the elevator together in silence up to the thirty-fifth floor. The security guard was alert and well trained. He did not spend his time watching the floors tick idly by. He watched Gene. He watched him, even as they approached the door that had been painted in impenetrable black.

The lock's small pinpoint of light changed from blistering red to emollient green when the security guard ran his pass over it.

The security guard pushed the door open and stepped inside while Gene stood in the doorway. The room was sparsely furnished with a computer, a desk, a telephone, a few books, and a mass of charts and clinical notes hanging like paper scales across two whole walls.

Two other doors led from the office. The security guard made sure they were secured and then stood in the corner and waited.

What's he doing?

'You're going to watch while I type?'

The guard remained as impassive as a stone pillar.

He must leave.

'Where am I going to go? Through doors that I can't open, that I don't have a key to? Now get out of my sight, or have you forgotten who I'm to become?'

The man tried to digest this uncomfortable information. Gene simply went about his work. He moved behind the wide hardwood desk, sat down and began working silently at the computer and without glancing back.

At first the guard did not move, but as the minutes ticked by and he watched Gene carefully, he took a chance and relaxed a little. After a while he checked that the two doors really were locked tight again before heading for the exit. On his way out he explained that he would be right outside.

The door closed, leaving Gene with the greater question. What was so particular about this room that they had wanted to keep him out of it?

He started with the layers of charts and clinical notes spread across the walls. They were not the results of genetic experiments, but embryology notes. These were fate maps.

A thousand embryos had been meticulously studied and mapped to show which clusters of cells were destined to develop into which parts of a future body as the genes kicked in.

The number of genes that made a man flesh was not even ten per cent of his total DNA. The remainder of his fate-filled thread was apparently redundant. But peer closer and there was order to the chaos. There was a purpose and it was an elegant and simple one. It was memory.

The millions of mutations in the DNA strands that Letha had earlier announced was occurring were the memories. Gene knew that the creation of a person was like shuffling two decks of playing cards. Sperm cells did not take whole chromosomes from existing cells: they selected pieces and constructed their own, new sets of twenty-three chromosomes. This genetic recombination, this meiosis of tiny single letter changes and genetic reorganizations were memories stored throughout the lengths of junk DNA, waiting to be read like tickertape, structuring the mind of the embryo so that the memories were embedded in the mind of the child at its conception.

Yet memories once they settled in the brain were not like a piece of videotape that could be played back on a television for the mind. Each memory was like a road map; where each town represented a colour, a shape or a smell. Genetic memory worked by imposing on the developing fetal brain a map of all the roads that linked the elements of memory, except for the sake of economy the names of the towns, the elements themselves, were missing.

As the child grew, so his experiences filled in the names of those towns with their colours and their shapes and their smells, completing the circuits and restoring the memories and the personality that went with it.

Gene now understood why there were gaps, and why Savage and Lawless were so concerned that their system had been failing Athanatos.

Should an offspring miss an experience and fail to fill in key elements, for example just by being colour blind, whole memories could fail to be resurrected and would be lost from the blood line for ever.

What he could not understand was how they could be so certain that what Cyclades possessed would counter this entropy to recollection. It seemed an act of desperation.

Gene shifted his attention to the ultrasound photos of embryonic development intently. What he found in the notes horrified him.

Every embryo was a child of *his*. Every deformed fetus with an arm where it shouldn't be or leg with no foot had been rendered as such because Lawless' process of increasing the load of memory committed to DNA was experimental and the results were sickening and cruel.

He pulled his file from the hook on the wall and reviewed it. Gene was Athanatos' ambitious experiment and greatest risk.

Although women could not create genetic memories, they kept traces of their fathers'. Athanatos had kept meticulous track of as many strands of Cyclades' descendants as he could through the ages, in anticipation of his return. His mother had been marked out as one such bloodline.

This confirmed everything he had suspected, that the intent of the process was to create a hybrid that was the body of Cyclades but the mind of Athanatos. A man who could father his own rebirth at will without the need for potions and elixirs. A man who would be truly immortal.

The embryos pictured on the walls were the consecutive iterations that proved Cyclades' memories were being successfully stripped out of his own DNA, leaving only those of Athanatos and the gene Cyclades used to return.

It was deduction, not memory, that told him that was why there were so many inexplicable gaps in his own memory. That was why there were holes that were collapsing into gaping chasms. Three thousand years of his life were fading away, crumbling in his mind. Shattering in his hands each time he tried to retrieve just a little more. He'd go to a place where he knew a vivid picture once existed, but now all that was there was darkness. As if the lights of his thoughts were being put out, one by one.

Yet what Gene had not suspected was that he had been a willing and able hand in the entire affair. His natural disposition *favoured* Athanatos. He had done this to himself. But the process which drew out Cyclades so that he could be erased was the very thing that gave him his sense that he somehow *was* Cyclades. His sense was a temporary and precarious one.

In truth he was the warring shades of both Cyclades *and* Athanatos. This was the seventh trial. The battle that had raged for over three thousand years was within him. He had *become* the battlefield.

And as his file made clear, he was not the only one facing the nightmare of conflicting impulses.

THE BROKEN PIECES

4.07 a.m. Saturday.

She'd blown North a kiss at the entrance to the Lincoln Tunnel and now he was ripping open her blouse to feel her small pert rented breasts tumble out into his enraged hands. She was young. Still vital. Not the haggard leather of used skank. Her hair was dark, her skin soft Puerto Rican caramel.

The insinuation of distant streetlight through the windshield gave just a hint at her flushed delicate features, a ray amid the gloom between two infested tenements.

Her beauty was more than he could bear. He gripped her tightly and thrust her back into the anonymity of the darkness.

'Careful!'

Her plea fell on stony ground.

'Hey, go easy.'

Th-thump.

'You're hurting me!'

Th-thump. Th-thump.

His knotted shoulders livid with animal rage, he loosed into the condom and held her tight until she choked for air.

Th-thump.

North would not move. He simply held her, his breathing laboured and ragged.

Th-thump.

She wrestled an arm free and slapped him but he would not let go.

Th-thump.

She tried a different approach.

Th-thump . . .

She gripped his neck and stroked him with her warm fingers, a suggestion that this all was somehow real. That she had somehow been satisfied.

North pulled away in terror.

He didn't hunger for lies. Had she asked, he would have admitted that he was barely conscious of the person who filled the limbs that staunched his need, but she was not so naïve as to ask and neither did she care.

'You didn't say you wanted it rough. That's double,' she said angrily.

North fished for more money. 'Tell Moira I wanted to see her again.'

'I told ya, no one's seen Moira in weeks. Maybe ya paid her too much. Maybe she's retired.'

North looked away in shame. 'Get out.'

'With pleasure, ya fuckin' psycho.'

She checked she still had her money and ran back out into the shadows leaving North to fester in his rupture. The sex had not healed him. His soul stirred, ever vengeful, ever watchful for that chink through which it might yet escape, but the task was futile. North wore his self-disgust in such heavy layers that the blades of his fury could do nothing but mutilate him from within.

Th-thump.

His fingers shaking uncontrollably, he tied a hurried knot in the rubber and threw it from the window as he pulled out into the road, only to swing his car around when he caught a fleeting glimpse in the mirror of another streetwalker scurrying from the darkness, scrabbling around in the dirt to retrieve his wasted seed.

What does she want with that?

He hit the brakes and bolted from the car, but by the time he got there she was gone. Now value was placed even on a used condom?

He didn't recognize this city. Not any more. Its claustrophobic streets pressed in on him, their thick vaporous fumes shrouding him from his place in the world. His life felt broken. It was as though he were a cluster of tesserae in search of a mosaic.

Ya fuckin' psycho.

He drove through the darkness, the face of his true father growing grotesquely from his own malleable features, glaring back at him through the rear-view mirror.

Ya fuckin' psycho.

Who was he, this man who knew both him and Gene?

Confusion heaped upon confusion. In the darkness that stretched before him, the waxen figure of Porter's corpse played ghostly tricks on the edges of his sight, seizing him with the burning need to flee for home.

Yet as North drove through the darkness, taking turn after aimless turn, he could find no light; he had uncovered instead the swingeing truth that he no longer knew where home was. He was immured in a labyrinth that was neither of his own making nor one he had entered of his own choosing. He was subject to its cruel whim, he was lost and he could find no way out of it.

5.22 a.m.

At the long front desk of the Pennsylvania Hotel he settled Porter's account before the night manager took him up to the shabby room and let him in to collect the Englishman's belongings.

Everything was just how Porter had left it. The towel was still discarded on the floor, product of his unsuccessful blanket. His reading glasses were arranged as though he were just about to return and resume his study of the journals.

What answers lay hidden within them?

North set the journals to one side, before deciding to place them inside the small black travel bag the Englishman had used to carry his passport and other slivers of identification. As he unzipped one of its compartments he found a collection of newspaper articles detailing what had happened at the museum, Porter's notes on how to trace him, and a magazine Porter had recently purchased.

A very familiar skull was pictured on its cover and Porter had circled the hole smashed into its temple.

North read the headline. It was promoting the American Museum of Natural History's *Faces from the Past* exhibit, not the Met, not the place where he had first encountered Gene.

What am I missing?

North thumbed open the magazine to read the article, much to the irritation of the night manager who checked his watch, his inconvenienced weight shifting from foot to swollen foot. 'Do you have to do that here?'

North was cold and sharp. 'You have somewhere you need to be?'

The night manager backed off and took to loitering out in the hall.

The Metropolitan Museum of Art sat more or less opposite the Natural History Museum across the lush expanse of Central Park. For the summer the two museums had entered into a partnership to promote each other's exhibits. This was unusual, the article went on, because the Met did not ordinarily concern itself with human remains; its focus was artistic and cultural.

North felt foolish. Why didn't he know that one simple fact about his own city?

The skull that had been placed on loan with the Met was displayed intentionally opposite the white marble form of

Protesilaos, the first Greek to die in the Trojan War, because the two artefacts mirrored each other. The bleached white bone was the battered skull of a warrior unearthed on Hissarlik, the modern Turkish hill where ancient Troy once stood.

The museum had then taken a copy of that skull, had placed markers at various points across its surface to work out the average tissue depth, and a sculptor had then used dark earthy clay to restore every twitching muscle, every slender sinew and every layer of soapy fat and smooth taut skin to slowly reconstruct the face of the man who truly had died at Troy.

This one skull at the Met offered a glimpse into the host of skulls that were undergoing similar facial reconstructions at the Museum of Natural History, a process full of surprises. The face of a 2,000-year-old Severnside farmer from England was a ringer for the man in the photograph labelled: 'Guy Gibbs, blood relative, Present Day'. There was a similar example on the next page. An Englishman from Cheddar who looked just like his ancestor, whose skull was over *nine* thousand years old.

Next to the article, Porter had clipped North's own photograph and the artist's impression of Gene. He'd also circled the peculiar birthmark that each one shared with the skull on the cover. It was starting to make sense.

North remembered stepping in the modelling clay that had been flung angrily at the marble floor, the glass eyeballs swimming in a sea of jasmine-scented perfume.

Gene destroyed the face.

North shook with the chill remembrance of that moment when he first stepped inside the museum and encountered Gene under the shadows of statues. He remembered the stiff fingers that clutched that shattered skull as though Gene, too, was held in the unforgiving grasp of his own ghastly realization, crushed under his thoughts in one almighty chaw like bone trapped in the maw of a rip-toothed hound intent on tasting greasy marrow.

A man reborn over and over, awaking each life to find his thoughts transferred from husk to husk: had Gene found himself holding the remains of his own head in his petrified hands?

Or mine?

But I don't have the birthmark. *Am I not Cyclades? Did Porter lie?*

Why had Porter not told him about this? Why had he held it back?

With unsteady hands North stuffed the magazine back into the travel bag. Porter had lived out of a suitcase. There wasn't much else to pack.

6.36 a.m.

In the snare of the Fourth Precinct, North's desk was his anchor and he clung to it. He clung to his leads stacked up in piles. He clung to the simple fax from the CSU that confirmed in clear uncompromising black and white that the print he had lifted from Cassandra Dybbuk's house in Troy was a positive match for prints lifted from the bloody glass fragments at the museum.

Eugene Dybbuk *was* Gene. It was a small victory but he took it.

He glanced across to Martinez's desk. Spread out across his whiteboard were the sketched mugshots of the assailants in Chinatown, composites from a host of eyewitness accounts. Some were better likenesses than others. The one of the older man was the most powerful of all, the most disturbingly familiar.

Why was his face easier to deal with than the messages Nancy, the PAA, had stuck to the telephone on his desk? His mother had called several times yesterday. Was it about his father's barbecue?

My father. Which father?

He couldn't deal with her right now. And in any event, it was too early. He left the note where it was, pushed away from his chair and tore the pictures from Martinez's corner of the squad room.

Laying them out neatly across his desk he studied them in meticulous detail; the shape of their eyes, the curve of their lips, the definition of their strong noses.

What was it about these faces that struck him as so peculiar? Was it that they all seemed somehow related?

Do I have brothers?

It was more than that. He reached into Porter's travel bag and plucked out the assortment of the Englishman's papers and placed them on his desk, shuffling through them until he found the magazine featuring the skull on its glossy cover.

The ragged hole where bone had been shattered featured prominently around the temple of one eye – the same place that both Porter and Gene bore birthmarks with striking similarity.

Yet none of these men bore such marks and, perhaps most distressingly of all, neither did he.

Porter did lie.

North sat heavily in his chair, the wind knocked from his sails.

Was he using me to get to Gene?

I have to see that skull.

He thumbed through the magazine and found the museum's opening times. The doors would remain firmly closed until ten o'clock.

'You found the skull?'

He peered up through sore eyes to find Martinez looming over him. He was offering a simple paper cup filled with black coffee and North took it with little gratitude.

'Perhaps. I'll find out in a couple of hours.'

'I see . . .'

The younger man took a seat but he was far from comfortable, the clouds of his own turmoil weathered his features and where the circles of his eyes gathered, his shroud of darkness began.

It felt as though North were looking into yet another mirror. He set the magazine to one side and drew Martinez's attention to the sketches. 'What do we know about *these* men?'

'Nothin'.' Martinez sipped his bitter coffee. North was not satisfied. 'Seriously, no one knows nothin'. It's like a freakin' miracle. I canvassed must be three city blocks. Nobody's talkin'. And your friend, Jimmy Peng? Disappeared off the face of the earth.'

North wasn't surprised.

'Whoever these guys are, they got Chinatown locked up tight. I dunno whether that makes me more curious or nervous.'

'Money can buy a lot of silence.'

Martinez grasped the implication. They were looking for more than just Gene.

North checked the time up on the wall. 'I thought you had today off? What are you doing here this early?'

Martinez flinched before swilling a little more of his drink. 'Ah, I couldn't sleep.'

It was a poor excuse.

Martinez remained quiet. His knee bounced up and down in well-fermented agitation, exposing the immaculate sheen of rarely worn black leather shoes.

Dress shoes. There would be a dress uniform to go with them hanging in his locker. Manny Siverio's funeral was in a few hours.

North hung his head. 'I should have remembered—'

'Hey, you got your own problems, right?'

You have no idea. Martinez's face remained an ambiguous mask as he waited for a meaningful reply, but he was to be disappointed. North chose not to respond.

Martinez did not press him further. Without warning he

leaned across the desk and scooped up one of Porter's journals, flicking through its old, worn pages. 'So your friend's been keeping diaries, huh?'

The scrawled handwriting made little sense to him. The smell that came with it piqued his curiosity. He put the tattered book to his nose and took a quick sniff. Whatever he could sense, clearly that was not it.

'Can you smell cheap-ass perfume?'

I should have changed my shirt.

North moved quickly to relieve him of his burden and set the journal conspicuously to one side along with the others.

Martinez wasn't so easily dissuaded. 'You been through those things?'

'Have *you* been through all the traffic tapes?'

Martinez shrugged. 'Most of 'em.'

'And?'

The younger detective reached into his jacket pocket and set three black and white photographs down on North's desk and fanned them out. They were worryingly blurry, almost useless, but they did show what appeared to be North on a bicycle in a collision with a Sebring sedan.

North felt the rush of adrenaline seize him from within. 'Did you get a clear shot of the plates?'

Martinez shook his head. 'I left the tape with TARU, they're tryin' to enhance the picture right now. If they get somethin' they're gonna run it by the DMV and let us know who the car's registered to, but it's not lookin' good.'

North drummed his fingers on the cold hard steel of his desktop. 'Thank you,' he said. 'That was good work.'

'Hey that's not the best part. I took a trip down to Columbia yesterday. Spoke with the Dean. Did you know Eugene Dybbuk was sponsored for his bachelor's degree?'

North surrendered to the seductive prickle of his own curiosity. 'Sponsored by who?'

'A bio-tech firm called A-Gen. You ever hear of 'em?'

North couldn't say that he had.

'It was no ordinary scholarship, they paid all his tuition, accommodation *and*, the Dean thinks, kept him rollin' in spendin' money. Sweet gig.'

'What kind of student was he?'

'Three point nine GPA. Straight A student.'

'So A-Gen got their money's worth.'

Martinez set his coffee cup down and reached for his notes. 'That's just it, on paper they didn't.'

'What do you mean *on paper*?'

'Usually the agreement goes like this: a firm sponsors a student, the student commits to 'em for a few years after they graduate, or they forfeit the money. Gene never went to work there. First he gets an internship at Cold Spring Harbor out on Long Island. Then he comes back to his alma mater for his master's and gets a job at Eric Kandel's Memory Pharmaceuticals working on drugs that slow down, stop and even reverse memory loss.'

Memory. It was all clicking into place.

North took to his own black notebook and found a clean page. 'What's at Cold Spring Harbor?'

'The Cold Spring Harbor Laboratory.'

'Which does what?'

'Genetics research. There's a whole complex. The Dean tells me one of the guys who discovered DNA used to run a school over there.'

North pictured all the well-thumbed genetics books that sat crowded along Gene's shelves back in his old room in Troy, so vivid he could almost feel their dusty pages. *Who discovered DNA? Watson and Crick.*

'Prestigious people.'

'James Watson? Eric Kandel? He's hangin' with Nobel Prize winners.'

'*Hanging* with them. It doesn't make him one. So he leaves Cold Spring Harbor—'

'You don't wanna know what he was doin' there?'

North didn't see why that was relevant. Gene was a geneticist, that part wasn't in question.

'He was investigatin' HERVs.'

North had no idea what that meant.

Martinez explained. 'Human endogenous retroviruses. Diseases that insert their DNA into *your* DNA, so whatever you catch, you end up passin' it on to *your kids*. Nasty little bastards. Gene was only interested in retroviruses that affected the brain. Memory viruses, y'see where I'm goin' with this?'

North froze.

Does he know about my memories? He can't know.

North kept his mouth shut.

Martinez recoiled from the fear written across his partner's face. He knew he'd hit a nerve but he couldn't fathom why. He took a different approach. 'Hey, all I'm sayin' is there's no tellin' what else that sonofabitch put in that syringe. You make sure they test you for everythin', y'know?'

Th-thump.

Ya fuckin' psycho.

North assured him that he would.

Th-thump.

He picked up his pen with a sharp sense of relief. His shame was buried well. 'You've been busy,' he said.

'Been learnin' a lot.'

'So, does Gene still work for Memory Pharmaceuticals?'

'No way. I spoke to the lady from Human Resources? She said they had to let him go.'

Had to? 'Did she say why?'

'They *suspected* he was leakin' their research to a competitor.'

Industrial espionage? North wrestled with the jumbled pieces of information. He could see a glimmer of logic. 'Perhaps he *was* working for A-Gen after all?'

Martinez said he thought it was a good bet.

'Did they bring any charges?'

'Not that she was aware of and we got nothin' on file. They just wanted him gone.'

'What about a last known address?'

'Student housing. Dead end.'

North scratched a thought into his notebook. A-Gen. 'Where's this firm based?'

'*That* I don't know. I didn't have time to do a search. Been dealin' with this Chinatown thing ever since y'know when.'

North let his chair take the full weight of his knotted back. It was good to discover that Martinez was so sharp, but what else were they missing? There had to be a paper trail somewhere.

Money?

'I wonder how Memory Pharmaceuticals paid Gene?'

Martinez was one step ahead. 'Regular paycheque. I already looked into it. But he's not with the bank whose account they used to pay into any more and they didn't have his details.'

'Someone does. He stood in front of me wearing two-hundred dollar tennis shoes. He's cashing cheques *somewhere*.'

'Well I ran his name through AutoTrack, he doesn't vote, he doesn't own a credit card, he doesn't have a mortgage, he doesn't even own a telephone—'

This isn't adding up. 'But Cassandra Dybbuk said her son calls her from time to time, the last time was as late as last year.'

'Not on any telephone that he *owns*.'

'So after he graduated he – what – just disappeared? How does he survive?'

Help me.

'Maybe he changed his surname?'

No. Why would he do that?

'Or maybe he's just the classic case of a paranoid schizophrenic?'

Ya fuckin' psycho.

North ran tense fingers across his clammy forehead in a desperate attempt to ease the passage of the Bull within.

'What're ya thinkin'?'

'Perhaps,' North reasoned with some reluctance, 'perhaps – what if someone's intentionally been trying to keep him hidden?'

Martinez found no comfort in that notion at all. 'Look,' he said, 'the only thing I could find for certain is that the DMV still has a car registered in his name. If they're tryin' to keep him outta the light, they haven't erased all trace.'

North remembered a car parked outside the Dybbuk family home.

'A bronze-coloured 1981 Camaro?'

Martinez was impressed.

North filled him in on a little more of its not so impressive detail. 'That heap hasn't moved in years.'

Gene was bankrolled. Cassandra Dybbuk was bankrolled. His mother.

North's attention settled back on the telephone and on the messages to return his mother's call. He peeled the Post-its from the receiver and held the slips of paper in his hand.

Martinez watched him uneasily. 'Y'know she called up here six times askin' f'you yesterday.'

'Did she say what about?'

Martinez shrugged. 'She's your mom. I guess she saw the Chinatown thing on the news, she got worried.'

Saw what? He'd been a cop for years; it wasn't as though he hadn't faced assault in the line of duty long before now. What would give her such concern that it would prompt her to call? *The mugshots?*

Th-thump.

North asked, 'Did any of these get broadcast last night?'

Martinez said that one of them had gone out in a late-night bulletin.

Th-thump.

'Do you know which one?'

Martinez fumbled around in the pile and pulled out the sheet of paper featuring the older male, the man North recognized from his nightmare as his biological father.

She recognized him, too.

Th-thump.

What else does she know?

Martinez tried to fathom North's curious demeanour. 'You all right?'

'Y'know Gene's mother told me that she was *paid* to give birth to him.'

Martinez winced but the chill within him would not distil into any sympathy. 'She was like a surrogate?'

North wasn't certain that was the right way to describe it. 'No, she played Mom and was paid to *raise* him too.'

Martinez wanted to know why.

'She said she just wanted the money.'

'That's cold.' The younger cop struggled with the harshness of this new scenario. 'Does Gene know about it?'

North said that he did.

'Man, that's gotta screw up any kid. Who's the father?'

'I don't know, but I do know he's *still* paying her.'

The tease of implication unfolded before them. Was this a real break, or just blind hope? Was the man who financed Gene's education through A-Gen the same man who had had him conceived and raised? The same man from Chinatown?

My biological father.

Th-thump.

It was Martinez's turn to check the time up on the wall.

7.21 a.m.

Martinez said he'd take care of the paperwork, but both men rose to their feet. 'Y'know they don't operate the lobster shift down at The Tombs no more, right?'

Of course North knew that. The Tombs, the New York

Criminal Court building at 100 Center Street just a few blocks away, used to operate a twenty-four hour arraignment system. Now it closed at 1 a.m. and there wouldn't be a judge in chambers to sign any warrants again until nine.

North collected the museum magazine but the mugshots held his attention.

What does my mother know?

He tucked them under his arm and fished out his car keys. 'I'm on the street. Are you done here for the day?'

The grim thought of the funeral weighed heavily on Martinez but his mind was already set. 'No. I'll be gone a couple hours, max,' he said. 'After that, 'til we're through, there's nowhere else I need to be.' He yanked out the chair at his desk. 'So we subpoena his old lady's bank records, see who's been paying her.'

'And we get a court order for Cassandra Dybbuk's telephone records,' North added. 'She said *he* calls *her,* she doesn't know his number to call him back.'

Martinez was sceptical. 'I doubt that.'

North agreed. 'But perhaps when he does call, he calls her from work.'

BAD BLOOD

Gene sat back in the office chair. He was not alone. There were others who were just like him.

Just like us.

They will understand.

Who were they? The notes and papers, the maps of fate and the secrets over which Megaera held sway were considerable, but they did not answer this one simple question.

We must know.

Since Gene's return from the museum they had all been watching him, wary of him; suspicious of his moves and of his motives.

His sudden rampage was something Lawless seemed to consider nothing more than the occasional and inconvenient side effect of the process. But it was Megaera who had demanded to know why he had jeopardized everything they were working towards by involving the detective.

He could barely remember the detective or the museum. As they sliced away at his memories and reordered his personality the fog through which he stumbled offered only the briefest glimpse of a lucid world. Yet blinded as he was to so many pieces of himself they had not robbed him of reason.

If Megaera had to ask the question, then clearly *he* was the keeper of this secret, not *they*. So why *had* he singled out the detective?

The numbers on the slip of paper.

The book in the library.

Had he already set aside the answer?

Gene put his ear to the door. The wood was thick, the sounds out in the hall beyond Megaera's small office were muffled. Was the security guard still there?

He had been here for hours – far longer than he had anticipated. It was unlikely they had forgotten about him. Perhaps they were still embroiled in their new crisis.

Or perhaps they waited to see what his next move would be.

He returned to the desk. There was one cupboard above it, there was one filing cabinet next to it, and one drawer built into it. All were locked.

There had to be a key here somewhere, *something* that would allow him to open either of the other two doors that the security guard had been so anxious to ensure remained locked. He did not care what lay beyond them – they meant escape.

Gene scoured the desk for something with which to pick any of the locks. There was nothing. He contemplated smashing open the drawer but the noise would attract attention.

Perhaps he could dismantle it.

Gene crawled up under the desk and rested his head against the back wall. The drawer was secured within a solid surround. There was no obvious way inside from the back.

The twitch of glinting metal, however, offered him everything he needed. A spare set of tiny silver keys dangled from a hook that was tucked up behind the lip on the overhang of the desk.

Inside the drawer were the keys to the filing cabinet and the cupboard. Inside the cupboard was a security pass.

*

Gene chose a door and let himself out through it.

He was met with the sound of faint cries echoing out from the crossroads of halls that flanked the sides of the long dark corridor that stretched ahead. Not the guttural sobbing of adults, but the distress of ignored infants, a cacophony of distant misery.

Gene reeled from the unexpected discovery. Clinical charts and experiments on paper were one thing. Living results were quite another.

Almost in spite of himself, he took a step towards the sound. This place was so desolate, so bleakly grey and cold. It was no place for children.

Our children.

Soon he was lost in the twists and turns of the labyrinth, with each breath his lungs filling with the smell of babies, the grim stench of soiled diapers, the faint nauseating odour of stale vomit and old formula and the sharp antiseptic sting of powders and ointments and oils.

He considered turning back but his curiosity was far too strong to allow it. Yet whatever his expectations had been, when he reached the windows he was unprepared to deal with what he found.

Rows of stark metal cots, their starched white blankets devoid of comfort, the infants that lay abandoned in these wretched bundles fighting for his attention when they sensed that a visitor had come.

Did they recognize him? Or was it merely blind desperation that fuelled their anxious attempts to steal his attention?

He inched closer to the cold sheets of glass to get a better look at them, and a few replied with their arms and legs flailing. But most did not. Some stared bleakly out into a void through sightless eyes, others had no limbs. Some were conjoined at the head or the back, distorted entanglements of crippled human fusion. These were the lucky ones.

What drew Gene's horrified attention the most were the infants that did not move. The fragile babies who seemed so exhausted from their unrelenting suffering that their small mouths flapped in a fixed, silent scream, their tiny feet and hands covered in sores from constant clawing at the rough material, weeping where their dehydrated eyes could not.

These were the next iterations of himself, the experiments that probed his genome for the signs of immortality, and it filled him with such revulsion that it squeezed the knots of his offal, bending him double and forcing him to retch.

He clung to the glass and steadied his nerve.

This is what it means to be Athanatos.

Does our work not inspire us?!

It repulses us!

You don't understand. But soon you'll be gone.

Gene marched quickly in his vain attempt to escape the battlefield of his mind. The duality of his nature was splitting further apart. Where an uneasy peace once reigned a war was now raging and would not cease.

We must continue our work—

We must leave—

'Shut up! Shut up! Shut up!'

A searing pain of seething conflict stabbed at every nerve buried in his throbbing skull. He clawed at his skin but the war would not stop.

Through gritted teeth he tried to make sense of what he was seeing. Nothing about these halls struck him as familiar. Perhaps the demon of these memories had been exorcized before – if they caught him he was left in no doubt that they would be again.

A scream of rage and agony cut through the mewling din of infants.

Was that us?

No. There were the sounds of a woman giving birth, lost in the maze of corridors. What more could she possibly add to this litter of misery?

Through the arched doorway to one of the small sterile rooms he caught his first glimpse of the birthing child, a mottled mess of infant flesh, amniotic fluid and blood.

For one joyous moment it quelled the voices.

The nurse checked its breathing, its gender and made a note that its left leg was missing before bundling it into a towel and carrying it through to the next room without so much as a thought for the exhausted shell of its sweat-drenched mother.

It was like watching the conveyor belt in a factory for human flesh.

The raging argument began anew.

'I don't know why we let them live either. When they're useless like that they're such a waste of space.'

Is that voice real?

Are we caught?

Gene's limbs seized as he contemplated the comment. It could so easily have come from the murk of his own duplicitous soul.

The footsteps drew near. She was not Megaera, her disassociated eyes told him that, she was the other one. Letha. Where had she sprung from?

She ran a thin pale finger through her auburn hair and with wistful eyes watched with him as the procedure was completed.

'You'd have this baby killed?' Gene asked.

'Interesting. They let you back in here. I thought after the last time you were to be excluded until you had completed the process.'

Gene faltered.

Letha needed nothing more. The conclusion was obvious. 'They didn't allow it, did they?'

Gene refused to answer but when she moved he blocked her progress. 'You didn't answer *my* question.'

'Though they tell me infants like that have a use,' she said, 'undoubtedly I would have had such useless flesh discarded.'

The sickening knot of an unwelcome question forced itself upon him. He could barely form the words.

'Is it mine?'

Letha seemed genuinely puzzled. 'It was not likely to be anybody else's.'

The deep reservoir of remorse that welled within him gushed uncontrollably to the surface. Gene flung her hard against the wall. 'What kind of woman *are* you?'

The outburst sent the medical staff beyond into a panic. They hurriedly began locking doors and scurrying into hiding.

She smiled that wistful, dreamlike smile. 'You should be glad that I'm not the one in control.'

Neither are we.

Letha was so much like her sister, Gene's compassion elicited nothing more than her contempt, but she made no move to woo him as Megaera had done. She had an altogether different agenda.

She wriggled free and grabbed the telephone receiver from the wall nearby and speed-dialled an internal code.

'Emergency,' she said. 'Gene's having another relapse. He's doing it again—'

Gene yanked the receiver from her hand and tore it from the wall. 'I want no part of *this*.'

She seemed puzzled. 'But you *are* this.'

'I am *not* Athanatos.' He flung the receiver at her feet.

'Then who are you?'

Her security pass dangled provocatively from her pocket. *Two cards will be useful.*

He snatched it before she could react. He would find his exit, but first there was something else he had to do.

*

Gene ran, not in blind panic but in careful control, keenly aware of every detail of his surroundings.

If he had left this place before, he could leave it again. Just as the code that had unlocked the door to his bedroom had lain buried in his mind, he was certain his knowledge of this building was there for the taking. There were only so many corridors and interconnecting doorways, only so many options. He couldn't be lost for ever.

Instinct will guide us.

He waved both security passes at random over the receivers on the walls as he went to keep the security grid distracted, but it was only on the fourth occasion that he actually passed through one.

Another stark corridor stretched before him and doors to more rooms than he possibly had time to explore. But from one corner he noticed the dim recess of a service elevator.

He moved quickly. He used one security pass on the door across the hall from the elevator while simultaneously he called for the car with his other hand.

Whoever was monitoring his progress on the security grid would not be able to determine which route he had taken to make his escape.

He listened to the rumble of the elevator make its slow ascent towards him and tried to remain calm. Each unexpected noise that echoed through the hall heightened his agitation. When the ding of the elevator's arrival brought its doors sliding back, Gene feared the worst – but the car was empty.

He stepped inside and selected three floors at random. When the doors closed he selected the fourth. When he stopped at the second destination he got off and looked for the emergency stairwell. He climbed one flight up to the next floor, found another elevator, and repeated the whole process all over again until his movements were so erratic that any security guards who might be trying to follow him would find it difficult.

The cloak of chaos hid him nicely, all the way to the long shadows of the third floor.

The atrium was empty.

Gene waited for a minute in the obscurity of one darkened corner just to make certain but no one came. When the sounds of the distant elevators faded into their shafts, he crept along the soft carpet and slipped quietly back into the library.

The lights were off and the blinds were drawn, but enough early daylight squeezed into the room to give him sufficient light to work.

He began the systematic hunt for the row that matched the Dewey decimal number he had left hidden for himself.

His search drew him to the medical section, to the volumes dedicated to psychology and the deconstruction of all manner of psychoses, where, next to Spira's hefty yellow tome on the treatment of dissociative identity disorder—

There's a gap.

He inched closer. A thin purple volume had been pushed deeper into the shelf. The code number on its spine appeared worn and faded; it matched, and when he pulled it out he noticed that the spine was peculiarly unlike any book he had ever seen before: this one had *hinges*.

There was a small brass clasp on the front. He flicked it open with his thumbnail and with unsteady fingers opened the small purple silk covers to see what lay hidden inside.

The book was not a book at all. It was a box he had a vague recollection of acquiring. Had it once contained an old surgical syringe? *Yes.* He had used that syringe. The lining that housed it had since been hastily cut out and in place of the syringe there were now a very slim notebook, a grey cellphone, switched off, and a small .22 calibre handgun that reeked of cordite.

He took the gun out first and checked its chamber. It was

loaded. He placed it in his pocket and turned his attention back to the box.

Inside the notebook he found his name on the first sheet with a table of numbers and letters marked out below it. Stapled to each subsequent page were more names, more tables and a succession of mottled monochrome chains, like a series of fuzzy barcodes. They were DNA fingerprints.

The DNA from a select group of individuals had been cut into small pieces using restriction enzymes and separated out by an electrical current on a bed of gel and a nylon membrane.

Twenty points on the DNA fragments had been chosen for comparison, twenty points where the radioactive chemicals, the probes, could bind to the DNA and determine whether there was a match.

We have been hunting.

They all bore similar hallmarks to his own. Yet one after the other, firm lines had been crossed through their names. All but the one on the final page, the fingerprint that had been labelled 'North'.

Help me?

He lifted the cellphone from the box and switched it on. After a moment it blinked and beeped and requested the code that would unlock it. He pushed the buttons by instinct, and then cycled through its menu, searching for the last number dialled.

Only one number was registered, the same anonymous number that was the sole entry in the handset's phonebook. Gene's thumb hovered over the button to connect. The opportunity to press it did not come.

The lights of the library flickered into life. The fast approach of heavy footfalls drew close.

They were here.

SHAME AND PUNISHMENT

9.45 a.m.

North sat behind the misted glass of his car across the street from his parents' small brown frame house in the heart of Greenpoint and watched it through the soak of rain swept Brooklyn grey.

I got away. He doesn't know I'm here.

He doesn't know?

He's on duty. We got all night. All night.

The echoes would not fade. The world had unfolded to an unexpected plan and the shift in perspective still smarted.

Ripping at her clothes. Throwing off her bra. Devouring a mouthful of her fleshy breasts. Teasing her nipples between my teeth, clawing fingers into her hungry soft, white skin. Handfuls of rounded ass, drawing her in to meet my rage. A frenzy of hardened animal lust. Hammering at the gates.

The front door opened.

In the spatter of unforgiving rain a woman stepped out on to the stoop, made her way down the steps and marched to the end of the street, her face hidden beneath her umbrella.

His mother. He checked his watch. He knew where she was going.

A thousand grunts and screams.

One block down. The Polish bakery on the corner.

The sweet taste of bitter secrecy.

Two cheese Danishes, perhaps a babka.

The unbridled need.

He tapped his pen nervously on the cover of Porter's Museum of Natural History magazine. The skull glared up at him from his lap.

Whose face was it that had tipped Gene over the edge?

He shifted his cellphone to the other ear. Finally someone from the museum came back on the line. 'This is Doctor Birch,' the abrupt voice announced. 'I'm afraid the object you're looking for has already been collected by courier to be returned to its owner.'

'Which owner?'

'Believe it or not, some contributors prefer to remain anonymous.'

North was unmoved. 'I can get a warrant.'

Birch made no attempt to sound reasonable. 'Detective, what happened at the Met caused our fledgling partnership with them to collapse and caused some of our contributors to withdraw their support.'

That's not my problem. 'Tampering with the physical evidence from a crime scene is a Class E felony punishable by three to five years' jail time. Do you understand what I'm telling you?'

'Do I need a lawyer? We took advice from our insurers; we liaised with your colleagues at the NYPD. We followed everything to the letter. We've done nothing wrong.'

North wasn't playing. He didn't care who had told him he could take back their exhibits from the Metropolitan Museum of Art, *no one* had deigned to clear it with him.

'I can be there by noon,' North explained. 'With a warrant. I'm sure you'd welcome the inconvenience. Or you can fax over to my office the details of *who* owns the skull, *where* I can contact them and *which* courier currently has possession of it.'

He listened to the reluctant sound of the curator writing everything down. 'Anything else?'

Yes. What did Gene see?

'Just send me everything you've got. Thank you.'

North gave him his fax details and hung up. He watched the rain-soaked street. His mother was on her way back carrying the pastries in a thin plastic bag.

Her edges were a little worn, but the slow march of age had been kind. She still had her figure. She still moved with grace. She dressed far younger than her fifty-two years. It wasn't something North had ever noticed about her before now but his mother was a very attractive woman.

It made him nervous.

She stroked the back of my neck. The closeness of our mutual crime.

He pulled out the sheet of paper he'd sandwiched in between the thick glossy pages of the magazine. The mugshot of his biological father.

I can't put this off any longer.

He waited until she was nearly at the house before he stepped out of the car, resolved to begin the unavoidable, excruciating process.

He made the long walk across the swirling street hoping he would never make it to the other side.

The rain seemed heavier somehow.

A shudder so violent that she cried out.

Water thudded into his shoulders and ran down his back in torrents, hammering him as though each drop carried with it a burden too heavy for even the sky to bear.

He tried to prepare himself. He was just a few short steps behind.

'Mom . . .' he said.

Elizabeth North heard the break in her son's troubled

voice. She turned around to face him, the fright washing over her.

'Jimmy . . .'

At first North couldn't move. Then the embarrassing awkwardness of the situation wouldn't let him stop. He fumbled with the mugshot, the rain lashing his cheeks like tears from a weeping god, and showed her the face of the man they both knew.

'Is there something you want to tell me?'

10.04 a.m.

'I thought you were going to that funeral up in the Bronx somewhere?'

New St Raymond's on a hundred and seventy-seventh. *What would I say to Manny Siverio's family?* 'No,' he said. *Too awkward.*

She set the pastries out on a plain white dish and threw the plastic bag in the trash. 'Did you eat already?'

North had no interest. He watched the puddles of rainwater settle around her feet on the faded kitchen floor.

'We've been calling you, and calling you. We were worried.'

You and Dad or you and him? 'Why didn't you tell me?'

She couldn't look at him. She glanced out the window but all that brought her was a view of her husband tinkering around in his tool shed at the far end of the back yard.

'It never seemed like the right time.'

'Does he know?'

She tried to find a corner to hide in. There wasn't one, just family photographs hanging on the walls. Three generations of North men giving service to the NYPD, a heritage crumbling under scrutiny.

'Of course he knows.'

'I grew up living a lie.'

'You grew up with *two* parents who love you. That's what

matters.' She marched to the small cherry wood sideboard near the back door and snatched a carton of Luckys from inside.

It was already open; when she reached inside for a pack, her fingers trembled so much she almost dropped it. When she got the cigarette lit at last she hid the pack in the folds of her coat. 'Don't tell your father.'

How many other things did she keep hidden? He'd never seen her smoke before now.

'Is that how you're always going to look at me from now on?'

'How am I looking at you?'

'You *judge* me.'

'What's there to judge? That my mom's a fucking tramp?'

The flat of her hand came fast and stinging, leaving an angry welt across his cheek. The remorse for her actions brewed almost without pause. She tried to make amends. 'I'm sorry . . . I'm sorry.'

He smacked her hand away.

Her voice was soft, but her words were hard. 'You've no right to look down your nose at me when you *don't know* what happened. You don't know what it takes to get a marriage to work because you've never *had* one.'

'Oh, I see what you're thinking. You think you can lay this off on someone else. It's their fault what *you* did, right, Mom?'

'It's *my* fault? Your dad's drinking and his floozies and his excuses—'

She's lying.

'What's wrong, Jimmy? Your dad not the hero you thought? Did he forget to tell you about all the times they came knocking on the door looking for him? You don't remember *Aunt* Ginny when you were five, brought you that little red train that Christmas? What side of the family is *Aunt* Ginny on? Why doesn't that *whore* write?'

It hurt to have the wind knocked from him so viciously. Everything was such a mess. She seemed to pity him.

'You don't know . . .'

Neither do you.

'What *I* did was get a little comfort. Find a little sanity. But I don't blame your father. You're *my* fault.'

North took the body blow. He looked her in the eye. 'So what am I to him? Dad's penance?'

She didn't know how to take that. All she knew was that it wrung tears from her eyes. 'You're his son.'

North thrust the mugshot back in her face. 'What's *his* name?'

She refused to look at the picture. 'If he didn't tell you then maybe he doesn't want you to know.'

'Too bad.'

'He's never been a part of your life.' She was hurting. 'Can't we talk about this later?'

'I'm working a *homicide*!'

His mother shook her head in disbelief and tied her dark hair up in the back, exposing the time-worn punctuation marks of her age, roots of white and silver waiting for the subversion that came from a bottle of dye.

She searched for a mug and a filter, then dug a spoon into the tub of earthy coffee grounds. She refused to face her son. 'He called himself Doctor Savage.'

'What was his first name?'

She grimaced at her own naïveté. 'He never told me. That was all part of our little game. Doctor Savage will see you now.' She went to the fridge; the milk was in a quart-sized bottle. 'He used to show up with his flash cars and always with the money.'

Savage. Is that my name, or my nature?

'How did you two meet?'

'I waited tables, and he didn't. He said he was a surgeon. I don't know if that was true. I never went to where he worked.'

'What about where he lived?'

'I have no idea. I think the Upper West Side. I know he had a parking permit for Columbia University so he was always up around that area.'

Columbia. Gene's alma mater.

'So what, he came here?'

His mother grew increasingly uncomfortable. She took her sopping coat off and threw it over the back of one of the dining chairs. 'There are a lot of hotels in Manhattan, honey.'

North couldn't help himself. There was a laugh in there somewhere, a cruel sardonic kind of spiteful laugh. His conception was a joke and he was its punch line.

'Where is he now?'

His mother shook her head. 'I haven't seen him since you were born.'

'Does he know about me?'

'I didn't think so.'

Her voice lost all trace of fight. She glanced out the window at the tool shed and fumbled for a spoon for the sugar. 'I have to get your dad's pills. He can't miss one.'

'I'll get them.'

'You know where they are?'

North didn't reply.

His mother, however, was wrestling with a different question. 'I don't understand,' she said. 'How did you know to ask?'

11.21 a.m.

The medicine cabinet in the bathroom was behind the mirror above the sink. Amid the jumble of packets and pots the beta-blockers were hard to miss.

North opened the Inderal and fished two pills out. He didn't replace the lid immediately.

Porter said they would stop the flashbacks.

The question remained: did he want them to stop?

Th-thump.

Could he afford to deny himself the answers that they gave?

Th-thump.

He cowered from his reflection in the mirror, petrified of eye contact with his own suspect image. His pallid skin stretched taut across his waxy face. Sweat and rainwater beaded on his cheeks, and from his forehead protruded two sharp, thick, glistening black horns.

The Bull was no longer in him. It *was* him.

Th-thump.

North's hands shook. He picked a few pills out of the container but he did not take them. He dared not take them. Instead he slipped them into his pocket, promising that he would not be weak.

The expression in the mirror suggested that he did not believe himself.

He took his father's dosage and crept downstairs. He collected his father's coffee and Danish and carried them out to him in the tool shed.

His father had such a loose, easy smile, it usually put North at ease, but not today. He had a newspaper laid out and was picking horses.

'Looks like your barbecue's going to get rained off,' North said.

'Ah, what's a little water? You been speakin' wid ya mom?' His heavy Brooklyn accent seemed thicker somehow today.

'Yeah.'

His father shook his head and carried on tuning in his little radio. 'Funny thing, life.'

No argument there.

'You know who I saw yesterday? Billy Mead's kid.'

North didn't know him.

'Sure ya do. Eddie Mead. His dad used to live right next door to the St Alphonsus Convent on Java. We all used a go over there play stickball wid a spaldeen, punchball, slapball, lose da ball. Shout over at da nuns: Hey, Sistah! Coudja trow da ball back? Okay, coudja pleeeeez trow it back?'

North wanted to say that it was before his time, but in truth it was nothing of the sort.

His dad took a slug of his coffee that he shouldn't even have and downed his beta-blockers.

He said: 'Ah dere was a bunch of us. Whole gang. Billy lived in one a dem tenement railroad apartments onna top floor. A block froma Astral, one block from da East River. Chicky lived over on Dupont Street. Schultzy over on Kingsland Avenue, which was great 'cos then we all got to go to Ralphie's. This little hole-in-the-wall candy store near Nassau Avenue, right behind Gerke's Gin Mill. Two-cent jelly bars and Dixie cups cos my girlfriend at the time used to like peelin' the cellophane off the lids and collectin' the pictures of da movie stars.'

North had no idea what his father was talking about. Not that it mattered. These were such gentle memories compared to his grim nightmare, suspiciously devoid of the black spots his mother said were tattooed on his father's character.

Was that the point of memories? *You can pick and choose.*

'Y'know, the docks were in full swing back den.'

The fifties.

'We had these cargo ships come in from all over the world. We'd go down to the banana boats and hassle the dock workers for bananas, then go sell 'em and blow it all on Eagle Street where this old guy owned a bicycle shop. And ya could rent a bike for twenty-five cents an hour. Pick the bike you wanted. Me an' Billy always fought over the black one 'cos it was the fastest.

'Then hightail it to Gus Walters's place over on Driggs Avenue, on the corner of Leonard Street. Second floor above the Park Inn bar and restaurant. His mother used to call it a saloon and mutter about any woman who set foot in there, which a course is why we was hangin' outta his window in the first place.'

He scratched a few more rings around the horses in the paper, took his Zippo out and lit up a Lucky, tuning in the radio to find another station.

North felt thoroughly alienated. The history of this man who he called father wasn't his history. It was on loan. He said, 'I didn't know any of this.'

His father seemed genuinely baffled. 'Why should ya? We all lead different lives, son.'

Sometimes not.

'So did Eddie say how his dad's doing?'

'Yeah, he ah, died about six months ago. Terrible thing.'

'Was he sick?'

'Nah, Eddie says Billy was out one day walkin' the dog. This guy just comes up to him. Wants his wallet. Billy don't want no trouble. He hands it over. Couple hundred bucks inside. Guy says hey, tanks. Then for no reason just stabs him in da fuckin' neck. Den and dere. Strings cut. Billy's gone.'

North said he was sorry. For what it was worth.

'Son, I was twenty-eight years on da job. You've seen it. Some people are just born that way. It's in deir nature. No one makes 'em like it. Dey're dead inside. Dey're just *born* evil.'

North nodded. *Yes.*

'But dat don't excuse it. Dey're under no obligation to act on it. Everyone's got a choice. Remember dat.'

How can you have a choice if you don't know the difference?

They listened to the radio and watched the rain hammer down on the yard. His father washed down a bite of his cheese Danish with more coffee, which he still wasn't supposed to have.

'Dis guy's got you worried.'

'Yes,' North said. 'Yes he has.'

'Good. Keeps ya on ya toes. But I promise ya dis, son, whatever set dis guy off, kook or not, you ain't half as worried as he is right now.'

THE HOUSE OF SECRETS

1.24 p.m.

Ploughing through the drizzle over the scoured Pulaski Bridge across Newtown Creek, between Greenpoint and Woodside, North caught a glimpse through the heavy spatter on his windshield of the legions of bleak headstones which marked the armies of rotting corpses that stood guard at Calvary, marched through New Calvary, then on to Mount Zion and beyond, their grim lines stretching from cemetery to cemetery, for gale-tossed mile upon mile.

What had put them in the ground? Age? Fate?

Everyone's got a choice.

He changed lanes, contemplating his exit. Home was close by. He could take a shower; scrub the filth from the encrusted walls of his apartment. Or he could answer his cellphone.

He fished the Nextel out, checked the caller ID and put it on hands free.

'How did the funeral go?'

'Well he didn't get up and it's too late now.'

North appreciated the comfort a little gallows humour could bring. 'I've put a name to a face,' he said. 'Savage. No first name. They think he may have a connection to Columbia University.'

'Columbia again?' He could hear Martinez writing it down. 'You think maybe that's where he and Gene met?'

How do I explain this? 'I think it runs deeper than that. Anyway, we need to do a search. Financial, DMV, property—'

'Maybe he lives up in the Barrio.'

East Harlem, or El Barrio, started at around East 100th Street and went on to East 135th Street over by the East River at the northern end of Manhattan. Crowded and raw, it was choked with the ache of slums.

Yet it also sat just a few straight blocks from Columbia University over on the west side.

North grew suspicious. Martinez sounded too cheerful for a man who had just attended his cousin's funeral.

'What makes you say that?' he asked.

'Oh, just that the kind man over at Cassandra Dybbuk's phone company pulled her records and found the only phone number that connects her to the city and it ain't St Cecilia's.'

One hundred and forty-one, Apartment 12C, East 118th Street, near the corner with Lexington.

1.57 p.m.

North gunned the Lumina across the jagged steel of the Triborough Bridge, careening through the sweep of heavy traffic, a blue strobe flashing violently on the dash. The grasping of the tyres finding grip in the wash of the rain cut through the engine's roar.

When he reached the other side he loosed a shrill burst from his siren. He tore through the busy intersection on to East 125th Street; the crumbling Hispanic brownstones threatening to crush him if he so much as slowed.

He swung the Lumina into the turn at Lexington to see a blaze of light coming the other way. A dark blue Ford Crown Victoria. Martinez had thundered up the FDR to meet him.

On 118th Street they parked side by side. At the brownstone marked 141 they climbed the steps, acutely aware that the eyes of the neighbourhood were watching them.

North unfastened the clip holding his Glock in the holster. 'Is this place in Gene's name?'

Martinez looked up to see if anyone was watching them from the filth of the upper floors. 'Nope, but unless this is a psychiatric hospital or a bank, it's the only private address that called Mom in the last nine months.'

2.06 p.m.

The heavy, chipped green door was well locked. North looked for the buzzer for a super or a building manager.

The name on the label read Saul Poisonberry. The man who came to answer the door was a repugnant, corpulent oaf with reddish stubble on his well-rounded chin that looked more like powdered egg had fused into his uneven, unwashed skin. He had a kind of wheezing leer about him, like a bloated small-time pornographer that would make even seasoned hookers retch at the prospect of putting his shrivelled parts anywhere near their own. Poisonberry mumbled something unpleasantly incoherent.

North stepped up and flashed him his shield. 'Apartment 12C.'

The super muttered something that sounded like the third floor. They took him at his garbled word.

When they crossed the threshold they both gagged at the stink. The fetor of urine and the pungent reek of old ammonia used for cooking up crack dragged their bile up for a quick sharp taste.

Th-thump.

The third floor was even worse. The stink of damp wafted from the decayed walls as they made their cautious way along the festering passage. Someone had heard them coming – Filthy needles lay scattered along the grim floor.

Th-thump.

The apartment was the third one along. They took up a spot, one each side of the door, drew their weapons and knocked on the faded wood where the number used to be.

No one came to answer. They could hear faint scratching sounds but nothing distinct.

North banged on the door a second time. 'Eugene Dybbuk? NYPD! We just want to talk to you!'

He winced at the lie. He didn't want to talk to him. Not really. At this moment the horror was that he didn't know what he wanted.

Th-thump.

He glanced over at Martinez who was straining to listen. He shook his head. He couldn't hear anyone inside.

North called out again. 'Don't do anything stupid, Eugene!'

Yet inside he was screaming for him to do exactly that and present him with the excuse.

Th-thump.

Martinez stepped away from the wall.

Th-thump.

North's finger tightened on the trigger.

Th-thump.

Martinez raised his foot and kicked the lock. The door flew open in a cloud of rotting splinters.

2.09 p.m.

The sudden hot reek of sick, putrefying human flesh overwhelmed Martinez with its rancorous misery when he followed North into the room. The repugnant stench gripped him so tightly that he spewed his puddle in the doorway.

North breathed through his mouth, the oppressive churn of his guts the least of his concerns. He crept forward, his Glock aimed at the back of the head of the man who sat immobile on the couch in front of him.

Yet as he drew closer, the crumple of darkened skin under his greasy, matted hair and the droning buzz of black flies told him that he was unlikely to be a threat.

The bacteria and digestive enzymes in his intestine had long since begun eating through his moistened internal organs and once supple bodily flesh, filling his cavities with the fluids of decay. The skin had blackened and the body bloated until it had quite literally burst apart. The dissolving fat and muscle had already begun seeping from his deflated ears. As North stepped cautiously around the arm of the threadbare couch he found that the deep blackened gash of the victim's savagely slit throat had become obscured. His face was sliding off his skull, but this was not Gene.

Martinez wiped his mouth, hiding in the shadow of his black humour. 'Think CPR would help?'

North wasn't listening. At the feet of the corpse, dancing in the draught that whistled through a broken floorboard, grimy pages torn from a handwritten notebook rattled like the dried prophesying leaves of a scrying Delphic oracle, skipping in a circle around the body of a young boy.

He was crossed-legged on the floor in a thin blue T-shirt and shorts, hunched over a small coffee table, facing in the direction of a muted television, its images of the Olympic Games crawling busily across the glass.

Funeral Games.

The boy's thin hand, his putrefying skin hanging limp from his white bones, still clutched the pen with which he had been writing in his own white-coloured notebook, just as North had done before him, just as Gene and Porter too, pouring out the memories like the ones that now lay scattered all around him. So enraptured with them was he, that he never even heard the knife's approach before it was plunged deep into the back of his neck.

His head had flopped forward. His brain had liquefied and the foul grey ooze had dripped out of his nose and mouth and pooled around his chin, where an eyeball had since slid down his cheek and glued itself to the paper. The edges of the mess were now lost under the brown crust of nocturnal visitations. The cockroaches had been out to feed.

North noticed a second notebook lying in the cheap paper shade of an upturned lamp; a husk, the parent of the dancing pages. He could read some parts from where he stood and they mirrored his own writing. Two bodies. Two more murdered aspects of himself. North felt violated.

He stooped to retrieve a few pages when he heard the noise, a scampering scratch on hard wood.

Martinez heard it too. Together they made their way cautiously along the hall towards the back rooms of the apartment. The scratching grew no louder, and neither did it change pace as they approached.

Martinez took the room on the right. North took the one on the left. He pushed its sticky door open to find a tiny grime-ridden bathroom where a large, sopping-wet rat had crawled up out of the toilet bowl and was chewing on the dead toes of a woman. Bone white maggots wriggled and writhed at its clawed feet as it freed them with every chomp and bite.

She had been on the toilet when the struggle began; her black thong had still been twisted around her ankles when someone had charged in. Her cheap hooker's clothes were soiled and shredded from the struggle.

It wasn't clear if she had been pushed or whether she had panicked, but she had crashed through an old glass shower divider where the sharp teeth of its shattering had sliced right into her neck.

Arterial spray had hosed the walls. When he peered closer to look at her blackened and collapsed face, North realized there was something horrifically familiar there.

He knew her. He'd had sex with her. He'd wanted more sex with her this morning but he couldn't find her and he'd had to settle for another. A hooker he knew simply as—

Moira.

'If only the dead could talk, huh?'

North glanced up to find Martinez queasy in the doorway, pulling his handkerchief from his pocket and cupping it over his nose.

'You gotta come take a look at this.'

North followed him into the back room where the stench of festering decay was so foul that he was forced to do the same.

2.30 p.m.

Along one wall four large black plastic trash cans stood in a line. When North found the courage to glance briefly inside the nearest one he was greeted with the squalid sight of hundreds upon hundreds of used and festering prophylactics, their discoloured contents alive with fungus and lice.

'They're all like that,' Martinez explained, crossing over to a rusted old refrigerator that was standing by the haze of a filthy window. 'I've seen this a few times. Hookers sellin' condoms to street gangs so they can salt the crime scene? Put the blame on somebody else. But this is like a whole freakin' industry.'

Against the opposite wall sat pieces of grim equipment North couldn't name that performed tasks that he couldn't fathom. The only things that he did recognize were the results that came from this chain of infested devices; tens of hundreds of DNA fingerprints arranged and catalogued.

On the wall behind the workbench were pinned notes and results, each one of them reminding whoever had been working here that *everything* had to be systematically evaluated and approved *by Gene.*

Martinez opened the icebox with care. It had long since ceased to function and he was determined not to be caught without his handkerchief to ward off the smell. 'There's only a few a these in here,' he said. 'Must be the special ones.'

He took his pen, gingerly stuck his hand inside and carefully lifted out yet another used condom flopped over the nib.

North felt utterly sick, his mind flashing with a merciless cascade of connections. He remembered the hooker scrabbling around in the dirt. How many other times had he tossed a used rubber from the car? How easy had he made it for Gene to find him through the hard brute force of industry?

These DNA fingerprints proved unequivocally that he was related to the dead man, the butchered child, the savaged hooker; he was related to Gene.

And how had he been hunted?

Stapled to the dangling condom was a photograph, a Polaroid of him caught in the carnal embrace of a now dead hooker, his name scrawled hastily along the bottom of it.

If only the dead could talk?

They were talking now.

SACRIFICE AT PHRYGIA

How many long drawn days had these flaming spirits now danced before my lying eyes? Two days? *Three*?

This Sibylline room filled with ghastly images of ghosts and shades and demons of stomach churning vulgarity, multiplied by this single oil lamp casting a thousand dancing phantoms in a flickering procession around my fevered husk. They beckoned me to join them in their ethereal gambol to pass through the solid things of earth and descend into their chthonic machinations where the walls moved and the insects spoke and the songs of silence were filled with the voices of distrust.

Such were the delirious purifying rituals of the Oracle of the Dead.

I writhed in the dirt, slave to the undulating rhythm of the terrible flame, clutching at my eyes pink with blood and stained with the kiss of fearful tears, finding courage to blink only when the ghosts left the walls and reached out their spectral arms to embrace my induced madness.

'When will the Oracle see me?' I cried out to the darkness.

When she sees you, the shadows whispered back.

I cowered. My fingers curled in the dust, finding only the dried scraps of my last meal, a heap of poisoned beans and sacrificial meats that had once sat sharply in my belly before

I heaved them across the sweep of this cold floor. When had that been? When had my sleepless fast begun? Two days ago? *Three*?

These immortal magicks and bitter brews, these vile and vaporous emetics had brought me to this shimmering edge; if only I could bring myself to look down. How the dancing shadows taunted me so.

'I *must* consult the Fates,' I pleaded.

And what if the Fates do not wish to be consulted by you?

The loud clap of a bolt and the throwing open of a door brought the world of wood smoke howling through its maw.

How long had those two beautiful young—

Were they boys or were they girls? They wore silks as green as grass and linens dipped in saffron. They wore gold on their toes and sandals of pink and one wore ribbons in – *his* hair?

How long had they stood watch over me? They made my skin twitch as though it crawled. Where had they sprung from with their locks soft as a wisp, their touch like that of the gods themselves? Were they real, or another trick of this burn of twilight? If they were of no substance, then how were they holding my hand? And why, though they reeked of perfume, did they have the strength of men?

I screamed as they dragged me out into the cold night air where the clash of cymbals rang, where the tambourines resounded, where Phrygian flute-players blew on the curves of droning reeds. The dancers twirled in the stinging air of Phrygian night, choked with the raging fumes of spitting, split wood fires, alive with orgiastic frenzy. Crested Corybantes banged on the skins of drums; plumed Curetes clashed shields and spears; Cabiri danced, and sang, and wailed at the night; the adoring frenzied whores of Cybele, men who believed they were women, so enraptured with orgiastic fervour that some had taken to slicing off their own genitals and tossing them in the fire in Cybele's reverence.

With my lonely solitude at an end, they threw me to my trembling knees before seven sacred thundering black bulls that ringed the altar at the temple of the Great Mother Cybele, whose domain guarded the entrance to the caves that led to Hades. Swollen tangles of muscle rippled beneath their thick, dark, sweat-drenched coats, where from their heavy brutish brows, horns sharp as blades protruded; my gifts to a god.

'Why do you come before us, Pamphylian? Why do you bring us these fine sacrifices?'

Whose voice was that? I could not see. *Pamphylian*. In the shadow of Mount Taurus I was born, that much was true, but I was not Pamphylian. To the darkness pricked only by the flicker of torchlight, atop the din of the drums and the spears and the wild dervish of dancers, I cried out: 'I died at Troy!'

The Sibylline priestesses stepped from the shadows; *real* women who seemed decidedly unmoved. '*All* Pamphylians are descended from the survivors of Troy these past seven hundred years. That is how your nation came to be.'

I struggled to my feet, the bulls watchful of my every move. 'Yet nothing is as it was!' I proclaimed in my unsteady haze. 'Towns have changed, buildings have vanished, and whole rivers have altered their course. I was dead. I should have reached the Elysian Fields by now but I am not there. I am here.' I shook with the fear of my memories, uncertain of my perceptions. Was there even ground beneath my twitching feet? 'I remember my body was dragged here from burning Troy, which now sits under the dirt at the bottom of this very mountain. *You* gave me that fate, here at Ida.'

The Sibylline priestesses were firm. 'We did not give you this fate. It is not within our power to give. We may have nursed you, but you are a child of Cybele. If the Great Mother, giver of life, has seen fit to raise you from the dust, as she did Attis, then who are you to question her?'

Attis, Cybele's son and lover, driven mad by her maternal lust, castrated himself and died, only to be raised again by her eternal power, and now watched over the heady columns of the temple where we stood.

'I must know who I am,' I begged. 'I must know what awaits me in my fate.'

'The Great Mother is life and her secrets are the secrets of life. Unknowable by men; known only to women.'

'As Athanatos knew when he came here in search of them from Babylon seven hundred years ago.'

Mere mention of his name gave them pause. I had never seen the flicker of uncertainty in the eyes of priestesses before.

I went further, lost to the stupor in which they had placed me. 'When the prince of Troy, King Priam's brother Tithonus, was given immortality by Zeus as a wish granted to his lover Eos, was it not here, on Mount Ida, that it happened?'

They said nothing. The shouts and the screams and the nagging of drums whirled all around us, but I did not give up.

'Not the Ida of my homeland,' I said. 'Not the Ida of Crete, birthplace of father Zeus, but *here*, with Mother Cybele. Did you think others would not come looking when the word went out that immortality could be found on the wild shores of Troy?'

The Sibylline priestesses gathered around the altar. 'What is your name?'

My chest heaved with the exhaustion of it all. 'Once, my name was Cyclades.'

Another flicker touched their noble faces; this time of recognition. 'We know of you, Cyclades.'

'Then you know what awaits me and how I may end it.'

The priestesses would not answer. They rinsed their hands and took up barley. The young one in the centre, the one with golden locks and robes of white, rose up among them and stretched her innocent arms to the sky. 'Hear me, oh great

Hades! Protector of the shades! Hear him, oh great Fates, weaver of lives! Let this man know his thread!'

With that, the other priestesses flung the barley, while the first lifted up the tail of the closest bull and taking an iron blade slit off its dangling black sack and heavy manhood in one fluid motion.

The Bull bellowed with pain as the first gush of its vitality loosed upon the altar. It bucked and it roared but the ropes held it fast. And with the strong reek of hot black blood loosed upon the hands of the high diviner she cut the fetid entrails from this ugly enraged beast and looked for favourable portents that might allow me to descend.

As the torchlight licked her face the others drew their blades and severed the tendons of the frenzied beast's neck to rob it of its strength. With hot blood flowing freely, they skinned it and carved away the meat. The thigh bones they wrapped in fat, a double fold sliced clean and topped with strips of flesh which they burned over the glowing embers of the fire, while the main carcass they roasted, pouring glistening wine over its crisping quarters.

I rocked on my heels with the pain of hunger as the flesh sizzled and grease oozed from the dark meat and amphorae of the finest olive oil were brought and poured upon the sizzling roast.

With the bones burned and the organs tasted, they banged their drums and shook with dancing and cut the meat into pieces, pierced with spits what morsels still needed to be cooked, roasted them and pulled them from the fire. While their mixing bowls they filled with wine poured in honour of the gods whose realm I was to enter and by whose hands my fate would soon be decided.

And with their fill taken, these Sibylline priestesses rose as one and lit the way to the precinct with flickering torches. Their greasy smiles broad from an appetite sated, they bade me stand and follow them, past the first forecourt where I had spent my purification days and on to the dark dank hole that burrowed into the very depths of stark Phrygian Ida. This hole in the earth was the gateway to Hades, the passage to the Fates and the terrifying horrors that awaited me, from where I could already hear the strange sounds from the chambers buried deep within.

'It is time,' they said as one. 'It is time for Cyclades to journey into the underworld.'

The black womb of Ida took me in her clammy embrace and pulled me through the slimy twists and vaporous turns of her chthonic whim, down, down into the depths of the earth, beneath the worms and the roots of trees, beneath the rocks and the sunless springs into a place of such vile bleakness that it could drive men to despair.

Here, the air was hot and sticky and smoke-filled; here whisperings of the spirits and cries of the forgotten were met with the grip of angry shades; here I came to the River Acheron, the river of woe, beyond which stood the tarnished Gates of the House of Hades.

I stood at the shoreline and felt its frigid waters lap at my toes, desolate and petrified, as through the veil of murk the wizened boatman came, decrepit old Charon on his gnarly skiff.

I clutched my silver obolus tightly and when he stretched out his withered hand I paid him with the coin. He said nothing, nor did he help me into his vessel. I staggered in my delirium and collapsed on to the seat while he stretched out his back and, with two sturdy oars, heaved me across the still waters.

Into the mists of Acheron we sailed, into this quiet reflective place where my exhausted limbs and my fading breath withered. I closed my eyes, the whirl of it all a heavy burden I could bear no longer.

When I awoke it was to shrill sounds. I was slumped on the far bank of Hades, surrounded by the angry shades of soldiers, their phantom armour burnished by the smiths of the underworld. I leaped to my feet and retreated before their spears of ash and flashing bronze.

A voice from the gloom asked: 'Do you not recognize them, Cyclades? Do you not know the faces of the men with whom you went to war?'

There was no Odysseus here, no Achilles or mighty Ajax. These were not the kings of Greece who led the way to Troy, nor the heroes of the war songs sung in their godlike honour. These were the anonymous men, the faceless men, the fathers of stolen daughters, the husbands of captured wives. These were the angry sons of Greece, men like me, the men who *fought* the war.

I looked away quickly and stepped back, lest they possess my soul, yet the shades retreated further. They scurried back to their holes and whimpered.

'They see in you something darker than Hades' shadow.'

The apparitions shrieked and cried from their vantage points in the ghostly murk of the underworld, revealing before me the Oracle who sat in the grey gloom beneath the Gates of Hades, divining the waters of her burnished krater.

Stretched behind her hooded head a vast pit had been dug into the earth, and somehow, far beyond my fathoming, the remaining fearsome bulls from Cybele's altar had been cast down to Hades before me, their throats slit to fill the pit with their hot black blood. Shadow feet and other revolting creatures were stooped around its edge, drinking their fill and gathering strength.

'Ancient violence longs to breed new violence,' said the Oracle. 'And when its fatal hour comes, the demon takes its toll. No war, no force, no prayer can hinder the revenge meted out by your hand.'

I inched up the cold muddy bank towards her with disquiet. 'My hand?'

'You made a vengeful pact, Cyclades, with Mother Cybele; you for justice, her for spite.'

Why would she not show me her face, this hunched crone at the crossroads of Hades? I reached out to her. 'What was my pact?'

'For Athanatos' crime against you and for his impertinence in seeking immortality she laid with the tempestuous god of his people, the Great Bull, Babylonian Adad, *Lord of Storms*! She carried his seed from their union and placed it inside you, where it could grow only in a bed of rage and churn through the ages, the most vengeful storm of all!'

A mighty roar went up from the spirits and the shadows. The shades around the pit screamed and howled and beat their breasts with filthy balled fists.

For my part, I stood transfixed in terror.

'Cyclades, you have been cast upon a chariot drawn by the Hours themselves. Each one of your lives to come will be an island, like those that lie circled to the north of mighty Crete; like a thread woven into the sea of time, each stitch of your thread will be the islands upon that sea, and you will awaken upon the shores of each stitch, and draw your thread further around the circle until the cycle of your fate is complete.'

This was never to stop? This was madness. Perhaps *I* was mad. 'A man's life blood is dark and mortal,' I pleaded. 'Once it meets the earth, what song can sing it back? None. Yet I have sprung back from wormed torment? I should be dead!'

'Death is a skill you will find elusive.' The Oracle washed her hands in the mixing bowl as if to wash her hands of me.

'Death finds me . . . disagreeable?'

She rose to her diminutive feet, her face still hidden in her shroud, and ferreted off into the darkness, her voice an echo of before. 'You dare deny your fate?'

She would leave me here? I ran after her. 'I deny it!' I cried.

'How can you deny a path you are already on?' she asked in warning as I chased after her into the swirling mists and ran into a web of bloody threads.

Thick red oozed from thousands upon thousands of sinewy tangled tendrils that punctured the mist in every direction. And in the pools that dripped beneath them the lives whose fate was spoken by each one unfolded across their glassy surfaces. It was as though I were a god looking down on the smallness of their existence.

Yet the threads were not static, they moved and they stretched, they knotted and they squeezed, and where the threads crossed, the lives of those below entangled. And where the threads met my flesh, they cut and sliced right through me and dragged me screaming to the edge of the pit that sunk beyond the bounds of Hades, where within the endless gaping mortar a mighty pestle extended into the bowels of the earth, the Spindle of Necessity on which all the revolutions of men turn.

Seven mighty circles of bronze revolved in slow orbits around it, a Siren on each one singing a hymn to the throne above, where sat the Three Fates, the daughters of Necessity, who made even Father Zeus tremble. Spinning the cycles of life and mortality, weaving the threads of destiny, Clotho spun the threads of the Past, Lachesis measured and weaved them in the Present, and Atropos sliced them off when their times had come.

'See the slicks of your rage, Cyclades!'

A dripping thread of destiny extended from my belly – though I clutched at it and tried to control my actions, it yanked me on to the first churning circle of fate. Blood oozed between my fingers and in the drips and pools between my feet I saw at once my past and I was broken.

Moira, my wife, my love.

She was the finished fate of me, the line the gods had seen fit to twine with my thread. I fell to my knees and wept over the cruel puddle of my life.

She was alive again in my blood. On the burning crags along the wild shores of Crete I stood with her and watched as King Idomeneus solemnly accompanied the body of his uncle Catreus, slain on Rhodes, back to Knossos; back to hold the funeral games that the honoured House of Minos held; the games where King Menelaus came to bid his grandfather goodbye.

I stood with her again and felt a little of her warmth, her joy at the chariot races, the spear throwing and the hurling of the iron ingots. How she gasped with the crowd and ran through the hard stone porticos and balconies of the palace, beneath the blood red columns, peering into the Labyrinth below to watch me run with the bulls – leaping over their sharp black horns, escaping the trample of hooves in the hot dry dust, while the mighty wooden gates blocked the paths before us, making true the sport.

And in the evening, when torch was set to funeral pyre, I watched her face against the flame and knew I would never see another face more beautiful than this. I would never find another heart whose truth made such pitiable things as me possible.

I stretched out my fingers to her, but all I met was blood.

The Oracle yanked at my oozing thread and dragged me further on; on through the puddles where Athanatos waited, on through the puddles where he struck. I slid through the blood of my memories, watching my vengeance unfurl through the ages, watching my rage and storm, filled with the burn of hate and fury, on and on from stitch to stitch, raging life to life!

I slumped at the feet of the Oracle, consumed and bitter and weeping. 'She means that much to you, Cyclades?'

'She is my vow.'

'Then cast your eye back over the circles of your life. Look at the blood, look at your vow!'

I did as I was bid, scowling at the sticky pools of my cruor through which I had crawled.

'If she means so much to you, why is she but a petal on this rampant sea of hate?'

'You do not understand.'

'Go find Athanatos. Rage on, Cyclades, if you must, if that will bring you peace. But know that you rage for *you*. You do not rage for me.'

I heard her words but could not believe she had spoken them. Stinging with sickness I looked up at the face of the Oracle and saw instead Moira weeping over me.

'My dearest Cyclades, was I nothing but heartache to you?'

My hands trembled, my body shook. I tried to hold her feet and kiss them but there was nothing there.

'I am a shade,' she said. 'I am a thought. I am a woman who touched you and whose touch you miss as though a part of you were missing. Why would rage honour that? I am the sweet air of spring. I am the dew upon the ground. I am the birds who dart for berries. I am the peace at sunlight's dawn. I am with you *every* day. So when you have finished raging, my love, and the grief has finally passed, remember *that* and celebrate *me*.'

When they set me sail upon the Styx and rode me down the bitter river of hate, she was gone and it was as though he had taken her from me all over again.

It was the rawest wound of all.

I gasped for air and choked back the tears of my madness. Surely the Oracle would see me soon?

Had the morning star yet led twilight into day and raised the sparkle in Niobe's tears, the springs that gush down the craggy rocks of Ida? Had the sun circled round again and lit the rugged mountain tops of far-flung Phrygia? Or did she sit trapped in shadow, mistress to the cold mountain air?

How many long-drawn days had these flaming spirits now danced before my lying eyes? Two days? *Three?*

I could not say, nor could I fathom.

3.08 p.m.

Everyone has a choice.

North clutched his handkerchief to his face, sick of the stench of death, wishing that he could get some relatively clean air out in the filth of the hall. He felt the gaping hole of loss shake the foundations of his chest as though his ribs were about to collapse in on him.

Moira.

Another Crime Scene Unit technician stepped inside the fetid back room of the apartment carrying a silver case of heavy equipment. He tried to strike up a conversation with North as he rummaged around in the putrefying green mess of used condoms, collecting lice and maggots with a small pair of tweezers, but North was somewhere else, anywhere else but here.

He overheard Martinez talking to Robert Ash in the tomb of the lounge. Time of death for all three vics was placed at around eight to ten days.

When the flashbulbs of evidence-gathering sizzled and popped North had had enough. He had to go.

He pushed past the heave of CSU investigators, but when he reached the door Martinez barred his path, his cloud of concern tinged with grim suspicion. 'What's Gene want with *you?*'

North said he didn't know.

'People are gonna want answers.'

'*You* want answers.'

'Fuckin' right I do.'

North didn't know what to say. He didn't know where to begin.

He could feel the eyes of everyone around him boring into the back of his head, burning, probing, trying to peel away the layers of his veneer and peer beneath his surface. It provoked rawness like North had never known. He turned on them.

That was when the telephone rang. The ordinary unremarkable black handset that belonged to apartment 12C.

Ash quickly pointed out that it hadn't been dusted for prints yet. North used his handkerchief and when the room fell silent he prised the receiver from its cradle and put it to his ear.

At first he heard nothing. After a moment, something that sounded like the rustling of clothes.

North was reluctant to say anything – whoever had called was going to know something was wrong as soon as he spoke. Yet as the silence grew, he felt forced to act.

'Who is this?' North asked firmly.

'Hello, Detective North.'

North met the expectant gazes around him as directly as he could. He took a quiet breath, the hairs on the back of his neck already starting to prickle. He tried to sound as calm as possible.

'Hello, Gene,' he said.

BOOK SEVEN

CHARACTER IS FATE

HERACLITUS

THE DOMINANT

Gene sat on his haunches hidden in one aisle of the library; the bodies of two dead security guards arranged neatly at his feet, thick dark slicks of blood pooled beneath their heads, the bullet holes small but savage.

He kept the cellphone pressed to his ear while he searched inside the jacket of the closest guard: a slim black wallet.

He listened to North's breathing and the scurry of activity hidden somewhere behind him at the end of the telephone line. He wasn't alone – North was not cast adrift like he had been, forced to make do with what he could find.

'I envy you.'

There was a reticence in North's voice, but the curiosity that ate away at him still spilled down the telephone line. 'Why would you envy me?'

The wallet held nothing important; a little money but that wasn't what he was after. Gene put it on a shelf and searched another pocket. 'How does it feel to be resurrected?'

The resounding silence from North was answer enough.

'Unnerving, isn't it? Nightmares that infect your every waking thought, consuming you until you become paralysed with fear.'

'Where are you?'

The abruptness of the question took Gene by surprise. His answer was faltering. 'You don't waste time.'

He set his new finds out on the floor. A Zippo lighter, a penknife, another security pass. *That's more like it.* 'Are they *all* dead?'

'Are *who* all dead, Gene?'

He reached inside the jacket of the second dead guard and retrieved another gun, a compact black SIG Sauer P245. *Better.* 'The others,' he said. 'The ones who were just like us.'

'Like *us*? How are you and I anything alike?' North asked bleakly. 'I didn't *butcher* four people.'

Gene rose to his feet and moved towards the center of the library, scouring the room until he found what he had been hunting for.

'Perhaps you didn't murder anyone in *recent* memory,' he replied simply.

'It's the only one that counts,' North said.

3.13 p.m.

Th-thump.

North gestured hurriedly to Martinez. The young detective was on his cellphone, urging the phone company to speed up the line trace.

Ash had inspected the telephone cradle already, but there was no caller display.

North resolved to keep his tone impassive and indomitable and the conversation alive. He was failing. He asked: 'How's Savage?'

Th-thump.

Gene did not answer. The only reply North could discern was the scratching of metal, the squeak of screws and the snapping of brittle plastic.

What's he doing?

North pressed him further. 'Savage,' he said, 'he's much older than I remember.'

It was not a comment that went unnoticed by the others in the room.

Eventually Gene replied, 'You have him worried.'

Th-thump.

Good. 'Why do *I* have him worried?'

'You're the experiment that didn't work; the one who would not remember. You're Savage's useless child that failed to achieve his dominance, but you found him nevertheless.'

I'm an experiment? The grip of fury was absolute. *An experiment.*

Don't bite.

Everyone has a choice.

'Perhaps I didn't want to remember.'

'And you wonder why I envy you? I wonder what it was like to have a *normal* life. A childhood untainted by the squalid nightmares of death, decay, butchery and sex running rampant in the mind of a three year old.'

North felt no pity. 'It didn't have to be like this.'

The reply was desperate. 'You think there was a choice? I'm not who you think I am.'

'No, Gene. You're not who *you* think you are.'

Martinez feverishly scribbled something down in his notebook and held it up for North to see.

'He's on a cellphone,' the note read.

He could be anywhere.

Gene removed the cover from the final smoke detector on the rear wall and dropped it at his feet. Using the penknife he carefully stripped the wires before unscrewing the dulled electrical contacts. Each one he kept pressed firmly to the glinting blade so that as he removed them from the sensor, the unit remained wired into the building's security network.

'Why hunt and kill if we're so *alike*?' North demanded.

Gene twisted the thin wires together to secure the circuit in a makeshift knot.

'Because I want this to end, this disease of remembering. I want to be whole again.'

He pocketed the knife and returned to the centre of the library, stepping over the two dead security guards as he did so.

'If you're a splinter from a former mind, did you ever think to ask yourself *which* mind?'

Gene ignored him. He was unpleasant. He studied the gleaming metal sprinklers dotted along the ceiling instead.

On the floor above the library, he remembered, sat the vats and canisters of chemicals used in the laboratories on the upper floors. Some were highly explosive: hydrogen, acetone and butanol. Others, like hydrochloric acid, scoured the air and corroded in clouds of gas.

Gene couldn't reach the sprinklers and he couldn't deactivate them. Each head relied on either a soldered link or a small glass tube to independently fracture under the intensity of billowing heat. He would have to think of something else.

Change the floor plan. Move the bookcases. Stop the sprinklers from reaching the corners of the room.

He watched the two security cameras. He would have to remain out of their sight too if this was to work.

'I don't know why I ever asked for your help. You don't understand,' he said.

'Here's what I understand, Gene; I understand that who we are is revealed to us not by what we think – but by what we *do*.'

'I already know what you're going to do.'

'And what's that?'

'You're going to kill me.'

3.16 p.m.

The line went dead.

North dialled star 69 and called the number that it gave him, but Gene wasn't answering. He slammed the receiver down angrily. 'Where is he?'

Martinez cupped his hand over his Nextel, 'They're tracin' the nearest cell tower now.'

'Forget the cell tower,' Ash interjected hastily. 'You'll be combing four city blocks. Tell them to check E911 capability You'll be accurate to fifty yards.'

Martinez shook his head when he disconnected his call. 'No E911. He's usin' an older handset registered to *this* address.'

'What about the cell tower?' North persisted.

'It's in midtown. Seventh Avenue. Somewhere north a Times Square.'

It's close enough to Hell's Kitchen.

Gene hadn't been heading for the Lincoln Tunnel when North had chased him from the museum; in his confusion he had panicked. He had gotten lost.

Gene stacked more books in one corner of the library until he was content with the size of his pyre. Sheltered from the sprinklers and cameras by the sturdy wall of rearranged bookshelves, he flicked open the Zippo and began his purifying blaze.

The flames licked the dry paper, taking a moment to find purchase before the pages of the tomes that sat along the top began to blacken and curl as though some infernal demon had taken to reading their esoteric contents.

If books were how mortals remembered, then perhaps this was the way they forgot.

Our father has much to answer for.

He retrieved the rolls of vellum and parchment, the meticulous records of an immortal lineage, and tossed them on the smouldering pyre.

On his way out he noticed that somebody had left an empty

plastic bottle that once contained mineral water disposed in the wastepaper basket.

He retrieved it quickly, scavenging a roll of Scotch tape from a further drawer to attach it to the barrel of one of the guns; a poor man's silencer, good for one shot.

At the emergency telephone hanging on the wall by the door he tapped in the code he'd seen Letha enter and disguised his voice. Gene, he said, was heading for ground level in his bid to escape.

He hung up the receiver, marched out into the hall, stepped into the elevator, and selected the button that would take him all the way to the top floor.

3.35 p.m.

North ploughed his Lumina through the thundering sheets of black greasy rain, Martinez trying to keep up behind, darting through the cantankerous jostle of densely packed traffic, flashing blue down the speeding sweep of the Henry Hudson Parkway.

North radioed Central and issued a *10-48*. The radio crackled in response, ordering the first half dozen available radio cars to patrol the eight blocks surrounding Seventh and Broadway at the Duffy Square end.

The grim black tempest that battered the city was quickly alive with the gathering flash of the reds and the blues.

North's Nextel chimed for his attention on the passenger seat. He switched it over to radio mode and heard the rumbling, harried voice of Martinez speeding alongside him.

'They're gettin' nothin' in the squad room. They ran the name Savage through AutoTrack and Accurint. Zip. And there's *no* firm called A-Gen listed anywhere in the city. It's like we're chasin' ghosts.'

If only.

'What about bio-tech firms with offices in and around the theatre district?'

'It's a bust. Maybe they already went out of business? Maybe it's just a front for a different firm.'

A-Gen. A for Athanatos? 'Or perhaps it's short for something else.'

He wouldn't be that blatant, would he?

'Fuck! What're you fuckin' insane? Can't ya see the flashing blue light?'

What?

North glanced across the storm swept lanes of traffic to see Martinez's car swerve to avoid a slower vehicle pulling out in front of him.

The colourful tirade was ceaseless. North clicked the Nextel back to cellphone mode and left him to it.

He pulled out his black notebook and spread it on the dash behind the wheel, restlessly flicking through its tattered pages, trying to find anything that would jog his memory, trying to keep one eye on the swirling road.

What am I forgetting?

Alert and cautious, Gene left the elevator. There was one security guard in the plush hall to meet him.

Quickly he raised the gun and fired. The plastic bottle flared like a neon tube and shattered at one end as the bullet emerged silently and drove into the security guard's skull.

A spray of blood peppered the walls as he collapsed to the floor without a sound.

A set of polished mahogany doors barred Gene's way and there seemed to be nowhere to wave his string of security passes, there were no number pads at which to key in his codes.

He ran his fingers over the unyielding wood, searching for a weakness, but it was only when the elevator doors closed behind him that he heard the heavy sound of the lock release.

He pushed open the doors gently, took his first quiet step into the marble reception room that lay beyond and came face to face with his Babylonian past.

Delicate dusty clay tablets covered with the intricate patterns of cuneiform hung proudly on the lapis tiles of the walls. He could read them as easily as he could read English, and it disturbed him. King lists and poetry and great epics, that marked the lives of heroes and meddling of the gods – Inanna, goddess of war and carnal lust; Gilgamesh, hero of all men, who braved the wrath of the gods in his hunt for immortality.

'Death is what the gods gave men; *Life* is what they kept for themselves.'

Gene watched his father creep from the shadows, his ebony walking cane striking the hard marble with each step. The thin pale face showed not surprise that Gene had come to him, but arrogant satisfaction that his son's instinct to kill was in perfect working order.

He knew we were coming.

'Isn't that what we were taught in Babylon?' Lawless asked. 'That Death has no face or voice until it shatters our lives, abandoning our spirits in the miserable black of *the land of no return*? I ask you, is that any way to live?'

Gene said nothing. He watched the withered old man and was repulsed.

Lawless knew that look. He turned his back on him. 'It's not *me* you hate,' he said.

He stepped into the gloom of his apartment confident that Gene would follow. 'Do you think that I don't share your revulsion when I look into the mirror? It's *age* that offends you, Gene, like it has always done; the decay and the corruption of remorseless, unforgiving time.'

'I hate you for *far* more than that,' Gene said, following darkly in his wake. 'I loved her.'

'Then why do you remember taking her?'

'I kissed her . . .'

'Do you remember *raping* her?'

Lawless's words cut like the rusted metal of a dull blade. Gene tried to defend against it but was torn anyway. 'I fought for her . . .' he said.

The withered old man gazed upon his son. 'And yet?'

And yet the answer was already there. Fully formed and terrifying. Gene stumbled over his words. 'I murdered her.'

'Yes. How easily we forget.' He turned his attention to the stone tablets and ran a shaking finger over the bumpy surfaces. 'I wrote this, so the records tell me. I have no recollection of it. It's lost. It destroys me to contemplate what else of me is missing; but at least together we can stem the flow.'

Lawless led Gene into the open expanse of the lounge, from where they could see the raging black storm that lashed the city and rattled the windows.

'You are in conflict,' Lawless explained. 'What is it the Hindus call it, Maya? The *self* is an illusion, a veil that blinds us to our true nature.

'The mind is an atlas filled with maps. Neurons search our selves according to their direction. People born with missing limbs feel phantoms move because they are born with an image of their body fully formed in their minds at birth.

'And like phantom limbs, you possess a phantom personality within you, which together we are purging, discarding like old clothes. My boy when *the process* is complete, in you we will have achieved what we set out to do all those years ago. We will have immortality without the need for potions, without the need for merciless gods. It will simply be our nature to endure.'

Gene's face suggested that he took little comfort in that notion.

'You seem disappointed. Were you looking for a different answer?'

'Gilgamesh failed,' Gene said.

'And they sung a song about the fool for millennia. Yet here we are. We have done what Gilgamesh could not. I have taken root, and I will not cease to flourish.' He took Gene's young hands in the gnarl of his own and stroked their backs with his thin wretched thumbs. 'A thousand hands need but one mind.' He looked deep into the turmoil he found in the eyes of his son. 'You don't need the gun.'

Gene regarded the clumsy silencer taped to the SIG Sauer with disdain. 'No,' he said. 'You are right.'

He tossed it aside. It clattered on the hard floor.

He watched the ferocious cyclone lashing the windows. If this was not *his* ire then why was he so compelled to do its bidding? He felt the rage of ages and with the bellow of angry phantoms in his ears he knew what he had to do.

He reached for his father's throat.

'This is going to hurt,' he said.

Before the violent unforgiving fingers of his son pressed down upon his thin windpipe, before the tears streamed down his pallid cheeks, before the flowers of bursting blood vessels bloomed across his pale eyes, Lawless smiled the faint wistful smile of resignation.

'It always does,' he said.

INTO THE STORM OF SPEARS

We angry sons of Greece who nurse such bitter rage – oh, Muses, sing the song of our fury! Let us knot the ropes of death around these Trojan necks and pluck them for our instruments; a funeral dirge to make us drunk with retribution.

Hear me when I say that I was there. I was there at dawn's first kiss when we set oar to glistening water. Long black ships of war, fast and agile, a furious swarm of insects, a thousand pentekontors skimming the wine dark sea, vowing to slake this thirst for Trojan blood.

I was there. One among fifty. The oarsmen to each vessel, stretching out our backs, how we heaved our mighty ships along the coast to tame the wild shores of the east and have them taste what they had served to us. How we vowed to make them gorge on bloody decimation. One year. Two! Laying waste to all in our path, isolating the harlot until her exposed flanks were nothing but a carcass awaiting the carver.

Weep, Troy, weep. We angry sons of Greece who nurse such bitter hatred shall see your towers topple, yanked like rotten teeth from your greedy, diseased mouth.

I was there. The day fifty thousand men poured forth from those black-beaked ships and marched upon the blustery plains that stretched before the frigid waters of swirling

Scamander. How the earth shook beneath the march of men and horses! How the glare of desperate daylight was diminished by the rage of long-haired Greeks. How the sky was black with spears and death arrived beneath their far-reaching shadows. How Protesilaos fell skewered into the ground, his young swirling blood first warning to us all.

Shriek, Trojans, shriek! Make the terrified din of war, like wild beasts with backs against craggy rocks. Bawl you mewling children and fall on to your knees. We hard-fought Greeks are braced for endless siege; we breathe as one, a mighty lion stalking you, our prey. So cower now behind your shields and choke upon these clouds of dust that swirl about our feet. One man who falls is nothing to the mighty who remain.

Agamemnon, king of all Greek kings, rally us with your battle cry! Promise us that father Zeus will never defend a Trojan. Let the vultures eat them raw.

Odysseus, wily king of all tacticians, stretch you plans before us! Promise us Athena will not throw us to the wolves. Let your traps ensnare the Trojans, corpses festering in the dust.

Achilles, king of all great warriors, show us that your blade is sharp! Promise us that Ares will not butcher us this day. Let us see you climb the ramparts, let us hear you roar.

We ten-tongued men of far-flung Greece stand with you on this plain. We Myrmidons and men of Argos, Aegina and Pherae. We Boeotian troops and Phthians, men of Ithaca and Locris. Lorian troops in long war shirts, and Epeans famed in battle. We Cypriots rage, we Phylacians too. We Cretans thirst for justice. We ten-tongued men of far-flung Greece will mete out the murderous sentence. Condemned you Trojans are this day when we slaughter all before us, and mark the path that casts your souls upon the road to Tartarus.

Hear the savage clash of armies and the slamming of the shields! Hear the pounding strength of fighting men, and the roar that struggle yields. The screams and cries of triumph and the choking of despair when the bronze awash with hot bright blood wages war for ten long years!

Oh, Muses, sing the song of our slaughter! Let us tell the tale of how men fought and died. Not kings, not us, but anonymous men, the savage beasts upon whose backs this tide of war was carried.

Hear me when I say that I despaired. I despaired at the prize of soulless work, to rend all men asunder, reducing limbs to bloody stumps. I despaired at the pound and blow, the thud of arrows raining down, puncturing breastplates, spearing flesh; the frothing blood where arms and legs were a rolling mess of carnage in the dust.

I despaired. One among thousands. The soldiers to each army, stretching out our arms, how we heaved our mighty spears across the plain to skewer these wild curs from the east. How we sliced their bellies and watched their bowels spill loose upon the ground. Pulling thrusting blades from the back of Trojan heads and using their tattered war shirts to wipe away their red.

Rage, Greeks, rage! That the greed of Trojan men brought such grim, degrading work as this to your door.

How we mortal sons of Greece were marked by so many graves. Oh, Muses, sing the song of our fallen. Let us stalk this field of corpses and drink from pools of cold black blood a toast to those too fetid for the pyre.

This I saw upon the blustery plain. Body piled upon body, their rotting ribs the clutch of Hades' wrenching fists grasping for more, bloated with the breed of flies feeding with the worms, seething in their carrion lust. Carnage, corpses and piles of armour, cracked black teeth with tongues gouged out. Broken limbs and cratered heads, fat and dust turned all to sludge. The grim bones of Trojan men lay scattered, like grey shoals of fish caught in Poseidon's net, not a patch of sand was left unscathed from when we first breached these plains, for now Scamander swirled with blood and wept with bitter tears of shame.

And on this crested ridge this night, overlooking the Trojan battlefield, we marvelled at the horror where a thousand fires blazed, the camps against the walls of Troy, her suckling allies who would not see her die.

In silence we marched upon them, prepared for the rule of fate. It was not over, no not yet, there were thirsts still left to sate.

This Trojan War, this harlot's greed, she wanted blood, she wanted me.

Gene stood before the rattling windows, peering out through the swirl of the storm-lashed city, watching the gathering flash and burn of red breed more and more patrol cars, through the streets stretched out below.

He listened to the sound of shallow breathing. He was being watched. 'Have you been there all this time?'

His visitor would not reply.

Gene didn't fear the scrutiny. 'Keep to the shadows, then, if you must stay,' he said.

Megaera, her long fiery hair swept back off her shoulders, stepped into the light but she was not alone. Familiar animal control poles looped with steel aircraft cables twitched in the hands of the security guards.

'What do you see from your Scaean Gates?' she asked.

Gene felt the chill of memory – that terrible tower from where Athanatos had seen the slaughter slice its way towards Troy. How long had these memories lain in blood now? Over three thousand years?

He watched the gathering figures behind him emerge as ghostly reflections in the glass. 'They're here for me,' he said.

He stepped away from the trembling windows to witness her directing two orderlies to pick up Lawless's body and transport it down to Savage in Theatre One. They quickly heaved it neatly on to the solid metal of a gurney and began to wheel it out slowly.

'Why didn't you stop me?'

'This is how it is,' Megaera explained, 'when we separate the strong from the weak; though I wouldn't have given you nearly as much freedom as he did. Do you feel better now that he's dead?'

'No. I answered my instinct, that's all.'

Megaera joined him at the soak of the window. 'Well, now answer *this*. You have a choice,' she said.

The lights of the ever growing army of squad cars whirled beneath the discharge of lightning that ruptured the black sky.

'What is my choice?'

She reached out to him and brushed a finger through his hair. 'I can make this madness end. These warring voices in your head, one Cyclades, one Athanatos, fighting for control of one body, a conflict raging in flesh; I offer you the chance to silence these voices and leave *one* as the dominant. One clear mind, one clear purpose. No more doubt. No more confusion. Complete the process or die.'

Megaera saw the conflict boil within him and pressed her advantage. 'Laws are for the small and the weak,' she said. 'In *this* society freedom is bought. We have deep pockets, our reach pervades. But I will not see this house crumble at the hands of the likes of you. Not as you are.'

Gene's ire grew. 'Then what would you have?'

'If you wish to succumb to the weak nature of your infected personality then we will give you up to them down there. You will rot in a jail cell, counting down the desiccated days to your unremarkable execution.'

Gene measured what she had to say. It was suitably unappealing.

'*Or*, you can do what you were born to do. Become more than any of us have ever been.'

'You sound just like him.'

'We are *all* him, the House of Athanatos. When we stand in a room of twelve people, we *are* those twelve people; one mind with twelve sets of grasping arms, twelve sets of peering eyes, all thinking and feeling the same thing. But there is only one head of this house. Now that we have made your mind pliant, like wax, all that remains is the final imprint to be impressed upon it, the proteins of memory from Lawless's mind to cement those you have had since your birth. The memories of Athanatos.'

Gene saw the flaw in the circling squad cars below. 'They will demand justice,' he said.

'And they can have it. We'll give them someone to answer for your crimes. We have so many to choose from.'

Change or die.

'Either way,' Megaera reflected with satisfaction, 'I achieve what I promised: that I would destroy you.'

AT THE CROSSROADS

4.27 p.m.

The relentless seethe of assaulting rain battered the traffic hunched bumper to bumper beneath the rugged glow of Times Square. The press was so merciless that North abandoned his Lumina and pounded the sidewalk on foot, his wilful eye probing every window, every doorway, every nook. Which one of these stark drenched buildings held Gene?

At the Duffy Square end he snatched up his Nextel and placed another call to the Fourth. He stayed on Broadway, his sight blurring through the sharp stabs of rain.

Lieutenant Hyland said, 'Yeah, you did have a fax come through.' North listened to the rustle of paper. 'The Natural History exhibits are being couriered to a firm called American Generation. Delivery's set for between five and seven this evening.'

American Generation? A-Gen. 'They're not bio-tech?'

'Just running a check on them now.' The sound of plastic keys being struck amid the commotion of the squad room did nothing to ease the acute tension of the wait.

North crossed the drench of the intersection and jogged exhausted down the next busy block past more flashes of radio car blues and reds.

'Not listed as bio-tech,' Hyland confirmed. 'They're

genealogists. They specialize in databases: births, deaths and marriage records from over a hundred countries, do paternity tests, fertility screenings; trace adopted kids. They also got the largest private genetic database in the country, bigger than the Federal government's. But they're definitely not listed as bio-tech.'

'Then what *are* they listed as?'

'An institute, noted for its philanthropy.'

Gene's Columbia scholarship.

'Where are they based?'

'Seven hundred and fifty, Seventh Avenue, at West Forty-Ninth Street.'

That's two blocks away.

North quickened his bone-weary pace. 'Which floor?'

'The whole building.'

4.33 p.m.

North forced his flagging legs through the slosh of unceasing rain; his clothes soaked and heavy, threatening to drag him down into the swirling murk of the drains.

He darted through the traffic at the final cross street, almost tripping over his sopping shoes, suffocating from the towering press of looming concrete towers that jutted up out of the ground like angry gnashing teeth, threatening to crush and consume him.

At the corner of Broadway and West 49th, North clung to the wall, the violent rain striking hammer blows on his tired bowed head, peals of black thunder rolling above him.

I can't do this any more.

He gasped and choked for air and through the wheeze of his suffocation he saw his fate towering before him.

Seven hundred and fifty, Seventh Avenue stretched into the sky, a stepped ziggurat of glass and steel that twisted in a spiral in its reach for the vault of the heavens. At street level its dark mouth sat gaping open, occasionally swallowing a car.

North pressed on, towards the group of men in dark suits who were gathered in its shelter like a disease in its gums.

Chinatown.

They saw him approach and moved to block his path. 'You can't come in here, this is private property.'

North looked the nearest one in the eye and saw the sudden flicker of recognition that crossed his face burst into an uncontrollable flood. He didn't just know North from Chinatown. He knew him from his past.

North didn't reach for his shield. He simply asked: 'Where's the front entrance?'

No one replied. A few attempted to appear intimidating but most of them knew it would take far more than that to dissuade him. Yet, collectively, they had given him far more than they realized.

'Thank you,' North replied.

They remained silent as they brought down the shutters on the mouth of the subterranean parking lot.

But it was too late: North had already seen the gleaming silver 2004 Chrysler Sebring sedan.

A gleaming stainless steel autopsy table lay in the centre of the room.

While Savage pulled on a pair of thin latex gloves and arrayed his burnished surgical instruments on the plain white cloth of the tray next to it, Lawless's corpse was wheeled in on the gurney, hidden beneath a starched white sheet.

The orderlies counted to three before lifting the body up on to the table and peeling the sheet back. Even death had failed to wipe the hint of perverse satisfaction from Lawless's thin face.

Savage pulled a blue surgical mask over his mouth and a

moulded polycarbonate face shield down over his eyes and goggles. He directed Gene and the others to do the same. This was grisly work. The bone, he said, will get everywhere.

Megaera and her cohort of twitchy security guards watched Gene do as he was asked first, before moving to do the same.

Gene observed Savage closely as he took a scalpel and with precision brought the glinting blade close to Lawless's left ear where a cluster of freckles disappeared into his hairline.

Savage pressed the scalpel into the cool dead flesh and did not stop until he felt the blade strike hard bone beneath. Holding Lawless's head with his free hand he then sliced its razor tip smoothly through the juicy tissue all the way around to the right ear.

This was the art of butchery. Savage grasped the upper edge of the wet incision and held it open as he forced the scalpel underneath, slashing away the connective tissue, until the meat of the scalp grew loose on the bone and he could insert his hand and fold the limp flap of dripping flesh over Lawless's face like a macabre bloody toupee pulled inside out. The calvarium, the domed upper portion of the skull which held the brain, lay exposed.

'Stryker.'

Gene took the scalpel from Savage's bloodied hand and exchanged it for the whirring bone saw. The semicircular serrated blade vibrated, hundreds of cycles per second, grinding deep into the dead bone.

'You can put the scalpel down now Gene,' Megaera instructed carefully.

Gene looked at the bloody blade and slowly did as he was told.

Savage had not exaggerated about the mess. Flecks of dead skull and deep red tissue filled the air and clung to his face mask as he carved into the bone in a zigzag pattern across Lawless's forehead, so that when he was done the skull cap would fit snugly back.

Finally, using a large metal skull chisel, he levered into the sawn groove, twisting and jemmying to prise the calvarium from the lower skull until with a dull moist pop he exposed Lawless's glistening inner workings, his meninges, the moist membranes which enclosed his crinkled grey brain matter beneath.

'It seems to be in good condition,' Savage observed. He indicated to Gene. 'Please spread the hemispheres apart for me.'

Gene's fingers trembled at the prospect. To touch the memories trapped within the curves of Lawless's wrinkled cortex, to hold the essence of who he was in his hands – this was not what he wanted but this was the fleshly prison to which he had been born.

The others watched every move.

Why haven't the alarms sounded yet?

Had they found the fire and extinguished it?

Reluctantly Gene reached over and gently parted the cold grey hemispheres of Lawless's brain while Savage inserted a long needle between them and into the top of the spinal column where he extracted his sample of cerebrospinal fluid, the glistening liquid which bathed the brain and the spinal cord.

Filled with proteins that were absorbed into the circulating blood, the cerebrospinal fluid was replaced every six to eight hours and conducted metabolic waste products, antibodies and the pathological products of disease away from the brain. It was the route through which the proteins of memory first travelled, the proteins which directed the meiosis of sperm cells, and the same slick which held the remnants of proteins which filled the caskets of memory – Lawless's last memories.

Savage set the syringe down on his tray. Holding the brain away from the interior skull, he severed its connections to the body with the glistening blood-soaked scalpel, slicing through the facial and auditory nerves, disconnecting the eyes.

Once Lawless's brain was completely detached, Savage sat it on the scale, noted its weight and placed it into a bucket of cold saline for storage.

To stop residual spinal fluid seeping out of Lawless's head, Savage directed Gene to stuff the empty skull with wads of paper towels. Then matching up the zigzag patterns replaced the calvarium and pulled the fleshy, bloodied scalp back over it tightly.

'I'll suture him later,' Savage remarked, removing his gloves and face mask. 'Let's finish our work.'

6.48 p.m.

The game of waiting was a long one.

The great spiralling ziggurat of 750 Seventh Avenue stood illuminated on all sides by a wash of red and blue, the greasy rain pounding on the hoods of the squad cars, hammering on the shoulders of a small army of NYPD and Emergency Service Unit officers.

Martinez had come out of the building having been told no one by the name of Eugene Dybbuk was inside.

'I think they're lying.'

North had no doubt. 'Of course they're lying.' North called Hyland for a warrant. No reply came for over an hour.

It left North with little else to do but watch and wonder which anonymous window Gene stood behind. He walked around the walls, probing for the weak spots, searching for a solution.

After a few minutes, he slogged back over to where Martinez had parked his Crown Victoria. An ESU officer in his dark bulky body armour, his Heckler and Koch MP5 slung from his shoulder, hunched angrily over the wet driver's side door, waiting.

Inside the car Martinez hung up his phone with bitter frustration. 'Hyland can't find a judge willing to sign the warrant.'

The ESU officer demanded to know why. His men were waiting to go in.

'He says these A-Gen people got everyone's dirty little secret. It's like they're untouchable. They grease the wheels of public office and they grease 'em thick.'

No shots fired inside the museum.

'For now all we do is keep the place surrounded.'

At the far end of the block a small white delivery truck emerged from the murk of grey and pulled up to the roadblock. The young driver nervously got out and started showing the two beat cops what he'd got stowed away behind the sliding door on the side.

North watched them quietly through the hammering rain; the courier was from the Natural History Museum.

The skull.

'Let's just give them what they want,' he said simply.

Martinez followed North's gaze over to the truck.

'So if he wants *me* I'll take him his gift,' added North. 'I'll knock on his door and if I get into any trouble I can always call for help.'

The ESU officer liked what he was hearing. Exigent circumstances.

'Right,' Martinez replied, realizing the implication. 'We won't need a warrant.'

'No one's untouchable,' North said.

7.04 p.m.

When they'd secured permission from the delivery company, the driver brought his vehicle slowly down to the front entrance. He pulled three cardboard boxes from a stack and set them neatly on a wheeled hand truck.

The sight of so many cops made him thoroughly nervous. With unsteady hands the thin young man handed North the white docket and quickly abandoned him in the rain.

North peered exhausted into the building; so many arrogant men going about their business as though no one could get to them.

He dug his hand into his pocket and pulled out the pills he'd taken from his father's medicine cabinet.

I can forget if I want to.

Th-thump.

'What are those?' Martinez asked at his side.

'Beta-blockers.'

Martinez grew increasingly alarmed. 'You got a heart condition?'

'No.' *I got other problems.*

Th-thump.

Everyone has a choice.

He watched the security guards watching him.

Th-thump.

'You really want to know what my connection is to Gene?' North threw the pills to the ground and watched them dissolve in the rain.

Martinez didn't say anything. He didn't have to.

North rearranged the boxes and tore open the one on top, casting the packaging aside until an ancient skull rolled out into his hand. He clutched it tightly. To finally hold it was such an odd experience. It was so old, so fragile, so pitted with memories. The teeth, worn and discoloured, had tiny holes drilled in them from where someone had extracted their pulp.

What did the face look like, the flesh of which once hung from the bones? The reconstruction had been destroyed by Gene, he'd seen that in the museum, but the docket said that there were records somewhere inside the box, photographs of the results that had been achieved.

North put down the skull and rummaged around until he found a small white envelope and emptied the contents out into his hand.

Polaroids of an earth-coloured clay head, from the back, in

profile and from the front. He handed the pictures to Martinez.

North had seen exactly what he had expected to find. The face staring back at him was his own.

Martinez was stunned. 'This sent him over the edge because it looks just like you?'

'I think he was more upset that it didn't look like *him*.'

'I don't understand.'

'You don't have to. It's just he and I go way back, that's all,' North replied.

He picked the skull back up. Acutely aware that every eye was upon him, he strode towards the American Generation building, through the thick glass doors which slid back smoothly, and into the foyer where the reception was even more hostile than the storm outside.

Under the shadow of two vast stone Babylonian winged bulls with human heads, North arrived at the front desk.

He said, 'If Mr Dybbuk isn't in today, I'm guessing Dr Savage isn't in either?'

The security guard was resolute. 'No, sir. He isn't.'

North explained that he understood. 'In any case, could you please place a call upstairs and let Athanatos know he has a visitor.'

The mere mention of the name set the guards on edge. For a moment it appeared as though they didn't know what to do.

'Who shall I say is calling?'

North set his skull down on the counter. 'Let him know that Cyclades is waiting for him.'

Gene sat at the ornate wooden writing desk in Lawless's apartment. Savage set a plain syringe down on the desk's leather surface and next to it a vial, its contents dark as glistening blood, each drop filled with the black blossoms of Athanatos' memory.

Gene regarded it with dread.

We do not have to remember.

His hand hovered over its plastic surface.

We do not have to remember.

The strong scent of Jasmine wafted towards him. Gene turned to find Megaera watching him coldly, dabbing on a little perfume.

He remembered the museum and knew that she did nothing without intent.

'I thought you lost your perfume bottle,' he said.

Megaera seemed surprised that he remembered. 'I have more than one,' she replied with some amusement. 'Does it trouble you?'

'You wanted to see me fail.'

'Of course. You still can, if you choose to.'

Gene did not answer. He picked up the vial and affixed to it the long glinting needle that it required.

He held the syringe in his trembling fingers and positioned its tip over a vein.

The telephone on the desk began to ring.

Megaera put her perfume down angrily and set the call to speakerphone. 'What is it?'

'There's a man downstairs,' the voice explained with clear agitation.

'Tell him to go away.'

'He calls himself Cyclades.'

Megaera shot both men a thunderous blast. Savage turned away, the implication weighing so heavily that the roll of his shoulders sagged.

Yet Gene's concern rested with the perfume bottle before him. A smile tugged at his lips.

It left Megaera worried. 'What does he want?' she asked.

'He wants to see Athanatos. Who should I send him to see?'

THE DYING DAYS

The wounds of war carve deep their marks in men. Only madness carves them deeper.

When mighty grief struck, Achilles fell – slayer of Hector, King Priam's finest son and scourge of all Greeks, slayer of Penthesileia, Queen of the Amazons, slayer of stout Memnon, general of the Ethiopian horde, son of King Priam's brother immortal Tithonus; when mighty grief struck, Achilles fell, downed by the winging arrows from the goat's horn bow of Paris, fat with indolence, root of King Menelaus' siege, blood gushing down his own legs like women dying ivory frothing red, when mighty grief struck Achilles fell, the might of such grief struck all Greeks.

When first I set eyes upon the Trojan plains, horsehair crest brushed and bristling on a glittering helmet of fine boar tusks, war shield jutting, shield to shield, man to man tight as a mason packs good strong blocks of granite that fight the ripping winds, we were as one, we were as the gods.

Look at us now, driven back to the scouring sea, driven against the bows of our black-beaked ships, driven to despair. Look at us, lost in a forest of ramparts made from the rotting bones of the fallen, buried in the fetid mud of ten years' struggle, racked with a withering plague from our enforced sleep with carrion. Look at mighty Ajax, slaughtering the cattle, wrapped in such unshakeable melancholy that the force of war had brought, and taking his own sword to carve himself a journey to Hades.

Look at us now, aghast at the unrelenting greed of the Trojans who cannot cease their grasping ways even when death glares at them from the beaches. Look at indolent Paris, dead – and yet another of Priam's miserable sons, Deiphobus, quickly takes Helen for his bride and still no Greek woman is returned to us. Where is the grace of the Trojans? It is nowhere, it is a myth.

We soldiers of Greece sit huddled by our fires each night, and weep like children for the wives we cannot see.

'Cyclades.'

I peered into the cold black of night and saw standing in the flicker of the fires my king, Idomeneus. Yet the proud man I knew from Knossos, who watched the Bull leaping with his heart filled with passion, was gone. The shine of his handsome face had dimmed.

So the punishments of war were just as harsh to kings. I felt somehow satisfied in that knowledge.

I stumbled to my feet. 'Great King,' I said. 'What is your bidding?'

'A man's tongue can be a glib and serpentine thing, can it not?'

'You have been drinking with King Odysseus?'

Was that a smile buried somewhere deep in his pensive face?

'You mourn for your Moira.'

The merest touch of her name upon my burning ears brought such terrible pain as to scour my flesh with fish-hooks. 'She is locked behind those walls,' I warned. 'While she is true, I rage still.'

'We all rage, Cyclades. That is not in question.'

What was it that troubled my king so? Idomeneus cast his eye upon his war-weary soldiers hunched around their fires.

'Come,' he said. 'Walk with me.'

We passed from the flicker of crackling flame until we reached the black shore and the cold spit of the sea.

'I have seen you leap bulls. I have seen you wrestle them; fine, powerful black beasts, their horns wrenched in your strong hands in the bowels of the Labyrinth of Knossos. You show courage. You show *no fear.*'

I was humbled that he remembered me.

'Does *that* man still breathe? Does the Bull leaper walk with me now? Or did this miserable war slay him long ago?'

I was insulted that he need ask. I was defiant. 'Great King, I have already asked what it is that you bid.'

King Idomeneus considered my words with grave concern. He stretched out his arm and commanded me to join him in King Odysseus' tent.

Standing before Odysseus' generous table amid a host of Greek commanders stood two grim-faced lords of Troy, men I had seen slay Greeks with glee, Antenor and Aeneas.

I reached for my blade but my king stayed my eager hand. 'You are a soldier,' he said. 'It is not for you to understand.'

The two grim-faced lords concluded their business. 'Then it is agreed, I receive half of Troy's wealth and one of my sons sits on the throne. The House of Aeneas is left untouched and his wealth remains intact.'

Wily King Odysseus spread out his hands over the glistening wine on the table. 'You have my word.'

'But what of Agamemnon's?'

'I speak for Agamemnon on this matter.'

Aeneas turned his back on the table and brought his gaze to rest on me instead. His dark eyes threatened to swallow my fate whole.

'And what of the man you are to leave on the beach?' he asked. 'What are *his* wishes?'

I did not understand. I looked to King Odysseus for an explanation. He supped his wine and ran a coarse hand through his rough beard. 'Cyclades, Idomeneus says you are the man for this wretched job. I trust his judgement. If you were to walk through the Scaean Gates right now and march on Troy, who would you have marked out?'

'What trick is this?'

Odysseus laughed at such a display of suspicion. 'Cyclades, you could be my cousin. This is no trick. When you march on Troy, who shall taste your bronze?'

There was only one man. 'The Babylonian,' I said, my breast surging with ire. 'This magician who calls himself Athanatos, who ripped out my heart and holds it yet; he is who I would have marked out above all others.'

Aeneas accepted my wish. He returned to the table with Antenor. 'The Palladium will be gone from Athena's temple by dawn. We shall say that Odysseus took it. From there your plan shall unfurl and the House of Priam will fall.'

I did not understand what it was they had agreed upon, but with the alliance concluded, Odysseus directed that the two grim-faced Trojans be escorted back to Troy.

I launched myself at Odysseus' table. 'Now we make pacts with Trojans?'

'We did not come to give special terms to Troy,' Odysseus assured me. 'We came to fight them to the death.'

Idomeneus quickly joined our side. 'Cyclades, if you are still desirous of war, we are with you. We shall honour our pact with the Trojans, the same way Paris honoured his with Menelaus.'

'Epeius has three days to deliver the fruit of our plan,' Odysseus ordered. 'But all depends on the glib and serpentine tongue of *one man* whom the Trojans will trust because they will know him *not to be a king.*'

*

The black palls of smoke hung low over the Greek encampment, abandoned and reduced to smouldering ashes.

With lips parched and broken I tore free from my rough bonds and scooped what liquid I could find from the shattered head of a plagued black bull; its clouded eyes the fruit for my hunger, the swill of its diseased and oozing innards the juice to slake my thirst.

I heard voices and ran from them, stumbling through the festering bones of a hundred corpses until I came crashing to my knees before the feet of Trojan men.

Bronze jabbed me in the shoulder. I clutched at my wound, the gush of red awash between my filthy fingers.

'What is your name? Speak!'

What is my name? In my fear I had forgotten it! I stumbled upon my words. 'M-my father comes from lands to the south. Though I was raised a Greek, My name is . . . *Sinon.*'

'Sinon . . . ?'

They did not believe me. What a fool I was. *Sinan*! I was to use the name *Sinan*! That was a name from these parts, a slave pressed into Greek servitude. Not Sinon. I would have to act quickly.

I pressed on, still unable to find the courage to look these men in the eye. 'There is nowhere left for me now,' I said, 'on sea or on land.'

'Where is your army?'

'They have gone,' I said with melancholy. 'The Greeks have fled.'

'Why have you been abandoned?'

Betrayal. Yes, they knew all about betrayal.

I said, 'I witnessed Odysseus murder the men who objected to this war. And when I revealed what I had learned it sowed so much fear throughout the ranks that it made the armies weak and there followed a plague and the Greeks clamoured to go home. And for tearing down the Palladium of Troy Odysseus, wretched man that he is, was forced to make a tribute to Pallas Athena so that she might watch over all Greek ships on their long journeys home.'

The Trojans were left in no doubt that the tribute of which I spoke was the towering wooden horse that had been left stranded on the beach. Big, like a ship, pine trees woven for its ribs, a wheel set under each foot, it immediately set the Trojans to quarrelling.

Laocoon, priest of Poseidon, saw nothing but grim portents in the offering, recounting his dream that while he was sacrificing a bull on the altar, two mighty intertwined snakes rose out of the foam of the sea to eat him and his heirs.

But while he wanted it burned where it stood, I argued that his portent was true, for it was the fate that awaited every Greek if the horse was dragged within the city walls to honour Athena.

It was now that I truly saw the Trojans for the first time. So desperate were they for some luck, so eager to snatch a morsel that might change the tide of their fate and end the misery that they had brought on themselves, that even in victory their greed would not allow them any other consideration but that which brought ruin on their enemies.

Lashing the horse with ropes they stretched out their backs and heaved to, and with the excited roar of Troy ringing in their ears, they dragged the mighty wooden horse through the Scaean Gates to stand before the Temple of Athena.

When the blanket of black night fell upon far-flung Troy, when their bellies were full and their hearts drunk with the celebrations that had lasted one full day, I roamed their wretched streets while they slept.

It was as I unfastened the pine bolts on the belly of the horse that the voice called out to me. 'What choice did we have?'

Was I caught? I moved slowly so as not to cause alarm

when I stepped down from the belly, but instead I found a woman, huddled beneath the looming nape of the horse, talking to it, weeping beneath it, touching the pine from which it was made, seeking her forgiveness.

'A thousand Greek women and for every face the hope of a remedy: to fight, or submit? To reject our captors, or give ground for an inch of comfort that would ease the burden of captivity. Know that the torments were long and they were harsh. Know that for those women born to comforts, the need to see those comforts once again led them astray from the start. Know that they convinced themselves that perhaps they could have a new life here, when in truth they were merely fighting to survive. The instinct to survive is greater than any man or any woman. So once more I ask, what choice did we have?'

I stepped from the shadows, uncertain that I should break this woman's prayer, but I could not help myself. I was drawn to ask the inevitable. 'Did they *all* succumb?'

The woman seemed startled. She rose quickly and turned away, pulling a hood over her face.

I reached out to her quickly. 'Please,' I begged.

She would not face me. 'For every mind, there is a malady; for every heart, a shameful tragedy. Some were strong. Some rebelled and paid the price. Helen grew to love her captors, as though they had borne her no evil; fooling herself into thinking that she could see some good within them if only to ease her pain. She was not herself. Her mind was pierced by wicked men as surely as they had used a spear to rend her from this world.'

'You *know* the others?'

'After ten years, I know *every* face.'

Could I trust her? Had she so succumbed to Trojan treachery that she would betray me? I felt it worth the risk. 'What of Moira?' I asked. 'Am I betrayed?'

'How little you know her! She fought, as brave as any warrior!'

I was too afraid to know, but still I pressed her further. 'Where is she?'

'She is dead . . .'

'How long?'

'Nine long years. She was the first to go. Athanatos took her, forced her to carry the child through which the blessing of the Oracle would supposedly grant him the gift of immortality, but she refused to bear the burden and cut it out of her womb. As she lay there bleeding, he dragged her screaming from his temple and cut off her head and stuck it on a spike at the gates to his tower. She is there still, and each morning I pray to her to give me the strength to continue.'

I sunk to my knees, my breath stolen, my chest a heaving mass of knotted muscle and flexing bone incapable of wringing out air. Moira had lain dead for *nine years*?

I had fought for nothing.

Eager to steal off into the night, free to roam, as only those who had collaborated were free to, I asked her, 'What is your name?'

Tears stained her once soft cheeks. She caught my eye by the lamplight and she wept. 'My name is Helen.'

She was as beautiful as they said. I was truly stricken for her when I asked, 'Please show me where I may light a beacon.'

Tremble, Athanatos! Tremble! You may fear the gods. Now fear me!

As the men from in the wooden horse throw open Trojan gates, the Greeks sail back from Tenedos enraged with murderous hate. Through the Scaean Gates they pile, through the Dardan Gates as well. Nothing quenches raging ire like the pound and hack of metal.

See the end of Troy; watch her burn into the ground! See her people buried in the pile of funeral mounds. The pop and hiss of Hades' pyres, the screams of Hector's ghost, the slaughter in the streets and temples, the Trojans made to roast!

Through the fire-ridden pillars that mark the reek of Trojan death, through the crackling tongues of dust-choked fire we Grecian warriors tread. Those who sleep shall never wake, those awake shall surely die. No noble victory for us Greeks when we are driven to destroy.

Quake, Athanatos! Quake! If you do not fear the gods, you will fear me!

See the end of Priam's reign; watch him slaughtered in the temple. See his grandson, baby Astyanax, hurled from the city wall. I come for you this night, my foe. I come to spill your blood. Like a strong wind whips a fire through a field of drying grain, so the sweep of your destruction shall reap the harvest of my blaze.

THE HEART OF
THE LABYRINTH

7.24 p.m.

The searing sting of the old scars of memory jabbed sharply behind North's eyes as he rode the elevator to the top.

He pulled away as though to fend off a blow and clutched at his face in agony. He pressed his fingers to his temple and found that they were covered in blood.

The mirror told him what he already suspected. The scars of his past were welling to the surface; the deathmarks of Cyclades emerging beneath his horns, sharp and primed.

Th-thump.

He simply did not know whether the blood on his fingers was real. Certainly it had been real in the past.

7.27 p.m.

When the elevator doors slid smoothly back, North stepped from the car clutching the skull of his former self.

The lights were out.

Th-thump.

A dim sliver of lamplight spilled from under the door at the end of the hall. North moved towards it with caution, his free hand moving towards his Glock.

The roll of the elevator doors snapped shut behind him in a thunderous echo, taking with them the light.

North stood in silence and waited for his eyes to adjust.

Th-thump.

The vibration of his cellphone rumbled in his jacket pocket. He thumbed the receive button and listened to Martinez's harried voice spring from the hands-free earpiece.

'Get outta there, man.'

North eased his fingers on to his gun. 'What's going on?'

'ESU sharp shooters spotted a fire on the third floor.'

He told him to call the fire department. Martinez explained that he already had. But as North took another step the signal faded and the connection died.

North eased back and hammered the button for the elevator car. Nothing happened. *I'll have to find the stairs.*

Th-thump.

He pulled out his Glock and edged towards the end of the hall. As he drew closer the wafting scent of jasmine percolated through the gap between the heavy wooden doors.

His aching mind was a flood of images and sensations, thoughts and emotions, darkness and ancient hatred. He let them be his guide when the doors cracked open before him.

7.31 p.m.

'Do you mourn for your life, Cyclades?'

North probed the unyielding darkness, aiming his Glock at the movement of shadows, the sky erupting in violent flashes of lightning through the rattling windows beyond.

He set the skull down on the writing desk, barely visible in the gloom. 'I'm only just getting to know myself,' he said.

'We share the same blood,' Gene remarked from the cold of

the darkness. 'It would not take much for you to mourn for mine.'

North jolted at the idea that in some small way he really was talking to himself.

'What are the gods, detective, but one God with a multiple personality? What are characters in a play, but the facets of just one gem? What are the faces in this room, but the branches of *one tree*; a cancer that when starved of blood will wither and die?'

Faces? Who else was in here?

Th-thump.

North whirled but all he saw were wheeling shadows.

Th-thump.

The shrill hammer and clang of a fire alarm blasted through the quiet, heralding the dim ignition of emergency lights.

Th-thump.

Gene stood only a few feet away, lodged between the familiar figure of the woman with the long fiery hair who had driven the Sebring sedan, and Savage, the man North knew to be his father.

They were gagged and trussed to their chairs. In one hand Gene held a bloody syringe, in the other a small black handgun. North snapped his Glock up and took aim.

7.35 p.m.

The windows rattled and the storm raged when North ordered Gene to do as he said. 'Put them down!'

Th-thump.

Gene would not listen. He breathed in the perfume deeply. 'Reminds me of Moira. Doesn't it you?'

'Put them down.'

'Which one killed Moira?' Gene pressed. 'This guilt-free desirous schemer? Or this soft fool indebted to his conscience?'

North watched his biological father struggle with his bonds, his familiar eyes awash with fear. Not for his fate at the hands of Gene, but for the hatred he saw in the eyes of his son.

What do you know of your life?

'Did I kill her?' Gene goaded.

The process.

'Or did *you*?'

The Bull.

'Plumb the depths, detective,' he warned. 'Not so simple when the prey multiplies is it?'

The blood of the innocent.

'You know what memories lie hidden in those far-flung shadows and spots.'

Help me.

'There is not a thing that separates you or me.'

Ya fuckin' psycho.

'There is not a memory that one of us does not share.'

I am Satan's Oath.

'To know who murdered Moira requires nothing but a mirror!'

What do you know of your life?

The process.

The Bull.

The blood of the innocent.

Help me.

Ya fuckin' psycho.

I am Satan's Oath.

The scent of jasmine grew stronger. The touch of Moira pricked his skin at the thought.

I am the sweet air of spring.

Remember that.

Remember me.

The window glass rattled and the storm raged. The building shook and the explosion of incandescent flame churned up from the billowing inferno on the floors far below.

And when the heat had melted and twisted and eaten, the windows cracked and the glass caved in.

The explosive rage of searing flame and the angry lash of the storm fused into a furious swirl, bringing Gene crashing into sheets of slicing glass.

North did not know, nor did he understand, how he remained on his feet. He was this storm's eye and its cutting blades swirled around him.

He aimed his gun at Gene.

Everyone's got a choice.

His finger tensed on the trigger.

Gene's battered form stirred. He raised his syringe and held it out. 'This is what we are. This is our end.'

'I will not live in the past,' North lied, thrusting the muzzle of his cold gun hard in Gene's face.

Everyone's got a choice.

His grip tightened.

Gene rose to his bloodied knees and he begged. 'We are changed,' he said.

'That's what I'm afraid of,' North replied.

THE ELYSIAN DREAMS
OF CYCLADES

I remember the day I was born.

The details are clearer now. A clarity that comes only in the telling. I remember the suckling sounds of lips upon a breast, the shrill gurgle of bloody birth upon wet straw. The hunger. The rivulets of bathing water running down my face. Olive oil rubbed gently into my skin. The smell of sweet-scented perfume. Like jasmine blossoms floating on a summer breeze. Thick honey oozing. Wine flowing like a river. The human animal can be such a tender creature.

I remember my father, big and sturdy, black hair oiled and twisted on his thick arms. Strong, like a bull. I remember he played with me in the dark dank places of the Labyrinth of Knossos where children were forbidden to be. He would swing me in his arms and I would try to see his face, but they would not let him remove his mask. So he held his head close and I would reach to the top of the skull and I would play with his horns instead.

I would see him again, if my fate had not been so shackled to flesh. But my prison is of my own making; I did this, and I do not know how to unmake it. From my father I took his rage, but only I am responsible for the wielding of it.

The building is burning. The hot naked flames are licking at my heels and they are so very hungry.

And I am left with one unanswerable question: does the man consume his past, or does the past consume the man? Revenge is the snake that eats its own tail. It is a circle. And a circle is always empty. Yet I cannot deny my nature. I cannot run from my fate. I am the snake eating his own tail. I stand here, the cold hard metal of my gun thrust into his familiar face, pressed to *his* temple; yet it may as well be my own.

All that remains lies within me and whether I choose to pull the trigger.

My name is Cyclades and I wanted to be justice. But I am not justice. I am wrath.

I am the storm.

SELECTED BIBLIOGRAPHY

This is by no means an exhaustive list of the sources I consulted but is intended as a good basis for further reading.

Aeschylus, *The Oresteia*, trans. Robert Fagles, Penguin, 1984.
  Prometheus Bound and Other Plays, trans. Philip Vellacott, Penguin, 1961.
Calvin, William H., *How Brains Think: Evolving Intelligence, Then and Now*, Weidenfeld & Nicolson, 1997.
Casey, Joan Francis, with Lynn Wilson, *The Flock: The Autobiography of a Multiple Personality*, Fawcett Columbine, 1991.
Cohen, Barry M., Esther Giller and Lynn Wilson (eds.), *Multiple Personality Disorder from the Inside Out*, Sidran, 1997.
Dawkins, Richard, *River Out of Eden*, Weidenfeld & Nicolson, 1995.
  The Selfish Gene, Oxford University Press, 1989.
Dennett, Daniel C., *Kinds Of Minds: Towards an Understanding of Consciousness*, Weidenfeld & Nicolson, 1996.
Gehlek, Rimpoche Nawang, *Good Life, Good Death: Tibetan Wisdom on Reincarnation*, Riverhead Books, 2001.
Goethe, Johann Wolfgang von, *Faust – Part One*, trans. Philip Wayne, Penguin, 1949.
  Faust – Part Two, trans. Philip Wayne, Penguin, 1959.
Grant, Joan and Denys Kelsey, *Many Lifetimes: Concerning Reincarnation and the Origins of Mental Health*, Gollancz, 1968.
Graves, Robert, *The Greek Myths*, Penguin, 1992.

Greenfield, Susan, *Brain Story*, BBC Books, 2000.

  The Human Brain: A Guided Tour, Weidenfeld & Nicolson, 1997.

Harpur, Patrick, *The Philosopher's Secret Fire*, Penguin, 2002.

Herrin, Judith, *Women in Purple: Rulers of Medieval Byzantium*, Phoenix Press, 2002.

Herodotus, *The Histories*, trans. Robin Waterfield, Oxford University Press, 1998.

Hesiod, *Theogony, Works and Days*, trans. M. L. West, Oxford University Press, 1999.

Hillman, James, *The Force of Character, and the Lasting Life*, Random House, 1999.

Homer, *The Iliad*, trans. Robert Fagles, Penguin, 1990.

Janowitz, Naomi, *Magic in the Roman World*, Routledge, 2001.

Jones, Steve, *In the Blood: God, Genes and Destiny*, Flamingo, 1997.

  The Language of the Genes, Flamingo, 1993.

  Y: The Descent of Men, Little, Brown, 2002.

Jones, Terry and Alan Ereira, *Crusades*, Penguin, 1996.

Kingsley, Peter, *In the Dark Places of Wisdom*, Element, 1999.

Lewis, Bernard, *The Assassins: A Radical Sect in Islam*, Weidenfeld & Nicolson, 1967.

Maclean, John, *The Idea of Immortality*, Kessinger, 1907.

Marlowe, Christopher, *Doctor Faustus and Other Plays*, Oxford University Press, 1998.

Marshall, Peter, *The Philosopher's Stone: A Quest for the Secrets of Alchemy*, Pan, 2001.

Moody, Raymond A., *Life After Life*, Rider, 2001.

Ogden, Daniel, *Greek and Roman Necromancy*, Princeton University Press, 2001.

Pinker, Steven, *The Blank Slate: The Modern Denial of Human Nature*, Allen Lane, 2002.

Plato, *The Republic*, trans. Desmond Lee, Penguin, 1987.

Ramachandran, V. S. and Sandra Blakeslee, *Phantom in the Brain: Human Nature and the Architecture of the Mind*, Fourth Estate, 1998.

Ridley, Matt, *Genome: The Autobiography of a Species in 23 Chapters*, Fourth Estate, 1999.

Rulandus, Martinus, *A Lexicon of Alchemy*, Zachariah Palthenus, 1612.

Schacter, Daniel L., *Searching for Memory: The Brain, the Mind and the Past*, Basic Books, 1996.

  The Seven Sins of Memory: How the Mind Forgets and

Remembers, Houghton Mifflin, 2001.

Schacter, Daniel L. and Elaine Scarry (eds.), *Memory, Brain and Belief*, Harvard University Press, 2001.

Schnabel, Jim, *Forever Young: Science and the Search for Immortality*, Bloomsbury, 1998.

Searle, John R., *The Mystery of Consciousness*, Granta Books, 1998.

Shroder, Tom, *Old Souls: The Scientific Evidence for Past Lives*, Simon & Schuster, 1999.

Sykes, Bryan, *The Seven Daughters of Eve*, Bantam Press, 2001.

Tacitus, *The Annals of Imperial Rome,* trans. Michael Grant, Penguin, 1961.

Teresi, Dick, *Lost Discoveries: The Ancient Roots of Modern Science – from the Babylonians to the Maya*, Simon & Schuster, 2002.

Vernant, Jean-Pierre, *The Universe, the Gods, and Mortals: Ancient Greek Myths*, Profile, 2001.

Virgil, *The Aeneid*, trans. David West, Penguin, 1991.

   The Eclogues, trans. Guy Lee, Penguin, 1984.

Von Franz, Marie-Louise, *Alchemical Active Imagination*, Shambhala, 1997.

Wade, Nicholas, *Life Script: The Genome and the New Medicine*, Simon & Schuster, 2001.

Weiner, Jonathan, *Time, Love, Memory: A Great Biologist and his Quest for the Origins of Behaviour*, Faber & Faber, 1999.

Wilson, Ian, *Past Lives: Unlocking the Secrets of Our Ancestors*, Cassell, 2001.

Woods, Michael and Mary B. Woods, *Ancient Medicine*, Runestone Press, 2000.